Dates and Dead Bodies

Dates and Dead Bodies

Imogen Knowed

Paperback ISBN: 979-8-9874825-2-0
Ebook ISBN: 978-1-972670-22-4

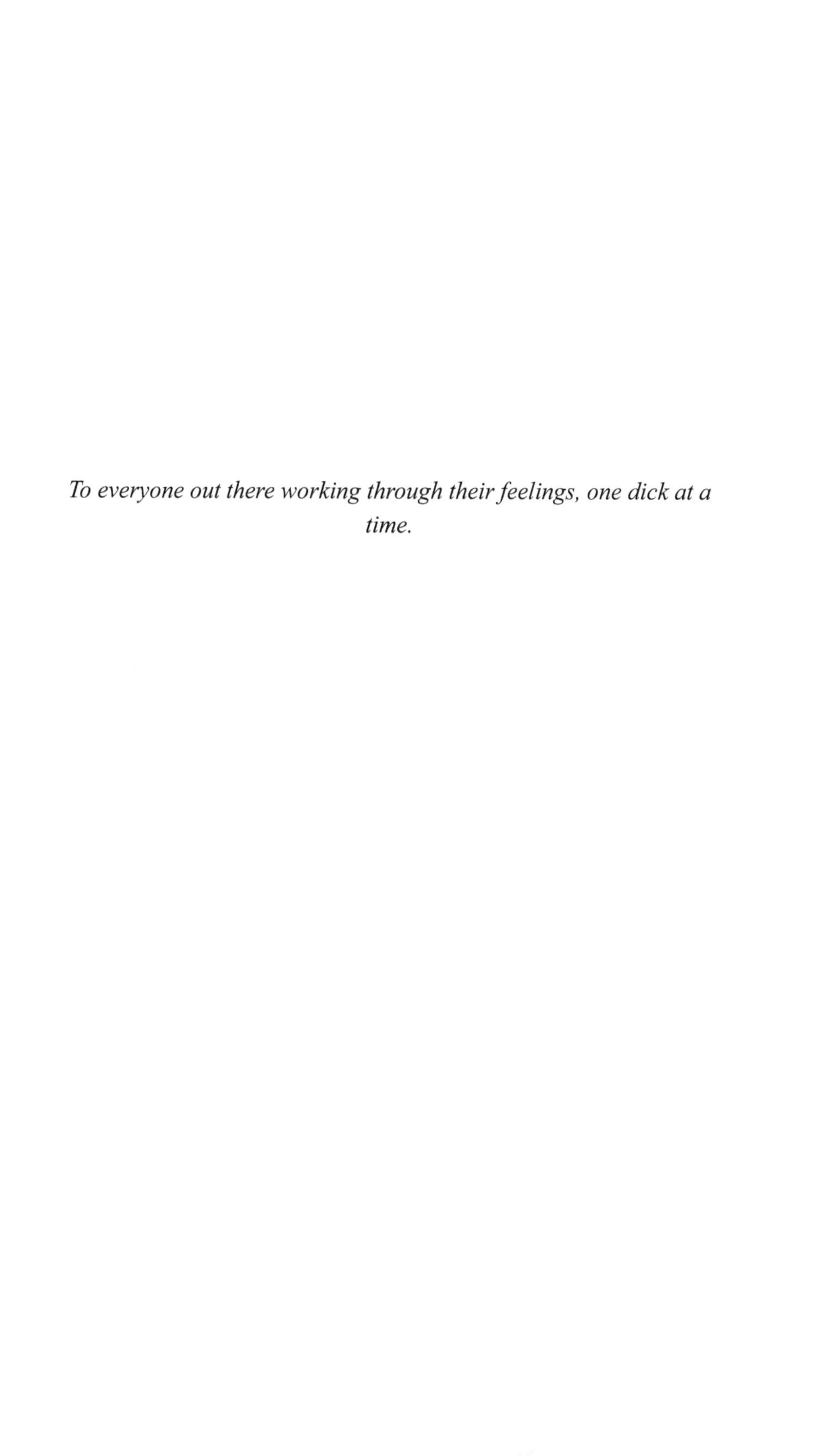

To everyone out there working through their feelings, one dick at a time.

Content Warnings

This book is about three things: mental health resulting from childhood trauma, solving a murder, and fucking. If that's not your vibe, maybe stop reading now.

This is a story, not a manual for how to live. These are flawed characters and written as such. The author does not necessarily condone the actions of these characters.

I'll start by assuring you, no harm comes to the dog, but he is fed table scraps.

The murder that the FMC sets out to solve is not described in great detail. Many people express gratitude over the victim's death.

This book has explicit descriptions of sexual acts among two, three, and four people. While all sex is consensual, some acts may be considered dubious or coerced. Unsafe sex without STD conversations ahead of time happens. There is reference to breeding and creampie kinks.

Childhood trauma is explored throughout. The adult characters discuss their past experiences with narcissistic parental abuse, parental abandonment, and physical abuse. The actual abuse is not described in great detail.

The main character has moments of negative self-talk, with some statements bordering on suicidal ideation and ableism. Some of her statements could be considered slut-shaming, but, in general, she is not ashamed and wears the term proudly. The book begins with her coming home after both of her parents died in a car accident, but it is not described in any amount of detail.

A secondary character in the book exhibits bullying behavior with insults that focus on slut-shaming and classism.

Some characters express internalized homophobia.

Cancer is mentioned throughout the book. Two characters (one adult MMC and one tertiary child character) are in remission. No character dies from cancer during the course of the book; however, one character is mentioned to have died before the book begins.

Pregnancy and infertility are discussed throughout the book. An MMC grapples with his feelings of infertility due to cancer. A tertiary character is pregnant throughout the book, and her baby is introduced at the end.

If you have any questions or comments about these content warnings, feel free to contact me. You can find my contact information at imogenknowed.com.

1

I fumble with the keys: a once familiar action now foreign and clumsy. The door swings open with a soft click, and I step inside, creaking the wood beneath my feet in the same spots as always. The urge to say, "Mom, Dad, I'm home," overwhelms me, and I crumple to the floor.

My purse falls open at my side, spilling its contents across the hardwood. My tears come freely in big wet plops as my lip gloss rolls under my mom's baby grand piano in the adjoining dining room. The sound of it moving away pulls at my chest as my vision blurs and my eyes cross to keep track of it.

Memories of my mother teaching me to play flood me. My hands ache as I envision playing for hours on end. *I hate that fucking thing.*

I'm a terrible daughter. Always have been. I'm so selfish. "I'm so sorry. I'm sorry I wasn't here." I wail, clutching my chest. The deep, swelling pain in my heart washes over my entire body. *I guess I've got to say goodbye to that lip gloss.*

Don't look at it. I focus on the grain of the hardwood directly in front of me, running my fingers over the crevices. *How many times had they stepped on this very spot? They'll never step here again.* I close my eyes, allowing the grief to engulf me.

Just as the sorrow is about to consume me, a knock at the door startles me. My eyes fly open, locking on the door—the unexpected intrusion: a welcome savior.

I hesitate to raise—unsure if I am ready to face anyone in my current state of vulnerability. I turn, now fully prone, and rest my forehead on the ground. I close my eyes, willing whomever it is to go the fuck away. *I don't deserve saving. I don't deserve happiness. I don't deserve to live.*

The knock sounds again, more insistent this time.

Curiosity and annoyance pique my interest, outweighing my grief and self-hatred. I shove myself upward with what feels like my last reserve of strength. I wipe my nose with my sleeve and draw a shaky breath as I try to compose myself. Presentable is likely a futile goal.

My hand rests on the doorknob as I steel myself and plaster on a brave face. With one deep breath, I turn the knob and slowly open the door, bracing myself for whoever it might be.

The warm, slightly more wrinkled than I remembered, smile of Mrs. Heart peeks around the creeping open door. Her kind blue eyes twinkle with affection and empathy. She holds a freshly baked apple pie—my favorite—with a crumbly top. Its sweet aroma wafts through the open door on the cool breeze. It envelops me in a comforting embrace. The scent elicits a familiar warmth despite the air's autumn chill. It's the same pie she brought over every time I needed comforting as a child. It healed every heartbreak. *Now, my heart is broken into a million pieces, which I doubt can ever be repaired.*

"Celeste, dear, I hope I'm not intruding. We thought you could use some pie." Mrs. Heart beams at me, her voice filled with warmth and love. At her feet, a Cavalier King Charles Spaniel wags its tail eagerly. The little dog's enthusiasm and big brown eyes momentarily push aside the heaviness in my heart and crack a smile on my face.

"Mrs. Heart." I smile, genuinely happy to see her. "And that can't be…Agatha?" I ask, referencing the dog below.

"Oh, no, dear. Agatha passed away years ago. This is Watson," she says, nodding toward the dog.

"Hello, Watson." The dog's entire back half swings with his tail when I say his name. I gesture to the foyer. "Come in."

Watson, needing no further invitation, rushes toward the purse splayed open on the floor, his claws clicking against the hardwood as his nose investigates the out-of-place items. When Mrs. Heart crosses the threshold, the aroma of cinnamon and baked apples intensifies—the nostalgia comforting. Mrs. Heart looks at my purse and frowns. She approaches me and wipes a tear off my cheek with her thumb.

She says nothing, just looks at me silently. But her eyes and touch say all she needs to say. I grip her hand against my face and nuzzle into it. Sobs explode from deep within me, and I lose myself to my tears once again.

I am distracted from my grief when something drops on my foot. Watson peers up at me with big brown eyes, waiting for praise. "Sweet boy, did you get that for me?" I lean down to grab the lip gloss he's dropped at my feet. *I love this lip gloss. I'm happy he got it for me.* I give him a scratch behind the ear, and he leans into my touch.

I compose myself yet again and gesture to the kitchen. "Let's cut that pie in the kitchen."

Mrs. Heart simply nods and shuffles through the foyer, then the dining room. She's been here many times—having cared for me since I was a baby, so she knows exactly where the kitchen is. I follow behind her slowly, unspeaking and broken. I avoid looking at the piano as I pass it.

"Thank you for looking after the house and…helping with the funeral arrangements," I choke out.

She waves off my thanks. "Oh, dear, of course! You think nothing of it."

Mrs. Heart didn't just help with the funeral arrangements; she took care of everything. I didn't even come home for it. I just kept working. *Avoiding. Denying.*

After putting down the pie, Mrs. Heart reaches out and pats my hand—her touch soft and reassuring. "I'm here for you, dear. Whenever you need anything, you know where to find me." My eyes well up with tears yet again, touched by the sincerity in Mrs. Heart's words. I feel the truth in them and know I don't have to face this nightmare alone. *She's always been here for me. I shouldn't have left her, too.*

Feeling grateful, I reply, “Thank you, Mrs. Heart. This means more to me than you know.”

Suck it up, Celeste. I shake myself to push past these tears. I gesture to the small kitchen table. “Why don’t we sit down and have a slice of this pie?” A genuine smile spreads across my face. “I could use the company.”

Mrs. Heart’s eyes crinkle with love. “That sounds wonderful, dear.” With a mischievous raised eyebrow, she asks, “Eat in the living room?” She’s given me this exact look so many times. Eating pie in the living room was our secret, shared rebellion against my mother’s “no eating in the living room” policy.

I laugh, and a glimmer of hope replaces the heaviness in my heart. “Yeah, I’d like that,” I respond. I *suppose I can eat wherever I want now.*

I cut two generous slices of pie. As I lift them from the tin, they collapse into crumbly, gooey piles of golden goodness onto the plates. I lean forward and inhale the cinnamon and baked apple aroma. I close my eyes and try to let it envelop me, hoping it can take me away from the pain I feel. While it eases the pain slightly, it doesn’t remove it, but perhaps eating it will.

I guide Mrs. Heart towards the living room. Watson trots happily behind us, his nose and eyes locked on the plates in our hands. I watch his tail sway high above his back, the hair arching like a perfectly groomed feather.

Mrs. Heart settles onto the couch and watches me intently—her eyes soft with compassion, patience, and love as she waits for me to sit. I perch on the opposite side of the sofa. Poised on the couch’s edge, I cradle my plate in one hand and my fork in the other. They tremble slightly in my hands as I continue to compose myself. Mrs. Heart does the same but doesn’t dig into her pie. It’s as if she’s waiting for something—perhaps waiting to see if I will break into tears again.

To show her I am okay, even though I am most assuredly not, I take a confident bite of my pie. I momentarily close my eyes and savor the flavors as they burst onto my tongue.

As if emboldened by my bite, Mrs. Heart does the same. I study her face. Since I've been gone, her hair has gone completely white. She must have given up dyeing it black at some point. Her skin, which used to be tanned by constant sunbathing, is now so pale that it's nearly translucent. But she still has that "beauty queen poise," and you'd never know she was in her eighties.

We eat silently, and tears threaten to fill my eyes yet again as each item in my house triggers another memory. Mrs. Heart opens her mouth to speak, but before she does, a wet nose nudges against my leg, drawing my attention. Mrs. Heart giggles at Watson as I reach down and scratch behind his ears. His soulful eyes and gently wagging tail once again tug a genuine smile onto my lips.

"You're a sweet one, aren't you, Watson?" I mutter. The little spaniel looks up at me as if I'm the most important person in the world, and for a moment, I feel like I might be. *A girl could get used to being looked at like this.*

I pat the couch at my side, between Mrs. Heart and me. Watson immediately jumps up. As if sensing my need for comfort, he rests his head on my lap. He's probably just angling for some pie, but it feels like genuine compassion. His warm presence is like a soothing balm to my troubled soul.

Mrs. Heart chuckles softly at Watson because it's almost impossible to look into his face and not do so. "He's always had a way of knowing just what someone needs."

I place my plate on the coffee table and stroke Watson's silky fur. With the plate gone, he shifts more of himself onto my lap. The weight on my shoulders eases with each stroke. For a moment, the grief that has consumed me recedes, replaced by a sense of connection and belonging.

"Thank you for coming to see me, Mrs. Heart," I say, thick with emotion. "Thank you for the pie. I…I really needed this." I rest my hand on Watson, noting his breath slowly lifting my hand.

Mrs. Heart rests her hand on mine. "That's what neighbors are for, dear."

Neighbor isn't a strong enough word. Family is much closer.

"I…I have to go to a lawyer's office tomorrow. He left a message this morning. He seemed…angry. I guess I've neglected my responsibilities long enough and have to meet with him…" I trail off, reflecting on the voicemail.

She places her plate down forcefully, finished with her pie. I'm surprised at the aggression. *Did I do something wrong?* "I'll show you where the law office is, dear. I know where it is." Her voice is tinged with a sharpness I'm not sure I understand. She looks at her plate, reflecting on something, then sighs. "So much loss this year." Guilt overwhelms me at how utterly selfish I've been.

I turn to her. "Oh, Mrs. Heart. Forgive me; I was so wrapped up in my…I am so sorry about John."

"Oh, no, dear, that's okay." She sniffles and dabs her eye with a hanky.

"I'm sorry I didn't come to his funeral," I choke out.

"It's okay, dear. I know you were busy."

Too busy to come to John's funeral? Too busy to come to my parents'? Too busy to be here for Mrs. Heart the way she is here for me? I am so selfish. Mom was right about me.

"That's…it wasn't an excuse; I should have been here. He was like a fa…" I croak, unable to finish my sentence.

"Dear, I've been so proud of all you've accomplished. I understand. Watson was here for me. And you're here now…if only…it had been under better circumstances…" *Why is she always so nice to me? Why does she always try to quell my guilt? I don't deserve her kindness or her love.*

We sit in silence for a long time, reflecting on the loss we've both experienced this year. Mrs. Heart's eyes twinkle with tears as she leans back on the couch, studying my face. Her soothing voice breaks the silence. "You know what always helps me when I'm feeling blue? Taking Watson for a walk around town."

Watson instantly perks up at the word "walk," his tail back to its whipping motion as he stares at me hopefully. I hesitate, and my gaze drifts to the door. The thought of venturing out, of facing the world, sends a flicker of apprehension through me. But the happiness radiating from the dog warms me to the idea. Watson paws at my leg, and his tail wags with even more expectant enthusiasm. I waver.

"I don't know," I murmur, uncertain. "I'm not sure I'm ready to—"

"Nonsense, dear," Mrs. Heart interjects, with a firm and encouraging tone. "A short walk will do you good. And Watson here won't take no for an answer. Will you, boy?"

As if on cue, Watson lets out a soft bark—his eyes fixed on me with a pleading expression that fully melts my resolve. I smile at him and nod in acquiescence. It's a face you can't say no to. What kind of monster could disappoint that sweet face? *I suppose it would be nice to get out of this house.*

"Alright, alright," I relent, pushing up from the couch. "I guess fresh air couldn't hurt."

Mrs. Heart beams, her face alight with satisfaction as she slowly rises to join me. "Nice work, Watson! While we're out, let's get some coffee to wash down our pie."

2

I breathe deeply, inhaling the crisp air. I stand on the porch and attempt to take in the beauty of the newly yellowed leaves, but Watson bounds down the steps, letting me know my dawdling is not appreciated. He holds his tail high as he leads the way down the familiar streets. He bounces on his paws, tugging eagerly at the leash in my hand.

We follow his lead and turn in the direction opposite Mrs. Heart's house. We cross in front of a two-story house that looks almost identical to my family's home, except mine is a pastel pink, while this one is a pastel blue. Multiple lawns have signs that say "Keep Goose Grove Quaint" stuck within them. I want to ask Mrs. Heart about it, but she speaks before I can.

"You know, dear, Ryan visits his dad quite often," Mrs. Heart says with a glint of mischief and a nod toward the blue house. "When was the last time you saw him?"

"Before I moved to California," I say while looking wistfully at the powder blue two-story. "We text each other occasionally, but it's mostly just silly memes."

"You two used to be so cute when you were little—inseparable. And when you were teens, I had to practically pry the two of you off each other."

"Mrs. Heart!" I interrupt.

"I always thought the two of you would get married," she laments. "Or Ryan would have at least become a doctor after all that studying the two of you supposedly did together, locked away in your room," she giggles.

"Mrs. Heart! You haven't changed, have you?" I laugh.

"Nope. I'm still the deceptively devilish old romantic I've always been," Mrs. Heart chuckles. *Romantic is one word for it. Perv is another.*

My gaze instinctively returns to my feet. The voice of my mother rings in my ear: *"Stop staring at your feet like a pathetic little mouse; what will people think?"* I pull my scarf tighter around my neck and nuzzle it, before hugging my arms around my chest.

Watson lets out a playful bark, raising my gaze. I search for what merited the outburst, but don't see anything that could have instigated it. I take in the sights. Goose Grove is always beautiful, but it really shines this time of year. The cool breeze nips at my nose as the gold leaves rustle overhead, solidifying that it's the first day of fall in upper Minnesota. *It is so beautiful. I have missed it.*

Watson's tail glides back and forth like a little metronome set to the rhythm of his feet. I take a deep breath, relishing the comforting presence of Mrs. Heart and Watson.

Mrs. Heart points to the biggest house on the street—the biggest in the town—with a white picket fence. "Oh, Celeste, do you remember when you and Nicole would have tea parties in her front yard? You two were joined at the hip back then."

I follow Mrs. Heart's gesture, and a recognition flickers over me. "I do," I say sadly. "We used to pretend we were attending one of her parents' galas."

"They're having another one next month; maybe you can go now that you're an adult," she chuckles.

"I don't think I'd be invited," I laugh, knowing I'm not exactly the type to be invited to those things. *Why would they want me there?*

"Nonsense. As your parents would tell it, you've got more money than the whole town combined. Even those stuck-up Astors.

Who, by the way, lost a lot of their wealth with some recent bad real estate deals. Serves them right for trying to own the entire town," she says conspiratorially. "But, you didn't hear it from me, of course."

"I don't know about that," I respond, not in the mood to elaborate on my current financial status. "I'm 'new money,' after all." And, attempting to change the subject away from my finances, I ask, "Is she still married to Marcus?"

"Yep, they've got a pair of adorable twins. Sweet kids. Took after their father more than their mother in that department," she laughs.

"Oh yeah, good for them," I say, a twinge of jealousy flitting through me.

"You know he's mayor now, right?" she asks, raising her eyebrow at me.

"Oh…wow. He's always been a charmer. Makes sense," I say with a sigh.

"What's with that wistful voice?" she asks.

"Oh, I don't know. Thinking about the past, I guess," I say, trailing off. Past mistakes, more like it. *If I hadn't left, would I have a family?*

As we continue our walk, Mrs. Heart regales me with more stories from my childhood, each a thread weaving together the tapestry of my past. I spot the old oak tree where Marcus carved our initials in a heart. In the distance, I see a lush park where Ryan and I often rollerbladed. It's been so long since I've been home, and so much has changed, but the scenery still contains whispers of the past. It invokes a melancholic nostalgia.

"You never did find Mr. or Ms. Right, did you?" she asks, yet it's more of a statement.

"Wasn't ever looking for one. 'Married to work,' as they say," I reply, putting my hands in my pockets and squeezing my fists. "I was too busy for anything more than casual flings." *Too busy for love. Too busy for my family.*

"I bet you'll be getting busy again in no time," she laughs, saying "getting busy" with a flourish and doing a little dance.

I sigh at her because she has talked to me in this way since I was old enough for her to do so. The dichotomy of the little old lady with a filthy mouth will never get old.

"I'm starting to…starting to think it was a mistake, though. I think…I think maybe I wish I had started a family," I admit.

"Well, you're still young, dear. There's still time for all that," she replies, patting my shoulder.

"Maybe…" I trail off. *Is it really not too late? Not that anyone would want me.*

Watson continues to trot at a steady pace, leading us to a place only he and Mrs. Heart seem to know. Occasionally, he pauses to sniff a fallen leaf or intimidate a wayward squirrel. His antics draw a laugh from me. *Mrs. Heart was right. A walk is doing me some good.*

As we approach the downtown region, the cozy homes give way to a variety of commercial buildings. Many of the buildings have been revitalized or entirely replaced. The once-quaint downtown area is now a patchwork of disparate building designs—some rustic, some colonial, some all metal and glass, and some unfinished, with just frames of future buildings.

To my left, right at the edge of the downtown region, is a vibrant splash of colorful foliage. "What is that?" I ask. Watson seems to spot the area at the exact moment. His ears perk up, and his nose twitches with curiosity.

"That's the community garden," Mrs. Heart states with pride. "I helped start it. Watson and I volunteer there most weeknights."

Watson darts forward, leash taut, and pulls me forward. I now smell what he does: fresh earth and flowers. "Hold your horses, Watson," I chuckle, holding onto the leash. "Don't rip my arm out of the socket."

Watson, undeterred, tugs insistently, zigzagging between rows of plants I don't know the name of. With each new scent, he pauses, sniffing deeply, then proceeds further into the garden.

"Supposedly, dogs see with their noses," I say, enjoying watching Watson explore. I breathe in the sweet smell of the garden and feel a warm glow of contentment settle over me. I like this place. *Maybe I'll get into gardening.*

"Hey there, Watson!" a deep male voice calls out. I follow the sound to spot Principal Gandy ambling toward us, waving gently. His smile is as warm as ever. He removes his hat, revealing hair now white with age, glinting in the sun against his dark mahogany skin.

"Good morning, Gus!" Mrs. Heart replies, her voice low and husky. She casually returns his wave with a flourish of fingers and bats her eyes. *Is she flirting?*

Watson trots over to Principal Gandy, his high-held tail now lowered and wagging furiously. He leans against the principal's legs and lifts his front paw, exposing his belly for pets. Principal Gandy bends down and reveals a weathered hand under a gardening glove. He groans as he bends, age obviously adding a bit of a kick to the bend, and gently pats Watson's chest.

"How're you doing, Regina?" Principal Gandy asks with a glint in his eye and a smoothness in his voice that hints at familiarity. He continues to pat Watson but doesn't break eye contact with Mrs. Heart. *What's going on with that look? Is dirty perv Mrs. Heart getting some?*

"Oh, my! Is that Celeste Moon? My most successful student is back!?" he exclaims, finally breaking his eyes from Mrs. Heart's blushing face and noticing me.

"Nice to see you, Principal Gandy," I say.

"Call me Gus, young lady! I'm not a principal anymore! I retired almost fifteen years ago. Tell me, is it true you're richer than the Astors and Adamses combined now?" he asks with a chuckle.

"Um…I…I…don't…" I stammer, unsure what to say.

"Ah, don't mind me. I'm just giving you a hard time," he laughs. "I have Google; I already know the answer." Watson breaks away and sniffs the earth with unbridled enthusiasm. "Well, looks like Watson doesn't have time for me today, Regina," he laughs.

"He's on a quest for doggy biscuits," Mrs. Hearts chuckles.

"Ah, taking her to the cafe, huh?" Gus asks Watson. Watson is having none of this banter and pulls his leash. He turns to me with those big brown eyes. It's like he's saying, "I'm done here, girl, let's get a move on!"

"Looks like it, Gus. See you tonight," Mrs. Heart says and gives him a side hug. He gives her a quick peck on the top of the head, and I just barely catch her youthful blush and giggle before Watson snaps me away.

"Tell my daughter to respond to my text when you see her!" Gus shouts after we're a few yards away. Mrs. Heart waves in affirmation.

"So, you and Principal Gandy, huh?" I ask, shouldering her affectionately.

"Yeah," she laughs and doesn't elaborate further, which is very much not like her. *Oh, she must really like him if she's not going to provide further detail.*

We cross the parking lot of Glendos's Grocery. It's still one of the few buildings in town with an actual parking lot, albeit only large enough to hold a few dozen or so cars. It's no longer the rundown store of my memory, but now a glossy interpretation of itself. *Glendos's Grocery got a glow-up.*

A grey-blond man wearing the grocer's signature green apron exits the automated doors, wiping his hands and looking worse for the wear. Watson spots him and barks, gently tugging me toward the door.

"Celeste, is that you?" he claims in a slightly British accent. I squint in the sun, trying to get a good look at him.

With a joyful yip, Watson bounds toward the older blondish man, and I follow. When he reaches the man, he nudges him with his soft nose, practically vibrating with enthusiasm.

"I'm sorry, Watson, I shoulda greeted you, too," the man laughs, bending down to give Watson a scratch behind the ears. "What a handsome boy," he coos, smooshing Watson's ears across his face before rising.

When he stands, I'm finally able to recognize him, but before I can say a thing, he grabs me in a big bear hug. "Celeste, as I live and breathe. It is you!" he beams, his accent just slightly peeking through.

Mrs. Heart approaches with a warm smile. "Good morning, Sean!"

"Mornin', Regina," he replies, still gripping my shoulders and marveling at me. "Gosh, you're still as beautiful as ever."

"Thanks, Mr. O'Connor," I blush.

"How are you doin', Duck?" he asks, concern washing over his still handsome face. "I'm so sorry about your folks."

"I'm okay. Thanks," I shrug, not wanting to elaborate.

"Where are you two off to?" he asks with a huge, handsome grin, finally releasing my shoulders.

Mrs. Heart answers for me, because I have no fucking clue. "Sarah's for some coffee and…" she lowers her voice, hiding her words from Watson, "treats."

"Ah, well, I wish I could join you and catch up, but I have to get back to work," he sighs sadly. "You stayin' at your parents?" he asks.

I just nod my head and fake a grin.

"Then I'll be seeing you around," he says, turning toward the door.

We say our goodbyes and continue on our path. Once Mr. O'Connor is out of earshot, Mrs. Heart laughs, "The whole town will know you're here now."

"Still the town gossip?" I ask, recalling how Mr. O'Connor has always used his beautiful face and charm to coax people into revealing everything to him.

"God, yes. Worse now that he works at the grocery store. Easier access to secrets," she laughs.

"Why…why does he work there? What happened to the orchard?" I ask, looking back at the store.

She shrugs. "He sold it a few years ago."

"That's weird," I say, recalling the time I spent there as a kid. "He loved that place."

She sighs, "Yeah, I don't know the whole story there, but I don't think he had much of a choice."

"Huh, Ryan never told me," I reflect, placing my hands back in my pocket, a new sense of sadness that I don't quite understand seeping into me. "I wonder why…"

"Well, I'm sure you'll get a chance to ask him soon enough. There's no way Sean's not calling him right now and telling him where you're headed," she chuckles, shaking her head.

3

"So, where's Watson taking us?" I ask Mrs. Heart. "You said, 'Sarah's'?"

"Sarah's cafe. It's just around the corner," Mrs. Heart nods, motioning to the corner a block ahead of us. "Let's get a drink and rest there for a while. These old bones are barkin.'"

"Gus's Sarah? She owns a cafe around here?"

"Yep. A few years ago, Sarah bought Shady's and turned it into the cutest little cafe," she responds. "You'd never know it used to be a dive bar. No more greasy food and bathroom glory holes!" she chuckles.

"It didn't have glory holes, Mrs. Heart!" I exclaim.

"It sure did. You must have never been in the men's room," she laughs.

"You had?" I ask.

"Sure, I have. Where do you think I met John?" she says with a side eye, which indicates she's joking, but there may be some truth to the joke.

Before I can ask more questions about that, she continues, "Sarah works there with her spouse, Andy. Andy uses they/them pronouns. Please don't go embarrassing me and misgender them. You'll recognize them by the hair dyed bright red and tattoos completely covering their arms," she says.

"Okay, thanks. I won't," I say with a nod.

"I don't recall an Andy. Are they new in town?"

"Oh, no, dear, it's Andy Astor."

"Oh, wow," I exclaim. I want to say, "She bagged an Astor?" but refrain.

"Yeah, that match surprised the whole town. But Andy's a good egg…despite their family." I didn't really know Andy when I was growing up. Before Nicole and I had our falling out in middle school, I would see them in passing. They'd occasionally make appearances during my and Nicole's tea parties, but mostly I just knew them as Nicole's twin sibling who lived behind a closed bedroom door and blasted music.

"What do we do with Watson while we go in?" I ask.

"Watson can go wherever he wants in this town," she says as if that answers my question…which I suppose it does.

Watson's excitement crescendos as we walk toward a cafe with the pink sign. The inviting scent of pastries and freshly brewed coffee ignites a spark in him, and his tail becomes a blur of happiness.

I push open the door, and a soft bell chimes above us. "Watson!" a pale, tattooed redhead, I assume to be Andy, cleaning a table, exclaims. Their smile reaches their eyes as they catch sight of Watson. "You're looking sharp today, aren't you?"

Watson responds by bounding up to them and greeting them with a gentle nudge of his head against their leg.

"Seriously, does everyone know Watson?" I ask.

"It's a small town, and he's a cute dog," the redhead, confirmed by the nametag to be named Andy, says.

I look around the cafe, and Sarah really has made it unrecognizable. It's quaint and pink, with possibly more plants than the community garden. It's really not the vibe I would expect from the metal-loving Sarah I remember. The rich, full-bodied scent of coffee wafts through the air, and this may be the coziest place I've ever been. I feel a sense of relaxation overwhelm me to the point I may pass out right here in the doorway.

"Andy, you remember Celeste Moon?" Mrs. Heart asks.

"Oh, yeah. Hey, Celeste," they say with a nod, but not really breaking eye contact with Watson. Watson flops over, and Andy says, "Okay, fine!" bending down to rub his belly. "I needed to go wash my hands anyway after bussing this table," they say with a chuckle.

My gaze drifts to the counter where Nicole Astor Adams stands—an elegant figure amidst the cutesy charm. Her blonde hair cascades perfectly over her flawless (presumed spray-tanned, because she's naturally as pale as Andy) shoulders.

Nicole converses with a beautiful woman standing sentinel behind the counter. There's a moment of hesitation before I recognize her. "Oh, wow! Is that Sarah?" I ask out loud.

Andy laughs, "Ha, I bet she's changed quite a bit."

Understatement of the century. She still has the same beautiful features and flawless dark skin, making her face almost instantly recognizable, but that's where the similarities to the girl I grew up with end. The Sarah I remember had a mohawk and wore spiked leather. This Sarah has sleek micro braids pulled into a bun atop her head and wears a pink, flowery dress that resembles one from a 1950s department store catalog.

Nicole, however, looks exactly how you'd expect her to have grown up to look: snobby. "Sarah, I really don't know how you stay in business!" Nicole says, her words dripping with honey and edged with steel. "Andy's trust fund must be running out by now. You really need to charge more for your coffee. Well, not this coffee. As I've mentioned before, you should look into those fresh organic beans I got at that gorgeous cafe in Minneapolis. They'd really step up the quality of your coffee. I already left the name of the cafe with you. I do hope you will call them."

"Of course, Nicole, I'll certainly consider it," Sarah responds in a calm voice that brings a flood of memories. Her smile never wavers, and you can see the stoicism of a debate champion in her, but her hands grip the edge of the countertop a touch too firmly. The strain in her polite tone is almost imperceptible, but having known Sarah since we were little girls, I can hear it. It's a reaction I recognize all too well, having known Nicole just as long and witnessed how others respond to her.

"Oh, Sarah! I know you could elevate this place if you just put in a bit more effort." Nicole's laugh is airy, a practiced melody of condescension. "Please consider it! I just want the best for this town. And for Andy, of course."

I catch Mrs. Heart's eye as we both observe Nicole, our shared glance carrying volumes without a single spoken word. It is a silent acknowledgment of the charade we know all too well. *Some things never change, I guess. Cunts stay cunty.*

Sarah's voice maintains an unwavering cheeriness. "Absolutely, Nicole. It's input from valued patrons like you that keeps us striving for the best." I stifle a chuckle because I know that's Sarah's extremely polite way of telling Nicole to fuck right off, but Nicole will never hear it.

Nicole continues, "Since we're family now," she cuts a snide glance at Andy, who stands and squares their shoulders, obviously contemplating whether to intervene, "I'd think you'd consider me more than just a patron."

Nicole seems satisfied with her last comment and turns her back to Sarah to view her phone as she awaits her coffee. Sarah and Andy both visibly relax. Andy walks toward the back and shares a loaded nod with Sarah before entering the backroom, presumably to wash their hands after playing with Watson.

Nicole looks up from her phone, and her eyes sweep across the room with the self-assurance of someone who owns it, even if just in spirit. And honestly, if Mrs. Heart hadn't just told me Sarah owned the place, it would be a safe assumption that Nicole did own it—since her parents own half the town. She casually brushes an invisible speck off her designer jacket, the movement as graceful as everything else about her.

Sarah spots me and lights up, waving and saying, "Celeste, oh, wow!"

I smile and walk toward her, ready to catch up, but I'm stopped in my tracks when Nicole locks her sights on me. She blocks my path to Sarah, and I brace myself for the verbal onslaught.

"Ah, Celeste! Darling, how absolutely delightful to see you here!" Nicole exclaims, her voice coated in feigned surprise. A smile is plastered on her lips, but her eyes hold that familiar calculating glint. She and I both know she's hated my guts since we were pre-teens.

I smile at Sarah apologetically, then brace for the verbal jousting coming my way by arming myself with a careful, neutral expression. Talking to Nicole is like trying to fuck on a minefield: dangerous yet still somehow arousing. If it weren't for our shared history, I'd be kind of into it.

"It's so nice to see that wealth hasn't changed that unassuming, low-maintenance, tomboy vibe you've always had," Nicole adds, waving her hand at me in that way one does when they want to dismiss something disgusting.

"Nicole, what a pleasant surprise," I reply, my tone measured and polite. *Smile, Celeste, don't let her get to you.*

"I did not know you were in town. I'm so sorry about your parents," she says with a level of empathy I didn't realize she was capable of. This is a sentiment, I suppose, I shall hear quite often. How I determine who actually means it is beyond me. She and my mother got along well, so I guess it is likely genuine.

"Thanks, Nicole," I say with a forced grin.

"We must get together while you are in town. How long are you here for? You'll be leaving after you sell the house, I presume?" Nicole asks.

"Actually, I think I'll be staying…indefinitely."

"Oh, really? Why on earth would you want to stay in that shabby old thing?! Don't you need to get back to your company?"

"Um…actually, I sold it. The company," I say nervously. *Fuck, here it comes.*

"Oh, got to be too much for you?" she asks with a smirk that is so vicious it's almost a sneer. She's not even trying to hide her arrogance.

Alright, bitch. Time to meet Celeste Fucking Moon, CEO and

Badass Bitch. I respond with a tone of authority and control, "Ha, no. I just needed a break from all the snobbery of the upper class. You know the type. The ones who mistake condescension for conversation and privilege for personality. Plus, I've already made soooo much money, what point is there in making more?" I shrug. "I'd much rather spend my time relaxing and maybe, I don't know, starting a family." *Shit, I shouldn't have said that last part.*

Nicole, never one to absorb an insult even when you don't veil the fact you're talking about her, says, "Oh, you're still single, Celeste?! I hate to break it to you, but it might be a little too late to start that family." *Mortal wound.*

"Maybe, but I've never had a problem finding men in this town willing to help me try. Speaking of…how's Marcus?"

She does actually bristle at this, and I'm proud to disarm her for the first time, maybe ever. The fact that I dated Marcus before her, took his virginity even, will always be a real sore spot for her. Why the high school quarterback, prom king, wanted to slum it with the rollerblading, video game-loving, tomboy nerd, she'll never understand. And that will always eat away at her. She'll always wonder what I had that she didn't and hate me even if she figures it out.

"Oh, he's wonderful. He's the mayor now, as I'm sure you know. He's really cleaning up this old town. Speaking of jobs, I have one to do. I can't just lollygag in a cafe all day like some people," Nicole responds. "Toodles, Celeste. Let's get dinner sometime."

"Goodbye, Nicole," I grin tightly back, eager for my heart rate to return to normal and speak to Sarah.

Mrs. Heart pats my back and sighs, "That girl will never change. Don't take it personally. She's actually gotten a lot worse since Marcus became mayor."

"Wow. Didn't think it was possible. What does she do for work? Micromanage the demons in hell?"

Mrs. Heart laughs with her belly as we approach the counter. "No, she works for the town. Some fancy title, I think she gave herself. Community Beauty Planner or something. She's part of the committee changing everything around here."

Sarah's face transforms when we reach her, the genuine warmth replacing the strained politeness that had shadowed her features moments ago.

I practically skip toward the counter and exclaim, "Hey, Sarah! Oh my God, this place! And you look fucking amazing!"

Sarah rushes around to greet me in a hug, squealing, "Oh my God, you too! I missed you. I'm so excited for you to be back!"

"Good morning, Sarah," Mrs. Heart greets, the ease of her demeanor reflecting the change in atmosphere.

"Good morning, Mrs. Heart. Watson," Sarah beams. She returns to her position behind the counter while saying, "Oh, my God, Celeste. I heard what you said to Nicole. An admirable effort. That jab about Marcus was an SS Rank, God-tier, finishing blow. I wish Andy had heard it," she laughs. "I cannot believe those two shared a womb."

"Thanks, Sarah," I reply, blushing at the praise.

"So, what can I get you two? Your usual, Mrs. Heart?" Sarah asks.

"Yes, please, dear," Mrs. Heart smiles warmly, "for me and Watson here."

"Oh, don't worry, we would never forget Watson's special treat," Sarah says, grinning down at the dog whose tail wags even more furiously now that he's heard the word "treat."

I stare at the sign above Sarah's head listing all the coffees available. I bite my lip, frozen in indecision. I request assistance, anxious that I'm taking too long. "Hm, do you have any recommendations?"

"Well, I always find a honey lavender latte to be the perfect calming palette cleanse after a spar with Nicole," she laughs.

"Oh, that sounds wonderful. I'll take your largest size," I say. I imagine the honey and lavender calming my nerves, and suspect this may be a drink I'll need often. I spot the reusable cups sporting the cafe's logo and grab a pink one. "Can I get it in this?"

"Absolutely. Feel free to sit wherever's open. Andy will bring the drinks to you shortly," Sarah says with a sincere smile that reminds me of why I've always liked her. "I'm bummed it's so busy right now," she pouts. "I wanna catch up!"

“Don’t worry, dear, I’m sure the two of you will have plenty of time for that,” Mrs. Heart says to her while shuffling to a corner booth.

“Yeah, I’m not going anywhere any time soon,” I smile, following Mrs. Heart.

“Awesome!” Sarah beams.

Mrs. Heart adds, “Oh, and your father said to return his text.”

Sarah rolls her eyes. “Gah! He just asked me a question about pumpkins. He knows I’m busy. Why can’t he just Google it himself?”

Mrs. Heart giggles, “You know how we old people are with technology, dear.”

Sarah groans loudly and pulls her phone from her pocket.

This doesn’t align with my memory of Principal Gandy. *I mean Gus.* “He said he knows how to use Google. And…doesn’t he have a PhD in library science?”

Mrs. Heart leans in to me and whispers as we settle into the booth, “He just sends her random questions throughout the day because he wants an excuse to talk to her.”

4

The booth we've chosen sits in the back corner of the cafe. I sit with my back to the wall and can see the entire cafe from this vantage point. Sarah has really transformed this place. The last time I sat in this spot, I was in a similar, and slimier, booth with Marcus. He and I spent many evenings that summer eating pizza and playing our Game Boys. I run my hand over the soft fabric of the bench, and I can almost feel the cracked, red vinyl sticking to the back of my bare legs, exposed by my shorts. I can also feel the fumbling hands of Marcus going up those shorts as he fingered me the first time. I wonder if he knows what a clit is by now. Judging by the fact that Nicole is still as angry as ever, I'm not so sure.

I scan the cafe, appreciating the various art and plants and taking note of the patrons, all of whom I don't recognize. The chairs are mismatched in style, but all look incredibly comfortable and adorable. Sarah must be a huge fan of pink—which, who can blame her?

My heart skips a beat when my eyes land on a handsome man at the table adjacent to ours. I immediately avert my gaze, not wanting to gape at him openly. I steal furtive glances, trying to see him without looking directly at him. Mrs. Heart is saying something, but I don't register it, too overcome with the lust building within me. A lust definitely not related to the memories of being poorly finger-banged in this seat 20 years ago.

I'm no stranger to lust, but I haven't felt a crush this instantaneous and intense since puberty. It can only be comparable to the moment Casper walked down those stairs at the local movie theater and asked Kat if he could keep her.

He's deeply engrossed in whatever he's typing on his laptop and doesn't notice us. AirPods peek out from behind his long, tousled, wavy black hair, and I brave a more direct stare since I don't think he'll even notice.

His brows are drawn together in concentration, the corners of his mouth tugging downwards ever so slightly, making him look serious and seriously handsome. His thin-rimmed glasses would make a less attractive man look old, but they make him look delicious. His faded graphic tee stretches over a wide, broad chest. I want to rip off those slutty little glasses and run my fingers through his hair while he types on my lap. *Fuck, Celeste, get it together. What's gotten into you? I wish it were him.*

"Celeste, dear, are you listening?" Mrs. Heart's voice breaks through my daze.

"Wha? Um, no, I'm sorry, what?" I say. *Do I need to wipe my mouth? Am I drooling?*

She smirks at me, and her eyes flit to the fucking hottest man alive. "That's Michael Nguyen," Mrs. Heart whispers to me, nodding subtly toward him without making it obvious. "He's a mystery writer."

A pink apron and an arm covered in tattoos of cats and flowers block my view of the hottie mystery writer. Andy places our drinks on the table and we thank them profusely. Watson, at our feet, watches Andy intently, sitting more still than I've ever seen him.

"Don't worry, Watson, I didn't forget you," Andy says and pulls a cookie-like treat from their pocket. They bend down and give it to the dog with a nice head pat. "How many times are you gonna make me wash my hands, boy?" Watson receives the treat with a characteristic enthusiasm for all things edible. Once the treat is in his mouth, he retreats to the space between my and Mrs. Heart's feet.

"Just like a man, give him what he wants, and he stops fawning over you," Andy laughs.

"Or is it that men are more like dogs?" Mrs. Heart retorts.

"You got me there, Mrs. H. Enjoy the drinks."

Once Andy leaves, I sneak a longer glance at Michael. He didn't even look up when Andy stood next to him, too absorbed in his work. I'm more confident in my ability to stare and dare to outright ogle him openly. His focused expression seems to shield him from the world. He is striking. The sunlight catches the faintest streaks of silver in his black hair—a distinguished touch. It's curious to witness someone so thoroughly ensconced in their imagination. Admirable. *Fucking hot as hell.*

Watson, with the contented air only a well-loved dog in possession of a fresh treat can attain, must suddenly sense an opportunity for social expansion beyond his immediate circle. With the treat still clenched between his teeth, he saunters over to Michael and gently nudges his leg.

Michael stops typing and looks down with a mild air of irritation. But there is something disarmingly adorable about Watson's large, pleading eyes that will erase any annoyance you may have with him. And there is something disarmingly adorable about the brilliant smile Michael beams at Watson that erases any semblance of brain cells I have left.

Now that his eyes have broken from the computer, the light hits them just right, revealing a brilliant amber. *Striking*. Michael, obviously not immune to the charms of big brown Cavalier eyes, says in a deep voice, warm with amusement, "Hey there, Watson!" The sound is smooth, like honey that drips right into my panties. *This dog DOES know everyone.*

"You want to help me write, boy?" Michael jokes, scratching behind Watson's floppy ears, eliciting a tail wag so vigorous it moves at a speed that rivals Michael's fingers—those, long, nimble, wedding-ring-free fingers.

Michael looks up at our table, smiling at Mrs. Heart. But when his gaze finds me, those gorgeous amber eyes, behind slutty little black-rimmed glasses, widen and lock on. A smile blooms deeper on his face.

No longer concerned with his laptop or the dog, Michael rises with fluid grace, and I forget to breathe.

"Seems like Watson knows how to pick his friends," Michael says, taking a step closer to me. His compliment, while directed to Watson, is definitely a compliment to me and surprisingly forward.

I chuckle, releasing my held breath. "He's quite the socialite."

Michael laughs, a rich sound that resonates in the close quarters of the cafe and vibrates my core. "I'm surprised we haven't elected him mayor yet." He reaches his hand out for me to shake. "I'm Michael Nguyen, and you are?"

"Celeste Moon," I say, and Michael's eyes go wide with the expression of someone who's heard my name before, when I take his hand. I ignore the look and continue, "I'm sorry that we've distracted you from your work."

"Trust me. I welcome the distraction. I was stuck, and I think talking to you might be the exact inspiration I need right now." *What a line.* I'd fan myself if that wouldn't be incredibly cheesy. "It's an honor to meet you, Celeste."

"Likewise," I grin at him.

I'm still shaking his hand, just smiling stupidly at him and refusing to let go. He doesn't seem to mind. I blush red and drop his hand, and ask, "So, um…Mrs. Heart says you're writing a mystery novel?"

"Yeah, it's just, whatever…" he says, waving his hand at the computer. He sits back down in his seat, scooting the chair closer to me and pushing his laptop to the other side of his table.

Watson puts his paws on Michael's knees, clearly indicating he is unhappy that the attention is not entirely directed at him. Michael resumes petting Watson, but does not break his gaze from me. He asks, "What about you, Celeste? What are you up to today?"

"Um, nothing right now. Reacquainting myself with the town. It's been a while since I've been back."

"Are you here visiting, or are you back for good?"

"Back for good," I say, feeling a bit disarmed by his intense stare.

"That's wonderful news," he says, smiling at me in a way that makes me feel like I'm on the menu. After a moment of pause, he says, "I'm trying to come up with a smooth way to say I know who you are and have played all your video games," while nervously brushing an invisible speck off his knee. "But everything I think of probably makes me sound like every other creepy guy who's been in love with your work for years."

"Well, most guys don't admit that so quickly. They usually pretend they don't know who I am or find a way to insult my work. So, you already don't sound like every other creepy guy."

"Oh, well, that's good to hear. Not that most guys are jerks, but that I haven't blown my chances yet," he says. He rambles slightly at me, a nervousness replacing his initial smoothness. "I haven't, have I? Is it presumptuous to assume I even have a chance?"

This rambly, nervous version of him is even hotter than the one with good pickup lines. I lean forward on the tabletop, completely overtaken by this disarmingly handsome man who's losing his cool over me. I sigh, "You absolutely have not blown your chances, and you absolutely are not presuming."

"Well, perhaps we can play games together sometime," he says, quirking an eyebrow, some of that smoothness returning.

"I'd very much like that," I say, blushing and thinking of all the other things we could do together.

5

A movement outside catches my attention. I glance up to see a man with tousled blond hair walking purposefully to the cafe. We lock eyes, and recognition instantly crosses his face. He lights up and bursts through the door, bringing a burst of chilled autumn air with him.

My heart flutters in time with the jingling bell above the door as Ryan O'Connor launches himself toward me. His wide grin is so infectious that it seems to ripple through the cafe, turning heads and drawing smiles.

"Star Girl!" his shout slices through the chatter as he rushes toward my table without even looking at another soul in the room. Michael's head snaps toward him, breaking his eye contact with me for the first time since Watson alerted him to my presence.

"Ry Guy!" I exclaim, unable to repress my genuine happiness at seeing my childhood friend. My response is so visceral, so genuinely charged with delight, it is as though the years of distance have simply dissolved.

With a boyish grin plastered across his face, Ryan closes the gap between us in a few eager strides. His arms open wide, uncaring how much space he takes up. His blue eyes sparkle with the same devilish mischief that has convinced me to do oh so many naughty things. I brace for impact, as the speed at which he approaches doesn't slow. Watson jumps up, his whole body wiggling as he runs toward Ryan, but Ryan doesn't address him.

Ryan grips my hand, yanking me from my seat, bumping me against Michael, and causing my coffee to wobble precariously on the table. Before I can even react, his arms are around me, strong and warm, lifting me from the ground and spinning me. The familiar press of his body against mine stirs a nostalgic, girly desire I hadn't felt in nearly two decades.

Laughter bubbles out of me, unbidden, as his joy radiates through the air. His laugh, deep and rich, wraps around me. My feet dangle for a brief, exhilarating moment before he gently sets me back down. His arms don't leave my body, still steadying me at my lower back and pulling me against him. The press of his slightly hardened cock pools a tingly gooeyness within me. Watson barks and jumps on our legs, trying to get our attention.

I grip Ryan's strong, solid shoulders instinctively, breathless, and look up to find his face close to mine, lit with an irrepressible grin.

His voice is alight with unguarded happiness. "I couldn't help it," he beams. "Fuck, I missed you."

The cafe melts away for a second, and my focus is fully on his heat, his smell, his touch. My heart races, not just from the spin but from the unexpected, unfiltered joy of the moment. His grin goes crooked with a devious smirk, and my body's reaction to it is practically Pavlovian. That smile has so often preceded an orgasm, I can't help but become aroused at the sight of it.

"Good to have you back in my orbit, Star Girl," Ryan claims, still not releasing me, but leaning me back so he can look at me.

"Missed you, too, Ry Guy," I respond, my heart doing a little dance at the exhilaration of his closeness.

I remain pressed against him, as we unabashedly study each other. His shoulders are broader, his chest fuller, and his eyes crinkle a bit more in the corners, but he looks exactly like the boy next door he's always been. Actually…he's much broader. His chest stretches his cable knit sweater to the limit, warping the pattern. No longer boyish, but a full man now. *I wonder how it feels to wrap my legs around his waist now.*

Fuck, I forgot about Michael. I turn to address Michael and apologize for the interruption in our conversation. Michael watches us silently with an introspective gaze, his flirty smile now gone. His deep amber eyes hold a flicker of disappointment that blinks away as quickly as it appeared, his expression settling back into one of quiet observation. *Does he think Ryan and I are an item?*

Ryan speaks before I can, positioning my body so I am facing him. "Goose Grove hasn't been the same without you, Celeste," Ryan proclaims, still not removing his hands from me. I notice our hips are locked together in a way that would be interpreted in no other way than sexual. His dick presses against my gut, and memories of days past flutter inside me.

I pull away from his hips before I do something stupid like kiss him, but his hands still linger on my shoulder and back, refusing to release me from his warm embrace. I bend slightly to pat Watson's head because this dog's need for attention is breaking my heart. Mrs. Heart calls him to her, and he receives his proper pets.

The scuff of Michael's chair returning to its original position turns me toward him. His eyes look down with an acceptance touched by a hint of sadness.

"Do you know—" I say to Ryan, attempting to direct the conversation to Michael.

But before I can finish my sentence, Ryan asks, "How long are you here for?"

"Forever. I'm staying," I say with a huge smile.

"No fucking way! Seriously?!" he asks with genuine surprise.

"Yeah, seriously," I say.

I look back at Michael and attempt to smile apologetically, but he's not looking at me anymore. He gently closes his laptop and gathers his belongings. *No! Don't leave.*

"Wow…that's…that's awesome…" Ryan says, staring deeply into my eyes. Ryan's fingers tap a silent rhythm on my back, each touch a note of familiarity and affection. The same tap he'd done a million times.

"We have so much catching up to do. I want to hear all about your life in California," Ryan says, hugging my head against his chest.

With my face buried in Ryan's hard pecs, I can barely see as Michael says something to Mrs. Heart before nodding to me and silently walking out the door. *Fuck.* I wanted to talk to him more, but this spot on Ryan's chest feels so familiar and comforting, it's hard to be sad.

When the bell jingles and the door closes, Ryan finally breaks his grip on me. *Was he waiting for Michael to leave before he let me go?*

Ryan, ever the tornado of energy, sweeps toward Mrs. Heart. "Mrs. Heart! How are you?" he booms, his voice rich with warmth. "Watson!" he says with equal joviality as he aggressively pets the pup.

"Ryan, dear!" she exclaims, the affection in her tone mirroring the fondness in her gaze. "I'm well, thank you. How about you? Your dad said something about you going viral," she says with a confused sense of understanding.

"Oh, yeah!" he chuckles, scratching the back of his neck. "Another one of my videos really blew up."

"Oh, that's nice, dear. I'm so proud of you," she replies with admiration, having nearly raised Ryan, too.

"I just wish my art could go viral when I keep my shirt on," he replies, rubbing the back of his head and looking to the ground.

"No need to be embarrassed, dear; whatever gets the eyes on your work, right?"

"Well, sometimes I wonder if the eyes are actually on the work," he laughs.

"He says your work is selling out! So they must be seeing it! And you're opening a gallery?"

He lets out a single "ha" before replying, "He told you about that? I haven't even announced it yet."

"Can't stop a proud father from bragging, dear," she says. *Especially not the local gossip.*

"I guess not…" he trails off and glances at his watch, nervous energy wafting off him.

"Celeste, I have to rush off, but we have to catch up properly. How about I come over tonight with dinner?" he asks.

"Sounds like a plan," I agree, my laughter subsiding into a warm smile.

"Okay, good, because I wasn't going to take no for an answer. I was prepared to be as absolutely obnoxious as possible," he chuckles. He squeezes my hand and kisses me on top of my head, before darting out the door with a final, "See ya, Star Girl!" and a salute.

The bell above the cafe door jangles a bright farewell as Ryan, with his usual flair for exits, slips out into the chilly, sunny afternoon. An emptiness hits me as I watch him go, my heart no longer buoyant from the reunion but heavy with regret.

The memory of Michael's expression as he closed his laptop to leave shoots through me, dropping a deep ache in my chest. As much as I love Ryan, I wish I could have had more time to speak to Michael.

"Quite the whirlwind, that one," Mrs. Heart observes, drawing my attention back to her.

"Always has been. He takes up all the energy in a room," I laugh, as I sit back in my seat. I trace the rim of my coffee cup absentmindedly, frowning to myself as I reflect on my actions over the last few minutes. "It was good to see him, though," I say and mean it.

Mrs. Heart grins at me mischievously.

"Don't say it," I appeal.

"Don't say what, dear?"

"Whatever pervy thing you are thinking about me and Ryan. Probably something about shirtless videos. You've been scheming to get me with him for at least 25 years. I know all your tricks." I exhale, leaning back.

Mrs. Heart feigns insult and clutches her nonexistent pearls. "Wouldn't dream of it, dear!"

"Sure," I utter, unconvinced.

"Indeed." Mrs. Heart nods, her gaze softening. She takes a dainty sip from her cup. "And what about Michael? He seemed quite taken with you."

My smile shifts, and I squirm in my seat, feeling my face flush. "I'm not sure. I wish we could've talked more. But, Ryan—"

"Cockblocked you like always?" she asks.

I laugh because, yes, that is exactly what Ryan has always done.

"Well, if you would permit this old woman one scheme," she says and slides a folded piece of paper across the table to me.

"What is this?" I ask, unfolding it.

It reads, "It was wonderful to meet, but I'd love to get to know you —Michael," followed by his number.

"He left this for me?" I whisper, unbelieving. "Really? Even after all…that?" I ask, waving toward where Ryan and I had been.

"He asked me to give it to you," she says with a smirk.

"Thank you, Mrs. Heart," I gush, my heart fluttering. I carefully refold the paper, tucking it into my purse. It seems like there's one cock in this town that won't get blocked by Ryan.

6

"Let me show you where the law office is, and then we can head back. Does that sound okay?" Mrs. Heart asks, as we exit the cafe.

"Sounds great," I respond as we turn to our left to walk deeper into the heart of town. With Watson leading the way, I marvel at the familiarity of the small town, taking note of the things that have changed. Many of the old-fashioned storefronts have been revamped, and I see a hint of an unfinished building towering in the distance. The trees that line the street remain, and there is still barely any place to park.

It feels surreal being back. Like stepping into a dream I once had.

We turn a corner, and I'm confronted with a building that stands out like a sore thumb. It does not look like a quaint building in the middle of a town populated by 19th-century storefronts. It seems more like something you'd see in downtown Minneapolis, except it's only two stories tall instead of a skyscraper. A granite sign claims, "Goose Grove Legal Group."

"Wow, it sticks out like a sore thumb. I don't think I really needed you to show me—" I say just as a door swings open, and I narrowly avoid a collision with the man stepping out onto the sidewalk.

"Oh, miss, I am so sorry," a devastatingly handsome man in a perfectly pressed suit exclaims, the surprise in his voice melting into a friendly smile as his eyes meet mine.

Jesus, did they start putting something in the water since I left? What is with all these handsome as fuck men? The sunlight catches the edges of his neatly styled hair, turning it a soft golden brown with interspersed strands of bright, shining gold threads. A five o'clock shadow outlines his chiseled jaw.

"James, you've always been bad at watching where you're going," Mrs. Heart chides with a chuckle, stepping forward to introduce me. "This is Celeste Moon." Still taken aback by almost being knocked over and by how hot this guy is, I don't say a damn thing, but I do at least manage a goofy smile.

His warm grin shows a hint of recognition. "Oh, yes, I know Celeste."

"You do?!" I ask, surprised, my words finally returning to me, but I still have absolutely no chill.

"You beat my grinding record. Really put me to shame," he says with a wry smile.

"WHAT?!" Mrs. Heart asks, the perv in her rearing its horny head.

"Oh, sorry, Mrs. H, that sounded…rail grinding! Rollerblades. Celeste challenged me to rail grinding back when we were kids. She was a few years younger than me, but she made it all the way down the old steps in Grove Park. Really put me to shame," he responds.

I laugh nervously, then exclaim as my memory catches up to me, "Oh! J-Money!"

"Well, James Montgomery…Esquire, now," James corrects, playfully lifting his chin. As if on cue, a faint autumn breeze catches his hair, accentuating his introduction. *Damn, did he do that on purpose?*

Ever the attentive canine companion, Watson sniffs curiously at James's polished shoes, eliciting the lawyer's gentle pat on the head. "Hey, Watson," he says, without breaking eye contact with me, his goofy grin matching mine. *These men and their eye contact.*

When Watson whimpers at him, he finally breaks eye contact with me and shifts his attention affectionately toward the dog. "I'm sorry, boy." He squats, not putting his knees quite on the ground, but giving the dog the aggressive belly rubs traditionally bestowed upon such a good boy, while asking, "Is this what you wanted, buddy?"

I wish I could see the way his ass looks right now, squatting like this. *The knees on this man.* I note that there is no wedding band on the hand rubbing Watson's belly. I can't help but notice the way his pants stretch at the crotch. *Oh, fuck, this man is ungodly hot.*

"So, how long are you in town for, Celeste?" he asks, rising to lean on the wall and jolting me from my lustful, crotch-staring stupor.

Before I can reply, the door swings open again, and this time, James has to jump out of the way. An older man with a starched collar and a tightly knotted tie barrels out. He looks surprised to see a bunch of people standing outside the door.

"James, why are you loitering?!" he barks.

"Just talking to these ladies and Watson," James says. The older man scowls in response. *He must not be a dog person—red flag.*

"Regina," the man says curtly, addressing Mrs. Heart.

"Dick," she replies with a nod and a coldness I don't think I've ever heard from her.

The tension coils in the air, a tangible contrast to the earlier calm.

Dick? "Oh, are you Richard Holbrook? I have a meeting with you tomorrow to go over my parents' estate," I chime in with a smile, hoping to break the tension.

Richard's eyes skim over me like an unwelcome draft, and he sneers at me. *What did I do?*

"So you must be Celeste Moon," he says, the words carrying an edge sharp enough to slice through me. "So your parents finally got you to come home, I see," he snickers.

A sharp pain shoots through me, stunning me. *Did...did he really just say that to me?*

My mouth hangs agape. A wave of discomfort washes over me. Once I recover from the shock, I square my shoulders and raise my chin—a resilience my mother demanded of me pulsing through my veins.

"Richard, that was uncall—" James says with a tone of authority, positioning his body between me and the other lawyer.

Richard cuts him off with a flick of his wrist to check his wristwatch. "I will see you tomorrow at 11 a.m. sharp, Ms. Moon." He storms off without a goodbye or a second glance.

We watch him leave, disarmed by the interaction and unsure how to turn the conversation.

Richard's words sting my eyes. I feel the pit of despair swirling around me, threatening to drag me under. I look to the ground, hiding my face behind my curtain of hair. *Don't you fucking cry.*

James's voice, warm and reassuring, breaks the silence. "Welcome back to The Grove, Celeste. I imagine a lot has changed since you were last here."

I look up to find James's amiable eyes waiting for me. They're that beautiful green that looks brown from certain angles. He leans casually against the doorframe of the law office again, a gentle smile softening his features. His open posture and warm smile are comforting. His eyes rake over me, shifting from friendly to downright lascivious, shifting me from impending grief to deep lust.

My cheeks warm as his eyes linger on me. "It certainly seems so," I reply, tucking a stray lock behind my ear.

"I assure you the hospitality isn't one of the things that have changed, despite all of that," he says, motioning toward Richard.

I simply nod in response, too stunned by him to say much else. I've never been this disarmed by a man before.

"They tore down that rail a few years ago, which is too bad. Otherwise, I would challenge you to a rematch," he jokes.

I laugh slightly at the thought. "I haven't skated in decades," I look him up and down, admiring his fit physique. I brave a wry smile and decide to try flirting. "I'm sure you'd dominate me," I say as seductively as my pounding heart will allow.

"I don't know, Celeste. I suspect you could dominate me," he smirks, lobbing my innuendo back at me, clearly picking up on it. *He's hitting on me, right?* "If you'd like, I can show you around town—show you some of the other changes they've made around here," he adds, his smirk quirking higher.

"I'd like that."

"I was just heading out for the day. I could show you around now, if you'd like. Then maybe we could get some dinner? That is, if Mrs. Heart and Watson don't mind my stealing you away."

Watson seems to catch the buoyant mood, his tail wagging energetically as he reaches up on James's leg.

Watson: Wingman.

"Seems like Watson approves," James quips, nodding towards the spirited spaniel and bending to rub his head. "Down, boy," he instructs, continuing to pet the dog as Watson lowers himself for belly rubs.

Since the dominant comment, Mrs. Heart has fidgeted with such girlish enthusiasm that she looks like she's about to burst at the seams. She practically sings, "Oh, that is quite all right with me, dears."

Fuck. I already told Ryan I'd eat dinner with him. I look at James's dazzling grin. The words railing and grinding flash through my head, and not in the rollerblading sense.

Before I can respond, a man rushes down the sidewalk toward us—nearly out of breath, his hands fluttering like panicked birds and booming, "James! You've got to help me with this mess, it's urgent!" He's an older man, what some may dub a "silver fox," with golden skin and salt-and-pepper hair.

James straightens and rises off the wall. "Daniel, I was just heading out for the day," James says, his tone a blend of surprise and patience that seems second nature to him.

"Please, it can't wait!" Daniel's insistence cuts through any pretense of departure, and James casts a questioning glance toward me. Disappointment clouds his beautiful green-brown eyes.

"It's okay. I already had plans for the night. Some other time?" I ask, giving him an out.

He looks at me apologetically, and I think he may protest, but he responds, "Sounds like your contact information is in the system. If you don't mind my using it for the nefarious purpose of contacting you socially, I'll text you."

"Oh, that'd be great," I reply, blushing.

"It was wonderful to see you again, Celeste," he grins. His eyes linger a bit longer than expected, a bit longer than is decent, and his grin widens.

James excuses himself, retreating into the law office with Daniel in tow. I turn to Mrs. Heart and swoon, "Holy fuck, that guy is hot." I practically melt onto the wall where he stood just to prop myself up.

"Quite the charmer, isn't he?" Mrs. Heart giggles, voice tinted with the wisdom of one who had seen many such scenes unfold along these cobbled paths.

"He is," I concede, my gaze lingering on the door, wishing he would return.

A flutter—excitement mingled with apprehension—dances through me, a delicate shiver in the crisp autumn air. "Does he charm all the ladies like that?" I ask, wondering if I should steer clear of him.

"Actually, no. Lots of broken hearts fluttering around that one, but I don't think I've ever heard anything about him being in anything serious," she says. "He's like you—focused on his work."

"Weird; I wonder why he'd be interested in me," I say, confused.

"I think it had something to do with grinding, dear," she giggles.

7

I rush to my purse and sift through it for my favorite lip gloss. *Where the fuck did I put it after Watson retrieved it?* I dash to the kitchen and find it next to the pie. I sprint back to the bathroom to apply it and check my hair. I brush out the curls, trying to make them look like a natural wave of my hair and not the result of a luxury multi-styler. *Thank you for your service, Dyson Airwrap.*

A playful knock at the door jolts me from my coiffing. I swipe on another layer of mascara and haphazardly sweep all my makeup off the counter into a little bag. I toss it under the sink, slamming the door behind it and not checking where it landed.

I give myself one last look, ensuring I look hot, but not on purpose, tucking my college sweatshirt into one side of my sweatpants. I don't want Ryan to think I tried too hard, but I also need him to find me irresistible.

I rush to the door, slide on my socks, and open it with a huge grin. "Ry Guy!" I exclaim.

"Star Girl!" he responds. He's wearing grey sweatpants and a sweatshirt matching mine—sweatshirts we collected when we went off to college together. *Why is he wearing grey sweatpants? What is he trying to do to me?*

Ryan leans against the doorframe, precariously balancing an overstuffed bag of Chinese takeout and a bottle of wine. His face breaks into that familiar, playful grin, the one that always promises a good time.

"Hope you've got an appetite," he says, as if we're picking up a conversation we just put on pause fifteen years ago.

Opening the door wider, I can't help the rush of warmth that floods through me. Nostalgia sweeps in like a gust from the past, stirring up memories of a much younger Ryan naked above me, kissing me, and crying about how lucky he was to have a friend like me.

"Well, I hope you're ready to get your ass whooped in Soulcalibur II," I say with a sly grin.

"No! You don't have that! I haven't played that since…high school, maybe," he reflects, his eyes wide open.

"I found it and my old GameCube in my bedroom," I say, making way for him to come in.

"Oh, we're going to your bedroom already, are we?" he jokes.

"No, goof. I brought it downstairs," I laugh.

"Ah, too bad; I was hoping you were harboring decades-long pent-up sexual frustration and were just going to throw yourself at me the moment I walked through the door."

"Still a painful flirt, I see."

"Still doesn't work, I see."

Ryan has been like this for as long as I can remember. I swear his first sentence had to have been, "Celeste, I know you want me." And I did. Sorta. We've had a sexually charged relationship since…forever. We spent the majority of our formative years teaching each other how to please the opposite sex while deriving pleasure from each other. No one ever understood our relationship—myself included.

"Come on in, make yourself at home," I say, though it's clear he already has. He practically lived here when we were kids—right up until we went off to college together—in which case, we actually lived together.

Ryan removes his coat and shoes and looks around. "It's been years since I've been in here."

Same.

He spots the piano in the dining room, now covered with a blanket. "Still can't look at it?"

"No," I say flatly.

He gives me a tight, pursed-lip smile and a nod, signaling he understands I don't want to discuss it further.

Settling onto one of the plush couches in the living room, I watch as Ryan carefully sets the wine on the coffee table. He unpacks the bag of takeout with a flair of ceremony. There's so much food.

"You never could resist overdoing it, could you?" I quip as he spreads the meal out.

"Overdoing it is my middle name," he retorts. Once he's done laying out the food, he adds, "Your mom would be so pissed at us right now." At the mention of my mom, he pauses, softens his tone, and asks, "How are you doing, Star Girl?"

"I'm still processing it."

He responds with a playful squeeze of my knee. Never one to dwell on the uncomfortable for long, he says, "Got your pork fried rice, white rice, and orange chicken, Celeste," winking.

Ryan and I were inseparable from childhood through college. Inseparable until I separated us…moving to California to start my company. He came back to Goose Grove, I moved to California, and then he just…stopped responding to my messages.

There was a long period of time during which we had absolutely no contact. Then, one day out of the blue, he messaged me a silly meme with the message, "Reminds me of you."

We still send each other a meme every few weeks or so, but that's about as deep as our relationship has been. I don't really know anything about his life now, other than what I've seen on social media. This morning was the first time I had seen him in person in nearly fifteen years since we parted ways.

"I can't believe you remember my favorite order," I say in disbelief.

"Of course I remember. I had to call it in at least once a week since you were too scared to phone in the orders," he laughs. "I could recite that script in my sleep—I probably do. I remembered your favorite wine, too." He pours us both a glass and leans back, smirking at me.

"I thought you swore this stuff off after rush week, when you cracked your head open rollerblading," I say.

He laughs. "I did, but that was a long time ago. Plus, gotta make my best girl happy."

"Oh, speaking of the skate park, I saw James Montgomery—J Money." I laugh at the silly nickname.

He chokes on his rice. "Oh yeah? And how'd that go?" An air of coldness frosts his voice.

"He told me the stairs were pulled up from the park! That's so sad!"

He sighs, "Yeah, it's a nice walking trail now, though. It is a bummer that there's nowhere good to skate now. I haven't seen a kid on rollerblades or a skateboard in over a decade."

I nearly drop my chopsticks. "Wait! Is the skate park gone, too?!"

"Unfortunately, yeah. Golden Wingspan Development paved it over a while back. It's apartments now. There's still a nice paved trail around Glendos Park, but there's nowhere to really do any tricks or anything."

"That's too bad. We used to have so much fun rollerblading. The skate park was the only cool place kids could hang out back then," I sigh. "What can kids do around here now?"

"Probably what we did when we weren't skating," he says slyly.

"Oh, you mean playing Soulcalibur II?" I ask, deflecting his innuendo.

"They're probably not playing a twenty-year-old video game; they're probably doing the other stuff we did," he says, raising an eyebrow at me, not letting me wiggle away from his verbal advances so easily.

Changing the subject, I say, "So, Mrs. Heart tells me you're a social media stripper—but the classy, arty kind," spooning pork fried rice into my mouth and stifling a grin.

He sighs. "She would say it that way."

I raise my eyebrows at him while I shovel more food into my face.

He groans and leans back on the couch. "A while back, I posted a video of myself painting shirtless, and it kind of took off. Someone bought my painting—paid more than I ever could have imagined. I tried posting videos with my shirt on, but no one watches those or buys those paintings." He raises his hands in defeat. "So, now I'm the shirtless art guy."

"The last time I saw you with your shirt off, everyone was begging you to put it back on. You were so scrawny and pale," I laugh, playfully shoving him by the shoulder.

"That is not true. I've always been hot. Besides, I don't recall you begging me to put it back on. In fact, I recall you begging me to take off the rest of my clothes."

"I think your memory is clouded by time, my friend," I say, hiding in my wine glass.

"There are a few things I don't remember about college. But my times with you are not on that list." A twinge of sadness coats his voice.

I look him up and down. "But I can see why people might want to see you with your shirt off now." I emphasize "might."

He flexes. "Oh, yeah, like what you see, do you?"

Yes, yes, I do.

"I have a confession. I actually follow your account," I say shyly.

He laughs, "I know."

"What? How!?"

"Some thirsty babe named 'MoonfireGamesCEO' likes all my videos and sends me lewd emojis. It was pretty obviously you, Celeste," he says, draping his arm around my shoulders. "Did you really think I didn't know it was you?"

"I just kind of assumed you had so many responses, you didn't see mine," I laugh. "I've had my notifications muted for so long, I guess I forgot most people don't."

He laughs at me. "What about you, Star Girl? How's Moonfire Games?"

"I sold it." I pause to tuck a stray curl behind my ear. "Well, I'm selling it—it's in the works. Hasn't been officially announced or anything, but the deal is done."

"Sold it!?" He blinks, the surprise evident on his face. "But that was your baby."

"Was," I say succinctly.

"What happened?"

"My parents died."

"Yeah, but why would you sell your company because of that?"

"I hadn't been home in so long. And, I never fixed things with them. Maybe I could have if I hadn't hidden behind it. I realized I used my company as a way to…I dunno…an excuse to not really live, maybe? I guess I realized life is too short. I don't want to be a woman who dies with no one to love, just a company to love…if that makes sense."

"I think it does."

We sit in silence, the weight of all the things unsaid between us hanging heavy in the air. Ryan breaks the silence, asking, "So, you don't have anyone in your life that you love right now?"

"No," I respond flatly.

He turns to me. "So, does that mean we can pick up where we left off?"

"I don't know, Ryan. I…I think I need to figure myself out. I think I need to figure out what I want in life. And…friends with benefits can get in the way of that."

"How so?"

"You know how so! Remember Marcus! He freaked out when he found out that you and I had been together."

"Well, Marcus was a tool. Still is a tool."

"I know that, but even after I explained that you and I stopped having sex the moment he and I started dating, he couldn't trust me around you. Let's face it. Guys aren't exactly lining up to marry the girl who's fucking the boy next door."

"You want to get married? I thought you were anti-marriage."

"People change, Ryan." I exhale. *You'd know that if you ever talked to me.*

I add, "I want kids. I want a family. Or at least I think I do. I've got no one. No family. Not even a cat. But I need to have the space to figure it out."

"Alright, Star Girl. I won't push it. But the door is always open. All you gotta do is say the magic word. You know what it is."

I do…Orion.

"What about you? Don't you want to find love?"

"I don't need to find love." He takes a sip of his wine and averts his gaze.

"Still insisting on the bachelor's life? I can't believe no one locked you down in all these years."

"Well, I was engaged for a bit…but it didn't work out."

I sit patiently waiting for him to elaborate, but he doesn't. He's never really been one to want to talk about this kind of stuff. Not about himself anyway. Not since his mom left.

Refusing to try to change a man who hasn't changed in twenty years, I ask, "Wanna play Soulcalibur?"

He laughs at me, "That's what you wanna do? Sure, Celeste, let's play."

8

“In your face!” I exclaim as I make Link deliver a final spinning sword attack, finishing off Ryan’s character, Ivy.

Ryan groans, slumping back in the chair. “Alright, alright. I let you win.”

“Let me win? Please,” I say, smirking. “You’ve always been terrible at this game.”

“Not true. I was good before you started ribbing me about my strategy.”

“Spamming the same move over and over is not a strategy!”

“It is when it gets a win,” he says with a smirk.

“Whatever, Ryan. Your moves are old and played out. I can see them coming a mile away—even when you spam them, you can’t win,” I laugh.

“Well, that I know for a fact to be untrue.”

“Okay, hotshot, show me.” I lean forward with my controller in position, ready to woop ass yet again.

“Alright.” He looks at me with a devilish grin. “Ope.” He exhales, reaching over and gently brushing a strand of hair away from my face, tucking it carefully behind my ear. His touch is light, but it sends a cascade of warmth through me, pooling somewhere deep inside.

"Thanks," I murmur, suddenly aware of just how close his hand lingers near my cheek. It's as if our years apart have collapsed into this single moment, the space between us charged with memories.

"Anytime." He flashes a boyish smile that melts through me—the same smile that has disarmed me since we were children.

I lean back and place my controller on the table. Without thinking, I reach out and put my hand on his strong jaw. His lip quivers at the gesture, and I want to pull him into me. Before logic can intervene, I call him "Orion."

Ryan needs no further permission; he's heard this magic word hundreds of times before—the code word we used to indicate we wanted to have sex. He closes the remaining distance between us. His lips meet mine in a kiss that feels like coming home. The kiss is tender and questioning, as if he's forgotten how to kiss, but I can tell he's waiting for me to reciprocate. When I return his kiss, his kiss deepens with more confidence. We've done this dance before, yet everything about it feels new and thrilling.

My hands find their way to his shoulders, and I pull his chest toward me. The urgency in our breaths mingle as we gasp for air and stumble over each other. Ryan pulls back just enough for me to catch a glimpse of the familiar twinkle in his eyes, one that's always signaled he's up to no good.

"See," he says. "Old moves work like a charm. That hair behind-the-ear move gets me a win every single time. I know you, Star Girl. But that's not all I remember how to do."

He pushes me back gently, hovering his body over me for just a moment before pressing his weight down on me. His fingers eagerly slide down the front of my sweatpants and slip into my panties. The overwhelming warmth of his touch sends shivers up my spine.

"I knew you'd be wet for me," he moans into my ear.

His fingertips flick against my clit, momentarily making me buck upward to meet their teasing touch. He applies a firm circular motion, reminiscent of the way he handled the video game controller. His touch evokes a familiar intimacy, and it feels like the years apart never happened as he expertly applies pressure in all the right places.

As he continues stimulating me with precision, my arousal grows stronger. His teeth graze along my throat as he nibbles softly, causing goosebumps to spread down my chest.

His warm breath brushes against my ear, and he whispers breathlessly, "You feel so good, Star Girl."

His strong arm wraps around my waist, pulling me impossibly close to him. His words are filled with longing and desire. "I missed the feel of you. I missed the taste of you. I missed you so much." He takes my earlobe into his mouth, sucking and nibbling it.

His hips grind against me in response to my pleasure. His movement further ignites me. With assertive motions, his hand moves faster —stroking and caressing.

"Come for me, Celeste. Let me hear that cute sound you make that I've missed so much," he commands.

The intensity of the sensation builds rapidly, and my body begins to tremble. The pleasure within me reaches a crescendo—and I'm consumed by an incredibly powerful release that leaves me trembling and weak in his embrace. I bask in my climax until he quips, "See, button spamming is a strategy."

"Shut up, dork. Did you bring a condom?" I need the feel of his cock inside me.

"If I say yes, are you going to think I'm presumptuous?"

"I already know you're presumptuous," I laugh.

He fumbles with his wallet and retrieves a condom. He pulls his erect cock from his pants and sheepishly unrolls the condom down his length. The corners of his mouth twitch into the cutest, embarrassed smile—the same smile he's done every single time he's put a condom on in front of me.

I tug my pants down, tossing them to the floor. I can't judge him for bringing a condom. I wore these pants specifically because I, too, knew this would happen, and they'd be easy to remove. He doesn't bother pulling his pants all the way off, and neither of us bothers removing our shirts.

He positions himself above me, knocking his tip at my entrance. His eyes search mine for confirmation as he asks, "Yeah?"

"Yes," I exhale, grabbing his muscular backside, aching to feel him fill me, and pulling his pants further down his taut ass.

He pushes into me gently but firmly, each inch of him stretching and filling me completely. A flood of delightful sensations overwhelms me as he reaches a spot that hasn't been reached since he and I were last together years ago. It's like his dick was built for me, hitting the perfect spot. It's been so long since I've felt this.

As he thrusts deeper into me, I wrap my arms around his neck. I pull him in for a passionate kiss and lock my legs around his waist. His body is thicker than when we were last together, more powerful, but still so amazingly familiar. He fits so perfectly.

"Celeste." My name escapes his lips in a breathy sigh.

I arch my back, urging him to go deeper within me. My nails sink into the flesh of his back as our rhythm intensifies. He moans in that way that I know signals he's close to his own orgasm.

With each thrust, he hits that perfect spot deep inside me that only he can reach—forcing a gasp of pain and pleasure out of me with each hit. He loses control, gripping me tightly as he groans through his climax—his hot release filling the condom and leaving his member twitching within me. With his final thrust, he achieves what only he and one vibrator I've owned can accomplish. I come from deep within myself, biting his shoulder as we ride our orgasms out together.

Gasping for breath, he collapses on top of me, spent and trembling. As we both recover from our passionate encounter, I run my fingers through his soft hair, recalling all the times we've done this on this couch. I'm not sure how I feel about the fact that I no longer have to worry about being caught.

9

Having gotten all the sexual tension out of the way, we spend the rest of the evening playing video games and reminiscing. Eventually, Ryan says, "It's getting a bit late. Should I go home? Or should I stay over?"

"I don't know. Your dad probably knows you're here. Will he… will he think we're together if you stay over?"

"Why does it matter?"

"Because your dad is the biggest gossip in town. And we all know Mrs. Heart can't keep her mouth shut. We're surrounded on both sides by the Goose Grove Grapevine."

"Celeste, are you ashamed of me?" He sarcastically feigns offense.

"I just…don't want this thing between us to block me from being able to start up something serious with someone else."

"I thought you said you weren't seeing anyone."

"I'm not, but there are a few guys that…"

"A few!?"

"Well, two."

"Who?"

"Um, I had a moment with Michael Nguyen, and then there's James Montgomery. I was thinking of exploring that."

"I see..." he pauses for a long time and bites at his lip.

"What? Is there something wrong with them? Are they bad guys or something?"

He smirks at me. "It's nothing, Star Girl. I just don't want to lose my friend with benefits."

His words hang between us. *Friend with benefits. Why does that phrase sting so much?*

"Ryan," I begin, but my voice fades as I examine his face for clues. My mind races through memories. There's a tug of uncertainty—caution that comes from knowing how tangled and messy things can become. "Are you certain that friends with benefits is what you want?" *Is that all he wants?*

His blue eyes fix on mine, as serious as I've ever seen them amidst their usual mirth. "Yeah. No strings, just like old times. Except it'll be a lot better for you because I have abs now." He laughs.

Just like old times. The phrase resonates with a mixture of sweetness and sorrow. *We were different people then, weren't we?* A battle brews within me. A battle between the lure of the familiar and the fear of repeating past mistakes. It's tempting, oh so tempting, to fall into a pattern that once brought us joy. *But at what cost?*

"Ryan," I say again, steadier this time, reaching for his hand. "It's not that simple anymore."

"Isn't it?" He squeezes my hand, his thumb tracing small circles on my skin. *It was never simple between us. Not really. We just pretended it was.*

I sigh. "We...probably should have talked about this a bit more before we jumped on each other."

His eyebrows furrow and his jaw twitches. "Are you saying you regret it?" he asks, his tone skirting on the edge of serious for once.

"No, I just..." I start, my voice carrying a tremor of vulnerability. "We've both changed, you know? Our lives...they're different now, and we never talked about my leaving."

"What's to talk about?" He shrugs.

"Ryan, I left, and then you didn't talk to me for years. You still barely talk to me. You just send me memes occasionally. Why?"

"You got busy."

How dare he? I tremble and clench my fist. "Don't. Don't blame me. That wasn't what happened. You stopped responding."

He sighs and looks at his feet. "Fine…I was hurt."

"Hurt? Why?"

"Celeste, you told me that the only thing you cared about was making your game."

No. NO. That's not what happened. "OUR GAME. You were supposed to come with me."

"I couldn't come to California. You knew that. I wanted you to come home with me. I was hurt you didn't want to come back."

"But—"

He cuts me off. "You were my best friend, and you didn't want to be with me."

"You weren't why I couldn't come back…you know that. It was my mo—"

"I know…I do. I didn't then. But I do now."

My heart pounds in my chest, and I realize I've been yelling. "Ryan…I'm sorry for yelling."

He tucks my hair behind my ear. "I missed you, Celeste. I miss you."

I lean into his touch. "I miss you, too, Ryan."

"How about this? I go home tonight, and you think about whether or not you want to do this again. If not, cool. We can be friends with no benefits, and Michael and James will never know. I can remain your dirty little secret."

"Ryan, you're not a—"

He cuts me off with a finger to my lips, the twinkle of a jokester returned to his eyes. "Shh, it's okay. I get it. I'm just teasing you, Star Girl." He leans in close, his breath warm against my ear. "But just so you know, I'll be your friend, with or without benefits. If they wanna date my best friend, they better make sure they deserve her." *So we're already back to best friends?*

I can't help but smile, even as I playfully shove him away. "You're impossible, you know that?"

"Impossibly charming, you mean?" He grins, standing up and stretching. "I just…I don't want to lose you again."

"You won't," I promise, clasping his hand. "But we need to be honest with each other, and with ourselves. About what we want, what we're ready for."

"Of course!" he says softly, his thumb caressing my knuckles. "I'll be honest with you, always. I always tell you everything." But the look in his eyes tells me that's not true. "And right now, honestly, I want to kiss you again."

I bite my lip, torn between the desire to give in and the need to protect my heart. "Ryan…"

"But I won't," he adds quickly, releasing my hand and stepping back with his hands in the air. I follow him to the door, my heart still racing from his words, his touch, his presence. "Not until you're sure it's what you want, too. I meant what I said, Celeste. I'll be your friend no matter what. I just hope…" He pauses, running a hand through his tousled hair. "I hope that someday, you'll want more than that." He always says things like this. Things that make it sound like he wants to be more than friends, more than friends with benefits, but when I press, he deflects.

"Ryan, what do you want—"

"I just really want to show you some of the moves I've picked up over the last ten years." And it seems he hasn't changed. He still deflects. He's been like this since his mother left. Every moment of vulnerability is instantly followed by his running away.

As he steps out into the cool night air, the dropping temperature makes me wrap my arms around myself. He turns to face me and rubs my arms to warm me. "Sweet dreams, Star Girl," he whispers, and pecks me on the cheek.

"You, too, Ry Guy," I whisper back. I want to reach out and pull him close one more time. I want to tell him to spend the night—to stay. I want us to be a real thing. Not just friends with benefits. But I know that'll never happen between us. So I resist, knowing that any further action between us will need to be thought out more carefully. The delicate balance of our rekindling friendship is at stake.

He smiles softly, and it is so tender my breath catches. Then he turns with a flourish and hops down the stairs—just like he always has, the same bounce, the same rhythm. I watch him go, my heart a jumble of emotions—longing, uncertainty, hope, fear. *What do I want?* The question echoes in my mind as I close the door.

I shut my eyes and reflect on our night together. I recall the weight of him pressed against me, the heat of his breath against my neck, and the way he whispered my name. I can still feel his press deep within me—an ache, an emptiness. It felt so right, so natural, so familiar.

But confusion and doubt swirl within me. *What if it's really not as simple as no strings attached? What if we've grown too far apart, changed too much?*

Ryan has never wanted more of me than this: a best friend whom he sleeps with. What distinguishes that from a girlfriend has never been clear to me. Nor why he insists on the distinction. But he's always stubbornly refused to be my boyfriend. He'd waffle between insisting we'd never be more than friends who fuck, even going so far as pushing me to date other guys, and then he'd get jealous when I did.

I wish things were easier between us. I wish I could go to sleep with his cock nocked in that place only he's ever reached every night. I wish we could just get over this multi-decade farce and commit to each other—fully. But, it appears time has not matured either of us, and we're still just going to be "fuck buddies."

I can't let myself hold out hope that we'll be more. But for the first time in my life, I think I want more— a family. So, I don't think I can settle for "just friends who fuck."

What does he want? It feels like he's not telling me something—like he's holding something back. *Some anger? Some sadness?* I can't tell.

Ryan's words replay in my mind: *"I'll be your friend no matter what." Is that really true?*

I suppose we need to start by repairing our friendship. We spent this entire night together, and all we did was discuss our shared past. We didn't learn about the people we have become. *What has changed? Has anything changed?* We didn't catch up; we reminisced. We need to work through what tore apart the friendship to begin with, and then we can think about the more complicated stuff. But we need to keep our hands off each other long enough to have an actual conversation.

10

As I open the door of Goose Grove Legal Group, the knot in my stomach tightens—a cocktail of dread and resolve churning inside me. I'm here to tie up the last loose ends of my parents' lives, a task I've put off for far too long. *I can't make Mrs. Heart do everything.*

In the lobby, I scan the placard that indicates the location of each lawyer's office. I make a note of James's office location and run my fingers over the J in his name. *What is wrong with me? I am acting like a schoolgirl scribbling her crush's name in her notebook.*

I note the location of Richard Holbrook's office—second floor. Looks like it may be right near James's. I wonder if I'll see James. *You're not here for dick, Celeste—even though dick would be much preferable to what I'm actually here for. Well, I guess I am here for Dick with a capital D.*

As I reach the top of the stairs, a door that I think is Richard's swings open before Nicole storms out. Red-rimmed eyes and blotchy cheeks mar her usually impeccable appearance. I don't know if I've ever seen her vulnerable, let alone so uncomposed before. She barrels toward me, ready to rush down the stairs, but my presence blocks her path.

"Nicole?" I can't help but halt mid-step, my own agenda momentarily forgotten. "Are you okay?" It's odd the instinct you have to check in on someone, even when they are a heinous cunt. Perhaps it's our shared past and fond memories of tea parties, but my empathy for her is on overdrive, and I have a strong desire to grab her and growl, "Who hurt you!?"

She gives me a brittle smile, dabbing at her eyes with the corner of her sleeve. "Oh, Celeste. It's just…estate matters, you know? They can be so overwhelming."

"Oh, yeah, I know what you mean." I offer a sympathetic nod, understanding all too well the complex emotions associated with estate matters.

She meets my eyes, and an expression of real compassion crosses her face. "Yeah, I really am sorry about your parents. Your dad was such a nice guy. He would have asked me if I was okay, too. Anyway, good luck with Holbrook." She forces a smile and brushes past me down the stairs, keeping her eyes on her feet and wiping at her eyes. "You'll need it."

"Thanks," I say, but she's already halfway down the stairs, so I don't think she hears me. Her composure further falters when she reaches the bottom. "Nicole," I call out, driven by an urge to bridge the gap high school squabbles once carved between us.

But she doesn't turn back; she just raises a hand in a half-hearted wave without looking back. "Goodbye, Celeste," she says, her voice trailing off as she turns the corner out of sight. Well, if I wasn't discombobulated before, I definitely am now. *What kind of man could make the ice queen herself crumple?*

"Okay, Celeste," I whisper to myself, "you've handled worse." And I have. I've stood in front of panels of tech bros, pitching my game, requesting funding, only to be met with eyes of pure rage and hatred. But I could hide behind my skill and my game—an armor I don't have at the moment. *What armor do I have against this man?* Likely none, considering he's already spotted my greatest insecurity—my shitty daughterness—and exploited it. I take a deep breath and shake myself off. "Seriously, you can do this," I whisper, hoping that no one can see or hear me talking to myself.

And with that self pep talk, I push open the door and step into the office of Goose Grove's own legal eagle—or perhaps vulture would be more apt.

"Ms. Moon," Richard acknowledges without fanfare, his voice as warm as the chill outside.

I attempt to match his coldness. "Mr. Holbrook."

The room looks like someone threw all the books from the shelves of a library in a fit of rage. I half expect Slimer to burst through a wall and take credit for the mess. His desk is littered with precariously positioned books and stationery. An avalanche of folders is just a breath away from burying us both in legal letterhead.

I feel like the world is collapsing around me, and I don't know if it's due to the mess or the fact that I'm finally confronting the last thing that would signal my parents are truly gone.

He gestures vaguely towards a chair that's seen better days and grunts. The cracked leather reminded me momentarily of the old booth at Shady's. *God, Celeste, don't think about being felt up by the mayor right now.*

I perch on the edge of the chair, not wanting to get too comfortable, but doubting I could, anyway. I want to be ready to spring out of this thing the moment I finish this conversation. Richard looks at me for a long moment, his gaze sharp and calculating. For the first time, I don't balk at his fierce stare and study his face. The skin around his left eye is discolored. I squint to see more clearly. It looks like it's the deep purple of a fresh black eye, haphazardly covered with makeup.

He notices my scrutiny, his hand flying to his eye with a slight wince, before quickly pulling his hand away and returning his gaze to the chaos of papers on his desk.

Do lawyers not have computers? Why does he have so many papers?

He shuffles through the sheets, grunting and sighing as if each word he reads is speaking to him. *Did I not come at the right time? Do we not have a meeting? Is he waiting for me to say something?* An extremely loud clock ticks away the seconds. Each one is heavy in my consciousness and increases my anxiety.

"Busy day?" I venture, my eyes scanning the disarray.

"Always," he replies curtly, flipping through a file.

"Thank you for meeting with me." I try to sound light and friendly. I'd like to get this started. This is worse than sitting in a doctor's office.

"Let's proceed," he cuts in with a tone that implies I've been the one dilly-dallying the whole time. *Thank God.* I couldn't sit here waiting for him to get on with this one second longer. This man seriously skeeves me out, and I can't help but wonder if there's a heart beating under that crisp suit.

Richard clears his throat and says, "Your parents left a rather comprehensive estate. It's quite fortunate for you, given the…distance in your relationship." His words pierce through my heart, a thinly veiled jab wrapped in legalese.

I was prepared for this. I knew he'd say something cruel.

"Time can really get away from us all," I say, forcing my voice to steady and squelching the tears. I might be a statue of non-response on the outside, but on the inside, I'm swimming in guilt. My heart pounds in my throat, and my inner demons threaten to drag me down into a depth so profoundly sad that I might fall into a pile on this floor and never get up. Melt my sad, pathetic ass right here into this floor until you can't distinguish me from the papers and grime.

But, I won't give this motherfucker the satisfaction of tears. I won't give him the satisfaction of a reaction. I steel myself and casually place my hands just under my legs at my sides. Luckily for me, I have a lot of practice in concealing my emotions by locking them away deep inside myself. I just need to channel that part of me.

"Indeed," he says, the corner of his mouth twitching with a shadow of a smirk. "Twenty years is quite the…extended holiday, Miss Moon." I must not look as statuesque as I believe, because his face is profoundly smug. He knows he got me with that barb.

I take a breath, pushing down the bubbling anguish. I'm here to settle affairs, not to justify my life choices to a man who probably catalogs his emotions in a filing cabinet for efficiency. And, as we can tell, he sucks at filing.

"Being a lawyer, I assume you can understand a career that takes a lot out of you," I offer, refusing to bite the bait he's dangling before me.

"Yes, but I am a lawyer. You make…video games. Not exactly important work, is it?" he says with a sneer. *Fuck, this guy knows how to cut you to the quick.* Which I should have known, given he made Nicole cry. *What did he say to her?*

Defending my career choice is something I've had to do numerous times. People don't see the value of art. They don't see the value of joy. They don't realize that sometimes, during the darkest times, when you can't do anything, a shining light in the form of a distraction can save your life. But I don't have the mental energy for my usual spiel on the merits of art and how making video games is actually fucking hard work, so instead, I'll deflect. I won't let him goad me into a debate on the merits of my former profession. And wallowing in my shittiness as a daughter is something I'll do when I'm not paying a douchebag hundreds of dollars an hour. I can afford it, but I'd rather spend my money on literally anything else.

"My parents' estate," I assert, trying to get him on topic.

He bombards me with a flurry of legal terms that swirl in my head. I have no idea what half of the things he is saying mean, but he speaks at such a pace that I cannot find a pause to interject any questions. The conversation feels like a full-frontal assault. And he's supposed to be helping me; he's supposed to be a civil servant, but instead of feeling helped, I feel like I'm playing defense against a Soulcalibur II character when Ryan is implementing his "patented random button mashing" assault.

I'm finally given a reprieve from his attack when his phone comes to life—playing "Walking on Sunshine" of all songs. *Is that seriously his ringtone?* Richard's hand darts out, silencing it before lifting it to his ear.

"One moment," he mutters, holding a finger up as if to silence me and turning slightly away. As if the tilt of his shoulder could shield my ears from the conversation he is about to have.

"Of course," I nod. Not that this jerk deserves my respect, but I pretend to study the paperwork he gave me out of respectful distraction. My eyes cross as the meaningless words swim in front of me, and I strain my ears to hear what he is whispering into the phone.

He suddenly stands and leaves the room, without shutting the door, and stands just outside it.

I pull out my phone and consider texting Ryan to see if he wants to get lunch. I contemplate how I can cleverly make a joke about washing the bad taste this meeting has left in my mouth out with either coffee or cock, when Richard's hushed tone rises slightly. "No, Marcus took care of it."

My ears perk up.

I catch only fragments of the conversation—words like "urgent" and "discreet"—each one making me strain harder to hear the next. Eavesdropping on his conversation incites an insatiable curiosity in me. *Is this what the dredges of unemployment stir in me? Is my new life's mission to eavesdrop on the phone calls of shady lawyers? Maybe I should hang out with Mr. O'Connor more—start a gossip gathering gang.*

His tone further piques my interest. *If this is so secret, why stand in the hall with the door open? What's so urgent?* He sounds angry. *Scared?* It's not the same forceful arrogance I've heard him speak with up to this point.

While pretending not to listen, I scan the room absentmindedly, only half absorbing what I'm seeing. My eyes stop on a framed picture on a bookshelf behind Richard's chair. I lean slightly to the left so that I can peek at it. I place my elbow on the chair, feigning nonchalance and trying to hide my nosiness. In the picture, Richard stands with a man, neither smiling. But his arm is slung around him. It's the man who urgently pulled James back to work yesterday afternoon. *What was his name? Daniel?*

Behind them is a banner for the annual Crimson and Gold Autumn Gala, where the town's elite rub shoulders under the guise of philanthropy. Nicole's parents host it every year, and they raise money for various causes. It is a moderately significant event, rivaling similar events held in the Twin Cities. I've heard it single-handedly keeps some of our more posh hotels and bed and breakfasts afloat for the entire year.

"Understood," Richard concludes. He puts his phone back in his pocket and stands silently, lost in thought for only a moment before returning.

Richard returns and sits back in his chair, shuffling the papers yet again, but more aggressively than before. The air in the room feels thick, soured further by Richard's mood, which honestly I didn't think was possible. "Now, where were we?" I am pretty sure he is asking himself, not me. "Ah, yes. Your inheritance," he says, leaning back slightly. "There are some formalities to attend to, but everything appears to be in order."

"Formalities," I echo, forcing a smile.

"Indeed," he replies, his lips twitching into what could be construed as a smirk if one squinted hard enough. "Your parents planned to leave everything to you, as I'm sure you understood. There is some business with their financial accounts that I still need to finalize, and the probate process will be wrapping up soon. For now, you may remain in the house until it is officially yours. I will contact you when it is completed." He hands me another stack of papers, not the ones he's been shuffling, and stands as if to dismiss me.

"Of course," I say, gathering my things and rising to my feet, excited to get the heck out of here. "Thank you for your time, Mr. Holbrook."

He hands me even more papers and a folder to put them all in. "Richard will do," he corrects me, but there's no warmth in it. It's a command masquerading as an offer of familiarity. I nod, because it seems the easiest thing to do, and make my way to the door.

"Goodbye," I manage, my hand closing around the doorknob.

"Good day, Ms. Moon," he says, already turning his attention back to the mountainous work on his desk.

11

The tension coiled in my neck eases as I step into the hallway. My fingers tighten around the thick folder, biting into my hands. I close my eyes, attempting to dam the tears welling in me. *It's okay, Celeste. It's all over.* My eyes fling open when I ram into something—or rather, someone—solid. And handsome.

"Oh, Celeste," James's deep, amused voice booms above me. He smirks down at me. His golden brown hair falls at the corner of his deep green-brown eyes. *Fuck he is handsome.*

"James." A smile of my own takes over my face. "Sorry, I didn't see you there, J. Money." I chuckle, stumbling.

"Clearly," he teases, gently bracing me to stop me from falling and spilling my documents all over the floor. "Do you ever look where you're going, or are you trying to orchestrate a meet-cute with me?"

"Are you always loitering near doorways, waiting to be rammed into by distracted women?" My heart pounds in my chest, and I forget everything but those warm eyes and the warm hand on my forearm.

James's grin doesn't waver. "Part of the charm of this small town. Never know what—or who—you might run into."

"Charming indeed." I adjust the papers in my arms, now secured by his help. His hand, which had lingered on my arm, bracing me, removes itself, and I feel the loss of it.

"Everything alright, though?" The levity in his tone gives way to genuine concern.

"Inheritance talk is…well…upsetting. But thanks for the save. Spilling all this all over the floor would have definitely burst me into tears."

"Yes. Well. Richard can be…prickly," James admits, his voice lowered as if sharing a secret.

"I think you mean 'a prick,'" I say under my breath and grimace at my inability to hold my tongue.

He chuckles slightly, and I am relieved he isn't put off by the comment. Lots of guys find me abrasive and perverted—downside of being raised by Mrs. Heart, I guess. "Tell me at least that he's a good lawyer," I say.

A shadow crosses his face, so fleeting I might have imagined it. "He knows the law well." He chuckles again, but this time it seems less genuine. He gives a wry smile, but there's a note of something else there—hesitation, maybe? It's enough to make me wonder what lies beneath his easy-going surface.

He looks around momentarily, as if trying to determine if anyone is overhearing our conversation. "Maybe I can help you with him. If you need anything, even just an ear or a distraction from all this," he nods toward the papers, "you know where to find me. That's my office." He points toward a door down the hall.

"Thanks, James. That's…really kind of you." I feel a flush of warmth as his smile broadens.

He looks at his watch. "Hey, I was about to go to lunch. Want to join me?"

"Um." I bite my lip, thinking about the fact that just last night, Ryan was inside me. Ryan did say he didn't care if I pursued James. But would James care that I just slept with Ryan?

He leans against the wall next to me. "Come on. You need a little distraction from all this." He taps my folder. "And I can distract with the best of them." Apparently, this leaning-on-the-wall thing is his signature move—and it makes sense because it works. This guy is disarmingly suave. The smile is so seductive that I suspect he is hinting at the two of us doing things that have absolutely nothing to do with legal proceedings, but might be illegal in a few states with outdated laws. *Anal. I'm thinking about anal.*

"Sure." The word comes out too wistful and swoony for my liking.

"Give me a minute to lock up, okay?" he says, with a final charming grin. "I'll meet you in the lobby downstairs?" His hand brushes my arm in a way that feels more intimate than a simple parting gesture, sending an unexpected warmth coursing through me.

"Okay," I sigh, clutching my papers to my chest like a gushy teenager.

"Okay," he parrots, turning to walk away, but not before grinning and looking me up and down. *Did he really just eye fuck me? The audacity of this guy—I fucking love it.*

I watch him leave. Eye fucking him now. That perfectly tailored suit hugs his trim waist and accentuates his broad shoulders. I cannot break my gaze from his ass. *What is wrong with me? Am I ovulating or something?*

I drift toward the stairs, and my thoughts drift to James's touch—light, reassuring, and unsettling all at once. What is it about this man that manages to stir up such intense feelings inside me? Something about him makes me want to just let him wrap me in his arms, call me a good girl, and then do whatever the fuck he wants to me.

I descend the staircase to the lobby and find a corner out of the flow of traffic—if there were traffic—to stand in. I pull out my phone to distract myself while I wait for James, but a voice of hushed urgency pulls at the edge of my awareness.

I turn the corner to find the source of the voice. Just barely in view, Nicole and Daniel are locked in what seems to be an intense exchange. They're obscured by a potted fiddle-leaf fig that's seen better days. I don't think they can see me, but I hug close to the wall to help conceal myself even further. *Didn't Nicole leave? Why is she still here?*

"Daniel, this can't wait any longer." Nicole's voice feigns a whisper, but the sharpness cuts through the silence, and it's a bit too loud. "We need to sort this out."

"Keep your voice down, Nicole." Daniel's gaze darts around the room. I pull back even further, attempting to hide from his sight. I look at my phone to feign absentmindedness—I'm probably being suspicious as fuck, though. He leans in close to her and whispers something inaudible.

"Fine, we'll discuss it later," Nicole concedes and storms past me through the door. She doesn't even acknowledge me, and if her purposefully ignoring me didn't seem on-brand for her, I'd suspect I had done an excellent job hiding.

James bounds down the stairs before I have too much time to think about what I just witnessed. "Ready, Celeste?" he asks, putting his hand on my elbow and leading me toward the door. *Boy, am I.*

Goose Grove is the kind of small town where everyone knows everyone. But, each person who passes by greets, smiles, or waves at James—making him feel like a celebrity in this small town. I feel a little flush of pleasure at the fact that I am with him. The smiles he brings to passersby give adorable Watson a run for his money, and I wonder who would win a popularity contest. *Cute as fuck dog versus hot as fuck lawyer: the showdown of the century.*

James darts ahead of me to open the door to Sarah's cafe. He holds it with the controlled flourish of a man who knows exactly how to woo a woman through small acts of chivalry. The bell jingles with that now familiar sound, and I find it oddly comforting. I wonder if Andy and Sarah find it annoying.

He gently presses his palm against the small of my lower back and guides me through the doorway. I look back at him and am once again disarmed by his smile—so genuine and warm—it's impossible not to feel a spark of something more stirring within me. Usually, a man putting his hand at the small of my back to lead me somewhere sends me into a feminist rage, but there's something about this man that drops all of my defenses. *Drops me to my knees. Drops my panties*. This touch, paired with that smile and handsome face, sends a quiver through me, eliciting some extremely illicit thoughts. My heart thuds, and I want this man to touch me more, all the time, in whatever way he chooses.

I scan the room for Sarah and am disappointed when I don't find her.

Andy is at the counter, taking orders. "James," they say with familiarity, "and Celeste," they say as if asking a question. They're obviously wondering why we're together.

"Hey, Ands, the usual, please," James replies, then asks me, "Celeste, what'll you have?" I note that the way he controls the conversation leaves no question about whether or not he'll be buying my lunch. I actually haven't had a suitor buy me a meal in years. It always felt wrong…given…you know the whole having a shit ton of money thing. But this small gesture of dominance is the exact kind of daddy energy I crave.

I order a sandwich and the same drink I got yesterday, pulling my cup out of my purse, grateful that I remembered it.

James weaves through the mismatched chairs to a table in the corner by the window. He pulls a chair out for me, and I sit with a thanks. A long plant spills from a pot above my head, and I have to push a vine aside to avoid placing my stack of papers on it. The afternoon sun spills in, glinting the gold of James's hair.

James sits and immediately speaks, "You know, I must admit, seeing you yesterday felt like something out of a movie. I almost didn't believe it." He grins wistfully at me.

I laugh, "Really? Why?"

"I've hoped I'd see you again one day for so long, and then suddenly you were there, for me to run right into."

"I'm surprised you even remembered me."

"Oh, trust me, Celeste. You're not someone anyone forgets. I certainly haven't."

"Oh, really? Beating your grinding record made that much of an impression on you?"

"As a matter of fact, it did. I was the king of that park…until you came along. You showed up with that pink helmet and a tutu over your jeans. I thought, 'Who is this girl? Who does she think she is? There's no way she can beat me.'"

I mock offense. "Oh, so you underestimated me?"

He leans forward, his smile even more jovial than before. "I did. But you didn't just beat me; you pulverized me." He chuckles, shaking his head. A humble expression of embarrassment breaks through his generally suave demeanor. "You really put me in my place. Taught me a lesson in misogyny, honestly." He laughs again.

"It's good you learned it young," I chuckle. He laughs as well.

His expression becomes more wistful, and his tone softens when he says, "You made it look so effortless, too. You were so joyous. You didn't care if you won or not. And you certainly didn't care what I thought of you. You were just out there, having fun. I watched you fly down that rail, and I was dumbstruck. I was in awe of you. You were amazing."

"You're exaggerating. I was nothing special."

"To me, you were something special. You were beautiful, smart, kind, and completely yourself. I was, let's call it, smitten. I secretly pined for you from afar for quite a while."

I laugh and nervously tuck my hair behind my ear."Smitten, huh? Why didn't you ever say anything?"

"You were with Ryan, and I was just the tool who went around calling himself J. Money. I didn't think you'd want anything to do with me. You were so…you. I graduated the next year and went off to college. I missed my chance. By the time I came back to town, you were gone. I never forgot you, though."

"I wasn't with Ryan…" I trail off.

"Oh, well, I wish I had known that back then," he laughs a little sadly. James shifts forward, resting his elbows on the table, his gaze earnest. "And now…It's incredible what you've accomplished since then. The games you've created…I don't play many video games, but

I've played all of yours. You are even more amazing than you were back then."

"Stop it," I manage to say through my laughter, a light blush warming my cheeks. It's both embarrassing and endearing to hear him speak of me in such a way. Praising my accomplishments will always endear someone to me.

He reaches across the table, grabbing my hands. I don't pull away. He looks at me more earnestly than he had up to this point. "And now that you are back. I apologize if I've been a bit forward with you, but I refuse to let you slip away again. I will not miss this chance." His words hit me like a thunderbolt.

He continues, "Celeste, I—" His words are cut short by the shrill ring of his phone. He frowns, pulling the device from his pocket with an apologetic look. "Let me just mute—Shit." He cuts himself off when he gets a glance at the phone. "Celeste, I'm so sorry. I have to take this. I will be right back. Please don't go anywhere." He rises from the table and rushes toward the door.

"No problem," I say to his disappearing back, trying to sound nonchalant even though I desperately want to know what he was about to say.

As he steps out onto the sidewalk, I can't help but watch him, noting the tension in his shoulders that wasn't there moments before. *Do lawyers always run off from conversations to have tense phone calls? This is the second I've witnessed today.*

Sarah brings our plates and coffee, putting them on the table in front of me just as he disappears from view. She asks, "Oh, is he coming back? Or should I box this up?"

"Oh, no, he'll be back." I look down at the tablecloth, avoiding eye contact as the heat rushes to my ears. "Thanks, Sarah."

"No prob," she says with a big smile.

I scrutinize my coffee and sandwich, unable to eat due to the disappointment burbling in my stomach. I wonder what things would have been like had James and I dated in high school. I knew lots of people thought Ryan and I were dating, but I never knew people actively chose not to pursue me due to my relationship with him. *Does that make me regret my time with Ryan? No. Of course not. Right?*

A faint jingle barely registers in my periphery, but I'm jolted from my contemplation by a smooth voice saying, "Mind if I join you?"

Glancing up, I find Michael sliding into the seat James vacated, a small smile playing on his lips.

12

"Oh, um, I…James will be back soon," I explain.

"Then I guess I'll just have to keep you company until he returns," Michael offers, tilting his head playfully. *What is with the men in this town? Do they all have master's degrees in flirting?*

"Did Mrs. Heart give you my number?" he asks.

"She did."

"Did you throw it away, or did you keep it?"

"I kept it." I tuck my hair behind my ear and blush.

"Well, that's good. Then, would it be too forward of me to request your number so the next time I'm lying awake yearning to hear your voice, I can call you—rather than desperately waiting for my phone to ring?" Michael is the second man in less than twenty minutes to confess his pining for me. *What is happening right now?*

"Oh, um, sure," I say.

He hands me his phone. "Can you send yourself a text?" As our fingers brush against each other, there is a change in his body language. It's almost like our touch sends a shiver down his spine and cracks his facade. In the place of a confident, smooth talker, there is actually an adorably nervous man trying his best to impress me. I smile softly at him, touched by his vulnerability.

"Yeah, I'll do that." I enter my number and text myself, "This is Michael. The adorable one with the striking amber eyes." I put a red heart emoji at the end, just to be extra clear that I am interested in him.

I'm impressed with my ability to brazenly hit on this man. Usually, I am more passive in my pursuits. Something about him just makes me want to devour him with my entire body.

He looks at the phone, and his grin is bashful, embarrassed, and so fucking cute. He lets out a breathy chuckle, adjusting his glasses. "Adorable, huh?"

"Yes, very."

"Thanks." He laughs and puts the phone in his back pocket. "But I've got nothing on you. Or Watson. Where's the little charmer?"

"Oh, I haven't seen him today, actually. I've had some errands to run." I don't elaborate. If I hear "I'm sorry for your loss" one more time, I might scream.

I ask, "Do you know why he's allowed in here? Mrs. Heart was being unusually coy about it."

"Oh, he got a letter from the mayor permitting him in every building in town."

"No! You're joking?"

"Nope. When the mayor's daughter went through chemo, Watson was the only thing that could comfort her. So, he's like a local hero."

"Really? I wonder why Mrs. Heart didn't tell me that."

He shrugs. "Possibly because she lost her husband to cancer around the same time. That's why he was in the hospital to begin with. Mrs. Heart snuck him into the hospital to say goodbye to Mr. Heart."

We sit quietly for a moment, allowing ourselves to feel empathy for Mrs. Heart's loss and pay our respects to the man who had once been a staple in the community.

"So, it was just last year? That means the mayor was…it was Marcus Adams's daughter?"

"Yeah, you know him?"

"Yeah, small towns and all…" I trail off, not elaborating on our past. *Marcus and Nicole's child had cancer?*

"Is…she still sick?" I ask, not really knowing how to formulate the question I want to ask.

"I don't know the specifics, but I see her around quite often. She seems to be doing well. I believe she is in remission."

"That's good." My feelings for Marcus are complicated, but, in general, he's always been a nice enough guy, and I wouldn't wish a sick child on my worst enemy, which might actually be Nicole, the child's mother.

Michael's eyes flicker momentarily towards the door, a subtle shift in his demeanor. It's quick, but it's there. James must be returning. Michael forces a smile at me, but it's wrapped in disappointment. It feels like a goodbye as the doorbell jingles yet again.

"Sorry about that," James says, striding towards us with a hurried yet graceful gait. There's a tension in his jaw that wasn't there before, a testament to whatever crisis has called him away—I assume it was work-related, but perhaps it was something else. Or the tension could be related to the fact that Michael is in his seat.

"Everything okay?" I inquire, watching as he comes to a halt beside our table. He leans down, and the scent of his cologne wraps around me, invading my space. The warmth from his body is tangible even though he doesn't touch me—until his hand finds its way to the back of my chair possessively.

"Not really," James admits and smiles at me apologetically. "I'm so sorry we keep getting interrupted, Celeste. Work emergency. I have to go handle it." His tone indicates reluctance, yet concession to responsibility.

He pretends to ignore Michael, but his eyes flicker toward him. Michael's mannerisms shift. He's fidgeting and less laid back. He doesn't appear intimidated exactly, but…it's something else that I can't quite place. Almost like he's holding back from saying something. There is some shared history between them that carries a lot of baggage.

"No problem, James. I understand," I say, trying to be supportive and not convey disappointment. I've had to do the same thing numerous times. "Duty calls," I say, and I know there is a slight downturn in my lips.

"Unfortunately." James stands tall again, his hand lingering on my chair. There's something about the gesture that feels charged and intentional. "Mikey," he says curtly, finally acknowledging Michael's presence. *Mikey?*

"Jamie," Michael responds, his tone matching the curtness.

"Feel free to have my sandwich," he says to Michael with a smirk, his voice carrying a somewhat haughty tone I've yet to hear from him.

"Before I go," James says, the bite in his voice softening as he addresses me. "Are you free tomorrow night? I promise I will leave my phone at home."

Michael scoffs, and James cuts him a side glance, but his body remains pointing at me.

"Tomorrow?" The word slips out, tinged with surprise. My hesitance isn't just about the suddenness of the invitation; Ryan's face flashes through my mind—the way his eyes held mine just last night.

"Sure, I mean, I think so." I manage a small smile while darting a glance at Michael. He's watching us, an unreadable expression on his face that doesn't quite mask the intensity in his amber eyes.

"Great. It's a date then." James's voice is smooth, but there's a tightness around his eyes, a subtle shift that suggests he's not as unaffected by Michael's presence as he'd like to appear.

"Here, write down your address. Getting your phone number from the system is one thing, but getting your address feels a bit stalkery," James laughs while handing me a pen and opening a small notebook he had in his breast pocket.

I write down my address, stifling the tremble in my hand fueled by nervous excitement. I'm surprised I can even write. I hand the notebook and pen back to James, and he returns them to his internal breast pocket.

"I'll see you at six tomorrow, Celeste," James says, grinning at me.

"Sounds good," I reply, but the words feel automatic, my thoughts still tangled with memories of Ryan and the unexpected charm of the man sitting across from me.

Michael leans back in his chair, crossing one leg over the other casually, yet there's a tension in his posture that mirrors James's. Their silent battle of wills is almost palpable, and I am caught in the crossfire of their attentions. I can't say I hate the attention.

"Enjoy your lunch, Celeste," James says. He squeezes my shoulder—a final touch that sends a jolt of lust through my body.

"Thanks, James. Good luck with work," I reply, wishing I could somehow keep his hand on my shoulder forever.

"Mikey," he says with a curt nod toward Michael.

"Jamie," Michael returns with a similar nod, his arms crossed over his chest.

As James strides out in that confident way that he walks, the lingering warmth from his touch fades. I turn back to Michael, acutely aware of the sticky situation I've gotten myself into with them.

"So, should I call you Mikey?" I ask.

"Oh, um, only James calls me that. I prefer Michael."

"Michael, it is," I say, smiling at him. I want to ask what's with the nicknames? What's with the scoff? But I don't. However, the interaction with James still hangs between us. They obviously have some shared history, which makes sense—everyone in this small town has shared history.

A knot grows in my stomach, and I feel like I must address the elephant in the room, but before I can say anything, Michael says, "What about the night after tomorrow? Are you free then, too?"

I blush. "I am."

"I've been wanting to try out this restaurant in Estelle. I know it's a bit of a drive, but it overlooks this gorgeous waterfall. Would you like to join me?"

Drive? The idea of being in a car for a long drive sends a shockwave of fear through me. Should I tell him? Maybe suggest something else?

The look he gives me—hopeful, unrushed—makes me melt. I want to spend every possible moment I can with this man, and if that means getting in a car, so be it.

"That sounds amazing, Michael. I'd love that."

"Wonderful. I'll text you to coordinate."

We sit like this, chatting about things two people trying to figure each other out do, for a long time. He doesn't do that thing most guys do, where they use the conversation as an excuse to tell me all the amazing things about themselves in hopes I'll sleep with them. He talks to me like he actually wants to get to know me. Like he's okay with just being with me here right now and isn't thinking about his next move, how he can rush things to the next chapter of our relationship.

I almost have to pry details about his life out of him—something I'm not used to, but enjoying. "So, you write mysteries?" I ask. "What kind do you write?"

"Small-town mysteries. Lots of secrets. Improbable murders. Suspicious people with suspiciously good banter."

"So, basically, like this," I say, waving my hands, indicating Goose Grove as a whole.

"Well. No one's died. And you're not suspicious."

I lean back, "I'm not suspicious?"

"Not to sound like a fanboy, but I know a little about you. I've played all your games."

I laugh, "Even Lunar Bloom? That one got ripped apart critically."

He nods. "I liked it."

I give him a skeptical look. "No one liked that one."

"I liked the characters," he laughs. "They really resonated with me."

I look at him, not believing his assertion, "Oh, yeah. Which character did you try to romance?"

He laughs, "Will you think less of me if I say all of them?"

"Ah, so you got the why choose achievement?"

"I did," he smiles coyly. "Are you currently working on any new games?"

"No. I um…sold Moonfire Games."

He lifts his eyes to meet mine, "Oh, yeah?" The question doesn't contain any judgment. He's asking merely to continue the conversation, make me to open up, and get to know me. But I feel judged. Not by him, per se. By everyone. I feel like a failure at the one thing I felt proved I wasn't. So, I guess, I feel judged by myself.

I lift my glass slowly, contemplating how much of my reasoning I want to reveal, while also recognizing that I don't really fully understand my reasoning. "Yeah, I…I needed a change after…" I trail off. "I'm not sure what I'm going to do now. It turns out doing nothing stresses me out."

He smiles at me knowingly, and I feel he may share some of the same anxieties I do. Something about that smile makes me want to open up. "I tend to drown myself in work. It turns down the volume on…all the feels." I laugh slightly at the sudden revelation. *God, Celeste, why don't you just trauma dump on him already? Cut to the chase and let him know he should avoid you at all costs.*

"I get that. The only time I'm not worrying is when I'm writing."

"Oh, yeah?"

He laughs slightly. "Yeah, it's nice to pretend to be someone else when you…"

"Don't really want to be yourself?"

He nods and chuckles, pulling at his collar. It seems he also thinks he has revealed too much about himself.

I attempt to bridge the gap. "Oh, I know that feeling all too well. That's why I made games. I couldn't stand being myself, so I made a new me."

He cocks a half-smile at me. "Well, I'm happy you're you, Celeste."

"I'm happy you're you, too, Michael."

13

I wake to the soft glow of light spilling through the windows of my childhood bedroom. Momentarily, I feel like a kid again, and my heart races as my surroundings enter my blurred vision. Trophies tower over me, repressive sentinels meant to remind me how I'll never be good enough. This room is like a time capsule to my childhood—a time in my life I don't care to remember. *I might as well get up. I gotta get out of here.*

Instinctively, I kiss my fingers and press them against the Back Street Boys Millennium poster by my door as I shuffle into the hallway. *Ha, old habits die hard.*

I stop at the door to my parents' room and consider opening it. But the closer I get to the door, the faster my heart races. *I'm not ready for that yet.*

I dart toward the stairs, running from the ghosts of my upbringing. *I think I'll sleep on the couch tonight. I can't do this every morning.*

The oppressive stares of the family photos lining the stairwell surround me. The bark of tears threatens my eyes.

I scurry down the steps, averting my eyes from the photos, but one still manages to catch my attention, freezing me in place: my eighth birthday party. Mrs. Heart's dog, Agatha, has her head buried deep in my cake, in shambles on the floor.

I reach out and trace my father's face. He'd just dropped the cake. I can still hear him singing as he entered, "Happy birthday to you, happ—, shit, Emily, I'm sorry." *He never apologized to me…only her. It was my cake, not hers.*

He's looking at my mother, her smile taut. You'd think she was fine, mildly amused, if you didn't know her. *She was so angry.* She was really good at hiding that anger when others were around.

I'm looking down at the table, crying softly to myself, trying my best to hide the tears. "*Stop crying. What kind of mother would people think I am if they see you crying?*"

I scan the faces of the other guests. Everyone else is looking at the cake and the dog, laughing hysterically, except Ryan. He's looking at me—consoling me. *He's always been such a great friend.* He's shorter than me here, super skinny, all elbows. From this angle, you can see the rattail he insisted made him cool. *It didn't.*

Where's Mr. Heart? Oh, yeah, he took this picture—always behind the camera. That's how he met Mrs. Heart, right? He was a photographer for one of her modeling shoots, right? I should ask her. Would it upset her to talk about him?

Why'd Mom display this picture? I suppose it would seem like a silly photo to an outsider—a fun moment. The dog is eating a cake, and everyone is laughing. But it doesn't bring back happy memories for me. Knowing my mom, she used this as a way to remind my dad daily of how he fucked up. I retrace my father's face, whispering, "I'm sorry, Dad. I'm sorry I let her chase me away."

Grief overwhelms me, encompassing me like a black cloud, swaying me, threatening to make me stumble down the stairs. I snatch the photo off the wall and throw it up the stairs. It smashes against my parents' bedroom door. *Shit, that was stupid. You're so stupid, Celeste.*

Maybe living in this house isn't the best way to deal with my grief. Is it grief or shame keeping me here? What's the difference?

I thought that being here would be a way to force myself to confront my grief, to deal with it head-on, since I know my usual inclination is to avoid—distract. *I want to be better.* I thought…I thought since I couldn't be here for my dad, I could at least be here for him now.

I rush the rest of the way down the stairs.

I weave through the boxes stacked in the foyer and dining room, making my way to the bathroom off the back den where my Dad kept his collectibles. I grip the sides of the sink and stare down the drain as I compose myself.

"Suck it up, Celeste," I mutter to myself, smacking my cheeks.

What should I do today? The loss of my perfectly structured schedule—my purpose—incites a different type of grief within me. *I'm nothing.*

Distraction. That's what I need.

Dick. That's a good source of distraction.

James's gorgeous smile flits through my mind as I recall our date tonight. *I'm going to fuck him. So what if he thinks I'm a slut for putting out on the first date?*

I look at my watch. *Shit. What should I do in the meantime? I have twelve hours to kill.*

Maybe I could find Ryan or Michael to spend the day with…No… that's not fair to them, Celeste.

I should probably get a hobby. I don't really need a job, but it could bring me a sense of structure and purpose. The only hobby I've ever had was playing and making video games. I probably shouldn't fall back into that trap of locking myself away from the world for months while I hyper-focus on making a video game, though. *Right?* That's the life I'm trying to leave behind.

Is there another hobby I can pick up that won't send me down the same dark path? The faces of Ryan, James, and Michael flit through my mind. *Is being a slut a hobby?* I should probably get a hobby that does involve ping-ponging between dicks.

Teeth brushed and basic skincare complete, I shuffle to the open boxes of clothing in the dining room. All my clothes and essential items were delivered yesterday afternoon after my impromptu lunch date with Michael. The rest of my belongings are in a storage facility at the edge of town. I don't feel comfortable removing my parents' things to make room for the stuff in storage.

I remove the first soft sweater and pair of jeans I can find, leaving a layer of clothes strewn across the tops of the boxes. I probably should spend the day unpacking. But, I really don't feel like doing that. *Fuck, I need to get my shit together: Make a plan—decide what I want the next ten years of my life to look like.*

Maybe I can wander around town. That might help me stumble into clarity—or at least a decent cup of coffee. *Or maybe I'll stumble into a fourth dude's line of vision.*

Dressed and half-heartedly styled, I resolve to go to the cafe for some breakfast and coffee. I don't need to have the next ten years planned out. I can settle for the next ten minutes, and going to the cafe will take at least an hour. *Yep. I'm winning at this "unemployed thing."*

I'd really like to reconnect with Sarah and maybe get to know Andy more. I probably should befriend someone who isn't a matronly figure, a dog, or a hot dude—even though both Sarah and Andy are exceptionally attractive, too.

With a determined nod, I grab my light coat and scarf from the hook by the door. I should probably go grocery shopping and get some basics like coffee after I get breakfast. Maybe Mrs. Heart would like to join me. I really enjoyed my walk with her and Watson the day before yesterday. I'll stop by her place first because I need her wisdom more than ever. Maybe she'll have tea. I need some caffeine right now, and waiting until I get to the cafe seems unbearable.

Stepping outside, the crisp autumn air greets me with an invigorating bite. Fall had always been my favorite time of year, and I really missed it in my season-less corner of California.

I step through the fallen leaves, making my way to Mrs. Heart's house next door. Each crunch reminds me of my dad's defiant reluctance to ever rake them. People often assumed it was laziness. *It drove my mother crazy*. But it was for the butterflies. He would rant about how the leaves should be left for the butterflies and wax poetic about how lawns are bad for the environment. It was the one argument with my mother that he won. Usually, she cared enough about things for both of them, and he didn't state much of an opinion on things. Usually, he conceded to whatever she wanted. But the butterflies were one cause he was passionate about, despite her wrath. *Why couldn't you have had that passion for me, Dad?* I shake my head, trying to avoid the dark path that thought was about to lead me down.

14

"Here we go!" I announce to the invisible audience that always follows me, and try to channel some of that famous self-assurance I always see in Ryan. I glance behind me at the door of Mr. O'Connor's house and wish Ryan would come bounding out of the door to be with me. *I'd love some comfort right now.*

As I reach Mrs. Heart's front porch, I pause for a moment, letting the nostalgia wash over me. Memories of sharing cookies and stories on this very stoop flood my mind, making me smile. Mrs. Heart and Ryan were always there for me. I knock and wait patiently. A single soft bark signals that someone is at the door, as Watson alerts Mrs. Heart to my presence.

The door cracks open, and Mrs. Heart peers at me before realizing it is me. She beams, "Celeste, dear!"

"Stay," she commands before opening the door further. Watson sits patiently a few feet away, staying like the goodest boy. "Come in, come in! I was just about to brew some tea." *Score.*

"Thanks, Mrs. Heart." When the door closes behind me, Watson rushes toward me to receive his praise for being so patient and obedient. I oblige him with a belly rub and a few "good boys." He has muddy feet today and is not as perfectly coiffed as he has been, but still as handsome as hell.

"How are you doing today, dear?" Mrs. Heart asks, leading me to the kitchen.

"Honestly? I'm feeling a bit…lost," I admit, settling into one of the frilly cushioned chairs at the small kitchen table.

"You can only be lost if you're trying to find something. What exactly are you trying to find, dear?" she asks. Watson paws at my feet, and I give him more scratches. Mrs. Heart places an adorable teacup and saucer in front of me, then pours tea from an equally adorable teapot into it. It's all frill and flowers, and I giggle at how feminine Mrs. Heart has always been despite her masculine profession.

Her hands are the only thing that ever hinted at the fact that she was a mechanic. If social media existed in her day, she could have given Ryan a run for his money when it came to creating thirst traps: a beauty queen in frilly pink, sipping tea, and repairing a carburetor. *I'd watch that. Fuck, I'd probably even subscribe to her OnlyFans.*

I lean back in the chair. I hold the delicate teacup and saucer in the specific way Mrs. Heart taught me and let the steaming tea comfort me with its radiating warmth. *Maybe it will be a good day.*

I take a sip of my tea, the warmth spreading through me like a cozy blanket. "So, Mrs. Heart," I begin, stirring the leaves in my cup as if they hold the answers to my tangled heart. "I…um, well, I slept with Ryan."

Mrs. Heart chuckles softly. "Oh dear. Well, we all could see that coming a mile away. Took you a bit longer than I expected, though. I would have assumed he would have been at your place on your first night back."

I grimace. "It was the first night." I put my head in my hands.

She laughs at me and pats my leg in reassurance. "What's the problem, dear? You two have been going at it like rabbits since…well before you should have been, if I'm being honest."

"It felt…nice, but now everything feels complicated. Like, what's next? I don't really know where he and I stand right now. He's always been so weird about our relationship. I fear age has not made either of us better at communicating. I also had this lunch date with James that turned into a surprise lunch date with Michael. So…I'm just so confused…what should I do?"

"You've got yourself quite the romantic entanglement," she observes, leaning forward.

"I'm sorry, Mrs. Heart. I'm always dumping my problems on you."

"Dear, I will always be here for you. And besides, your love life is more interesting than my soaps. Go ahead, you can talk to me about it."

"Well, James is charming, and I am so intensely drawn to him. The chemistry with him is electric. But then I found myself having lunch with Michael instead, and he and I…I don't know how to explain it. I feel so…seen by him," I grimace, covering my face. "And he's so sweet, and every time he looks at me, I melt a little. And he's so fucking adorably hot. Possibly the hottest man alive. I just want to lick both of them. They have such different pulls on me I can't even explain it."

"Ah, my dear Celeste, it sounds like you're simply exploring your options." She takes a sip of her tea, her smile warm and inviting.

"And Ryan, you know how he's been ever since his mom left… he'll never feel settled in a relationship. Has he been single this whole time?"

"He was engaged to Angela Martinez for a while." A pang of jealousy tightens my chest.

Angela and I were cordial acquaintances back in the day. We'd occasionally end up at the same parties, but we were never close. I'm not sure why. I suppose we each had our own friends at the time. She and Ryan had been similarly acquainted. *How did they even end up together? So much happened while I've been gone.*

"Engaged? Why'd they break up?"

"I wouldn't know, dear, it was a few years ago. Before he started his internet videos."

"Why is that making me jealous!?"

"Envy is a tricky thing," she replies gently, reaching out to pat my hand.

"I know he's had to have been with tons of women since he and I parted ways forever ago. I mean, look at him. But is it wrong to want to be the only one he's ever been with?" I ask, searching her face for wisdom.

"Not at all, dear, but it's a thought you can't dwell on. No amount of anguish will ever change the past."

"Yeah, I know. Also, I know I'm being a bit of a hypocrite. I wasn't exactly chaste the last few decades. Far from it. And now I'm over here scheming up ways to meet up with Michael and James."

"Remember, we can't always control our feelings, Celeste. It's ok to feel so-called 'negative' emotions."

"We can't always control our emotions, but we can always control our actions," I recite. It's a motto she's preached to me since I was a child. "I know. I know. Thank you, Mrs. Heart." I pause for a long moment, trying to determine what is actually bothering me. "I just…I don't know what to do. *Should I just pick one of them and focus my attention on him? Or maybe I shouldn't be dating at all right now.* For the first time in my life, I'm thinking about love and commitment and babies and am eager to pursue something, but maybe I'm just trying to fill a void."

Mrs. Heart leans back, her expression thoughtful. "It's okay to not jump into anything. It's okay to not have everything figured out. To wait and see where your heart takes you."

"But, I can't just lead them on while I work my shit out, can I?"

"Just make sure you're honest with them about where you are emotionally."

"Gaaah! What should I do!?" I wail, covering my face again, the various possibilities of my future swirling in my head. *I feel like a horny, lost teenager again.*

Mrs. Heart giggles at me slightly. "I can't make the choice for you, dear."

"Do I have to choose? Between them, I mean?"

She reflects for a moment. "No, you can play the field a bit."

"Play the field!? You make it sound so easy!"

"Well, it can be fun! Think of it as sampling different flavors. Like at the ice cream parlor." Her blue eyes twinkle, and she smirks in that way she does when she recalls her youth. "Before I got married, I had about five different men I was deciding between at any given time."

"Mrs. Heart, really?!"

"Oh, yes, you don't get the crown of Ms. Goose Grove without having multiple admirers knocking at your door. I was quite the slut. Still am." She laughs more devilishly this time.

"Speaking of, what's going on with you and Gus?" I ask.

"Gus has been a great comfort to me," she says coyly.

"What's with this coy, demure, noncommittal response, Mrs. Heart? You've never been one to shy away from speaking bluntly about such things?"

"Yes, well, this is about your sex-scapades, dear, not mine." She blushes.

"So, you admit you're having sex-scapades with Principal Gandy?"

"Yes, I admit Gus is one of the men I am currently seeing," she says matter-of-factly.

"One of?!"

"I told you, dear, I'm still quite the slut." She laughs, again. "But we are not talking about me. We are talking about you. Enjoy the company, and see where your heart leads you. But be open with them. Don't hide them from each other."

"I wonder if they would even go for that. Michael knew I was on a date with James and didn't seem concerned. In fact, it seemed to spur him on," I say, feeling a flicker of hope. "I definitely need to talk to them. Especially Ryan."

"They're all nice boys. But for the record, I'm team Ryan," she advises, her tone light.

"Thanks, Mrs. Heart. You always know how to make things seem less daunting," I reply, smiling gratefully.

She's always been my guiding voice of reason. The one person I could feel safe with when the world felt unsafe—when the world felt like it was out to get me. She's like the mother I never had. Well, the mother I wish I had had, anyway.

"That's what I'm here for, love. But above all, make sure to use protection, dear. I'd really hate for you to be the cause of a clap outbreak in Goose Grove."

I groan, putting my face in my hands again.

15

I handwash the teacups for Mrs. Heart as she remains at the table, nibbling a cracker and passing a piece down to Watson. "Dear, would you mind taking Watson for his walk today?" she asks.

"Sure, but why don't you want to take him?" I ask.

"I pulled my back during my date with Gus last night." She reaches for her back, groaning and smiling wryly at me. *She does seem a bit less active than usual this morning.*

"Oh, no, do you need anything?"

"No, dear, I'll be fine. I just need some rest and ice."

After a few more moments of conversation, I stand to leave. This visit with Mrs. Heart was a good idea. She's always known exactly how to ease my mind, and I feel lighter than I did when I arrived.

"Wanna go for a walk, boy?" I ask, enjoying the thrill he shows as I put his harness and leash on him. He does a cute little anticipatory spin at the door while waiting for me to open it—excitement overtaking him.

With Watson trotting eagerly beside me, I step back into the crisp autumn air and feel strangely empowered—buoyed by Mrs. Heart's encouragement.

I look around, appreciating my surroundings. This town really is beautiful in the fall when the leaves start changing. I can't help but smile at the sight—the trees display their vibrant coats of gold and green, not yet the stunning orange and red I love so much, but still gorgeous.

"It sure is beautiful, huh, boy?" I march forward off the porch with conviction. I'll figure out a hobby and/or job later. For now, I'll live in the present. I'll appreciate the beauty of the town and do some casual, non-committal flirting.

I let out a deep breath. "Alright," I say to Watson as he sniffs around. "Let's go see if any of the neighborhood bachelors are lurking about, huh? Can you sniff 'em out for me? Preferably, don't find me anymore, though. Three is enough." Watson just walks forward, tail wagging like a flag, ignoring my musings.

As we walk through the familiar yet changed streets, I feel a weird sense of anticipation, like one of the men I am looking for could be lurking around any corner, just waiting to sweep me off my feet and distract me from my life. And, I honestly don't know which I would prefer to run into. The charming James with his lingering touches? The thoughtful and observant Michael? Or the fun and familiar Ryan?

I always have a weird sense that someone is watching me. Some unknown force is hovering over me, judging my every move, ensuring I'm perfect at all times. For the first time, I feel like it's for someone… well, three someones. I suck in my gut, poke out my chest (not that you can see it with this coat), and hold my face just right, hoping my double chin isn't showing. *Don't scowl; no one could ever love you if you look angry all the time.*

"What would you do, Watson?" I ask, knowing he won't respond. But he looks at me and wags his tail more excitedly. The little dog just likes to be acknowledged.

"Maybe I just need to take a leap," I muse aloud, glancing at Watson, who looks up at me with those big, trusting eyes. "Like Mrs. Heart said. Date them all—see where it leads. It's not like I'm signing a lifelong contract here. Well, just James and Michael—Ryan doesn't want anything serious." My heart aches at the thought.

I can feel a spark of excitement creeping in as I imagine what it would be like to enjoy dating without the pressure of commitment. Could I juggle the complexities of a non-monogamous sexual relationship with three men?

"Why not?" I chuckle softly, shaking my head. With renewed purpose, and let's face it, horniness, I quicken my pace, hoping to run into one of them.

As soon as Watson and I step into Sarah's cafe, I scan the cozy space for Michael. My heart flutters at the thought of seeing him, but my shoulders drop when I don't spot him. I was really hoping to see him at the table, typing away, ready to be distracted by my presence. I don't know why I expected him here. It's not like he lives here.

I force a smile and approach the counter. Beth, the woman behind the counter, informs me that she works here part-time, and Andy and Sarah had to step out for some errands. Hopefully, they get back soon. I was hoping I'd at least get to chat with one of them. *Man, is today going to result in me just being at home alone with a dog, wallowing in self-pity, and avoiding unpacking?* I place my now-usual coffee order, along with a light breakfast of fruit, eggs, and toast.

I sit at a table and look around, hoping Michael will reveal himself to me, hidden in some corner that I couldn't see until seated. *It's okay. I can always text him.*

My fingers fumble with my phone as I consider sending him a quick text. "Hey! Just at the cafe. Wish you were here!" I type, then pause, biting my lip. *What if he thinks I'm too eager?* I delete the message. Or maybe I should be extra eager and type something like, "Thinking about your dick in my mouth." I chuckle at myself, imagining Michael's face if I did send something like that. It would actually be a fun experiment to send it to each of them and see how they respond.

But I couldn't send that text to James if I wanted to. *Ugh, why didn't I get James's number?* I groan quietly, shaking my head at my own missed opportunity. I'm feeling a bit like Michael said he had when I had his number and he did not have mine.

My resolve to date three men begins to waver. But before I can think too hard about it, Sarah exits the back and approaches with my order. *Oh, good. She is here.*

"Here's your order, Celeste!" she says, her cheerful voice cutting through my growing disappointment, as she places my coffee and plate in front of me.

"Thanks so much, Sarah." I move the plate closer to me.

Sarah looks around. "All by yourself today?" she asks with a wry smile on her face.

"Yeah," I sigh.

"It's a bit slow today," she says, taking a seat. Watson puts his head on her knee as she sits. "Hi, boy," she says while petting him. "I can't resist petting that adorable face. Don't let me forget to wash my hands before I return to work, okay, boy?" She returns her attention to me. "I was just thinking about you! Watching Michael and James vie for your attention yesterday was the highlight of my and Andy's day."

I laugh lightly, gently poking my scrambled eggs with my fork, embarrassed. "Oh gosh, it was so awkward."

"Awkward or not, you coming into town and shaking things up has been the most exciting thing that's happened around here in a while." She winks, leaning in as if sharing a juicy secret. "You've got them both twisted around your finger. But the local scuttlebutt says Ryan was spotted leaving your house the other night…late and with an unusual pep in his step." She raises her eyebrow at me expectantly.

"Let me guess. Mr. O'Connor told you?" I quip, rolling my eyes, knowing Ryan's dad is and will always be the town gossip.

"He sure did!" she laughs. "He's been going around telling everyone that the two of you are back together."

"We were never together," I sigh, slightly annoyed. "Ryan always insisted we remain just friends—so that's all we have ever been and will ever be." My voice clips, pushing back an emotion I need to hold in tight.

Andy comes up, putting their hand on the small of Sarah's back and asks, "Is that so?"

"Yes!" I say a bit too curtly.

"Andy, you wouldn't know, since you ran with different circles back then—" Sarah begins to explain, but Andy cuts her off.

"And by that you mean kept myself locked in my room until college and never talked to anyone?" they ask with a self-deprecating joke.

Sarah sighs. "Yes, but anyway, the whole 'are Ryan and Celeste a thing?' is one of the great mysteries of Goose Grove."

"I said the same thing to Sarah, that I just wanted to be friends, but I was desperately in love with her. That was when I thought she wouldn't be interested in me," Andy says with a smirk.

"Yeah, but you were so transparent, Andy. It was pretty obvious that wasn't what you wanted," Sarah laughs.

"I'm sorry, but you were just too cute in that frilly apron. Perfect woman," Andy replies.

Sara blushes and leans into Andy's touch. They smile so warmly at each other that I can almost feel the love beaming off of them. Sarah shakes herself from Andy's gaze and says, "Anyway, back on topic. So, which one are you going to choose? Michael or James?"

"Or Ryan?" Andy says with a slight scoff. I'm not sure what that's about.

"Umm, do I have to choose?" I reply.

"No! Just make sure you have all your dates in here so we can spy on you," Sarah laughs.

"Honestly, I never thought I'd see the day that someone got their hooks in James," Andy says, sitting in the chair next to Sarah.

I see this as an opportunity to get some dirt on the men I'm currently interested in. Sarah and Andy seem like they appreciate gossip just as much as Mr. O'Connor. "So, James doesn't date?"

"Not really. He's been relentlessly pursued by quite a few locals. But he's never been one to really settle down. He's always too busy with work. I was surprised to see him so doggedly pursuing you," Sarah says reflectively.

"He's a bit of a rolling stone, I'd say," Andy says, reflecting on James.

"What about Michael? What's his story?" I ask, leaning forward, forgetting my breakfast entirely.

Sarah and Andy look at each other, as if silently asking how to answer this question. Sarah speaks up. "He's here a lot. He loves our mochas. I only know of him dating one other person, but that was a while ago."

I'm starting to feel a bit bad about collecting this data on these men. *Small towns are generally all up in everyone's business, and this type of information isn't particularly secret...right?*

Watson whines at Sarah, annoyed no one is paying attention to him. "Where's Mrs. Heart, by the way?" Sarah asks absentmindedly, petting him.

"She hurt her back and asked me to walk Watson for her," I say.

"Oh no, I hope she's okay!" Sarah says. "It was so nice to see her out and about with you the other day. I haven't seen her that happy in a while. John's death really affected her. After she sold the dealership, she didn't leave her house for quite a while."

"But your dad roping her into starting that community garden really seemed to cheer her up," Andy adds, looking toward Sarah.

"That's not the only thing my dad does to cheer her up," Sarah says with a bleh face.

I feel like such an ass. Mrs. Heart has been focusing on me since I came here, and I haven't taken the time to ask her about what she's been up to over the last few years. She and Mr. Heart owned a car dealership in town. He was the jovial salesman, and she was the drop-dead gorgeous mechanic. They even sold calendars featuring her.

I'm just like my mother; I only ever think of myself. I push the thought away.

"Who owns the dealership now?" I ask.

Sarah answers, "Oh, it's not there anymore. I think Golden Wing-Span Development bought it. They're buying everything. They're planning to make it an apartment complex, but the town has been really pushing back on it."

Andy adds, "Lots of red tape is holding it up. People think an apartment complex would really harsh the vibe of the small town. Daniel and Marcus have been trying to make us a not-so-small town since Marcus became Mayor."

"Daniel?" I ask.

"Oh, sorry. Daniel Stevens. He runs Golden WingSpan Development," Andy adds. "He and Marcus are like besties or something. I wouldn't be surprised if Marcus is cutting all that red tape for him."

Oh, that's the guy Nicole was talking to.

"Oh, that's…that doesn't sound like the Marcus I remember," I reply. The golden boy I recall was always super honest. Too honest sometimes.

"Well, he's got a lot of ambition," Sarah replies. *Yes, he was always ambitious.*

"It's probably just my sister's ambition," Andy sighs, "She's been bitching about living in this 'backwoods town' since we were kids. Marcus is a good guy, but…my sister can be really…persuasive."

Sarah adds, "This quarter's town hall meeting is coming up in November. I'm pretty sure the revitalization plans—"

"Gentrification plans!" Andy interjects, which, given their trust fund upbringing, is pretty refreshing.

Sarah rolls her eyes at their interruption and continues, "I'm pretty sure the plans are on the agenda. The whole town will be there voicing their dissent. You should go, Celeste! It'll be a good opportunity for you to get reacquainted with everyone and with the town's goings on."

"Oh, yeah, that's a good idea," I reply. I suppose I should try to integrate myself into the town.

16

Okay. Now what? I stand outside the cafe, dog leash in hand, and scan my surroundings, unsure what to do. My chat with Andy and Sarah was invigorating while it lasted, but once the brunch traffic picked up and they had to get back to work, I found myself alone with just a dog and my thoughts.

"What do you think we should do, Watson?" As if he actually understands me, he begins walking in the direction that would lead us home. I guess I'm at the point of directionless depression that I just let a dog choose what I do. I look toward the direction of the law office. "You sure you don't want to go that way?" I ask Watson, who, despite my personification of him, does not actually respond and continues to trot along, his ears bouncing ever so slightly with each step. "Alright, I guess I should go home and unpack," I say dejectedly.

My phone buzzes in my pocket, and the thrill of anticipation has me opening it quickly. It's a newsletter from an author I follow and, while smut is probably something I do need in my life right now, I am supremely disappointed it isn't an actual, real-life dick.

I continue to grip my phone and open up the texting app. Maybe I should text Michael. Something casual like "Hey, how's your day going?" Nothing too heavy.

Don't be so desperate, Celeste. No one will ever love you if you are so needy.

Or I can text Ryan. I bet he'd help me unpack. I could request his help under the guise of needing big, strong arms to help move things. He'd help me without the pretense, which is what makes texting him a really easy and safe bet.

I look up from my phone, and we're approaching the community garden area. A tall, tan, dark-haired man with an unmistakable, election-winning smile approaches me. His eyes are locked on me, and he is definitely walking toward me with the intent to talk to me.

Marcus. Fuck. My stomach flips in a surprising mix of anticipation and apprehension. His easy stride and confident demeanor still have a way of catching me off guard. As much as I'm interested in seeing how hot he stayed up close, I don't really want to talk to the first guy who ever truly broke my heart. *Am I bitter still? Fuck yes!*

"Celeste!" he calls out, stepping forward with that easy confidence of his, hands casually tucked into his coat pockets. He's dressed as if he's going to a business meeting, so I guess that means he hasn't been gardening.

"Hey, Marcus," I reply, trying to sound casual while keeping my heartbeat steady. My stomach does a little flip. There's something about him that brings back a flood of memories: good, bad, and a little horny.

"Welcome back to The Grove," he says, walking awkwardly to me, arms out. *Oh, uh, okay, I guess we're on hugging terms?* We hug, with just our shoulders, keeping our pelvises as far away from each other as possible while also avoiding my tits.

After that incredibly uncomfortable hug, his gaze flickers down to Watson, who's sniffing his polished shoes enthusiastically. "Where's Mrs. Heart, Watson?" He pets the dog. I notice Watson doesn't jump on him, likely knowing that Marcus wouldn't appreciate those muddy paws all over his nice suit.

"She's not feeling well, so I'm walking Watson for her," I say, gesturing down to my furry sidekick.

"It's nice to see you, Celeste. You're looking well." I may be reading too much into the look he gives me, but I think he eyes me in a way a married man should not.

"Thanks, Marcus, you look well…as well," I grimace, attempting to maintain my composure. I can't help but notice how the lines around his eyes have deepened, but he looks dignified in age. *Damn him. He's still remarkably hot.* I bet he won the election on that handsome face alone. "Congrats on becoming mayor."

"Thanks, Celeste. I don't know if you remember, but you actually encouraged me to run."

"What? That can't be true." I shake my head.

"Yeah, when you broke up with me, you said something like, 'you could run this town.'" He laughs and looks around as if he's afraid his constituents will see him laughing.

I look at him, confused. "Marcus, you broke up with me."

"That can't be true…I recall being pretty heartbroken." He looks upward as if trying to recall the memory.

"It doesn't matter anymore," I respond, because this feels like a weird thing to be talking about. *But, for the record, he broke up with me, and I'm still mad about it.*

"Yes, I suppose it doesn't." He smiles at me in that disarming way. Watson pulls at the leash, oblivious to the discomfort I am feeling right now, and tries to reach a nearby bush.

"I've run into Nicole a few times," I say, trying to steer the conversation to something that feels more appropriate. "How long have the two of you been married?"

His smile twitches in a way that indicates he's forcing it to stay on his face. The way a politician does. "About fifteen years now."

"Children?" I ask, knowing the answer.

"Two. Twins. They just started middle school, if you can believe it."

"Wow, we're getting old." I laugh.

"Tell me about it…" He runs a hand through his perfectly styled hair, a gesture I remember well from our high school days. We just look at each other the way you'd expect two people who fucked twenty years ago and haven't spoken since might.

He leans in slightly, lowering his voice as if sharing a secret. "You should come by the town hall sometime. I'd love to catch up properly and run some things by you." The words are all business, but the way he's eyeing me seems lurid. "Also, it'd be great to catch up, reminisce about the old times."

I swallow hard, unsure of how to respond. Memories flood my mind—lazy summer afternoons spent under the old oak tree we carved our initials in, watching him play football, making love in his car, and declaring our love for each other. He was the first person who ever told me he loved me. Literally, since I never heard it from my parents.

"I don't think Nicole would like that very much," I say, my pulse quickening, and I'm worried I'm misreading the situation.

He raises an eyebrow, teasing. "I don't think she'll mind." There's a flicker of something in his gaze, a longing that sends a rush of conflicting emotions through me.

"And why is that?"

"She's just as invested in the plans I have for this town as I am."

"Well, umm. I'm not sure I'll be able to find the time."

He shrugs. "It's just a chat, Celeste."

I chuckle softly, but inside, I'm wrestling with the idea of re-entering his orbit. Could I handle the complexities of our past?

"Just think about it." His gaze lingers on mine, and I can almost feel his hands on my body. "You might find it…invigorating."

"Invigorating," I repeat, feeling the weight of his words settle in my chest. I can't deny the pull I feel, but the skepticism remains. "I'll think about it."

Watson pulls hard at the leash, jerking me away from Marcus.

"That's all I ask." He steps back and cuts me a glance I can't quite read. "Now, I should let you get back to your walk before Watson rips that leash in two."

"Not sure what he's so excited about," I say, chuckling as Watson gives a determined tug on his leash. It's as if he understands the urgency of the moment and wants me to get away from this man as soon as possible. *Thanks, Watty.*

"Take care, Celeste." Marcus flashes that million-dollar smile again. There's a lingering resonance in his tone.

"See you around, Marcus." I smile reluctantly, not wanting to commit too much of my emotions to that whirlwind of a man.

"Okay, Watson!" I laugh as he pulls at the leash, his little paws practically dancing on the sidewalk. "And just so you know, Watson, even though Marcus is still devastatingly handsome, that's not a roller-coaster I plan on riding again. I'm all for playing the field, but not with someone's husband." *I hate Nicole, but there are lines I don't cross.*

I follow Watson into the community garden. "Maybe I should take up gardening," I say to Watson. "It could be a new hobby, right? Or at least something to distract me from all this..." I wave my hand vaguely, referencing my whole mess of a life.

Watson drags me through the garden. He tugs harder, nearly pulling my arm out of its socket. "Jeez, boy. I get it, but calm down."

I'm trying to appreciate the scenery because I really like the vibe of this place. It's chill—despite the insistent dog and horny, disheveled billionaire currently ripping through it. There are a few people tending to plots of land, and they all look so...content. I wonder if they could use another pair of hands. Maybe gardening, not romance, is the answer to all of my problems. *Perhaps I should scrap this whole 'Celeste the Slut' idea and focus on 'Celeste the Chill as Fuck Gardener.'*

Watson is a pup on a mission, pulling me deeper into the garden, yanking my arm, and stopping my mind from focusing on a single thought too long.

"Hey there, Celeste!" Principal Gandy waves from his plot, his hands smudged with dirt, but his smile bright as ever. "How's your day going?"

"Pretty good! Just enjoying some time with Watson."

"Where's Regina?"

"At home, resting her hurt back. I'm walking Watson for her," I say as I gesture to the enthusiastic pup, but he won't let me stop to chat. How this little dog can pull so hard is beyond me.

"She hurt her back?"

"Sorry, Principal Gandy, he's got somewhere to be," I say with a chuckle.

"Call me Gus, young lady! I'm not the Principal anymore," he calls back as I'm dragged further into the garden.

"Right, sorry! See ya, Gus!" I wave. He lowers himself back down to tend to his plot.

"Alright, Watson," I say, "Where do you want to get to so badly?" I let him pull me deep into the garden, no longer resisting.

17

I tug the leash gently, urging Watson to slow down, but he's having none of it. "Calm down, boy!" I chuckle as he pulls so desperately that his front legs aren't even touching the ground.

Watson doesn't usually tug like this. "What has gotten into you? Is it a squirrel or something?" I ask, shaking my head. As we round a bend, the bushes ahead rustle. Watson halts, his body tense, and lets out a series of frantic barks directed at the bustling bush. A cat rushes by. "It was just a cat, Watson. Why are you so upset?"

But Watson doesn't even look at the cat; he just resumes tugging me toward the bush, barking at it.

He stops at the edge of the foliage and resumes barking maniacally.

"Watson!" I gasp.

His barks sound urgent, almost frantic, and I peer past him into the shrubbery. My heart races as I lean closer, curiosity getting the better of me. Then I see it.

"Is that…?"

I step forward, pushing branches aside, and the world around me blurs. There, partially hidden beneath a pile of fertilizer bags, is Richard Holbrook.

My breath catches in my throat, and an icy wave of disbelief washes over me. Garden shears protrude grotesquely from his stomach, glinting menacingly in the morning sun.

My body understands what I'm seeing before my brain does. When my mind finally catches up with the panic stirring in my chest, a ringing in my ears accompanies the pounding of my heart.

Then it truly hits me. "No! No, no, no!" I croak out, the sound slipping from my lips and catching in my throat.

Watson goes wild at my side, barking frantically, his small body vibrating with energy. I can barely hold onto his leash. Everything feels surreal, like I'm stuck in some twisted version of reality where this isn't really happening.

The world darkens around me, a panic attack threatening to engulf me. I tug Watson toward me. I sink to the ground and attempt to use his warmth for comfort, pulling him to my chest. But he refuses to calm down. "Calm down, buddy! Calm down!" I try to soothe him, try to soothe myself, but my hands tremble.

I cling to Watson, feeling the warmth of his fur as it grounds me amidst the chaos. My mind races, struggling to grasp this grim discovery. *How could this be happening? What is Richard doing here?*

"He's dead. He's dead," I mutter, shaking my head as though willing the truth to change.

"Help!" I shout. "Help!"

I pull Watson into my lap, and he finally calms down, nuzzling into me. "Watson," I whisper, holding him tightly against me, his soft fur offering a fragile comfort.

I need to pull myself together, but all I can think about is the shock of it—Richard Holbrook, dead in the community garden. *What on earth have I walked into?*

Principal Gandy rushes toward me, "Celeste, what on earth is going on? Are you okay?"

"Richard Holbrook. He's dead. In the bushes," I sputter out.

"What?" he asks, confused.

My heart races faster, and I feel like I might black out. In the periphery of my consciousness, hurried footsteps pound behind me. I look toward the sound to see Ryan pushing through a small crowd that has begun gather, his face a mix of worry and determination. His movement is almost clumsy and panicked as he tries to reach me. *Why is he here?*

"Celeste!" Ryan calls out, urgency lacing his voice as he reaches me. Before I can respond, he wraps his arms around me, burying my head in his chest, and petting me. The warmth of his presence offers a small comfort against the chill of the morning air. *Always here to save me.*

He pulls back so he can hold my face in his hands. "What's going on?" he asks, his blue eyes scanning my face for answers. "Are you okay?"

"Watson. He found…Mr. Holbrook. Garden shears," I manage to say, my voice quivering. I return my face to his protective chest, grateful for his steady support.

Principal Gandy approaches the bush to peek behind the leaves tentatively. "Oh, my God. He's dead," he croaks. His usual calm demeanor is frazzled.

"Just breathe, alright? You're safe," Ryan whispers as his grip tightens on me and he pets the back of my head.

"Did you call the cops?" James's voice asks calmly above me. *When did he get here?* I peek out of Ryan's embrace to see James's hand gripping his phone as if ready to call the police himself. Ryan subtly shifts his body to position himself between James and me, blocking James from my view.

"Back off a bit," Ryan states, his voice quiet yet firm. "Let's not overwhelm her right now."

"Ryan, someone has to call—" James protests, but Ryan cuts him off.

"I know. Just give her a second to catch her breath. She's going to pass out." His voice softens as he returns his attention to me. *He knows me so well.* "Breathe, Star Girl. Breathe."

"He's stabbed. Murdered," I stammer, as my tears soak Ryan's shirt.

James replies in a consoling voice, "Okay, Celeste. It's okay, I've got it." I peek from outside Ryan's chest to watch James walk away and dial his phone.

As Ryan's protective grip tightens around me, returning my eyes to his chest again, murmurs from the crowd begin to seep into my awareness. Snippets of side conversations, as onlookers whisper to each other about their suspicions concerning Richard Holbrook's death, reach me.

"Not surprised someone killed him…" a woman's voice whispers.

"Holbrook…murdered," James says sternly from the street into his phone.

"Total sleazebag," another voice in the crowd adds, dripping with disdain.

"Half the town probably wanted him dead," a third voice chimes in.

The voices swirl within my head, and I wish they would all just shut up. My heart sinks further with each whispered accusation. It feels like a weight pressing down on me, getting heavier with each voice that shows no remorse for the dead man I just found.

"Isn't that the Moon girl? When did she come home?" a phantom voice whispers from the crowd.

"Must be here because of her parents' accident," someone responds, and I wish they would shut the fuck up. I don't want to think about my parents' death right now…ever actually.

"Community garden…yes…send someone right away." James's voice remains calm, cool, and collected.

My breath quickens, and I'm suffocating.

"Celeste," Ryan says gently, drawing my attention back to him, pushing me away slightly so he can hold my cheeks between his palms and look in my eyes. "Focus on me, okay? What do you need right now?"

"I just…I don't know." My voice is small, almost drowned out by the murmuring crowd. "Everything feels…too much." A paw scratches at my chest with a whimper, and I lift Watson to hug him tighter.

"Okay, we'll take it one step at a time," Ryan whispers.

He pulls me back, pressing Watson between us. "Remember the box breathing you taught me? Let's do that, okay?" Flashes of comforting him after his mother left flit through my mind. I nod in affirmation.

"In two, three, four. Hold two, three, four. Out two, three, four. Hold two, three, four," Ryan chants, as I breathe in the scent of him at the rhythm he's set.

I overhear more snippets of conversation—the words "business dealings" and "lawsuits." Each mention of Richard's name sends a fresh wave of unease through me. *Why would someone hurt him? And why here, in this peaceful garden?* I thought this could have been my safe space…where I could go to grieve and work through my feelings…but now.

I frantically search for the source of all the whispering. I want to scream at them to shut the fuck up. Ryan pulls my attention back when he says gently, "Don't listen to them. Listen to my heartbeat. Feel the ground underneath you." I do as I'm told, placing my ear on his chest.

James returns and makes a suggestion. "Let's get you some water. The cops will be here soon and will want to speak to her."

Ryan makes a noise as if he's about to yell at James for breaking into our de-escalation ritual, but I reply, "Water sounds good." Though I doubt I could keep anything down.

I attempt to pull away from Ryan, but he refuses to let me go. "Don't worry, I got you," Ryan says, his protectiveness starting to stifle me. "I won't let anything happen to you."

"Thanks," I whisper as we move upward together.

I must have dropped Watson's leash, because James has it in his hand. "Good boy," James says as Watson follows obediently behind us.

All I can do is cling to Ryan, with James following closely behind. I'm grateful that they are here with me.

18

I'm not sure how I got here, but I'm sitting on a bench, a cup of water in hand. I am trying to drown out the noise with my scarf wrapped around my head.

The crowd buzzes around me like a swarm of bees, their whispers swirling into an indistinct hum. Watson sits in my lap, and I cling tightly to him. He sits tense, protective. Ryan sits equally tense and protective beside me, one hand gripping me close to him, the other absentmindedly stroking Watson.

The crowd of onlookers has gotten larger, and I wonder if the whole town is here. The back of the crowd parts as a tall figure approaches through the throng of onlookers.

"Move aside," a deep, steady, and commanding voice calls out. An older man, wearing a khaki uniform of the Goose Grove Police Department, emerges from the crowd. He strides towards us, a presence that clears the path with effortless authority.

His sharp brown eyes scan the scene, missing nothing, even as they settle on me with a look that is stern yet somehow reassuring.

He moves to stand in front of me. "Celeste Moon?" His tone is professional, but there's a hint of empathy underlying it. He's done this before: dealt with hysterical women after a tragedy.

"Yes," I manage to reply, swallowing hard as my heart races at the thought of answering questions. *Please don't make me describe what I saw.*

"I'm Sheriff Kim. Can we talk?" He gestures toward a bench further away in a quieter corner of the garden, away from the gathering crowd. I nod, feeling Ryan's grip tighten on my shoulder before he reluctantly lets me go.

"Don't worry. I'll be right here," Ryan assures me, his voice low and protective. I stand and take a breath, trying to steady myself.

"I'd like to speak with her alone, Mr. O'Connor," Sheriff Kim says.

Ryan looks like he's going to protest, but he balks at the authoritative stare of Sheriff Kim. "Okay." Ryan takes Watson's leash. "I'll watch Watson for you."

Ryan's hand lingers on me and falls away as I follow Sheriff Kim.

James, who had been standing nearby, turns on his heels and pushes toward us. He grabs my elbow, steadying me. "I'm her lawyer!" he says firmly.

What? No, he's not. I look at him, confused. Sheriff Kim simply nods at James.

I whisper, "I have a lawyer in California."

He asserts, "Well, they're not here right now. So, I'm going to protect you."

The warmth of his body against mine makes me want to argue less.

James helps me sit on the bench, his hands gentle and firm. I'm happy he's helping me because I'm still unsteady on my feet as the world spins around me. He sits next to me.

"Tell me what you saw," Sheriff Kim urges.

I open my mouth, but the words are stuck somewhere between my throat and my racing mind. "It's okay, Celeste. Take your time," James says with a nod, placing a hand on my knee.

"I—uh, Watson was tugging on his leash," I stammer, the absurdity of such a detail striking me at this moment. "He never does that." I laugh. *Why am I laughing? A man is dead.*

"Right," Sheriff Kim says, nodding as if taking mental notes. "And then?" James squeezes my leg reassuringly.

"Then he...he barked at those bushes," I continue, pointing toward the bushes.

Ryan perks up, thinking I'm pointing at him, then looks behind himself, realizing what I'm actually pointing at.

My voice wobbles, and I try to swallow down the tremor. "I thought maybe there was a squirrel. But it was a cat." I stop and look around for the cat. "I don't know where the cat is now. I hope it's okay." I look frantically and rise from my seat, ready to start a cat search party.

"That's Callie. She's the garden's pest control and lives upstairs. Look, she's okay," James reassures me, pointing to a cat in a window above.

"Oh, good. I was worried..." I trail off, sitting back down, as if the entirety of the Earth's gravitational force pulls me toward it. Now unsure why I thought something bad had happened to the cat, I stare at the ground and try to get my wits back.

"Keep going," Sheriff Kim urges.

"But Watson didn't care about the cat. He wanted the bush. Then I found...Richard." The name sits heavily on my tongue. "I found him in the bush. He was..." My breath hitches again, the memory flooding back—fertilizer stacked on him, hiding nearly everything but his face and the glint of the shears.

"Take your time," Sheriff Kim encourages gently, and I appreciate the way he softens his demeanor just enough to let me know I can breathe. James places his hand on my back, a reassuring presence, and rubs in small circles. I look toward Ryan. His face is wracked with worry. He and Watson pace, both anxious to reunite with me.

"His stomach...it was..." I close my eyes briefly, forcing myself to remember. "There were garden shears," I say, gesturing to my stomach. I shake my head, struggling to keep the images at bay. "He's...he's dead?" I ask, knowing the truth but hoping there's a different answer.

"Did you notice anything unusual before that? Any arguments, strange behavior?"

"No, I saw Marcus and Principal Gandy...Gus Gandy...he's not a Principal anymore. Why can't I remember that? But...nothing else."

"Marcus Adams? The Mayor?" Sheriff Kim asks for clarification.

"Yes, Marcus Adams," I say with a swallow and a nod. I wince, worried I may have implicated Marcus and Gus.

Sheriff Kim simply hums in response and he jots something down in his notebook. His face is unreadable, the perfect poker face.

A sharp feminine voice cuts through the din of the onlookers, "Alright. Alright, everyone! Step back!"

I turn to see a woman ushering the onlookers further away. Her short, curly hair bounces with each step. She's wearing a police uniform and is heavily pregnant. She looks familiar, but I'm not sure if I know her. The town is small and I knew most of its residents at least tangentially, but I am terrible at remembering faces.

"Please give us some space!" she calls out, scanning the crowd. "This is a crime scene now, and we need to secure it."

The crowd shuffles back as she pushes everyone away. "Stand back, Ryan," she says more curtly than she does to the others.

He asks her nervously, "Angela, can I—"

"I said 'Stand back,'" she says with an authority he doesn't want to challenge. They share a look that is charged with history, but he moves back without a further word.

Oh, it's Angela. Ryan's ex-fiance, Angela. Is that his baby? No. That's impossible. I squint at her, trying to see if she's wearing a wedding ring. *God, Celeste, you seriously have more important things to worry about than the paternity of Angela's fetus.*

As everyone backs away, they keep their eyes on the bush where Richard's body lies, but Ryan and Watson keep their eyes locked on me.

Angela approaches me, and an expression of recognition crosses her face. She glances back at Ryan. "Hey, Celeste," she says, without any emotion. "Nice to see you. I wish it had been under better circumstances."

"I've been hearing that a lot lately," I reply, forcing a smile. My life has been encapsulated by death, and people apologizing that it's brought us together.

"Right." She gives a sympathetic nod, and I'm happy she doesn't say she's sorry for my loss of parents.

I realize the rudeness of my response and add, "Thanks, Angela. It's nice to see you, too."

She nods at me with a tight smile and returns her attention to the crowd. She says firmly, motioning with both hands, "Everyone, please keep moving back."

Of all the onlookers she attempts to corral, Ryan is the most reluctant. He hovers on the edge of the zone she has forced everyone toward. His usually relaxed demeanor is replaced by something tense and edgy. He has Watson's leash gripped tightly in one hand and the other shoved deep in his pocket. He paces like an animal in a cage. The uneasy expression on his face tenses further when James puts his arm around my shoulder.

"Celeste," Ryan calls, taking a tentative step forward before being stopped by Angela.

"Stand back, Ryan," she says with a voice of annoyed familiarity, placing her body between us.

"Are you okay?" he shouts, arching to see around her shoulder. He's doing that thing where he's projecting his anxiety on me. Trying to take care of me when it's he who needs to be taken care of.

James glares at Ryan, their eyes locking in a silent standoff, and he tightens his grip around my shoulders, almost as if he's egging Ryan on.

When Angela moves away from Ryan to corral other citizens, Ryan and Watson, unable to be restrained any longer, break from the crowd and rush toward me. Angela doesn't notice, and I suspect that when she does, she might actually tase him.

Before he can get to me, James suggests, "Ryan, maybe you should go find somewhere to sit and calm down now," his tone smooth yet edged with impatience.

"Why? She clearly needs support," Ryan shoots back, his voice rising slightly.

"And how is your anxious energy doing that exactly?" James scoffs, his posture stiffening.

Angela, having noted Ryan's approach, follows him, annoyed. She looks at me, her expression softening. Then, with the voice of a woman tired of men's shit, she says, "Gentleman. I understand you both are very protective of Celeste. Let's focus on what matters, shall we?"

My gaze flickers between Ryan and James, both of whom seem to deflate slightly under Angela's authoritative presence.

James asks, "Is there anything else you need to ask her, Sheriff?"

"No, that's it for now," Sheriff Kim says, closing his notebook. At that, Ryan sighs in relief and stands next to me on the side opposite James.

"If there's anything you remember, anything at all, Celeste, you call me, okay?" Sheriff Kim says as he hands me a card.

"Okay," I say, thumbing the card. I stare at it but don't see anything on the card. My eyes somehow look through it, unable to concentrate on it. My mind races, and I try to think of any last details I could tell him, but I can barely focus on anything. *What happened to Richard Holbrook? Who did this? Why?*

Watson paws my leg, and I lean down to pat him. His big brown eyes look up at me, filled with concern that makes my heart ache. If only this sweet pup could help me make sense of what just happened.

James and I rise as James shakes the Sheriff's hand. I drift toward Ryan, away from James.

"Celeste, are you alright?" Ryan's voice cuts through my foggy thoughts as he places his hands gently on my face. His face is creased with worry.

"Spectacular," I manage to joke, though it comes out more strained than I intended. I take a deep breath. "Honestly? Not really," I admit, glancing back at Richard's body, now obscured by a group of officers I never saw appear that are now gathered around the body. "I thought Goose Grove was supposed to be peaceful." Ryan puts his arm around me and leads me toward the street, pulling me away from James and Sheriff Kim and furtively glancing at Angela.

James walks purposefully beside us. He unbuttons his blazer and runs his hands through his hair. He reaches into his jacket pocket and hands me a card. "Celeste, here is my card. If the police come to talk to you, please call me, okay?" *Looks like I managed to get James's number after all.*

"Why would she call you?" Ryan asks curtly, his fingers digging gently into my shoulder.

"Because I'm a lawyer, Ryan," James says with an exacerbated eye roll. "Seriously, Celeste. Please don't speak to the cops without a lawyer. I don't have to be your lawyer, but I will be there for you."

Richard was my lawyer, and now he's dead.

19

I lie on the couch, watching the ceiling fan spin as thoughts spin through my head. Watson nestles beside me, squeezed between my hip and the cushions. I run my fingers through his silky fur, trying to find comfort in the sensation. It doesn't calm my nerves, however—each stroke somehow reminding me of the body I found in the bushes.

My mind flits between the ghastly sight and a desperation to determine what actually happened to Richard Holbrook. "Who could have killed him, boy?" I ask Watson.

Watson offers no answers, only the steady rhythm of his breathing and an occasional nuzzle against my palm when I stop petting him. He opens his eyes to look at me for a moment, and those big brown eyes seek mine only momentarily before closing—as if he couldn't care less about the murder of Richard Holbrook. And, I suppose he couldn't care less.

"Well, you're no help," I mumble to him as I continue to stroke him, now extending the pets from back to belly—a reward for absolutely nothing other than being adorable and a comfort.

The fact that I ran into Marcus outside the garden right before finding Richard's body will not leave me. *Could Marcus have murdered him? But why would he? Marcus is the mayor. Mayors are corrupt, right?*

Maybe it has something to do with Nicole. Marcus doesn't seem particularly loyal to Nicole, but perhaps he's loyal enough to kill a man who made his wife cry. That doesn't really seem like something Marcus would do, though. He was always a bit self-centered, and I don't really see him putting his own life on the line for anyone—wife or not. *But that was twenty years ago.*

Who else was there? Principal Gandy. A few other people I don't know. So many people materialized around me after I started screaming. Ryan and James certainly got there quickly. *But...how long had Richard been lying there dead?* Someone being there when I found the body wouldn't necessarily implicate them. *Would it?*

A gentle clinking stirs me from my rumination as Mrs. Heart enters the room with a tray. Upon the tray is my mother's old tea set—a gift from Mrs. Heart many years ago, and cookies. She smiles warmly at me when I lift to peer at her. I sit upright and place my elbows on my knees, annoying Watson as he shifts to get comfortable now that I am no longer pinning him against the back of the couch.

"Mrs. Heart, that's not too heavy for you, is it? Is your back okay?" I ask, rising to help her with the tray, but she waves me off with a chuckle.

"Dear, this weighs hardly a thing," she assures me, though I catch the subtle grimace that betrays the ache in her back when she bends to set the tray on the coffee table.

I eye her suspiciously but decide not to challenge her. "Thank you," I say, and pick up a teacup and saucer. I watch attentively as she fills my cup. I try to ground myself in the moment and embrace the warm aroma of tea that wafts toward me as she pours, but the antsiness within me is hard to quell.

"I'll always be here to bring you some tea and company, dear," she says, patting my shoulder gently before sitting beside me. "How are you doing? Still spiraling?" she asks with all the warmth of a woman who has watched over me my whole life. *The mother I never had.*

"I still can't get the image of him out of my head. I've never seen a dead body before. And I can't help but wonder who killed him," I say, staring blankly in front of me.

She shutters. "Oh, dear, try not to get yourself worked up over it. The police will find the murderer in due time," she says, attempting to turn me from ruminating on the subject I've harped on the last few days.

I take a sip, letting the liquid courage bolster my resolve. "I can't help it. I feel like I found him for a reason. Like, I need to solve this. I know that's weird."

"Dear, I think you are perhaps feeling a bit directionless and latching onto this murder as a way to find direction," she says warmly. Her eyes indicate she is worried about me, and I know I should focus on other things. I attempt a lighthearted grin, hoping to ease Mrs. Heart's tension.

"I know you're right. Just like how I was ready to make being the town hoe my life's purpose," I confess, with a laugh. I am quite ridiculous, and it's probably best that I hook my wagon to something more productive than sleeping with every man I meet—*like solving a murder? No.* I'm not some amateur sleuth stumbling upon dead bodies multiple times a year and nosing my way into the investigation. *Or am I?*

"You don't have to have a direction, dear. You are allowed to just exist without being productive."

"I know…" I say this because she's said this to me a million times, but the anxiety that bubbles in me can't absorb the logic. My head knows it, but my heart doesn't.

"When was the last time you spoke to any of the boys?" Mrs. Heart asks, hopeful that we'll change the subject to my love life.

"I was supposed to go on dates with James and Michael, but I canceled them. And I've been dodging texts from both of them for the last few days…and Ryan." The teacup in my hands trembles slightly, betraying the storm whirling within me. "I feel badly. I know Ryan is likely losing his mind with worry."

Her warm smile doesn't falter as she gives my knee a comforting squeeze. "Oh, Celeste, dear, there's nothing wrong with taking a little time for yourself, especially under these circumstances. Their feelings are theirs to manage. You can't be there for them if you're not there for yourself first."

I nod, the knot in my stomach loosening ever so slightly. "I know," I say, because she's told me this a million times, too. "I just feel like I'm ghosting them. I need to suck it up."

"They'll understand if you need space. You've had a traumatic experience," she advises, gesturing to my cup, encouraging me to drink. "And if they don't, well, they're not worth the worry."

"You make it sound so simple," I force a smile, my insides twisting with anxiety. I don't mean to sound dismissive, and I worry that I do. *Is Mrs. Heart mad at me now, too?*

"Well, you know what I always say, 'Keep it simple, stupid,'" she says, rising slowly, her hand resting briefly on her lower back—it must hurt more than she's letting on. "Will you be okay if I leave for a bit to go rest at home?"

"Yes, I'm feeling much better. Thank you for taking care of me."

"I'll always take care of you, my dear girl," she says with a smile that reminds me of all the times she's had to care for me. "I'll leave Watson here with you so you won't be by yourself, though," she says as she rises.

"Thanks, Mrs. Heart. I appreciate that. He doesn't look like he wants to go anywhere anyway," I say, motioning to the sleeping dog snoring beside me.

"Don't give him too many t-r-e-a-t-s, okay?" she says, eyeing me suspiciously.

"Okay," I laugh, both of us knowing I probably will.

She shuffles out the front door without further word. The soft click of the door closing behind her leaves a sinking loneliness in my heart until I look down at Watson, who perks up at the sound of the door. I hug him to my chest. "You're going to keep me company while she naps, if that's okay, boy."

Watson lets out a loud, happy snort at the attention. His companionship is exactly what I need right now. I hug tighter and tears well in my eyes. *She always knows what I need. Love. From anyone. Maybe I should get a little Watson of my own. Be a dog mama instead of a baby mama.*

Snap out of it, Celeste! Fake it till you make it—and you always make it. I shake my head and wipe my tears on Watson. "I can't wallow anymore, Watson! I need to get my shit together. I am Celeste Fucking Moon! Not a sad sack who lies around and moons over men… and thinks about the dead body she found in a garden…"

He looks at me with those big eyes and wagging tail, his energy matching mine now. He paws at me as if to say, "Yeah, that's the spirit."

Knowing Mrs. Heart, she's taught him a few tricks. "High-five, Watson!" I say, and he paws my hand. "Good boy!" I pet him aggressively, riling him up. *God, what a pathetic mess I've become.* Pretending I'm receiving a pep talk from a dog. *Sorry, Mom, I'll suck it up.*

I bounce to my feet and continue my pep talk to try to pump myself up. "Time to figure out what the fuck I'm going to do with myself," I say out loud to both myself and Watson. "Let's go through all my possible futures and just pick one! I can always change my mind, but I just need some direction."

Watson, further spurred by the shift in my mood, hops off the couch with sprightly energy. He begins darting around the living room, ready to play. *Zoomies.*

Over the last few days, since he's practically lived here while he and Mrs. Heart kept me company, Watson's been bringing various toys over. *Look at you, Celeste, already got a guy moving in with you.* He snatches up his favorite squeaky toy—a hedgehog wearing a detective's hat—and presents it to me with a wagging tail and expectant eyes.

"Is this your way of telling me that I should solve the murder?" I ask with a chuckle. I accept the toy and squeeze it before tossing it into the dining room on the opposite side of the foyer. Watson rushes toward the toy and weaves through the table's chairs and various unpacked boxes to get his toy. He shakes the hedgehog in his mouth and tosses it upward slightly, not yet bringing it back.

"Well, I guess one option for my future is to solve this crime. What do you say? Will you be the Watson to my Holmes? Come on, bring it back, boy!" He freezes in place, mid-roughhousing. Then darts back to me and drops it at my feet with an expectant wag. His excitement melts away some of my weariness.

"I suppose before we solve the mystery of Richard's death, we should solve the mystery of my love life," I say to Watson, then throw the hedgehog again. He once again is off to the hunt.

He returns the toy to me. "Which man should I choose, Watson?" I ask as he tilts his head at me, considering my words—and waiting for me to throw the toy again. "Or should I choose at all? Mrs. Heart says there's no rush to do so."

Watson's attention darts from the hedgehog in my hand to the front door, and he barks louder and lower than you'd think a little dog like him could.

"What is it, boy?" I ask as my eyes meet the door.

The doorbell's chime slices through the quiet hum of the living room fan, interrupting our game of "fetch and figure your life out." My stomach somersaults at the idea of having to speak to someone other than Watson right now, and for a split second, I consider pretending we're not home. Watson rushes to the door and barks again. I know that I won't be able to pretend no one is here. Whomever it is knows Watson wouldn't be here unless I were. It's probably Ryan, and I suppose some of his company wouldn't be too bad right now.

Nothing like an orgasm to distract you from your worries.

20

"Coming!" I say as I toss the toy to the floor, but Watson is no longer concerned with it. His undivided attention is on the front door. I look through the peephole, and it is Sheriff Kim. *Shit. What does he want?* I pause, my hand hovering over the doorknob, the cool metal seeming to pulse with my own trepidation.

James's number flashes in my mind. I guess he's my lawyer now. *Should I call him? No.* I shake off the thought. I have nothing to hide—I don't need a lawyer. I probably do need a lawyer, actually. But the guilt gnaws at me for ignoring his texts, the unread messages piling up. He told me not to talk to the cops without him, but I don't really feel like navigating any of my suitors' emotions right now. Nor do I feel like explaining why I've been ghosting him.

"Stay," I command Watson while pointing to the base of the stairs about 10 feet away from the front door. He obediently rushes to the spot and stands still as a statue. *What a good boy.* "Deep breaths, Celeste," I mutter to myself, and with a fortitude mustered from I-don't-know-where, I open the door.

Sheriff Kim stands there, a figure cut from stone. He scans the inside of my home, already taking in more than I'd like. Beside him, Angela offers a smile that doesn't quite reach her eyes, and I can tell she's wrestling with the awkwardness between us. I don't know what happened with the history between her and Ryan, but the ex-friends-with-benefits of your ex-fiancé is definitely a weird dynamic.

"Officers." My voice wobbles slightly as I step aside, gesturing them into the house. "Please, come in."

"Ms. Moon," Sheriff Kim says, his voice gruff but not unkind, as he steps across the threshold with a nod. Angela follows, offering me another strained smile.

As I shut the door, Watson breaks his impersonation of a dog statue and rushes toward them, tail wagging. "Good boy, Watson," Sheriff Kim says, leaning down to give him a pat on the top of the head.

"Such an obedient little guard dog," Angela says when she squats down to pay her petting dues. She groans at the strain of lowering her super-pregnant body. *It seems this dog can break anyone, even the fuzz.*

"Can I get you anything? Coffee? Tea?" I ask, remembering Mrs. Heart's tray now sitting abandoned on the coffee table, the tea likely cold.

"We're fine, thank you," Sheriff Kim declines for both of them, his gaze sweeping the house. He looks around as if he can see every molecule of the room, and I feel almost naked as he looks at the mess I've accumulated around the living room, where I've stationed myself the last few days.

Angela lingers near the edge of the entryway with a conflicted expression.

"Let's sit," I suggest, trying to sound more hospitable than cornered. I motion them to the couch that's not covered in my blankets and tissues.

Angela strains to lower herself into the couch, bracing on the armrest. She must be due any day now. Sheriff Kim waits for her to sit, watching her, I presume, to see if she needs assistance, before sitting on the side opposite her.

I sit in the middle of the messy couch. I feel fucking flanked by the fuzz.

Watson trots over to investigate our guests further. He hops between them and sniffs at them, his nose twitching with curiosity.

Angela pats him absentmindedly before removing a notebook from a breast pocket. Sheriff Kim's notebook is already in his hand as he leans forward, elbows on knees, ready to write down my every word.

"Is this about Richard?" I ask, attempting to mask the quiver bubbling in my voice. Watson seems to decide they're not here to play with him and leaps to my side.

"Yes. Deputy Martinez and I have a few questions," Sheriff Kim responds.

"Of course." I nod, folding my hands to stop them from shaking. "I'll help however I can." *Why am I freaking out? I didn't do anything wrong.*

Sheriff Kim clears his throat, and the sound pierces through me. Watson curls up in my lap, the weight of his body against my legs soothes me, and gives me something to do with my hands. *What a good boy.*

"Ms. Moon," Sheriff Kim begins, "where were you the night of September twenty-third? Tuesday?"

"Are you saying Richard was killed Tuesday night?"

Angela smirks at me, and I'm unsure if she thinks I'm being dense or clever.

He responds, "It appears Richard Holbrook was murdered the night before you found his body, so Tuesday night, yes. So, where were you Tuesday night?"

I draw in a slow breath, feeling the weight of Watson against my leg. "I was here at home. Alone," I say, realizing too late the possible implications of the statement.

"Can anyone corroborate that?" he asks, pen poised over his notebook.

"No." I wonder if maybe one of the local busybodies saw me, but they wouldn't have any way to say I had been here all night. "My stuff was delivered that day, but that was mid-afternoon." I gesture to the pile of boxes stacked around the dining room.

Sheriff Kim and Angela glance toward the boxes, then each scribbles something down in their notebooks, their expressions unreadable. For a moment, Angela pauses with a furrowed brow. I suspect she'll say, "That's it, I've cracked the case! Celeste Moon killed him in the dining room with the messy pile of boxes!" but she places her hand on her heavily pregnant belly instead, her grimace deepening. I note a wedding ring on the hand atop her belly. *So I guess she moved on from Ryan. Good for her.*

Sheriff Kim breaks his gaze from me to look at her, his expression softening. It's a quick look, but I can tell in that moment that he must care quite deeply for her.

"You met with Richard on Tuesday, correct? Approximately what time was that?" he asks, returning his attention to me now that his partner doesn't appear to be in labor.

"11 am. I was there until maybe 11:45, 12:00 pm. I'm not sure. I met with James and we went to lunch. He could maybe confirm the time." *Shit, I really should have called James. Maybe it's not too late to tell them I need my lawyer. Would that make me look guilty?* "We went to the cafe. Sarah's cafe."

"And, how did that meeting go? The meeting with Richard?" Sheriff Kim asks, unrelenting in his pursuit.

"It was...uncomfortable," I admit, in the most diplomatic way I can—my mind racing through the list of ways Richard showed me his less-than-charming personality.

"Uncomfortable how?" Kim prompts, leaning back slightly, and somehow this movement makes him feel more intimidating.

"Well, it's upsetting to discuss the affairs of my parents, and let's just say he was not a kind man," I state, choosing my words with care, aware anything I reveal could unravel further into a tapestry of suspicion. *Kind of a douche, more like it. Fuck, I should have called James. He would know how to respond.*

"Could you elaborate on that?"

"He was brusque. He made snide comments about my not being home in so long..." My eyes well up thinking about it.

"And, did his comments make you angry?" he asks.

"No, they made me sad," I respond truthfully. They both write in their notebooks. The scratching sound almost cuts into me.

"And the money that your parents left you—was the amount sufficient for your needs?"

"I don't need money. I have enough."

Sheriff Kim scrutinizes my face for a moment. He and Angela share a quick knowing glance.

"How's your business doing, Celeste? Is it profitable?" *Why is he asking me this?*

"It's not my business anymore. I sold it. The papers are signed, and the closing should finalize in the coming weeks."

"Do you need the money from the sale for something specific?"

"No, I sold it to come back here. I'm…I'm not sure what you are implying. I am well off financially."

"So, you didn't come back to town to collect your inheritance?"

"I mean, I guess I kind of did. I felt like I needed…needed to… come home."

"Why did you need to come home?"

Why is he asking me this? I can't think about this right now. "Because, because, I had to…" I say, my voice cracking up. "Because I…because I wasn't here. And I should have been." Big fat tears well in my eyes, blurring my vision, as I fail to stifle the intense guilt that surfaces whenever I think of my parents. *Because I'm a terrible daughter, always have been. A disappointment. A failure. Made Mrs. Heart deal with it, because I'm too fucking pathetic to do it myself.*

"Is it true you had not only not been back to Goose Grove in nearly 20 years, but you also hadn't spoken to your parents in nearly just as long? Why is that, Celeste?"

"I…I…I don't see how that is relevant to the investigation," I stammer, all of my defenses now fully down. I am rattled to my core.

Sheriff Kim's focus on me intensifies, as if he's waiting to see how I react. He says nothing. He merely waits. The silence kills me, and I answer the question, "I…I have spoken to them. We just didn't speak very frequently. They'd call me when they needed…they'd call me occasionally." How do you explain that you avoided your mother's calls because every second of speaking to her made you feel like you were somehow being attacked, even when she wasn't yelling? "I was very busy with my business. It is very important to me."

"Is?" he asks.

"Was. Sorry."

"But you sold it?"

I get the implication: *Important enough to never see your parents, but easy to part with?* "Priorities…change after tragedy."

"So, your return had nothing to do with the 4.5 million dollars that moved from your parents' account the day before you came to town?"

"Wait…what?!"

He doesn't say anything. He just stares at me—watching me—watching the emotions run through my face.

I ask for clarification, "What do you mean 4.5 million dollars was moved from my parents' account?"

"Money was transferred from their account to an unmarked overseas one. Had you initiated that transfer, Ms. Moon?"

"No…" I say, my voice breaking. "I didn't even know how much money was in the accounts. I only cared about the house."

"You didn't ask Richard about the money?"

"No, I only cared about the house. I don't need money…" *Did I ask him about the money?* I was so flustered during our meeting that I don't recall asking him anything. *What did I ask him?*

"Do you have overseas accounts, Ms. Moon?" he asks pointedly. My heart races, and panic sets in. *Fuck, they suspect me of something, but I don't know what. Do they think I murdered Richard? Shit. I really, really should have called James.*

"Am…am I a suspect?" I ask, confused.

"We're just following up with everyone who was in the area," he responds.

"Is that a yes?"

"You are someone who may have further information." His voice is firm, but not unkind. It's still a non-answer, and I know the non-answer means I'm a suspect. *Otherwise, he would just reassure me that I am not, right?*

"So I am a suspect. Is it because I found the body? Am I the only suspect? If not, who else is a suspect?"

"I cannot discuss that with you, Ms. Moon," he says. "Please answer the question."

I really need James right now. "Um…I think. I think I shouldn't answer any more of your questions without my lawyer present."

"We're just trying to figure out some discrepancies with your parents' accounts."

I steel myself, putting up the protective barrier that I have mastered. I remove all emotion from my body and become another: Celeste Fucking Moon, CEO and Badass Bitch. *Well, ex-CEO.* In a voice of calm authority, "I'm sorry, Sheriff Kim, but I won't be speaking with you further without my lawyer present. I ask that you and Deputy Martinez please leave my home."

They seem taken aback by the extreme shift in my body language and tone. I probably look more suspicious now. He probably thinks I'm a cold bitch who killed her parents and Richard Holbrook.

"You mean your parents' home?" he asks, attempting to disarm me.

"Please leave," I insist, standing. Watson jumps down to my side. He's picked up on my mood shift, and if he weren't so damn adorable, he'd almost look protectively menacing.

Sheriff Kim resigns to the fact that I will not be speaking further with him and says, "Thank you, Ms. Moon." He closes his notebook with a soft thud. "We'll be in touch if we have more questions. For now, please do not leave town."

As he rises from the seat, I want to grab him by the shoulders and say, "Stop fucking with me, copper. Just tell it to me straight," like I'm some gangster in a 1920s film.

I look to Angela, her face revealing no clues, but a flash of sadness hits her when she locks eyes with me. She grips the arm of the couch and heaves herself from the seat to stand with Sheriff Kim. He shifts his hand slightly, readying it just in case she needs assistance rising. The way he is so subtly watching out for her makes me wonder how a man who is so unconsciously caring could have disarmed me so thoroughly.

"Thank you for your cooperation, Ms. Moon," Angela adds after she completes her ascent.

I nod, feeling hollow as I escort them through the door. A breeze picks up, swirling around me and removing the last vestige of warmth within me. It's as if it wraps me in a shroud of cold and solitude.

I stand on the porch, watching them walk silently to their car. They look at each other in a way that conveys they can speak to each other without words. They enter the cop car and stay idling in my driveway, watching me as I pull out my phone and text James. "The cops were here. I spoke to them without you. I'm sorry. I think I am a suspect." Three dots almost immediately appear under the message.

The officers back down the driveway, and tears build in my eyes, the moment they are no longer facing me. I white-knuckle the phone, watching the dots bounce as James types something.

"Celeste," I hear a shout. I look up just as my phone chimes. Ryan runs across his dad's yard to me, his gaze locked on the leaving car. I note Angela watching him as the car drives away.

The sight of him breaks the damn and the tears pour down my face. I stuff the phone in my back pocket as Ryan rushes me. I bury my face in his shoulder, crying.

21

Ryan's tousled blond hair brushes against my face when he pulls back to look at me, putting my face between his hands the way he always does. "What's going on? Are you ok?" My phone chimes incessantly in my back pocket. The removal of his warmth, combined with the chill of the air, leaves me shivering.

"Ryan, I think they think I killed Richard."

"What? But why would you have killed Richard?"

"I don't know. I found his body, and he's an asshole…I guess it makes sense."

He pulls me inside the house. "Come on. Let's go sit down." Watson weaves beside us, awaiting acknowledgement from Ryan, while Ryan leads me to the clean couch.

Ryan kneels in front of me as I continue to cry, ignoring Watson's bids for attention.

I feel bad for the dog whose excitement to see Ryan is being ignored. "Say 'hi' to Watson, Ryan." His little tail is wagging so furiously that I think he might burst if Ryan doesn't acknowledge him soon.

Ryan removes one hand from me to rub Watson's now upturned belly. "Hey, buddy. Sorry," he says, not breaking his gaze from me.

Ryan tucks the hair behind my ears and pets my head. He spots the tea set. "Want some tea?"

"No, I need a stiff drink," I chuckle, but the sound is strained. Surprisingly, Ryan doesn't make a stiff dick joke—he must be worried about me.

"Well, I can definitely make that happen," Ryan says, settling beside me on the couch. He's close enough that I can smell the faint scent of pine and paint on his clothes—a combination that I've begun to associate with him.

He wipes tears from my face. "I'm guessing the liquor is where it's always been. Still puke at the smell of vodka?"

"I'll take a rum and Coke, please. There's probably some Coke in the fridge in the basement."

"No prob, Star Girl." He stands to make a drink.

"Thanks, Ryan. Really. I just didn't expect to be…a suspect."

"I didn't expect it either. Come on, Watson. That basement has always scared me. I need you to protect me." Watson leaps at the attention he's been so desperate for and hurriedly follows Ryan as they leave to make me a drink.

Ryan returns with two rum and Cokes and sits beside me. Watson leaps into my lap and immediately lies across us. Ryan hands me the drink and then wraps an arm around me as I sip it.

Ryan's warmth radiates through his embrace, and his touch always has the capacity to…do things to me. Even at my worst moments, my body instinctively craves him. *It's Pavlovian.* I lean into the solidity of his presence, finding solace as his arms encircle me. Watson, annoyed that the shift in body weight no longer provides him with stable bedding, sits to my other side.

Ryan's breath is a whisper against my cheek. "Hey," he murmurs, the pad of his thumb brushing away an errant tear. "You're going to be okay, Celeste."

He kisses me—so gentle, so fleeting, like he hasn't done it a million times before. It's meant to soothe, to comfort, but the lust it fires within me is filled with a longing to wrap my entire body around him. I want to engulf him.

"Ryan—" I start.

"Shh," he hushes, pulling back just enough to search my face with those ocean-blue eyes. "We're friends, Celeste. This is what friends do, right? They look out for each other."

"Friends," I echo, my heart stopping in my throat. The word hangs between us, heavy with all the things left unsaid. Friends don't usually send my pulse racing with a simple peck on the lips. They don't soak my panties with a simple brush of hair from my face.

But that's all this is, isn't it? Ryan being Ryan—playful, affectionate, never crossing the line from friends who fuck to lovers who make love. *Just two kids with mommy issues comforting each other with sex.*

"Exactly," he says with an easy smile, though I catch a flicker of something more behind his carefree facade. Perhaps that's just me being hopeful—like always. *Desperate for love.*

"Friends who kiss to calm the nerves," I tease, hoping to coax out the truth hidden beneath his jests.

A corner of his mouth quirks upward, and he gives a casual shrug. "New technique I'm trying out. Patent pending."

I chuckle at this, but study his face. *Does Ryan really want to be just friends, or does he want more? Why can't we talk about this? Why does my throat close up and my brain lock up whenever I want to ask about us?* You'd think by now I would be over this. But time and space haven't softened this mental block.

Ryan, master of deflection, has already moved on to a new topic. "Anyway, you've got bigger fish to fry than decoding my world-class comforting skills."

I sigh, "True. I need to figure out who actually killed Richard." Clearing my name, finding out who wanted Richard dead—it's a puzzle I need to piece together, and romantic entanglements can't cloud my focus. *Not now.*

"Wait. What? No. That's not what I meant. You don't need to solve this…"

"Yes, I do, Ryan! It's been eating at me for the last few days. I feel like this is something I have to do. And now that they think I did it, I… I just have to."

He sips his drink and stares at the door, thinking. “Are you sure they think you did it? Honestly, half the town has a reason to want that son-of-a-bitch dead.”

“What? Even you?”

Ryan looks at me, startled, caught red-handed with something. “Me? Of course not!” he says, and I can tell there is something he’s not telling me.

My phone buzzes again in my back pocket. *Shit. I forgot about James.*

“Fuck,” I mutter under my breath, scrolling through the missed messages from James—a string of increasingly concerned texts. There are also a few missed calls from Michael. My finger hovers over the screen, hesitating. “I messaged James right before you showed up, telling him the cops questioned me. He’s probably freaking out… lawyerly.”

I start to type out a response, trying to find the right words to explain my radio silence. But before I can hit send, Ryan puts his hand on my chin, placing his drink on the coffee table.

“Hey, don’t worry about all that legal stuff right now,” he says, his blue eyes boring into me. “The cops are already gone. Whatever he’s got to say doesn’t need to be said to you right now. You should try to relax.”

I raise an eyebrow at him skeptically. “And how exactly do you propose I relax?”

An impish grin spreads across his face. “I know just the thing to take your mind off it.” He waggles his eyebrows.

I shake my head and laugh at him. This guy finds a way to wrap everything in innuendo. And he still knows how to calm me, after all these years. We’ve fallen right back into our old habits of comforting each other with sex. We lost our virginity to each other the day his mother left, and we’ve been at it like this ever since. If we’re in the same room and sad, we’re fucking.

“Oh, yeah? What’s this brilliant plan of yours?” I set my phone down and give him my full attention—turning my body toward him, inviting what I know is about to come.

Ryan angles toward me, placing his hand on my inner thigh and locking eyes with me. He cocks a sly smile that tells me I was not wrong to read the innuendo laced in the original statement. I can almost feel the air between us cackle with the electricity that draws us together. He leans in even closer, the sexual tension building within me, and the heat radiating from his body. He whispers into my ear, "I'm going to lap at that pussy until my tongue is the only thing you can think about."

Before I can respond, his lips capture mine. The suddenness of it leaves me breathless, and I find myself surrendering to his embrace, my worries momentarily forgotten. Watson jumps from the couch, annoyed at our jostling, and goes somewhere out of sight. The squeak of the hedgehog toy in the distance tells me he's found something to occupy his time.

Ryan's hands tangle in my hair as he deepens the kiss and grips me firmly against his body. I respond with equal fervor. I wrap my legs around his waist, rubbing myself against his abdomen. I work frantically at the buttons of his shirt, finally revealing his toned chest. *Fuck he got hot.*

The long scar that reaches from his chest to below his beltline, curving around his belly button, points below his pants as if telling me exactly where I should put my mouth. I trace it with my fingers and look up at him. "Do you want to talk about it?" I ask.

"Not much to say…I'm in remission. Well, and I can't get you pregnant. So we don't need condoms," he says nervously, rubbing the spot behind his neck.

I look up at him, and I know he wants to move on from the topic as quickly as possible. Ryan loves attention. However, he doesn't love the attention that comes with his vulnerability. And you don't really get more vulnerable than cancer. I know about the scar. He got testicular cancer that spread to his lymph nodes right before he started texting me memes. I only know because I'm the thirsty babe who follows his social media and likes all his videos—videos he only began to help him reclaim his love of his body and spread awareness of the cancer that almost took his life.

Why did he not open up to me, even when he went through this? I look in his eyes, which stare down at me. I sense a falter in his brave facade, as if he might cry, and I am overwhelmed with empathy for him. *Is he trying to be brave for me? Why did he try to hide this from me? Was he really that mad at me?*

"Don't look at me like that. I'm fine," he says, his voice growing a little cold and his words clipped. I'm slightly taken aback at the tone.

He softens his tone and grabs my face between his hands when he says, "I'm sorry. I still get a bit defensive about it. And now isn't about cheering me up. It's about cheering you up."

He kisses me again, harder, even more passionately than before. My phone continues to chime insistently, but the sound fades into the background, no longer important. Ryan's touch sends my senses reeling, and every nerve ending cries out for more.

Slowly, Ryan peels away my shirt, lifting it over my head as his eyes devour my chest. With one hand, he deftly unsnaps my bra, setting my breasts free. His other hand is back in my hair, forcing my mouth onto his. My own hands fumbling with the button of his jeans, desperate to grab his cock in my hand and shove it into me.

The outside world ceases to exist as we give in to the passion that consumes us. He explores my breasts with a skilled hand while his tongue teases and tantalizes each nipple. As he kneels in front of me, he gently slides his fingers up along my inner thighs. My body lurches forward, trying to bring his touch to me. With the weight of his body, he leans me back further into the couch.

He hooks his hands under my knees and pulls me forward, placing me on the edge of the couch. He rips my sweatpants and panties from my body with the eagerness of a man starved.

My anticipation grows as Ryan positions himself between my legs. He lunges toward me, and I gasp when he softly parts my folds with his tongue, tentative and teasing. A direct contrast to the speed at which he lunged forward—as if he is holding himself back. I bite my lip and moan out, fisting his hair in my hands, unable to stop myself.

"I've always loved the way you do that," he says, locking eyes with me momentarily before shoving his fingers deep within me. He watches my face react, and I can see the smile on his lips from behind my mound. Emboldened by my reaction, he more aggressively flicks his tongue on my clit, before pulling it into a deep suck. He moans, vibrating against me.

As I writhe on his face, I forget about the missed messages, the murder investigation, and the complications that await me beyond these four walls. The sensation of his tongue flicking back and forth against my clit is electrifying, and I grind up against his face. "That's right, fuck my face, Star Girl," Ryan says, his mouth full as my body takes over. As my desire grows, his fingers within me quicken the pace at which they prod against my G-spot.

As wave after wave of pleasure courses through me, I can no longer focus on anything but the sensations Ryan is evoking. My orgasm explodes on his face, my climax rippling through my body. I cry out his name, and I can feel him smile as I grind into my release.

In this moment, there is only Ryan and the exquisite pleasure he brings. *Mission accomplished. I'm fully distracted.*

I take a moment to relish the pleasure before I ask, "We don't need condoms? Does that mean you've been tested recently?"

"Yep. Negative all around."

"Wonderful." That's enough confirmation for me. I push him back. "Stand," I command, and with a pleased look on his face, he does so. Breathing heavily, I yank down his already unzipped pants to reveal his throbbing erection.

I look up at his face, and his smile is anticipatory, sweet, and so sexy. I return the smile, as I take his tip into my mouth with a flick of my tongue on the head, and slowly part my lips with it.

I twirl my tongue around the head, and pull back to admire his cock. I consider for a moment whether it would be appropriate to grab his scrotum. My hand hovers and, as if sensing what I am thinking, he says, "It's okay. I got implants. You can touch them. It doesn't hurt."

I wrap his balls and base between my thumb and forefinger, and he moans so loudly for a moment I am afraid I am hurting him, but the thrust forward, causing his dick to nearly poke me in the eye, says otherwise. With my other hand, I squeeze tightly around his shaft, not yet in my mouth. I lick my lips and part my mouth wider, opening my throat and thrusting his whole member into my mouth while pressing my thumb against his taint. He moans again, and I think he might actually come already.

I take it all the way to the back of my throat, letting him feel the deepness of the action. Before pulling in a deep suck, while locking eyes with him. His knees buckle, and I grip his ass, steadying him. I suck and bob on his cock, letting him hit the back of my throat while tears well in my eyes.

He moans, "Oh, Star Girl. You're so good at that. You've always known exactly what I…"

My phone continues to light up with incoming messages. But I'm too lost in the throes of passion to care, my mind solely focused on the man who makes me feel more alive than I have in years.

"Oh, fuck, Celeste. Yes. I'm coming," he warns, as his body tightens. He gently pulls my hair as his orgasm shoots into me. I close my eyes, remembering the taste of him. Each spurt spurs a feeling of nostalgia.

A sudden, sharp knock at the door startles us, freezing us in place. His member is still in my mouth, still spurting down the back of my throat.

"Fuck," Ryan says as his final burst releases into me.

The sound of the knock echoes through the house like a gunshot. "Celeste?!" James calls from behind the door.

I swallow and look panicked at Ryan. "Just a minute!" I call out, hoping to buy us some time as we both wipe the evidence of what we've just done from our mouths with the backs of our hands.

22

"Ryan, he cannot know about this!" I say as I scramble to put my clothes back on.

Ryan looks hurt and says, "Yeah, of course," as he pulls up his pants.

"Where's my bra? I can't find it." I rush around, panicking, frantically looking for it.

Ryan looks around. "I don't know. I don't see it."

Clothed sans bra, I run my fingers through my hair, trying to tame the evidence of our passion. Ryan smooths down his own hair, his eyes darting around the room to make sure we haven't left any telltale signs.

Another knock, more insistent this time. I rush to the opposite couch and throw the blanket across it, trying to make it look less slovenly.

My heart races as I make my way to the door, Ryan close behind me. I try to compose myself so I can meet James. I take a deep breath.

"Must not make J Money wait," Ryan murmurs, his hand on the small of my back, pushing me slightly toward James's knocking. I am acutely aware of Ryan's presence behind me as I open the door.

James stands there, concern tinging his flush appearance. His eyes flicker to Ryan quickly before returning to me. In that brief moment, I read hurt and confusion on his face. He quickly composes himself, however, and says in an apologetic and smooth tone, "Celeste, I'm sorry to drop by unannounced." Then, with a hint of less confidence, he adds, "I tried calling, but you didn't answer. I was worried."

I clear my throat, trying to appear nonchalant and noting the coating still residing there. I really don't want him to know that mere seconds ago, Ryan was coating my tonsils. *Will I have cum voice? Is cum voice a thing?*

"James, hi. It's okay, I was just…" I stumble over my words, my attempt at casualness falling flat—*cum voice apparently being a thing.* My cheeks burn as James's eyes flick between Ryan and me, understanding etched on his face. We aren't fooling anyone, particularly not observant James.

James gives me a single, curt nod. He glares at Ryan, who smirks at him, challenging him to say something. Ryan, usually playful and silly, stands with a powerful and possessive presence that I didn't even realize he was capable of. I've never seen him like this, and I wonder if maybe I don't know him as well as I once did. A great deal can change in so many years.

"I understand. I hope I'm not interrupting anything…important," James says, emphasizing the last word, a subtle jab at Ryan.

I shake my head, stepping aside to invite him in. "No, no, it's fine. Please, come in." James darts a glance at Ryan, as if to say, "See, you're not important," and I feel bad about my choice of words.

"I was just comforting Celeste," Ryan says with a smirk, then runs his fingers along the corners of his mouth, wiping them. An obvious implication of how exactly he comforted me. I glare at him. I could fucking kick him in that huge dick right now. *What has gotten into him?*

As James enters, I catch a whiff of his cologne, and despite just having come, I am aroused again. If he had not knocked, I know Ryan and I would have done more than oral, and my body does ache to have a dick inside it.

"I'm sorry I didn't pick up. Was there something you wanted to talk about?" I ask, trying to steer the conversation away from the obvious elephant in the room.

James's expression grows serious when he sighs. He says, "I wanted to talk to you about the police questioning."

I nod. "Let's sit down," I suggest, motioning towards the couch—the one I just came on. *I should have fooled around with Ryan on the other couch.* James takes a seat, his posture relaxed yet attentive. Ryan hangs back, behind the sofa, and doesn't sit.

I sit with James, and he angles toward me in the same way Ryan had before jumping me, and I wonder if James will jump me. *I wish James would jump me.*

I squeeze my legs together and glance up at Ryan. He's standing awkwardly behind me with his arms crossed over his chest. His looming presence is a reminder that he recently loomed over me with his dick down my throat. *Concentrate, Celeste, stop being a needy, emotionally wrecked slut.*

"It's crucial you don't say anything else to the police without a lawyer present," he advises. His voice is firm, and his stern expression tells me I should listen. "Even seemingly innocent statements can be misrepresented, twisted, to be used against you. You could implicate yourself without realizing it. If I'm with you, I can protect you from that." His voice is softer now, and I know he really does want to protect me.

"Yes, I'm sorry. I understand. I won't speak to them without you again," I say obediently.

His eyes lock on mine, and he gives me a grateful grin. "Good," he responds, and his smirk and tone imply there is a "girl" right on the tip of his tongue. I inhale his scent and wish he would call me a good girl, bend me over this couch while Ryan watches. Or, better yet, Ryan comes down my throat again. The thought makes my chest heave, and I clear my throat. *I'll be a good girl, I promise.*

James continues by clearly outlining the steps I should take to protect myself should I find myself in the presence of the police again.

As James explains the legal intricacies of my situation, I find it quite challenging to focus on his words. I do my best to recall the questions the police asked and my responses, but my eyes linger on his bobbing Adam's apple, and I can feel the tension from Ryan behind me. Not to mention Ryan's lingering heat pressed against me. The air in the room feels thick with unspoken emotions, and my lust is spurred on by it. I nod, my mind struggling to absorb the weight of his advice.

Ryan shifts his stance. His arms are crossed tightly against his chest. His tension is palpable. I get a distinct sense that these two dislike each other for reasons that extend past this little love triangle thing I'm trying to orchestrate. He groans at something James says, an impatience that's not especially uncharacteristic. He's never been one for being quiet for long.

James pauses, his gaze flickering briefly to Ryan before settling back on me. He stops his pontification and sighs in defeat. "Celeste, I'm sorry, when you texted me, I thought…" as if acknowledging the obvious sexual undercurrent between Ryan and me, he continues, "I shouldn't have come over. I didn't realize Ryan would be here." The implication that he knows what Ryan and I were up to is clear, and I feel my cheeks flush with a mixture of embarrassment and arousal.

Watson jumps on the couch next to James, my bra in his mouth, and drops it in James's lap.

Ryan laughs. "Well, I didn't tell him about us, Celeste. Watson did." He leans forward and places his hand on my shoulder. I shoot daggers at Ryan with my eyes.

James places my bra on the coffee table and pets Watson on the head. "Are the two of you together?" James asks flatly.

"We're just friends!" I bark. "Friends who—"

Ryan steps forward, interrupting me. "Celeste doesn't have to explain herself to you." His tone is protective and unyielding. "She's been through enough interrogation today."

James raised an eyebrow, his expression a mask of calm. "I'm not asking for explanations. Celeste is free to do whatever she wants," he clarifies, his words carefully chosen. "I merely want to protect her…as her lawyer."

"Is that all you want to be to her, James? Her lawyer?"

"We all know that I want to be more than just her lawyer. Is her friend all you want to be, Ryan?" James asks, his voice more snide than before.

They stare at each other in a silent battle of wills. Ryan's stance tightens. His arms clench harder against his chest, and he becomes more defensive. James, on the other hand, exudes a quiet confidence, his demeanor unruffled by the mounting anxiety coming off of Ryan. In fact, he seems to relish in it.

I clear my throat, desperate to break the suffocating silence, and my throat still feels like it has cum in it. "I appreciate your concern, James," I manage, my voice sounding strained. "And your legal advice: I'll make sure to follow it."

James nods, his attention reluctantly shifting back to me. "Good. Remember, Celeste, I'm here to help you in any way I can. Don't hesitate to reach out. And I still owe you that dinner date," he adds with a slight, confident chuckle.

James stands to leave, and as much as I would like him to stay, a wave of relief washes over me. I'm not enjoying this little standoff between him and Ryan. Even though Ryan was the only one who seemed to be ready to fight.

I stand to walk James out. He squeezes my elbow. "I'll text you about dinner." He looks at Ryan with a smirk before turning toward the door.

I follow him, but Ryan lingers, still behind the couch. Ryan releases his arms from around his chest and leans forward to place both hands on the couch's back. He looks down at the coffee table where my bra is, seemingly lost in thought. His presence up to this point had been looming protectively, possessively behind me. But now he remains behind the couch and looks a bit defeated.

I say goodbye to James and lock the door behind him. Ryan and I obviously need to talk. That standoff was a bit much, and he's definitely avoiding talking about a lot of things with me.

Before I can even turn around and speak to him, Ryan is pressing himself against me and pinning me to the door. He wraps his arms around me, hugging me and nuzzling into the back of my neck, while jamming his once again hard cock against me. I press back on his cock, forgetting what I wanted to talk to him about, as my pussy begs for him.

23

"Why don't we continue what we started in your room?" he asks, his hot breath tickling my ear as he presses his rock-hard erection into my back, the firmness impossible to ignore. The combination of his breath on my ear and cock on my back sends an electric jolt straight to my core. He nuzzles into the back of my neck. My resolve to confront him and demand we talk about our relationship melts away, pooling in my panties.

His strong arms explore my body. He slips one hand beneath my shirt, pinching at my tender nipple. His other hand finds its way into my sweatpants, deftly teasing my clit. I instinctively arch my back, grinding against his insistent bulge, and brace against the door—smooshing my face into it.

I don't want to go to the room. In fact, I want to fuck him right here.

"Or," he pauses, as if reading my thoughts, "we can do it right here against this door," he whispers seductively in my ear, his voice husky with need. He grabs the waistband of my pants and yanks them down to my ankles, revealing my wet, aching pussy. "Do you want me to fuck you against this door, Celeste?"

I close my eyes and push my face into the door, biting my lip.

His zipper unzips.

"Yes," I gasp, my voice hoarse with need, the head of his thick cock teases at my entrance.

"I want to feel the warm embrace of your wet cunt. Do I need a condom, Celeste?"

I brace myself against the cool wood of the door as he grips my hips firmly. "No. Fuck me, Ryan."

He plunges deep inside me, filling me completely. The intensity at which he pounds into me sends a wave of pleasure through me, and I wail out as he hits my most sensitive spot inside.

James is probably still close enough to hear me. Fuck. Is that why Ryan wants to fuck me against the door? So James can hear?

I bite my lip, trying to muffle a wail of pleasure as his fingers return to their mark. He deftly rubs my clit with an open palm, his fingers pressing perfectly around my entire front as our bodies rock together in sync with our ragged breaths. His free hand caresses my breasts, rolling and squeezing my swollen nipple between his thumb and forefinger in a way that ignites chills all over my body.

"Oh, Star Girl. You feel so good. You're so wet for me," he moans into my ear.

My face presses against the door as I grind backward against him. It would be uncomfortable, but all I can think about is the feeling of him pounding into me and rubbing me. My nails rake against the door as I try to brace myself against the onslaught of sensations.

Each thrust is harder, better, deeper, and I cannot stifle the sounds that escape me.

"Seeing stars, Star Girl?" he asks as he thrusts into me again.

"Yes," I moan in response, unable to form any coherent words as pleasure consumes me whole. Each thrust really does send a spark of stars into my eyes.

He pounds into me relentlessly in his pursuit of our shared climax. His actions speak of experience—delicious knowledge of how to make a woman beg for release—as if he'd mastered the art of sex.

"Come on my cock, Star Girl," he growls in my ear, "I want to feel you clench around me." With a final plunge, he reaches depths within me that send me over the edge. The intensity of my orgasm crashes over me like a tidal wave, and I feel my walls grip tighter around his thick length.

"That's my Star Girl," he moans into my ear, his own release twitching within me and filling me with his warmth. "You're mine," he whispers as he collapses onto my shoulder.

We lean against the door, breathless for a few long moments. He kisses my shoulder and neck softly before saying, "You feel so good," then removing himself from me. "You okay?"

I nod.

"I'm going to go clean up," he says, walking away and leaving me feeling slightly abandoned.

I pull up my pants, and Watson emerges from somewhere deep within the house. He sits and tilts his head at me, his big brown eyes full of judgement. "Don't you judge me, mister." At that, he turns and jumps to the couch to fall asleep.

Ryan returns, his clothes returned to all their proper position. "Want me to stay the night? We can play some more Soulcalibur. Or we can watch TV? Or I can comfort you more," he says that last suggestion with a smirk. "It's up to you."

He always does this after sex, bombards me with a bunch of questions, eager to continue to please me.

What do I want? Do I want him to stay? "I...I think we need to talk," I manage.

Ryan's brow furrows, concern etched into his handsome features, at the phrase I'm sure every man dreads. "About what? Was I too rough?"

I shake my head. "No, we need to talk about us," I say, and as I see panic cross his face, I add, "Are you serious about this friends-with-benefits thing? That's all you want?"

"Yeah, why?"

"So, if I date other men, you won't be mad?"

"Nope," he says succinctly and without emotion.

"Are you sure, because you seem a little mad about James. And you called me yours—"

He grabs me. "I'm sure, Celeste. I enjoy being with you. But, I want to just be friends."

"So, I could date the whole town…sleep with the whole town, and you'd be okay with that?"

He bristles. "Planning on sleeping with the whole town?"

"Well, not the whole town," I chuckle.

"Celeste, as long as I get to still have you as my friend, I'm happy. I'm especially happy if you'll keep sucking my dick, because fuck that's the best head I've had in a long time. That door fucking was pretty amazing, too."

I lightly smack his shoulder. "Alright, goof. Fine."

"Does that mean I can kiss you freely now?"

"Sure." I shrug.

He pulls me to him with a smile and kisses me passionately, looking relieved that the conversation is over.

I want to ask him about his life since we last saw each other. I want to ask about his cancer. I want to ask about him and Angela. I want to ask why he ghosted me only to send me memes. I want to ask if and why he and James dislike each other. I want to ask what the fuck is up with him. But I think I'm scared to learn. I'm scared to ask. I don't want to fight, and honestly, I don't know if I have the energy to try to pull him out of the shell he's built around himself since we were kids—since his mom left.

"So, video games?" he asks, breaking away and tugging me toward the living room.

"Actually, I…I think I need some time alone," I manage. "To process everything. I'm probably just going to go to sleep."

Disappointment etches into his handsome features as he furrows his brow. "Are you sure, Celeste? It's early. I can stay if you need me." He's always trying to take care of me. *But what about him? Does he not need to be taken care of?*

I shake my head. "No, it's okay. I just need some time to think." I reach out, caressing his bicep. "Thank you, though. For being here. And for the two orgasms. I feel much better," I say with a giggle.

He nods. "Alright. Why don't I come by tomorrow and help you unpack? You really gotta get on that, Celeste." He glances around and takes in the sight of the multitude of boxes. "These arms can do more than pin you down, you know? They can also lift heavy boxes." He flexes slightly with a laugh.

My hand still on his arm, I squeeze. "I can definitely use your help," I laugh while making a face that exaggerates being impressed by his big arm. "Maybe not tomorrow, though. I'll message you and let you know."

"Sure, just let me know. Let me know if you need anything else, okay? I'm here for whatever."

"Thanks, Ryan," I say with appreciation.

With a final, lingering look, he turns and makes his way to the door. "See ya, Star Girl," he says as he leaves, bounding down the porch steps and jogging toward his dad's house.

Why does he only want friendship? I've never gotten a straight answer out of him, and I doubt I ever will.

I sink onto the couch, my head falling into my hands as I try to make sense of the whirlwind that has become my life. *Ryan and I are fucking like rabbits, and I'm a murder suspect. And then there's James. And Michael!*

Watson jumps up and sits with me. "Thanks for ratting us out to James," I say to him scratching behind his ear. "But, it seems like James doesn't care about me and Ryan. And Ryan says he doesn't care about James…so that just leaves…"

My phone suddenly lights up. Michael's name flashes across the screen, as if summoned by my thoughts of him. *Another complication.*

I hesitate for a moment, afraid to answer, worried about how I will explain the radio silence and cancellation of our plans.

I answer the phone anyway. "Hello, Michael," I say.

"Celeste, I've been trying to reach you." His tone is dripping with concern. "The police have been asking questions about Richard's death, and I'm pretty sure they're going to be visiting you soon."

I close my eyes and sigh out, "Yeah, they've been here already. I seem to be a suspect."

"Shit. Do you know what kind of evidence they have on you? They obviously don't have anything conclusive, otherwise they would have arrested you."

"No, I have no idea."

"It's probably just circumstantial at this point. If you want, I can meet up with you, and we can discuss this—murder mysteries are kind of my thing, after all."

I want to meet with Michael, but I don't want to lead him on. He needs to know about my feelings for James and what is going on with Ryan.

"Michael, umm…you know that I am exploring something with James, right?"

"Yes."

"And…Ryan and I…we have a…umm…friends with benefits thing." I place my face in my hands, embarrassed and ready for him to tell me he wants nothing to do with my slutty ass.

"Celeste. I…does that mean you don't want to spend time with me?"

"Oh, no, I do. I just…are you okay with…with not being exclusive?"

He pauses for a moment, and I brace myself. "I will have you; however, you will let me." A shock shoots through me. I didn't expect that.

"Are you sure?"

"Yes. I am very sure."

Am I really about to start dating three guys? Why not? They all seem to be okay with me being with each of them.

I resolve not to choose between them. *Why should I?* Like Mrs. Heart said, "Why choose?"

"In that case," I reply, my mind already racing with the implications. "When and where?"

As Michael rattles off the details, I find myself only half-listening, my thoughts drifting back to the complicated web of emotions that has ensnared me. The feel of Ryan's cock in my mouth and then slamming deep inside me, the smell of James's cologne, and the look of Michael's beautiful amber eyes all blend together.

I wish I could have them all at once. All of them inside me.

I end the call, promising to meet Michael at the cafe tomorrow.

I've gotten clear go-aheads from Michael and Ryan. That just leaves James.

I open my phone and text James. "James. I'm sorry again about ghosting you today. I would love to have dinner with you soon if you are still interested."

"Absolutely. I'm a bit busy with work right now. Any specific day work best for you?"

"Nope, I'm free…for like, forever."

"Ha. If that's the case, I'll make reservations and send you a calendar invite with all the info," he replies.

"So formal. Is this a business meeting?"

"Well, I'm a busy man who lives by his calendar, and I gotta make sure no one books over the most important date of my life. Plus, the restaurant sends the calendar invite when I make the reservation," he replies with a winky face.

I stare at the phone. Unsure what to say. How to ask what I want to ask. I decide just to be blunt and go for it. I channel Celeste Fucking Moon. "James, I need you to know that I have a sexual relationship with Ryan right now. If that is going to be a problem, I need you to tell me right now."

After a few moments, the following response appears, "Like I said. I'm not missing my shot this time."

"And, I am planning to pursue a relationship with Michael Nguyen. Are you ok with that?"

"It is not a problem, Celeste. As long as I get to spend time with you, I don't care who else is with you."

"Ok," I respond with a thumbs-up emoji. *Alright. Well, it looks like they're all okay with this—whatever this is.*

He texts, "Actually, I have a question for you."

"Yeah?" *Oh, no. Here it comes. He's going to say he does have a problem with it.*

"The Crimson and Gold Gala is the night after tomorrow. Would you do me the honor of being my guest?"

"You go to that?"

"Not usually, but I'm the guest of honor this time. My charity is the focus this year. It'll actually be a great help to have a date. Keep all the local singles off me while I'm trying to work."

"Sure, James. I can bat them away with a stick for you."

"You're the best. Thanks," he replies with a kissy face emoji that makes my heart flutter.

"Still black tie?"

"Yeah, is that ok? I know this is short notice."

"It's great. I've got something I can wear," I type, looking at the pile of boxes surrounding the piano. One of them has my dresses in it.

"Great. I'll pick you up at 5."

Shit. He'll have to drive me. I don't really like cars after...after my parents. But it's not that far. No highways. It's not like I can walk there in heels.

I shake my head, repressing the worry. *It's fine, Celeste. It's fine. Just get drunk and ride a dick. Don't focus on riding in a car.*

I stroke Watson and take a deep breath, ready to face whatever, whoever, comes next. Hopefully, it's me.

24

Michael doesn't see me approaching, his focus lasered in on whatever he's working on.

"Hi there," I say with a smile as I slide into the chair across from him.

Michael looks up, the light glinting off his glasses, and his amber eyes warm as they meet mine. The smile on his face is infectious, and a girl can get used to a man being so happy to see her. "Celeste, I'm glad you could make it." He sets his pen down, closes the notebook, and shuts his laptop.

I glance around the cafe, relishing the change of scenery. "It's nice to get out for a bit. Especially after…" My voice trails off as images of Richard's corpse flash in my mind.

Michael leans forward slightly, his brow furrowing with concern, his voice low and gentle. "I can only imagine how unsettling it must have been to stumble upon something like that."

I nod, my fingers absently tracing the pattern on the tablecloth. "I just can't figure out why the police would think I did this…it wasn't me, obviously." The images that flash through my mind this time focus on the point at which the garden shears were buried in Richard's stomach—a shiver runs down my spine.

"I know, Celeste. Of all the people in this town, you likely have the least motive."

"Yeah, I literally just met him! Why would I want him dead?"

"I don't know. There must be a reason they suspect you."

"Because I found the body…"

"That can't be the only reason."

"Maybe because I was one of the last people who saw him alive?"

Michael's gaze is distant as he contemplates what I said. "All of that feels pretty flimsy to me."

I bite my lip, unsure how much of my conversation with the police I should reveal. I'm not sure if I am overreacting and I don't want him to think I'm overemotinal. I'm also worried my telling him about my conversation with the cops will make him suspicious of me. I imagine him saying, *'Oh, thanks for telling me. I'm going to leave now because you're obviously bad news.'*

"What is it?" he asks.

"Well, I believe they think I had financial motivation. Apparently, some money was moved from my parents' account to an offshore account. They asked me if I had any offshore accounts and seemed to think I am having money problems. That I sold my company and came here for my inheritance."

"It's not illegal to have offshore accounts—"

I interrupt him. "I don't have any offshore accounts…that I know of. I'll admit I kind of give my accountant free rein to do whatever, but she'd tell me if she put money in an offshore account. But I didn't move that money! I'd have no reason to. In fact, the only reason they even had that money was because I gave it to them."

I put my face in my hands and stare at the pattern on the tablecloth. I want to cry. I continue, "Fuck. I'm so stupid. I really shouldn't have talked to them without James. He explicitly told me not to, and I did it anyway."

"Is James your lawyer?"

"Yeah, he kind of volunteered himself. He was nearby when I found the body and tagged along when I initially spoke to the police."

"Sounds like him. Ever the white knight," he says with an air of annoyance.

"What do you mean?"

"Oh, umm…James likes to be the knight in shining armor for 'damsels in distress' is all."

"You know him well?"

He clears his throat. "Um. Yeah, I know him pretty well," he says, his voice clipped. It's obvious he doesn't want to say any more about James. There's a history between those two that I'm interested to learn more about. "He's a good lawyer. He'll take care of you. Don't worry, Celeste."

In what seems like an attempt at changing the subject, he meets my eyes again, a glimmer of determination in their depths. "I suspect they don't think it was you who transferred the money," Michael muses.

My curiosity piques at his words. "What do you mean?" I ask, leaning closer.

"Well, I don't have any proof, but there have been some rumblings that Richard has been using his position as a lawyer to steal money from people," he whispers.

"But, how could he do that?"

"I don't know exactly. But he's handled a lot of wills and trusts around here. Land deals, too. He could easily delay probate and trick clients into moving money to accounts he owns. Most people don't read all the fine print. He could even be doing it legally."

I think for a moment, reflecting on how much of my parents' accounts he had access to. He said that we were in "probate." I barely know what that means. I have no idea what a reasonable time would be —I just trusted him. Everything I know about the process is what he told me. Not that I absorbed most of what he was telling me. *Is that what he did?*

"He could be using people's ignorance of the process and grief to deceive them…" I say, tracing the flower on the tablecloth and feeling guilty for how much I trusted him. "I shouldn't have trusted him. I should have done more research." *Too trusting, Celeste. So stupid.*

Michael puts his hand on mine, stopping my tracing, "Hey. If that's what he did, it's not your fault."

"But, if he stole all that money from my parents, it's because I couldn't handle my emotions. I let him manipulate me." *I'm too sensitive. I need to improve my self-control.*

"Celeste, you're allowed to be upset. You're allowed to trust and not know everything."

"I was weak. I failed them. Like I always do," I say, my eyes welling up.

"Celeste, it's okay to need help sometimes. What isn't okay is him taking advantage of that. If he did, that's on him. Not on you."

I look up at Michael, and the softness in his expression makes the words sink in. I sniffle, the tears not yet falling. I smile at him, realizing that no one has ever broken me out of one of my self-blame spirals before.

"Thanks, Michael," I say, feeling better after his words of affirmation.

Michael smiles, still holding my hand. "Of course." He adds, "By the way, I agree with the cops. This is about finances, but not yours."

"What do you mean?" I ask.

"Well, I'm sure you've heard about Golden Wingspan Development."

His words spark a realization in my mind. "Yeah, this Daniel guy has this whole beautification effort for the town."

"Gentrification is more like it," Michael says, echoing the sentiment I heard from Andy. "But I digress. Anyway, until very recently, the efforts were going full speed ahead, but all of a sudden, they stopped. Buildings left half-finished."

"What does that have to do with Richard?"

"I don't know how all of it works, but I do know Richard was part of the whole thing. It was like him and Daniel and Marcus running it all. Maybe Richard has something to do with why all the efforts have been stalled lately. Maybe he doesn't just take money from clients, he also takes money from friends."

"That seems like a stretch," I murmur, my thoughts racing. "Maybe there's some red tape that's held it up."

Michael nods, a glimmer in his eyes. "That could be… I think a lot of that financial information is public record. I can look into this," he says, writing some things down in his notebook.

"So, are you and I going to crack this case wide open? Clear my name?" I ask with a slight chuckle.

"Oh, sorry…was I doing that amateur sleuth thing all the characters in my book do?" he says with a chuckle.

"A little. But, I was, too," I remark, a smile tugging at my lips, "Maybe my next career can be a private investigator. Ever consider a career change? Want to start a sleuthing business with me?" I laugh.

Michael chuckles softly, shaking his head. "I'll stick to writing mysteries, I think. I don't want to end up like my characters, sticking my nose in everything and then being almost murdered at least five times a year." He laughs louder at himself.

I wish I knew more about his books. His charm disarms me, and I admit, "So, I googled you."

He leans forward, flattered, "Oh, you did? Were you investigating me?"

"I was trying to find your books. I couldn't find any mystery books written by a Michael Nguyen. I'm assuming you use a pen name," I ask, raising my eyebrow. "Obviously, you don't have to tell me what it is…" I say, waving my hands, realizing I may have overstepped by bringing it up.

"Oh, no, it's okay. It's no secret around here. Everyone knows who I am. I write under the pen name Thomas M. Nguyen," he says with a shy smile.

"Wait a minute…Thomas M. Nguyen? Did you write the Archibald Jones Murder Mysteries?!" I ask, recalling the name.

He chuckles nervously and says, "Yeah, that was me."

"Oh my God, I devoured that whole series last year. I couldn't get enough of them."

Michael recoils slightly at the praise, his mouth twitching tightly.

"Why the pen name? It's really close to your own name."

"It's my father's name…" he says flatly, in a tone I haven't heard from him before.

Maybe he wants to change the subject, "I'm…I'm sorry. I seem to have made you uncomfortable. We don't have to talk about your books, Michael."

"Oh, no, Celeste, I'm sorry. I do have a somewhat complicated relationship with my work and an extremely complicated relationship with my father. But mostly, I'm embarrassed. For you…of all people to call me amazing. It's a bit overwhelming, is all. It's a sort of…what is the word? Cognitive dissonance?"

I look at him quizzically.

He continues, "Well, for years I heard things like, 'Yeah, you made it on the New York Times Best Sellers List, but they made Celeste Moon's game into a movie. You're not the most successful creative to come out of Goose Grove and definitely not Minnesota. Do better, Son!"

Now I grimace. I recognize that kind of motivation from a parent. "He really said that? I'm sorry, Michael…" I feel bad that my work was used to diminish his accomplishments, and now I am ashamed of my success. *Is Michael jealous of me? Does he secretly hate me?* I look down at the table, my finger once again tracing the pattern on the tablecloth.

Realization dawns on Michael's face, and he reaches ahead to grab my hand, "Oh, no, no, don't misunderstand, Celeste. Those words did not deter me; they drove me. I admired you. I idolized you. I worshiped you…" Michael realizes what he said, and his face flushes. He trails off, stuttering, "I mean, I…it was not a competition. Of all the people my dad tried to pit me against…It was…you know what I mean…ha, I'm supposed to be a writer but I can't find the words…I should just go hide under a rock now." He pulls at the neck of his shirt, as if it's tightening around him.

I melt at this. It is so damn adorable, and I want to comfort him. I would also like to hear a bit more about how he feels about me. I turn my hand upside down to grab his. His fidgeting stops. His eyes lock on our hands, then rest on my face, curious, expectant, afraid.

"You worshiped me, huh?" I purr, leaning forward, seductively. I have something akin to a praise or worship kink, so this is probably the hottest conversation I've ever had. *It doesn't hurt that Michael is the hottest man I've seen.*

Michael looks at me for a moment before he realizes what's happening. He transforms into a man on a mission. "Well, how could I not? You're so impressive. A genius. And…" he clears his throat, "fucking gorgeous."

I smirk, my cheeks now warming with a blush. The sparkle in his eyes and the sincerity of his words are ingratiating him to me. "I was a bit coy the other day when I said I liked your games. They helped me through a pretty dark time. I played Lunar Bloom when my book sales were tanking and I was trying to figure out if I really wanted to continue being a writer. The whole idea of working toward the person you want to be, not the person other people want you to be…it…it changed my brain chemistry. It made me realize why I was doing these things that were making me miserable. It inspired me to go to therapy and really figure out what I wanted out of life. Not what others wanted for me."

I feel a flush of warmth at his words, a smile tugging at the corners of my mouth. He continues, "Your world, your story…it really resonated with me."

His words wrap around me like a warm embrace, and I find myself getting lost in the sincerity of his gaze. It's rare to encounter someone who truly understands the passion and dedication that goes into creating something meaningful. I blush and squeeze my legs together, wanting to wrap them around this man. "That means a lot coming from a writer whose work sucked me in so deep I actually took time off work to read it." I smile warmly at him. "You have no idea how big a deal that was for me. It was the first vacation I had taken…ever."

The way Michael shifts in his seat makes me think that I'm not the only one who gets off on praise. "And…Lunar Bloom. It helped me see that my father was a narcissist. It opened my eyes. It really helped me heal from…from all of that. Heal from having a narcissist parent. Well, I suppose you understand."

What does he mean by that? How would I understand?

I must look confused, because he says, "Oh, sorry, I just assumed from the subtext…ha. Maybe I just read too much into it. I projected. Read too much into it. I tend to do that." He tugs at the neck of his shirt again, which I now notice is a nervous tic of his.

The cafe begins to empty around us, the once-bustling space now filled with a quiet intimacy. Michael glances at his watch, a flicker of reluctance crossing his features.

"Sarah's is closing up soon," he says, adjusting his glasses—another nervous tic.

I nod, realizing that we've lost track of time in our enthusiasm. A sudden idea takes hold, and before I can second-guess myself, the words tumble out. "Why don't we continue this conversation at my place?"

Michael's eyes widen slightly, a mix of surprise and delight dancing within those gorgeous amber eyes. "Are you sure? I wouldn't want to impose," he says, shifting the glasses on his face. *So fucking cute.*

"Not at all," I assure him, gathering my things and rising from the table a bit too eagerly.

Andy approaches the table beside us to clear the plates and gives me a grin and a wink. Then looks to Sarah, giving her a slight head nod in Michael's direction, obviously signalling to Sarah that the slut of Goose Grove has caught another one.

As we exit the cafe, Sarah gives me a smile and a discreet thumbs up. I suspect I'll have to tell her and Andy all about this in the near future.

A flutter of anticipation swirls in my chest, and I know we'll be doing a lot more than talking.

25

As we approach my front door, a sudden hesitation grips me. Inviting Michael inside feels like crossing not only the threshold to my home, but some invisible threshold of my love life. If I walk through this door with him, we will have sex.

Is it okay to be so cavalier with this? It's not like I'm some virgin. I've had tons of sex. Ryan, obviously...and the last was...gosh? Adley, during the Game Developers Conference? Shit, that was over a year ago? That can't be. Can it? Perhaps it's because I genuinely like Michael, and I don't want this to just be a one-night stand.

But what do I want?

Babies?

The crisp air nips at my nose. I had forgotten how cold it can get in Minnesota this time of year. Living in Southern California for so long has made me quite a wuss about the cold.

My hand hovers near the doorknob, key poised just outside the lock, as I grapple with the implications. I look toward Ryan's dad's house. I*s he there now? Is he watching me through the window, fuming?*

Michael must sense my hesitation, because he smiles at me gently and says, "Celeste, we could finish our conversation some other time. I don't have to come in." His tone is reassuring, understanding, and respectful. It eases my apprehension and solidifies my desire to sleep with him. *I bet he'd be a really good dad. Stop thinking about babies, Celeste.*

I take a deep breath and return his smile, stating firmly, "No, I want you to come in." A look of relief washes over his face as if he had been holding his breath to see what I would say, as if he expected to be sent home.

It's time for a new Celeste. It's time to take what I want. It's time to stop being sad and start feeling good. It's time to stop running toward some invisible, unattainable goal and live in the moment.

With newfound resolve, I turn the key and push open the door, beckoning Michael inside. I'm happy I cleaned up the living room earlier today.

We step into the warmth of my foyer. He rubs his hands together in an attempt to heat them. It's that time of year when the weather can turn on you in an instant, with temperatures dropping or rising dozens of degrees, making it nearly impossible to plan your attire appropriately. "I've never been a big fan of the cold," he says as we remove our shoes and jackets and place them by the door.

"Me either. Um…maybe we could be totally extra and sit by the fire, a personal protest against the cold?"

"That sounds nice," he says with a suave smile. I can see excitement and hesitation in his eyes. Our connection and attraction have been growing since the moment we met—an inexplicable sexual pull. There's something about this man that, despite my just meeting him, feels familiar, perhaps because he reminds me of me a bit.

He just feels…safe—like he'd never hurt me. And safe is something I'm not used to feeling. However, we both seem to be a bit unsure how to push from the casually flirting to the outright ravishing each other part of our relationship.

Alcohol. Alcohol always works to calm my nerves.

"Do you drink wine, Michael?" I ask.

"I do."

"White or red?"

"Either, but I prefer white. The sweeter the better."

"Well, that makes this easy because all I have is Riesling: it's as sweet as it gets. Um, it's a gas fireplace. There's a remote on the mantle. Could you get it started, and I'll get the wine?" I ask. "Also, there are some pillows and things in the chest over there if you want to go ahead and get comfy."

"Oh, great," he says, already walking toward the fireplace.

I swerve through the boxes piled in the dining room and don't let my gaze land on the piano as I escape to the kitchen. My heart is racing, and I attempt to compose myself. *Am I really going to do this? Am I going to fuck this man I just met by the fire?*

What is it with me and having sex in this living room? Why does inviting these men to my bedroom seem so scary?

I find a bucket and fill it with ice. I get one of the many bottles of Riesling I purchased at the grocery store earlier today. Since I can't get alcohol or groceries delivered in this town, I needed to stock up. I probably should have also gotten groceries, but a girl has priorities. *Mine are wine and more wine.* I needed to get in and out of there as fast as possible because I didn't want Mr. O'Connor to corner me and ask me about my plans for the day. *To fuck someone who's not your son. Back off, Nosey.*

I grab two wine glasses, and before I return, I rush to the bathroom to check my reflection and ensure I am presentable and penetrable.

"You can do this, Celeste," I say to myself in the mirror. "It's just sex. People do this all the time." *You've fucked tons of people. Well, not tons. More like tens.*

Why am I so nervous? How can this man make me feel so comfortable and so scared at the same time? I think I'm scared he won't like me after he sleeps with me. Disappear and say, "Thanks for the fuck, slut, see ya!" Wouldn't be the first time. But this might be the first time it would devastate me. Michael feels...special. Different. *Do I want to risk this?*

No one will ever love you if you keep this up, Celeste.

No. Stop.

I grip the edges of the sink and stare into my reflected eyes. "You are lovable. You are…and if not, at least you're fuckable." *Gah! Stop. Just go fuck this super hot dude and worry about tomorrow, tomorrow.*

I shove myself through the bathroom door and snatch up the bucket and glasses from the kitchen counter.

In the living room, Michael has arranged quite a cozy scene. He's placed various poofs and pillows on a blanket in a way that really makes me want to get snuggly. I chuckle, thinking it looks like he's made himself a little omega nest. He's standing next to the pile, unsure, looking down at it.

"Oh, wow, I expected you to just throw two pillows on the floor," I say with a laugh.

"Oh, did I do too much?" he asks.

"Absolutely not. There's no such thing as too many pillows. Make yourself at home," I say, gesturing towards the pillow pile he's created. "You don't read the omegaverse by chance, do you?"

"No, why?"

I laugh, "No reason."

"Okay," he chuckles at me, confusion crossing his face, but he doesn't press. He settles in, sinking into the cushions, and looking a little uncomfortable due to his long limbs. I join him, nestling into the opposite end, our bodies angled towards each other.

I open the wine and pour us over full glasses. I take a sip and place mine on a coaster on the coffee table behind us.

"You know, I've been here before…" Michael says.

"Oh, yeah?"

"Yeah, when my sister was a kid, your mom gave her piano lessons. She was such a beautiful player. Your mother, not my sister. She was terrible. Do you play?"

I cringe thinking about the piano. I wish he hadn't brought it up.

"Much to my mother's chagrin, I played games, not music."

"Ha, mine, too. Well, my dad's."

"I guess we showed them, though, huh? Those games weren't a waste of time," I say sadly.

"Well, maybe you showed your mother more than I showed my

dad," he says with a chuckle. "My dad never really saw them as my inspiration, more like the thing I did instead of working."

Flashes of memories of my mother yelling at me for being lazy zip through my head. Memories I repress—I try to forget. The ones that ultimately stopped me from coming home all those years.

In a moment of weakness, I reveal too much, say more than I should. "Actually, I can play. I just don't. If I sit on that bench, my heart instantly starts racing. I can't even place my fingers on the keys without them shaking."

Michael tilts his head to the side, inviting me to elaborate, his attention fully invested in me. I continue, "She'd make me sit there until it was perfect. But the longer I sat, the worse I got."

"Of course, exhaustion makes things harder," he says, almost holding his breath as he waits for me to continue to open up.

I never understood how she could be so gentle with her students and so harsh with me. I'd think of the days when I wasn't allowed to get up from that chair. I couldn't eat, drink, or even go to the bathroom until it was perfect. Once, I peed on the bench and…that was the worst day of my life.

Tears well in my eyes. I pinch my wrist, trying to run from the memory. *Not now, Celeste. Suck it up. Don't think about that. Don't think about what a disgusting failure you are. What a fucking disappointment you'll always be.*

Michael places his hand on my back. We sit in the uncomfortable silence. The flickering light of the fire dances across our features. The glare of his glasses draws my attention to his eyes. In this light, I realize it's not their color that draws me to them. It's the way they look at me. He looks at me with the eyes of a man who wants to know me, not mold me.

He doesn't say anything, just lets me sit with my thoughts. But I don't want to think. Not about that fucking piano. Not about my fucking mother. I want to feel. Feel better. He'll make me feel better. Sex always does. In moments like these, I shift from the powerful, assured—well, feigned assured—Celeste Fucking Moon, to a whimpering, needy baby. *I need him to make me feel better.*

26

I repress the sadness and admire the way the fire highlights his black hair and reflects off his slutty little glasses. *Does he know how hot those glasses make him look? He must, right?*

I lean closer to him, my heart quickening as the space between us diminishes. I place my head on his shoulder and my hand casually on his leg, a bit higher up on his thigh than one would if they were trying to be platonic, and press my breasts into him.

I sit like this, nuzzling into his neck, letting my breath casually flick against him. He squirms at my touch, obviously becoming aroused by my not-so-causal seduction. However, he seems unsure of how to proceed, nervous and cautious.

He finally breaks, his voice low and pensive when he whispers, "Celeste," his voice almost breaking from lust and anticipation.

"Hmm?" I ask seductively, expectation lacing through me.

"I feel like I've been waiting for you my entire life," he says. His words penetrate deep within me, igniting a deep lust that I don't often feel for others. Other than Ryan, I usually have to work hard to arouse myself.

"Oh yeah?" I murmur, my breath catching in my throat.

Michael reaches out, his fingers gently brushing against my cheek, skipping my heart. "For so long, I've wondered what it would be like to kiss you—to feel the softness of your lips against mine. May…may I kiss you?"

"Absolutely," I whisper.

That coy smile tugs at the corners of his mouth. He leans in and meets his lips with mine in a tender kiss. It's slow, deliberate, as if he's savoring the most delicious meal.

I melt into his embrace and grip his hair, wanting to hold his face against mine for the rest of my life. "God, you are so fucking hot," I say. "I love your hair."

"I thought I was adorable," he says.

I press into him, wanting every surface of my body to touch his. "Well, I couldn't type 'from the hottest fucking dude you've ever seen.' That would have shown my hand too quickly. You never would have texted me."

He laughs, "Oh, I would have still texted you."

Wanting to engulf him with my body, I straddle him, wrapping my legs around him. The surprise on his face is apparent. "You are so beautiful," he says, his eyes watering with adoration. I kiss his Adam's apple, and his moan vibrates on my lips, causing a tingle throughout my entire body. Tentatively, he cradles my ass, as if he's unsure if he can touch me.

Usually, I gravitate to sexually aggressive lovers—people who take from me. I've never approached a potential lover. I always let them come to me. And, if I'm honest with myself, I usually give it up to anyone who shows any sexual interest in me. Their attraction to me makes me attracted to them. So, I'm not really sure how to sleep with someone who doesn't just take what they want from me—someone who takes their time with me.

"What do you like, Michael?" I ask, wanting to please him, and kiss his jaw.

"You. I like you," he says with a gasp.

"That's not what I mean," I giggle and brush my lips against his jaw. He moans with each touch of my lips. He clenches my body, as if each time our bodies touch is the best thing that's ever happened to him.

I clarify, "I mean, sexually, what do you like?"

"I knew what you meant," he moans. "My answer remains the same. You. I like you."

I pull back to look at his face. I've never seen such need, such devotion, and the look is so intoxicating. I tease, "So, you're saying I could do anything I wanted to you?" I look at him incredulously.

"Yes, anything. As long as it is you doing it, I am happy."

I slam back into him and kiss his mouth hard, tangling my tongue with his. *No more waiting. I'm taking him.*

His hands reach up my back, gripping me. It feels like he's afraid to touch me intimately, letting me take the lead.

"What…what do you like?" he asks between gasped breaths.

"I…I don't know, actually. No one has ever asked," I say, realization dawning on me. He looks at me as if I've just said the most ridiculous thing.

I've never been one to take charge sexually; I've always let whoever I was with lead the way. I just always did whatever they wanted. And if I'm being fully honest, Ryan is the only person who's ever mastered the art of getting me off, having learned my body long ago. I feel a bit hypocritical asking Michael to answer a question I don't know the answer to. I worry he will lecture me about the double standard of expecting him to answer me when I cannot answer him.

"Let's find out together," he says, this time kissing me. "May I take off your clothes?" he asks.

"Yes, may I take off yours?" I parrot back with a slight giggle.

"As I said, you can do whatever you want." The need in his voice is apparent. He wants me to do whatever I want to him.

He lifts my shirt over my head and pauses to admire my chest. "Wow," he says, staring at me. He kisses my collarbone, and I grind in his lap.

He removes his glasses so I can pull his shirt over his head. *Holy shit. I knew this guy was buff, but…holy shit.* "Wow," I say, mimicking him accidentally. I run my finger along his collarbone and down between his pecs, causing him to shiver. *Fuck, this guy has abs for days.* He's all lean muscle, but each one is clearly defined.

Tentatively, he unbuttons my pants. I stand so he can glide them down my hips. He kisses my knees and thighs. I start to lower myself back down, but he stops me. "Wait," he says, holding me in place.

He pulls me closer, kissing my hip bones and around my pelvis. He kisses my mound over my panties, and I grip his hair. My need and desire rip through each kiss. For each kiss he places atop my panties, he follows with three more elsewhere. The tentative nature in which he appreciates me is so arousing and in sharp contrast to the hurried, possessive way Ryan takes me.

I've never had a lover relish in me before; generally, it's mechanical, with the goal of getting off as fast as possible. But this…this is meant to appreciate, savor—not devour. This is meant to arouse me, not satisfy him.

He slowly lowers my panties and tentatively slips his tongue to my clit. "Oh, God," I wail. My arousal has built so high that I nearly come from the sensation.

His hands drift from my thighs to my spread lips. He kisses, and I wonder if these were the lips he was referencing earlier.

"So perfect. You taste so good," he says, smiling up at me, then slipping a finger into me. "Is this what you like, Celeste? Me at your feet?"

"I do like this, yes," I sigh out. He smiles and hooks a finger inside me, causing another wail of pleasure.

"Right there? That's it, isn't it?" He presses into me, at the perfect spot, testing his hypothesis.

I wail again. "Yes, oh, God. Yes."

He continues his efforts on me until I am undone, thrusting on his face and wailing.

As I orgasm, I fold over, barely able to stand up. I sink to the floor, and he brings me into his arms, holding me, letting me recover from the pleasure. He cradles me against him and just…waits.

"Even in my wildest dreams, I couldn't imagine how beautiful you would sound coming on my face," he says, kissing my neck.

Eager to please him now, I ask, "Can I sit on your cock now, Michael?"

"Oh, God, please do," he moans into my neck and cups my breast.

I turn to him, on my hands and knees, and release his cock from his pants. I study it momentarily, marveling at it. *Is everything about this man pretty? Damn.*

"Do you have a condom?" I ask, and he nods. "Give it to me." He obliges. He leans back on his palms and moans, thrusting into my hand as I roll it slowly down his length.

I straddle him, sinking onto him. His eyes alight as he fills me. "Holy fuck," he sighs out. "I can't…I can't believe this is actually happening. You feel…so…amazing."

A writer at a loss for words over me.

I shift and rotate, rolling on him, hugging him tight against me. *Oh my God. From this angle, he hits….Oh God.*

I rise and sink. A gasp escapes me with each thrust. I quicken my pace, probing the spot deep within me.

Michael grips my shoulders, but I escape his grasp as my body moves faster, harder, sinking him deeper into me.

"Celeste, it's…it's too much. I'm sorry, I don't know if I can last much…"

"Come for me, Michael. Show me exactly how good this feels."

He buries his face in my shoulder. "But…you…I want you to come on me. I had this whole plan." He laughs at himself, but a moan breaks it as I bounce harder. At this angle, he's hitting exactly where I want, and the pressure within me is building so fast I'm about to come again.

I grip his hair and look at his face. "Don't worry, Michael. I'm gonna."

He relaxes and lets me take him. He lets his orgasm come to him, and the look on that pretty face while that pretty cock twitches in me, releasing into me, is the last thing I need to come.

He grips my ass and whimpers into my shoulder, as I scream out, "Holy fuck, Michael!"

My orgasm crashes over me hard and fast and continues to pulsate through me after he is spent. My uterus flutters, likely aching for the seed of this gorgeous man to fill it up.

I collapse onto him, my arms limp at my side, my face resting against his shoulder. We sit like that for a long time, him still inside me as we pant, lowering our heart rate. I realize my mouth is open on his shoulder, as I goofily sit here, about to drool in a post-orgasm daze. I wipe my mouth and compose myself so I can look at him.

"This was not how I expected this day to go," he laughs when my eyes meet his. "I thought we'd be talking about Richard's murder."

I let out a sighing "ha" before saying, "Sorry, I definitely had an ulterior motive."

"Wait, so you met me with this in mind?"

"Kinda, yeah," I say, running my finger down his chest.

"That's the best compliment I've ever received," he says wistfully.

27

Four orgasms later, I'm standing smitten, leaning against my door frame the next morning with barely enough strength to stand.

"Thanks for the amazing night, Celeste," Michael says, turning on his heels on the porch and leaning in to kiss me on the cheek.

"Thank you, Michael," I say, giggling at the way his hair brushes against my cheek.

He adjusts his glasses and pulls his jacket tighter as the morning air picks up a chill. I love that he's as much of a baby about the cold as I am. The leaves have started taking on that beautiful red hue, and his black hair and blue jacket against the backdrop make a picture I wish I could immortalize in my brain.

He checks his phone. "Oh, it's October first. The Glendos Haunted Mansion opens up next week. Want to go with me?"

"Oh, awesome! They still do that?"

"Yep. But in the last few years, they've really ramped it up. It's not just the elementary school kids running it. The high school kids volunteer now, and they…they'll scare the pants off you."

"I'd love to do that, Michael. As long as you promise to protect me from the scary high schoolers."

"What? I invited you so you could protect me!"

"Well, I'm a notorious scaredy cat, so if bravery is required to hang out with you, I fear we may not be a great match."

"I suppose I'll have to man up, then," he says with a laugh, but his smile falters and his laugh halts, as if the phrase triggers something within him. He looks pensive and contemplative for a moment, adjusting his glasses.

God, that nervous tic is so cute. I jump upon him and wrap my arms around his neck. "If last night told me anything, it's that you're plenty man enough." I kiss his Adam's apple, and he trembles, stifling a giggle. I whisper into his neck, "God, that dick is magic."

He wraps his hands around my lower back, then, as if bravery overtakes him, he moves his hands to my ass and lifts me so he can kiss me long and hard. "Fuck, I wish I didn't have a deadline. I'd stay here with you all day if I could."

I hang on him, just admiring his face. "It's okay. We'll do this again." Then, my anxiety takes over, "Right?"

"Definitely. Plus, we gotta solve that murder, right?"

I laugh. "Yeah. Thanks, Michael. I really appreciate your help."

"For you: anything, Celeste." He kisses me on the forehead, and I grin at him like a lovestruck dork. "I'll let you know what I find out about the revitalization effort records." He kisses me on the cheek. "Don't worry, Celeste, we'll figure this out together." He kisses me on the other cheek, and my smile is so big my face hurts.

"Thanks, Michael." I pull away with a pout and bat my eyes at him. "See ya."

He sighs and pulls me back to him. "God, you're making it even harder to leave." We giggle and kiss, not wanting to break away from each other.

And just when I think we might go back inside and fuck again, a booming, slightly British-accented voice calls from my left. "Michael Nguyen, fancy seeing you here, lad." *Fuck.*

We break apart, and I feel like a middle schooler caught dancing too close at the school dance. I pull my robe tight around me, hoping to cover my tits that I'm noticing have rock-hard nipples in this wind and are spilling out a bit.

"Hey, Mr. O'Connor," I yell and wave, then whisper to Michael, "Run."

"Alright," he says, giving me a final peck on the cheek before bounding down the stairs. He waves to Mr. O'Connor and rushes away toward the downtown area. As they cross paths, Michael lies, "Sorry, gotta rush to the dentist. I'll talk to you later," dodging the notorious snoop's approach.

Mr. O'Connor walks across the yard toward me, a smirk of judgment slapped across his face. "Morning, Duck. It's nice to see ya outside again. How ya doin', girlie?"

"I'm doing okay."

"Ah, well, that's good to hear," he turns to watch Michael's disappearing form, walking as fast as his long legs will take him. "Ryan told me you were feelin' better." *God, I hope Ryan didn't tell him what got me feeling better: his son's dick.*

I choke on the thought momentarily and ask, "How about you? How are you doing? What are you up to today?"

"Alright. They finally opened the garden back up, so I'll be headin' that way with Regina today. I've got some mums and cabbage I'm eager to get back to. I hope they are alright."

As if on cue, I hear a bark from my right as Watson greets me. Mrs. Heart is locking up, but Watson is tugging on his leash to run toward us. "Hold your horses, Watty," she laughs. "I'm excited to see Celeste, too, but I gotta lock up first."

We exchange greetings and wait for her to join us on my porch. I pull my robe closed further. I really wish the clothes I had on under here provided better coverage. I forgot how this town was about front porch mingling.

"Morning, dear. What are you up to today?"

Fuck. I don't know. I respond with a shrug, "Oh, nothing much. Contemplating my place in the universe and drinking wine."

They both look at me with the level of concern you'd expect from a pair of surrogate parents. It's as if the twenty years I've been gone never even happened, and I'm a teenager who needs gentle parenting again.

Mr. O'Connor looks at me incredulously, "You sure you're doing okay, Duck?"

Not ready to face the judgment of these two, I change the subject. "Yep. I'm great!" I breathe into my hand and fake a grimace, pretending I smell something bad. "Well, I'm gonna go brush my teeth and get ready for the day. Don't worry about me, you two! I'm ga-reat!"

They look at each other and begin to protest, but I slink into the house, "Have fun at the garden! I'll see you two later."

I close the door, blocking their protests. I lean with my back against the door and slide to the ground. I place my face in my hands and succumb to the despair I've been running from.

I don't deserve their concern.

I'm pathetic. I'm a mess. I'm a failure.

I just need to suck it the fuck up.

The repressive walls of this godforsaken house close around me as the memories press down upon me.

Weak. Pathetic. Slut.

Failure.

Disappointment.

"I know! I fucking know!" I yell at the house. "You can shut the fuck up now." My eyes flit to the piano. I rush to the dining room and stack the boxes more tightly around it, hiding it further from sight.

I just need to make it to Friday. Then I can go to the Gala with James and forget everything again.

28

I clutch James's arm a little tighter as we step through the grand double doors, my heartbeat skips like a nervous teenager's. The charity gala sprawls before us—a sea of silk dresses, tailored suits, and champagne flutes. I used to attend events like this all the time in California, but being here, at this one, in my hometown, I feel extremely out of place. James places his hand atop mine and throws me a grin, obviously sensing my discomfort.

"You okay?" James whispers, his breath warm against my ear. He normally looks put together and is usually wearing a suit, but tonight, in his tux with a freshly shaved face, he looks positively stunning.

"Fine," I lie, adjusting the strap of my dress with my free hand. "Just feeling out of place."

He chuckles, the sound deep and private. "Ha. I know how you feel. I don't usually come to this thing, but I couldn't refuse this year… obviously. But I assure you, you belong here more than I do."

"James, you're the guest of honor."

"Yeah, but I still feel…too poor to be here."

"Well, I'm neuvo riche. I might as well be poor," I say with a laugh.

"I promise to rescue you if any of the old money corners you," he laughs.

"My hero," I say, and mean it more than he knows. "Oh shit," I say, remembering our text conversation.

"What? Is something wrong?"

"Oh, I just forgot my stick. How am I gonna bat away all your suitors?"

He chuckles, then looks me up and down lasciviously. "That dress is all the stick you need, Celeste."

I look down at the sparkling gold, backless gown I'm wearing. "Oh, this old thing?" I say with a fake air of pretension. "I just happened to have this lying around," I smirk, and mean that honestly. It was in a box I had lying in my dining room.

"Well, lucky me," he says into my ear. Then, more quietly, he whispers, "Perhaps I can see it lying around later."

I blush at the obvious pickup line and simply respond, "Perhaps." And honestly, I'm not sure what could go so wrong tonight that would stop that from being an inevitable conclusion, because I want him so badly I literally ache. I want nothing more than for this man to rip this dress off me, bend me over, and fuck me until I pass out, pleased and spent.

Being with James so soon after Michael feels like worshiper whiplash. Michael is thoughtful, unassuming, and he waits for me—but since all I can think about is wrapping myself around him, he doesn't have to wait too long. When he left the other day, I wanted him to stay longer—just have him move in and cuddle with me for the rest of our lives. I got so depressed, I almost texted Ryan to come over and fuck the loneliness out of me. But before I could message Ryan, I got a text from Michael thanking me for the fantastic time. We've been continuously texting since.

Guilt almost made me cancel this date. I'm feeling so close to Michael that this feels like cheating. But…I felt bad canceling on James. And now I'm happy I didn't, because being this close to James reminds me I'm not out here trying to catch feelings. *I'm out here trying to catch dick and run from my feelings.*

James has this vibe. I don't know what it is specifically. Daddy energy, maybe? But it's distinctly different from Michael, and my draw to him is different. Where Michael makes me want to chase him down and sit on his face, James makes me want to run and be taken, over, and over, and over. Loudly. A little painfully.

And then there's Ryan…he's just Ryan. Comfortable. Easy. *Mostly.*

Grand Oak Hall has been transformed from the dusty community center of my youth into something much more…expensive. Marble floors gleam under my heels, reflecting the soft glow from crystal chandeliers that definitely weren't here when I attended my high school prom.

The Crimson and Gold Gala is a fall staple in Goose Grove. All the quote-unquote elite of the region gather to drink wine and get a tax write-offs in the form of a charitable donation. This year, the charity they're raising money for is the Domestic Violence Justice Initiative. It's a charitable foundation that provides legal services to victims of domestic violence, which James founded.

James may say he feels like he doesn't belong here, but he guides me through clusters of Goose Grove's supposed finest with the ease of someone who belongs. I am not the only one who wants to bend to his will. People fawn over him, circle him, and giggle at him like he's the funniest guy that ever walked this earth.

His tux is crisp against my bare shoulder, and I catch at least three women tracking our movement with barely concealed interest. *Looks like my dress isn't quite a big enough stick.* I don't blame them. James in formal wear is like a painting come to life—all clean lines and perfect proportions. He looks like that tuxedo…no, all tuxedos were explicitly designed with him in mind.

"Champagne?" A server materializes before us, balancing a tray of bubbling flutes.

"Please," I say, perhaps too eagerly, earning another smile from James as he takes two glasses.

"To rekindling old friendships," he offers as he hands me my drink.

"Were we friends?" I tease.

"I suppose not," he responds with a laugh. "How about 'to catching the ones that got away'?"

"To catching the ones that got away," I parrot, clinking my glass against his.

We weave between tables draped in deep crimson cloth, each one crowned with a centerpiece of seasonal blooms and flickering candles. The room hums with conversation and the subtle notes of a string quartet tucked away in the corner. I look around but am unable to find the players.

"Celeste Moon! Well, I never!" A woman with hair the exact color and texture of spun sugar approaches, arms outstretched. "Marcus mentioned you were in town, but I didn't believe it." I follow her gaze to where Marcus stands holding court, his silver-streaked hair catching the light as he throws his head back in laughter at something his companion said. Nicole stands at his side, her smile fixed like it's been painted on. They both look gorgeous, like the prom queen and king they once were. *Is that where they stood when they were crowned?*

I search desperately for a name to match the face. *Why am I so bad at remembering people?*

James, sensing my panic, smoothly intervenes. "Mrs. Adams, you look lovely tonight. That color brings out your eyes."

"Oh, you," she giggles, actually giggles, at James. "Always the charmer."

Marcus's mom—of course.

I look at Marcus again, trying to reconcile the man before me with the boy I once knew. His face has filled out, the sharp angles of youth softened slightly by success and good living. His tux probably costs more than my first car.

Nicole stands slightly behind him, her blonde hair twisted into an elaborate updo that must require industrial-strength hairspray to maintain. She's beautiful, in that way that makes you surprised she never left this small town to be a model.

Twenty years ago, Marcus and I would sneak down to Willow Creek with a six-pack his older brother bought us, talking about how we'd leave Goose Grove behind and see the world. I did. He didn't. Now that I think about it, Nicole always talked about leaving this "shit hole," as she called it, too. I wonder why they stayed?

"Now, Celeste," Marcus's mom turns back to me, eyes sharp with curiosity, "I'm so sorry to hear about your parents. They were such nice people."

"Yeah," I say through gritted teeth. "Thank you for your sympathies."

"I'm sorry that we got you back under such awful circumstances, but I thought this little 'ole town would never see you again. What's kept you away all these years?"

I take a sip of champagne to buy time. The question follows me everywhere, like a persistent shadow. "Building a business is such a commitment. It's hard to break away," I say finally, the rehearsed answer slipping out easily. I don't mention the existential crisis that ultimately led me to have a meltdown in a board meeting.

"Well, your parents were so proud, I'm sure they understood," she says out of the corner of her eye, implying that she knows my parents didn't understand. "Anyway, we're all thrilled you're back." I'm not entirely convinced she's being truthful. "I always knew you'd be a success. You were a spitfire and never took any crap from my Marcus. You would have been good for him…" she says in that weird, wistful way a passive-aggressive, disappointed parent does. I look to him: the Mayor, rich, successful. *So, you're not good enough either, huh? Or maybe it's Nicole that's not good enough.*

"Oh well," she says with a shrug. Then, her face changes to the conspiratorial look of a gossip collecting data, "You're in such handsome company, though! You two make quite the pair. I suppose this means the rumors of you with the O'Connor and Nguyen boys are just that…rumors?" She raises her eyebrow at me, waiting for me to spill my tea all over her multi-thousand-dollar dress.

James's hand finds the small of my back, a gentle pressure that steadies me. "Handsome company? Oh, Mrs. Adams, you flatter me. And after you've already donated such a large sum to DVJI! A man could get used to this kind of attention," he says with a wink that makes Mrs. Adams flutter like a teenager.

"Oh, James, you shameless flirt," she says, swatting at his chest, giggling a bit too loudly. She looks around and notes the eyes that have landed on her.

"Well, you two have a good night," she says as she drifts away, embarrassed, presumably to report back to the town gossip mill.

"Is she one of the women I'm supposed to be batting away for you?" I ask.

"Yeah." James leans closer. "Thank you. That's the shortest conversation I've ever had with her."

"I don't think I actually did anything," I say with a laugh.

He laughs, and the sound warms me more than the champagne. We continue our circuit of the room, stopping occasionally to chat with various Goose Grove dignitaries. James seems to know everyone, remembering details about their families and their hobbies. It's mesmerizing to watch him work a room, like observing a master artist.

Various people regale me with stories of James's pro bono work, his passion for helping others shining through with every word. I find myself drawn to his compassionate nature and the way he speaks of his work.

When we break away from a group, I say, "For someone who says he doesn't belong, you sure do shmooze with the best of them."

"Well, you know, gotta' play the part if I want them to donate," he says, leaning down with a whisper.

Finally alone, I ask, "What made you decide to get into this line of work, James?"

"My mother," he confides, his eyes glistening with emotion. "My father wasn't a good man. He was abusive. When she was finally able to leave, he got everything. All because she had a shit lawyer. Seeing what she endured, I can't let that happen to anyone else. I've known since I was little that I was going to help people who needed it."

My fingers intertwine with his. This beautiful, intelligent man is working to help others. "That's admirable, James," I say softly, my voice filled with genuine appreciation. "Your mother must be incredibly proud of the man you've become." The warmth in his smile is palpable, and I feel a connection deepening between us.

"I wish I had more time to help…Richard worked me…never mind…" he says. He looks me deep in my eyes, and I nearly melt.

"I have to say, I was surprised you decided to come to this with me. I know the last week was tough for you. What made you decide to come out?" *Ah, so he's a subject changer. I bet this serves him well in the courtroom.*

I laugh softly, smoothing out my dress. "Well, I thought you might prove to be a good distraction," I pause for effect. "And if not a distraction, at least you could be my lawyer."

James matches my playful tone. "Distraction is my middle name. Just check the card I gave you. But if a distraction is what you need, believe me, I can occupy your mind," he arches an eyebrow knowingly. The seductive words and tone cause me to blush, and I know that my breasts, their tops bare in this dress, have flushed as red as my face.

He looks around for a moment, then quietly guides me to a corner of the room that's slightly out of eyeshot from everyone.

I look to him, hoping for an explanation. "I just wanted a little time alone with you," he says, positively pinning me against a wall. "I've wanted to kiss you for over twenty years, Celeste. I don't know if I can wait much longer, especially when you're…" he eye fucks me, "wearing that dress."

James leans forward, his eyes sparkling mischievously as he places his hand above my head against the wall. He leans closer to me, putting his thumb on my chin, tilting it to face him.

"Oh, yeah," I say, biting my lip and looking downward.

He waits a moment, studying my face, searching for signs of protest, before he leans in and presses a deep kiss against my lips. The world around us fades away as I melt into his touch, savoring the softness of his lips and the gentle caress of his hand on my cheek.

He brings his body even closer to mine, his hand not on my chin, wrapping around my waist and pulling me toward him, pushing against me on the wall.

"James," I say, breaking away for breath. "People will see." I glance around, looking to see if anyone is looking.

He clears his throat and backs away, smoothing out his tux, "I'm sorry, Celeste. That was…inappropriate."

I reach forward, gently grabbing his tie. "Don't be sorry." I pull him down toward me, and his eyes alight with delight. "Just, if you kept kissing me, I wouldn't have been able to stop kissing you back."

He smirks. "Oh, yeah?" And leans forward as if he plans to kiss me again.

"Yeah, but save it for when you take me home."

Before he can respond, a deep male voice booms from behind us, causing James to turn from me, "James! There you are." A stout, balding man barrels toward James, drink in hand, spilling it as he stumbles toward us.

"Fuck," James whispers to himself. I giggle at his change in expression when he says, "Judge Harmon, to what do I owe the pleasure?" He says while placing his hand on my back.

"James, my boy, I've been looking all over for you," the judge says, clapping James's shoulder and spilling a little more of his drink, which I can now tell is whiskey.

"Judge Harmon, have you met Celeste Moon?" James asks.

"I don't believe I've had the pleasure," he says, extending a hand and stumbling slightly as he shakes mine.

"Nice to meet you," I grin at the man who seems jovial despite being a total mess.

"Celeste recently moved back to town," James explains. "She's the brilliant mind behind MoonScape Games."

"Oh, yes, I've heard all about Ms. Moon from Marcus," Judge Harmon says, leaning forward and looking at me like he knows all my secrets. "Speaking of Marcus, I really need your help settling a bet, James. Marcus doesn't believe that I shot a 72 during our last round. I need you to come set him straight for me," he says, gesturing toward Marcus at the other side of the room.

James's hand is still firm at my back, and he looks at me to gauge my reaction.

"You go," I respond with a giggle, amused by this judge's antics. "I'm just going to the restroom. I'll find you soon."

"Duty calls," James whispers, giving me a look that makes my cheeks warm.

He comically follows the drunk Judge who yells across the hall, "Marcus, James is going to tell you…"

29

I emerge from the restroom and glance around to find James. He's in deep conversation with Judge Harmon and Marcus. Their animated gestures suggest they're debating something more important than golf scores. I probably shouldn't interject myself. I'll give him a few more minutes before I approach.

I feel like a million eyes are boring into me as I stand by myself in the middle of the room. I weave through the crowd toward the refreshment table, using a sudden urge to nosh as an excuse to escape their gaze and hopefully avoid being pulled into any conversations.

I don't mind the momentary solitude. Social gatherings have always drained me, even when they don't involve navigating the complex waters of my hometown's snobs.

The table looks like it's auditioning for a food magazine spread—delicate pastries filled with colorful mousses, tiny skewers of shrimp, and geometric stacks of cheese assortments. I know we're going to get dinner soon, but I feel the intense need to stuff my face.

A waiter passes me, and I decide that getting shit-faced is also something I want to do. I grab a glass of champagne and sip it casually despite wanting to down the entire thing.

I select a few food items that look yummy enough and position myself near a large fern. It provides partial cover while still allowing me to observe the room. *Still the wallflower, huh, Celesete?*

I hear the gritted voice of Nicole along with the clacking of her heels. "…not the time or place." She appears at the table from which I got my snacks.

"…never is with you. But you've been avoiding me, and we need to talk," the man, whom I've learned is Daniel Stevens, appears next to her. They don't look at each other as they talk, and if I weren't so close, I wouldn't even realize they were talking to each other.

They don't notice me, half-hidden by my strategic fern. They select drinks and a few appetizers. Nicole plucks at some shrimp—her nails are perfectly painted the same red as the bottom of her shoes—then subtly nods her head toward an area behind my fern.

After they tensely and quietly select items, they position themselves at the corner of the standing table closest to my hiding spot. *Don't mind me, just snooping.* They don't look at each other. It's as if they want to talk without appearing to be talking.

I pretend to be fascinated by the elaborate ice sculpture slowly melting at this end of the table. It's hard to make out what they're saying, but their hushed voices begin to rise as their emotions get the better of them.

"Are you absolutely sure he hasn't seen anything?" Daniel asks.

"He hasn't said a word. If he *had* noticed, trust me, I'd know," Nicole responds.

I look down at my plate of partially eaten party provisions and try to mind my own damn business. *But they're making it soooo hard. They're being so suspicious.*

Daniel sighs. "Still. One slip, and—"

Nicole cuts him off. "I've been careful. I don't use my usual routine. I even changed how I log everything."

I shouldn't be listening. I should move away and find James or literally anyone else to talk to. But something in their tone—that particular pitch that people use when they're discussing things they shouldn't—triggers my curiosity.

"Not so loud," he says, shushing her.

They sit in silence for a long moment, and I suspect maybe they are done talking until Nicole murmurs, "God, if Marcus finds out." She pops a shrimp into her mouth and chews slowly, staring at Marcus in the center of the room.

Daniel nods, lips barely moving. "He won't. Unless someone starts putting the pieces together."

"I'm scared. The cops have been asking a lot of questions. Won't they figure it out?" Nicole asks.

"They're just asking about Richard's involvement in the Riverside Development Project," he says. "They shouldn't be able to connect that to us. We just have to keep our story straight. Don't panic."

Nicole sighs loudly. She pops another shrimp and says, "I just hate feeling like I have to look over my shoulder all the time."

Daniel leans closer. "Once we're through the holidays, it'll be easier."

"I don't know if I can do it anymore," she says. "If Marcus finds out what we did, I'll never see my kids again. And now that Richard—"

"Nicole, I—" Daniel cuts her off, but stops abruptly as an older woman approaches the table. The two lighten their postures and disperse from each other. I remain where I am. My mouth is gummy and dry, and my heart sinks into my stomach. I sip my champagne, trying to compose myself. I take a small step away, processing what I've just heard.

I shouldn't have heard that.

What were they talking about? They're hiding something related to the Riverside Development Project. *What is that?* It must be related to the revitalization project everyone's always going off about. Daniel's company is implementing that, right? *Didn't Mrs. Heart say Nicole was part of some town improvement committee? Are they the reason all the plans are held up? And what does Richard have to do with it?*

"Find anything good?" James's voice startles me from my thoughts as he appears at my side, nodding toward the refreshment table. *Did he know I was snooping?*

He's perusing the table, and I suspect he's referencing the food, not the conversation I just overheard. "That cheese thing is better than it looks," I say, gesturing vaguely at the spread. "Did you settle the bet?"

"No. By the time we got to Marcus, Judge Harmond had forgotten all about it." James selects a small tart from the display. "Which is honestly for the best, because he definitely did not golf a 72 and I didn't really want to deal with his wrath if I had told the truth."

"His wrath? He seemed so nice," I say.

"That's because he's drunk. But that is a judge who will hold a petty grudge," he says, sighing and taking a sip of his champagne. "And he'd make me pay for it in the courtroom."

"Not particularly fair. Judiciously…"

"Well, unfortunately, as much as it claims to be, the law isn't fair," James states flatly, and I can tell there's quite a lot of personal anguish behind that statement.

I glance back toward Marcus, who's now deep in conversation with an older man I don't recognize. Nicole stands beside him, her plastered-on smile returned to her face. I run through the conversation I overheard between her and Daniel. "Hey, do you know much about the Riverside Development Project?"

If I weren't watching James so closely, I might have missed the brief tightening around his eyes before his expression returned to neutral. "Some. Why do you ask?"

"Just curious. I've heard people chatting about it tonight. Sounds like a big change for Goose Grove."

"It is." James takes a sip of his champagne. "Marcus…Mayor Adams has been pushing hard for it. Says it'll bring in new tax revenue, create jobs."

"And you disagree?" I prompt, noting the careful neutrality in his voice.

"I think development is inevitable, but I have some concerns." He shrugs slightly. "But then, I'm a lawyer. Having concerns is practically in my job description. I wish some of that development were more about the community and less about profit, but I suppose it's a necessary evil."

Before I can press further, the chime of a fork against glass cuts through the room's chatter. We turn to see Marcus stepping onto a small raised platform at the front of the hall, his mayoral smile gleaming under the lights.

"Ladies and gentlemen," he begins, his voice carrying that same confident resonance I remember from high school, "I want to thank you all for coming tonight to support the Domestic Violence Justice Initiative."

As he continues with practiced charm, I watch James watching him. There's something in James's posture—a slight tension, a watchfulness—that makes me think there's more to their relationship than professional acquaintance. Not friendship, exactly, but something with edges. He could just be nervous about the success of tonight.

I should tell James what I overheard. But the words stick in my throat. *What if I misunderstood? What if it's nothing but small-town drama? Or what if it's something worse?* The champagne bubbles tickle my nose as I take another sip, buying time to sort through my thoughts. My eyes continuously focus on Nicole.

For now, I decide, I'll keep what I heard to myself—at least until I understand more about what I hear. *I'll talk to Michael about it.*

"You okay?" James whispers, his shoulder pressing lightly against mine as we listen to Marcus's speech. His eyes are glued to me in concern. I must be making a weird face or something as I sit here contemplating.

"Just thinking," I reply, offering him a smile I hope doesn't reveal my inner turmoil, as Marcus concludes his speech to enthusiastic applause. I don't want to detract from James's moment with my amateur sleuth bullshit.

A waiter announces dinner will be served shortly. James guides me toward a lavish floral arrangement that mark our table, his hand on my lower back warming my body. "I'm glad you're here," he whispers, and something in his tone makes me turn to study his face. There's warmth there, certainly, but also something else—a tightness around his eyes, a shadow that passes so quickly I might have imagined it.

"Everything okay?" I ask as we take our seats.

"Perfect," he says, but his eyes scan the room briefly before returning to mine. "Just some work stress. Nothing that matters tonight."

I nod, not entirely convinced but unwilling to press. We settle at our table, draped in the same deep crimson cloth as the others. It's adorned with a centerpiece of white roses and sprigs of something fragrant. The china plates bear the town seal—a goose in flight over stylized waves—and the silverware is heavy in my hand, the kind that makes me conscious of my table manners.

Perhaps it's the three glasses of champagne I've had up to this moment, but I feel less intimidated than I have up until now. My fingers trail over the crisp crimson tablecloth, and I take a moment to marvel at how strange life can be. I used to dream of coming here when I was a kid. Now I dream of leaving.

James leans close, and I catch the scent of his cologne. His smile is downright dazzling. It's the kind of smile that rakes over my entire body. It makes me forget about my worries for my future. It makes me forget my shame around my estrangement from my parents. And it makes me forget about Richard Holbrooke, Nicole, Daniel, all of it. For a moment, I'm just a woman enjoying dinner with a man who makes her feel like he can protect her, then fuck all her cares away.

I'm seated between James and the county treasurer's wife. I've already forgotten her name. I hate to remember her only in reference to her husband. It feels distinctly anti-feminist of me, but I've forgotten his name, as well, so that makes up for it, right? Her diamond earrings catch the light every time she turns her head to laugh just a beat too late at someone's joke. She's putting on airs, trying to impress everyone at this table, and I'm finding her very off-putting.

James's knee occasionally brushes against mine under the table—each touch sends a small current through me. It's distracting and delicious. He seems distracted as well, but not by me. His mind is elsewhere. His eyes keep drifting across the room, and his responses to questions are just a fraction delayed, like there's a buffer between his thoughts and his words.

"So, Celeste," the treasurer's wife says, turning those glittering earrings toward me, "I hear you sold your company for quite a sum. You must have exciting investment plans for Goose Grove."

And there it is—the real reason half the town's elite have been so welcoming. They smell money and opportunity.

"Actually, I'm taking some time to settle in before making any decisions," I reply, cutting into the perfectly cooked salmon on my plate. "My parents' house needs quite a bit of work."

"Oh, but surely a woman of your means isn't planning to stay in that old place permanently? The east side has some lovely new developments." By "east side," she means the part of town where the new money lives in houses with professional landscaping, three-car garages, and plots adjoining a lake. My parents' home, with its slightly sagging porch and overgrown garden, sits firmly on the west side—historic, charming, and perpetually one harsh winter away from needing significant repairs.

I place my silverware on the plate and bring my hands to my lap, twisting the tablecloth in my grip.

"I'm quite attached to it, actually," I lie, not really knowing the answer to why I feel the need to keep myself imprisoned within its walls. James's hand covers mine under the table. *Does he realize I don't want to talk about this?*

"The salmon is excellent," James comments to no one in particular—an attempt to change the subject for me.

"Oh, yes, quite excellent," she replies. The rest of the table now begins to boisterously chatter about the quality of the food before it drifts to conversations about personal chefs and various other rich people shit.

I smile at him. "How'd you do that?"

"Do what?" he asks.

"Save me. You keep saving me."

He shrugs. "I guess an Ivy League education was good for something."

"Was that a humble brag?"

"That depends. Are you impressed?"

"A little."

"Hmm. What could I say that would impress you a lot?"

I tap my lip, pretending to think on it, "I'm not sure. I guess you'll just have to work really hard to find out."

His hand returns to my leg and drifts upward under my skirt. "Oh, Celeste. I'll work as hard as you need me to."

A loud laugh catches my attention across the room, where Marcus holds court at the head table. Even at dinner, he manages to be the center of attention, his laugh carrying over the general conversation.

"He sure does know how to sap all the attention in the room," James says.

"Always has," I respond.

Nicole sits beside him, picking at her food and smiling politely at whatever the woman next to her is saying. There's something almost theatrical about their performance as Goose Grove's power couple—too perfect, too rehearsed. But it's weird to see Nicole have to take a backseat to Marcus. She was the Regina George of my high school, so to see her not the center of attention, but beside it…it's weird. It sparks an odd feeling in my chest that I can't quite place.

Marcus meets my eye across the room and gives me a small, private smile—the same one that used to make seventeen-year-old me weak in the knees. It still carries a certain power, a pull of shared history, but now it feels laced with hurt feelings and ulterior motives.

Marcus stands and whispers something to Nicole, as they both look at me. She nods. He kisses her cheek, pulled tight by a fake smile, and walks toward me.

Fuck. I really don't want to talk to him.

30

Marcus weaves through the various tables, shaking hands but not stopping, in that way a man on a mission does. I lean toward James and whisper, "Fuck, he's coming over here. I really don't want to talk to him."

James jokes, "What? Got a problem with handsome men with dazzling smiles?"

"No, I've got a problem with men who broke up with me in high school," I respond.

"He says you broke up with him," James smirks.

"What!? He said that?"

"Yeah, he did," James says, smiling at the approaching Marcus.

Why would Marcus have told James that? First, it's not true, and second, why were they talking about me?

"Mayor Adams!" the woman beside me says cheerily.

"Gloria, you're looking lovely," Marcus says to the woman at my side, letting her take his hand in both hers as they shake. His other is casually leaning on the back of her chair. *Gloria, her name was Gloria. God, I could never be a politician with this awful ability to remember names.*

"Why, thank you, Mayor Adams," she blushes.

"If you'll excuse me, Gloria, I was hoping to talk to Ms. Moon here," he says with a smile, gesturing to me.

"Oh, no, that's okay," she says, flustered. *Lady, it was a polite compliment; he wasn't proposing marriage. Calm the fuck down.*

I squeeze James's leg under the table and hide my face toward him, whispering, "God, this guy."

James raises his eyebrow at me, looking as if I've lost my damn mind, but places his hand over mine in silent reassurance.

Marcus looks around for something until he finds a nearby chair, pulling it toward us. Gloria and I scootch apart to provide him a bit more room. I bump into James's chair.

"Celeste, I didn't expect to see you here," he says to me as he sits.

"Hey, Marcus," I say, grimacing.

"James, congratulations on tonight's success."

"Thanks, Marcus," James responds. "But tonight's not about me. It's about giving people a safe way out."

"Really. It was a hell of a night. I heard there was a substantial donation from an anonymous donor. Congratulations," Marcus says, his eyes flicking toward me.

James appears surprised for a moment, looking down at me, as well. I revert my gaze to the centerpiece, pretending not to be listening to them.

"Thanks, Marcus. I had a lot of help," James replies.

"Sure, sure. But you're the heart of it," Marcus responds. He's always been like this. Overly complimentary, even when you try to get him to stop. It was what initially drew me to him, and I suppose what got him elected.

He asks James, "We still on for tomorrow morning?"

"Yep, I'll be there at six," James replies.

"What are you two doing tomorrow so early? Golfing?" I ask with a laugh.

"He wishes," James says.

"Ha, yeah, I can't ever get James to stop working long enough to come play with me. But, no, just some business matters," Marcus replies. "But maybe we could have that talk over golf. Judge Harmon got you out there, so I know it's possible."

"Marcus, you know as well as I do it wasn't my choice to accept his 'strongly encouraged' invitation," James replies with an air of annoyance.

"I suppose it also wasn't your choice to let him win?"

James simply looks at him with pursed lips.

"Sorry, buddy. I'll drop it," Marcus says, realizing James doesn't want to continue discussing this. *Oh, are these two friends? I suppose that makes sense. This is a small town.*

Marcus returns his attention to me and says to James while looking at me, "Anyway, I didn't know you knew Celeste!"

I respond, "We just met."

"Oh, yeah?" Marcus asks, obviously wanting me to elaborate. I don't.

James begins, "Yeah—" but I squeeze his leg and he stops.

They both look at me, waiting for me to say something, but I don't. I just sit there, waiting for him to leave.

Marcus, never one comfortable with my silence, speaks up, "Well, anyway, Celeste, I'm happy to see you here. I've been wanting to talk to you."

"About what, Marcus?" I ask, my eyes fixed on the centerpiece. *Who designed this thing? It's kind of hideous. I bet it was Nicole.*

"First, I wanted to see how you were doing after the…umm…incident with Richard," he says with a level of awkwardness I hadn't quite expected.

"I'm fine," I respond curtly.

"Oh. Well, I'm happy to hear that. I was worried after you found the…found him that you'd be traumatized."

"Nope," I say flatly.

"Have the police spoken to you already? I asked Sheriff Kim to check in on you."

"You told the police to question me?" I ask, my voice rising.

Is Marcus the reason they suspect me? Why would he do that? Did

Marcus kill Richard, and now he's trying to pin it on me: the girl with no family, no one who would care if she got locked away.

"No, no. I asked them to make sure you were okay," he responds, putting his hands up. "Seeing a dead body can be—"

"I'm fine, Marcus," I reply, cutting him off. "I barely saw anything. That's what I told the police."

"Oh, you didn't really see anything? That's great," he says, nodding his head. *Is he trying to find out if I saw anything incriminating?* "Well, I know Sheriff Kim can be intimidating when he gets into his investigation mode. And I'm sure Angela isn't exactly playing good cop with you, given the whole Ryan thing. So, if you think of anything, you can come to me."

"Why would I come to you?" I ask, legitimately confused.

"I can go with you if you need to talk to them. Help smooth things out. Sheriff Kim and I go way back."

James chimes in and places his hand on the back of my chair, "I'm representing her, Marcus; she's in good hands."

"That's a relief," Marcus says, his mouth tight as if he doesn't actually feel it. Marcus's tone shifts, and he's back to his saccharine politician self.

What the fuck is up with him?

There's a lull, and for a moment I can feel Marcus studying me—like he's ticking off changes since high school. Finally, Marcus clears his throat. "Well, I should keep circulating, or Nicole will have my head. Don't let me monopolize your evening. Celeste, please stop by the town hall sometime. I want to discuss some investment opportunities and the revitalization project with you. See you tomorrow, James."

He fixes James with a nod, but holds my gaze for just a beat longer—enough to make me squirm, but not enough to say why. Then he glides away, hand already extended toward the next table's attendees.

"He was being weird, right?" I ask James.

"Yeah, I've never seen him so flustered before," James laughs. "Seems like you have a way with the men around here, Celeste."

That or he's guilty of murder.

What is going on? Why are the cops focusing on me? Is it because of Marcus? Is he trying to pin this on me? Why would he do that? Did he kill Richard? Did Nicole and Daniel kill Richard, and is he trying to cover it up? Is that what they were talking about?

James is sipping his water, his eyes darting around the room distractedly. *I know he's worried about the success of this gala, but is there something else going on?*

Questions about who killed Richard won't stop nagging at me. I should ask James about Richard.

I ask tentatively, "James…did you know Richard well?"

He doesn't quite meet my gaze, looking off in the distance at something or someone. "I suppose I knew him well enough. Well, as well as I would have liked, at least."

"So you didn't like him?"

James chuckles, "No one liked him." James leans back in his chair, his expression growing pensive. "Richard was a shrewd lawyer and businessman," he admits, his tone measured. "When I was younger, I admired him greatly. But…he had a reputation for being ruthless and self-serving. There have been rumors of some shady practices, but nothing concrete."

I nod, absorbing the information. "I can't help but wonder if his murder had something to do with his work."

James takes my hand in his. "It's possible. But let's not let speculation ruin our evening. The police are investigating, and I'm sure they'll get to the bottom of it."

For a fleeting moment, a flicker of doubt crosses my mind. *Could James have had something to do with Richard's death?* He seems so sincere, so genuine, but the thought lingers. I push it aside, I'm afraid and I feel like I can trust him. I need to trust him, because right now, I'm scared and need someone.

"I'm worried they're going to pin the murder on me," I say, my fear beginning to overwhelm me.

James turns to me, his focus entirely on me now, "Celeste, I'm sorry. I didn't mean to dismiss your worries."

"The police implied that he stole money from his clients. From me, specifically," I say with a stammer.

He looks around to ensure no one can hear us. He reaches under my chair, grabs its leg, and pulls me closer to him. It's so fucking hot, and I frantically look around to see if anyone heard the needy whimper that escapes me.

James heard it. He smirks, but doesn't mention it. Instead, he whispers with concern, "What exactly did they say?" His lawyer hat is now officially on.

"Something about 4.5 million dollars being moved from my parents' account. It seems like they think I am having money trouble. Maybe they think Richard stole that money, and then I killed him because of it. I don't even know how to check the accounts to see if any of that is true. I don't know why they would think I have money trouble. It's all been so…I've just been avoiding thinking about it."

"Celeste, I promise I will look into this for you. I will get to the bottom of it. I'll find out about the money and find out what exactly the police know."

"And now I'm worried that Marcus is trying to pin this murder on me for some reason, and I don't know why. Why would he do that? We haven't spoken in twenty years."

"Celeste, I don't think that's what's happening. My judgement may be clouded by our friendship, but I don't think Marcus is the kind of guy to do that. But don't worry. I will take care of you. I assure you, I would die before I let them convict you of Richard's murder. Even if you had killed him, there's no way I will let you see a single day in a cell."

"Oh, yeah? Are you really such a good lawyer that you could get me off a murder charge that I committed?"

"Yeah, I am," he says with such matter-of-factness that I don't think he's joking.

I whisper, "Just so you know, I didn't actually kill him."

James's joviality falters slightly, and he leans in, his voice lowering to a conspiratorial whisper, "Celeste, I know you didn't kill him. There are significantly more likely suspects." He glances around as if these alleged suspects might be eavesdropping right now.

"Then why are the cops focusing on me?" I ask with a bit of a whine.

"Detective Kim is a good man and a good detective. He's just covering all his bases. It's his job to ask questions. It might feel like he's focusing his investigation on you, but it feels like that to everyone when they're being questioned by the police."

I nod, trying to believe what he is saying and trying to let the words sink in to a place that eases my anxiety.

"Don't worry, Celeste. I don't lose when it comes to protecting what is mine." One hand sits on the back of my chair, the other is now firmly on my thigh. *When did it get there?* I was so anxious I didn't notice. His words are laced with a flirtatious undertone, and I can't help but feel a thrill at the idea of James looking out for me.

He continues, "But as your lawyer, I must insist that if the police approach you again, you don't say anything without me present, okay? I can't protect you if I'm not with you." His hand now reaches to my upper back, stroking the spot where my neck meets my back protectively.

"Okay," I say, slightly dejected.

He puts his hand on my chin, yet again, making me look at him.

"That's a good girl," he says in a breathy tone. He looks me in the eye, waiting to see the reaction I have to being called such, and my breath once again quickens. His thumb traces my jaw and stops just behind my ear. My whole body feels the words wash over me.

"What'll you do if I disobey?" I ask, in a slightly defiant tone.

"Well, you already have. I guess you'll find out when I take you home." He sips his water and places his hand on the small of my back between the chair. He whispers into my ear, "I'm not needed here anymore, and I only had a few sips of champagne a few hours ago. I can leave whenever you're ready for me to take care of you. Do you want me to take care of you, Celeste?"

I know by the way his hand shifts up my thigh that he's not talking about my legal troubles anymore.

31

The key sticks in the lock—it always does when the temperature drops below forty—and I jiggle it with practiced patience until the door swings open. "Welcome to my boxes," I say with a self-deprecating smile as I step into the entryway, flicking on the lights.

Feeling instantly stifled by the heat, I remove my dress coat and hook it on the brass hooks my father installed thirty years ago.

"Still unpacking?" James asks, closing the door behind him. He unbuttons his tux jacket, adjusting to the extreme change in temperature.

"I haven't started," I admit. "To say I've been dragging my feet is an understatement." I bend to unstrap my shoes, I reach for the table, but James catches my hand first, allowing me to lean on him as I do so.

"What's stopping you?" James asks, loosening his tie with a gentle tug that draws my eye to the column of his throat. "Bad memories?"

Something about the way he says it makes me feel like he isn't judging me for the mess, but empathizing with the emotional baggage that comes with going through my parents' stuff to make way for mine.

Instead of addressing his question, I ask. "Can I get you something to drink?" and move toward the kitchen. He steps out of his shoes and places them next to mine. "I have wine, or there's probably some of my dad's whiskey downstairs, though I can't guarantee its quality."

"Wine would be perfect," he says, following me but pausing to examine the row of family photos on the hallway wall. "What's this award?" he asks, pointing to a picture of a solemn-faced girl holding a trophy.

"Seventh grade. International Piano competition," I feel a flush of old shame. "I...got first place."

"You must be good," he says with a smile that warms me from the inside out.

"Nope. I just worked hard. I don't play anymore," I say, wanting to change the subject. "I'll be right back." I must be doing that thing where my voice drops and I sound like a total bitch, because he looks at me as if he's trying to read me. I scurry away to the kitchen to avoid further discussions. I want to get undressed physically, not mentally—laying all my trauma bare.

In the kitchen, I uncork a bottle of Riesling. As I pour, my mind flickers back to the tense exchange I witnessed between Nicole and Daniel and that awkward interaction with Marcus. Questions hover on the tip of my tongue, but I swallow them back. I don't want my suspicions and curiosity to ruin the night.

I carry our glasses into the living room, where James stands, hands in his pockets. His unbuttoned jacket reveals suspenders, which are so fucking hot. I was the type of girl who found Steve Urkel to be hotter than Stefan, and I always thought it was the glasses, but in this moment, I think it might have been the suspenders.

We settle on the sofa that faces the fireplace, close enough that our shoulders touch. I consider lighting it, but it invokes memories of Michael that don't feel appropriate to have right now. My boxes loom in the room across the foyer. The piano peeks from behind them, and I turn my body so I can't see it. I only want to see James right now. *I don't want to think about that. I just want to think about James.*

"Thank you for coming tonight," James says, his voice lower, more intimate in the quiet of my living room. "Those functions are always more bearable with the right company."

"You're welcome."

"And…that sizable donation from an anonymous donor…" He smiles, and I notice a small dimple in his left cheek I've somehow missed until now. "Thank you for that, too."

"I don't know what you're talking about…" I say, sipping my wine and looking at the fire.

"You know nothing about the 6 million dollar donation that came in when you spent an inordinate amount of time in the bathroom?"

"James, it's impolite to discuss a woman's bathroom distress… especially if you plan on seducing her."

He laughs. "Okay, Celeste. I hope you're feeling better from whatever distress you were experiencing."

His eyes soften as he sets his wine glass on the coffee table. "Celeste." Just my name, but the way he says it—like it's something precious held on his tongue—makes my heart skip.

He gently strokes the back of my hand, and I watch his fingertips trace up my skin, mesmerized by their gentle exploration. "All evening, it's taken every ounce of my willpower to stop from touching you," he confesses.

"What stopped you?" I ask, my voice huskier than intended.

His smile turns playful. "Professional decorum. And the fact that what I want to do with you requires significantly more privacy than a charity gala can provide." He circles my wrist with his fingers, his thumb now on my pulse point, amplifying the sensation.

Heat blooms in my chest, spreading outward until I'm sure he must feel it radiating from me. His eyes darken as they hold mine, his body angling toward me on the sofa.

"And what exactly do you want to do?"

In answer, he lifts my hand to his lips, pressing a kiss to my knuckles that sends shivers up my arm. "Unleash twenty years of yearning on you," he murmurs against my skin.

His seduction technique is devastatingly effective. I lean toward him, drawn by an invisible force that's tied me to him since I ran into him on the street. There's something about this man. Every smirk sends lightning straight to my loins. It's a primal desire. "That's…a lot of yearning. I'm not sure I can handle it."

His laugh is soft, warm against my cheek. "Oh, baby, I bet you can handle it," he says, his voice now husky with lust. He inhales my scent and moans into my neck. "Celeste, can I please have you now?"

I gasp as he places a tender peck on my neck. "Absolutely."

He pulls back and stares into my eyes for a moment before he closes the distance between us. I thread my fingers through his hair, pulling him closer as the kiss deepens. He tastes of wine, his tongue teasing mine in a dance that grows more urgent with each passing second.

His hands frame my face with a tenderness that contrasts with the growing hunger in his kiss. I shift closer, wanting to cover my whole body with his heat.

"You are the most extraordinary creature," he says, his voice rough with desire. His thumb traces my lower lip, still sensitive from his kiss.

"I'm nothing special," I whisper, and it's both an invitation and a challenge. I want him to prove it to me. I want him to heal the part of me that will never think she's good enough, but I doubt he can. I struggle to find anything even worth loving.

His eyes open in surprise, before softening in understanding. He stands, offering me his hand. I place my hand in his and stand by his side.

"I'll show you exactly how special you are, Celeste," he murmurs. His eyes roam down my body, and I can't help but follow his gaze. The sparkles of my dress reflect in his eyes for a moment. Paired with the slight buzz I have from all the champagne and wine, it feels like I'm in a dream. *This can't be real.*

James scrutinizes my shoulder for a moment and gently moves the strap to the side, causing it to fall down my arm. The dress stays put for the most part, only drooping a bit and exposing the top half of my breasts. He kisses my shoulder gently where the strap had been. Then down to the top part of my breast. He drops the other strap and kisses there, but this time, his hand reaches behind me, unhooking the clasp above the zipper.

"Unzip it for me. I want to watch it fall to the ground," he says, stepping back. Without hesitation, I do as I'm told.

I unzip it slowly. It peels away from my body as the zipper works its way down my back. I'm not wearing a bra with this dress. With each inch exposed, James's eyes widen. He loosens his tie further, as if it's choking him. When I'm almost done removing it, I worry he'll be disappointed in my body.

When my dress hits the floor, I step out of it, kicking it to the side, uncaring about what happens to it, despite it literally being the most expensive dress I own.

"Exquisite," James says, reaching toward me and gently stroking my stomach, focusing on the swell under my belly button. "You're even more perfect than I imagined."

"You imagined me naked?" I ask, shivering at his touch.

"Every night since I was seventeen." His admission sends a fresh wave of heat through me. The dress offered support for my breasts that I now no longer have, so they hang slightly. I wrap my arms around my chest, attempting to lift my breasts. If he's imagined this since we were teenagers, I doubt he imagined me with middle-aged sagging tits.

"Please don't hide from me, baby," he breathes, placing his hands on my arms. I loosen my grip, letting him part my arms for me. He holds my hands out, devouring my whole body with his eyes. "So beautiful, so perfect." His touch runs from my hands up my arms, tickling. He stops to circle my nipple and cup my breast gently.

He moves forward, kissing the area between my neck and shoulder, his lips worshiping me as he trails kisses across my collarbone and up my neck.

One hand cups my breast, thumb circling the sensitive peak, while the other gently holds at my hip. His mouth replaces his hand at my breast, tongue and teeth teasing until I'm writhing beneath him, my hands clutching at his shoulders. He moans as he takes my nipple into his mouth.

He turns me, pushing me gently back down to the couch, kneeling before me, and continuing his quest to cover my body with kisses. I moan softly as his hands and mouth explore my breasts, lavishing them with attention. He teases my nipples until I'm arching off the couch, desperate for more.

"So responsive," he praises huskily. "I love how your body reacts to my touch."

His fingers dance lower, skimming over my trembling stomach. I'm panting now, aching for him to touch me where I need him most.

"Oh, James," I whimper, threading my fingers through his hair.

Smiling against my skin, he kisses a trail down my stomach, dipping his tongue into my navel. He hooks his fingers in my panties and drags them down my legs.

I gasp as his fingers trace up my inner thighs, teasing me with feather-light touches. He parts my legs further, exposing me to his hungry gaze. He kisses my inner thigh, teasing me, making me writhe against his touch. His hand grazes ever so slightly across my clit, making me jolt upward.

His finger hovers slightly at my entrance, tracing small circles before he finally sinks a finger into me. "Oh, gorgeous, you're already so wet for me," he groans appreciatively, kissing my knee and plunging another finger inside me. Hooking them forward and caressing my G-spot. "I bet you taste so good."

I wail when his mouth is on me, his tongue lapping at my sensitive folds. I cry out at the intense pleasure, my hips bucking against his face. He holds me down firmly, taking his time as he explores every inch of my sex.

"Oh, J Money, that's perfect," I moan, fisting my hands in his hair and teasing him with the old nickname. His tongue swirls around my clit.

"Oh, so we're in a teasing mood, are we?" he whispers, pulling back from me slightly and removing his fingers.

I whimper at the loss of his mouth. "No, no! I'm sorry," I beg, running my fingers through his hair. "Please don't stop."

"Oh, baby, you're so pretty when you beg. Say my name for real."

"Please. James. Please don't stop."

He smirks and slides his fingers back inside me. He pumps them slowly, curling them to hit that perfect spot. "God, you're so tight. I can't wait to feel you wrapped around me," he growls, capturing my lips in a searing kiss. I can taste myself on his tongue as he claims my mouth possessively.

His fingers pick up speed, thrusting deeper as his thumb rubs tight circles on my clit. He places teasing kisses around my thighs, getting close, but not close enough.

The sensation sends me flying, pleasure coiling tighter and tighter in my core.

"So perfect," he says as he looks down at my body trembling on his hand. "That's it, gorgeous. Let go for me," he coaxes. "I want to feel you come undone."

"Please, James," I whimper, needing his mouth upon me.

"Okay, baby, I'll stop teasing you," he smirks, and his mouth returns to its mark. I grip his head, thrusting into him, lifting from the couch.

One more deep suck and expert stroke of his finger, and I completely shatter. "James!" I cry out, as ecstasy crashes over me in intense waves. He works me through it, drawing out my pleasure until I collapse back onto the cushions, boneless and sated. My head lulled back on the back of the couch.

"You're incredible," he murmurs, kissing his way back up my body. "I need to be inside you, Celeste. I need to feel you wrapped around me."

Still hazy with bliss, I breathe out, "Yes, I need you, too."

He stands and removes his jacket, folding it and placing it on the coffee table. He hovers over me and pulls his suspenders to the sides before slowly untucking and unbuttoning his shirt, allowing me to drink him in as I recover. *Fuck, suspenders are so fucking hot.*

I bite my lip as I watch the muscles of his chest undulate as he tosses his shirt upon the pile that represents my dress. Before he has a chance to remove his pants, I lean forward, grabbing his zipper. "You're taking too long," I say, eagerly unzipping them. I want to see his cock.

"Hold on just a sec," he says, stroking my chin before I can release his member from his pants. He reaches into his jacket on the table and pulls out a wallet. The glint of a condom rapper shines in his hands.

He hovers in front of me, and together we quickly remove the rest of his clothing. His impressive cock stands to attention, and before I have too much time to admire it, he is rolling a condom down it and covering my body with his.

I feel the blunt head of his erection pressing against my entrance, and I tilt my hips in invitation. He wraps his hand around the back of my neck and, with a groan, pushes forward, sliding into my slick heat inch by delicious inch.

He exhales once he's fully sheathed within me. "God, you feel amazing, Celeste."

He pauses and simply takes in the sensation of himself inside me. His eyes meet mine, filled with awe and desire. "I've wanted this for so long," he whispers, his voice cracking with adoration. He almost sounds as if he might cry. I wrap my legs around him, pulling him in deeper. "You're so beautiful. I adore you."

"Fuck me, James," I beg, my hips arching upwards, craving more of him. He lets out a low growl and obliges, moving inside me in a slow, sensual rhythm. His strokes intensify, driving us both higher and higher.

"You're perfect," he breathes against my skin as he thrusts deeper, filling me completely. "Absolutely flawless." His hands roam my body possessively, gripping my hips, my breasts, threading through my hair. He seems to be everywhere at once, surrounding me, consuming me with his passion.

I moan and writhe beneath him, meeting his every movement, urging him on with breathy pleas. "More," I gasp. "Don't stop." The coil of pleasure winds tighter and tighter in my core as he drives into me relentlessly.

He hitches my leg higher over his hip, changing the angle so he can penetrate even deeper. I moan loudly as he hits that perfect spot inside me over and over.

"Yes, right there," I pant, my nails digging into his shoulders.

"There, like that, baby?"

"Yes. Don't stop, please…"

"Never," he vows. "I'll never stop showing you how incredible you are, how much I adore you." His hand snakes between our bodies to rub my clit. I whimper at the added stimulation, my inner muscles fluttering around him.

He feels me tightening and redoubles his efforts, stroking and circling my clit as he pounds into me faster. "That's it, baby. Come for me again. Show me how much you like my cock. God, you're so beautiful."

I melt under his loving worship, surrendering completely. The coil inside me winds tighter and tighter until it finally snaps. "Oooooooh, fuck," I cry out as my release crashes over me in intense waves of ecstasy even deeper than the orgasm I had moments ago.

He follows me over the edge with a guttural groan, his hips stuttering as he grips me against him, pulling my face to his chest and kissing the top of my head. We cling to each other as the aftershocks slowly subside, the crackling fire the only sound besides our ragged breathing.

32

I'm feeling a little claustrophobic today. I've spent the last few hours staring at the boxes in the dining room. James left late last night to attend an early morning meeting with Marcus today. I wish he had stayed over. I can't stand being in this house alone.

I woke up early this morning to a twinge in my back, likely due to all these nights spent on the couch. I couldn't fall back asleep, so I resolved to spend the day unpacking—finally going through my parents' stuff and making way for mine.

I planned to start with the kitchen, but the moment I opened a cabinet, I got overwhelmed, cried, and texted Ryan, "SOS, Damsel in distress and in need of big, strong arms to move boxes and an impartial brain to make hard decisions about donating stuff."

Ryan almost immediately responded with, "Knight in shining armor on the way with arms and, despite popular belief, a brain."

"Could you maybe fuck the sad out of me, too?" I asked.

"Definitely. Be there in two shakes of a Wiimote," he responded, remembering our incredibly dorky phrase from college.

So, now, I'm sitting on my porch, waiting for him and trying to avoid the avalanche of emotions that overwhelm me whenever I look at my parents' stuff.

The gate to Mrs. Heart's backyard opens, and Watson rushes out, sniffing around the perimeter and barking at a squirrel encroaching on his territory.

He spots me and bolts in my direction, stopping at my feet with a full-body tail wag.

"Well, hello there, handsome!" I coo, reaching down to scratch behind his ears. Watson's soft fur and enthusiastic greeting have become a comforting constant in my life. He always rushes out to meet me if I'm around, after barking at squirrels and inspecting his territory's perimeter first, of course.

Not far behind, Mrs. Heart closes the gate, "Watson, you know you're not supposed to leave our yard. Celeste, I swear, you moving next door has set his training back," she says with a giggle.

She shuffles across her yard toward me, and it's evident that her back is still bothering her. *It's been a while. I hope she's okay. But she's probably overdoing it in the garden.* I worry she'll struggle up the stairs and rush to her. She waves me off, "Stop fussing over me," she says.

I take a seat at the top of the stairs next to Watson. He flops over, showing me his belly. I rub it profusely, and Mrs. Heart sits on the stairs at his other side. She looks at me with mischievous curiosity. "I noticed a car driving out of the driveway really late last night." She chuckles with a teasing grin. "Which bachelor did you have over?"

Watson flops so that his head rests on her leg and his feet are on me. *I guess I get the bad end.* We both stroke his belly absentmindedly. This dog really must think he's the center of everyone's universe. *What a charmed life.*

"James," I say with a bit of a swoon in my voice, thinking about last night.

"Oh, dear, let me go get my tea, and then you need to spill your tea. Is that how the saying goes?" she asks, grabbing the stair rail to pull herself back up.

"Yeah, it does," I laugh. "I'll get it, though! No need to stand!"

She scoffs at me and wants to protest, but I've already leaped to my feet. I'm halfway across the yard before she can say anything.

She sighs loud enough for me to hear, and, before I enter her house, she shouts, "Fine, fine. The kettle should be all set in the kitchen, you know where I keep everything."

"Be right back," I say, leaning out the door I'm already walking through.

I enter the kitchen and spot the teapot. The rest of her tea set is just as easy to find. I arrange two teacups on saucers, but before I can pour the tea, I notice a pile of bills tucked into the corner on the counter. They have large, ominous, red writing on them stating things like "final notice." *Is Mrs. Heart struggling with money? Did she not make money on the sale of the dealership when John passed?* I assumed Mrs. Heart was doing well financially. She always refused money from me. The sale of the dealership should have set her up for life. *I should ask her about it.*

If she needs help, maybe she'll actually let me help her. She's never let me give her money—a trait she certainly didn't share with my parents—and a trait I gave up arguing over years ago. I'm not sure why she wouldn't take my money.

With an uncharacteristic amount of control, I don't look at the pile too long. I respect Mrs. Heart too much to snoop. *I will ask her about it when I get back outside, though.*

I pour the two cups of tea. I decide against the entire tray and choose to just carry the saucers. I regret the decision almost immediately when I reach the front door and am not able to open it. I've already spilled a little tea into the saucers. I have the genius idea to place them on the ground so I can open the door. It becomes an annoying dance of saucer and door juggling, but I'm finally able to close the door behind me and begin my journey back to my porch.

Once I'm finally done with this dumb side mission and turn to my porch, I spot Sarah standing at the base of my stairs chatting with Mrs. Heart, while Andy tosses a stick for Watson.

"Hey, you two! If I had known you would be here, I would have gotten more tea," I say, still doing my damndest not to spill, and slowly progress toward my porch with precariously poised porcelain in hand.

"Aw, thanks, but no need, we come packin'," Sarah says, pointing at thermoses attached to their hips. "We were just out for a walk and decided to stop and chat."

"And play with Watson, of course," Andy says, tossing the stick.

"Of course," I say, sitting next to Mrs. Heart and giving her one of the teacups and saucers.

"Celeste was just about to tell me of her night at the Gala with James," Mrs. Heart says, sipping her tea conspiratorially.

"Well, well, well, it seems the uncatchable James finally got caught! When's the wedding? I know I'm invited, but can Sarah be my plus one?" Andy says playfully, as they toss the stick for Watson again.

Sarah just shakes her head at their joke. I feel my cheeks flush, a mix of embarrassment and amusement.

I'm unable to hide my own smile. "We're just enjoying each other's company."

Sarah raises her eyebrows and says, "Details, Celeste! We need to know everything!"

I shake my head, a soft laugh escaping my lips. "You two are incorrigible, you know that?"

Andy flicks their red hair out of their eye, their attention no longer on the game of fetch and they move to stand next to Sarah, awaiting more details from me. Watson looks positively dejected. Once he realizes Andy will no longer be throwing the stick, he returns to his position between me and Mrs. Heart, pawing at my leg for pets.

Andy adds, "Come on, Celeste, we need to know what happened. James has been breaking hearts for years. He's the fish no one's been able to catch. I've never known him to take someone on an actual date, and I've known him since the two of us played Little League together."

"Oh, really?" I ask, unsure if I should be flattered. "Well, it wasn't exactly a date. I just went with him to the Gala."

"That's a date, dear. A fancy date," Mrs. Heart laughs. "You're looking a bit starry-eyed. I've never seen this look on your face post-coitus."

"Maybe Ryan isn't the stud he thinks he is," Andy laughs.

"I'm not starry-eyed," I protest, but the warmth in my cheeks betrays me. "And come on, Andy, Ryan is great." Andy scoffs in a way that seems to hold a bit of history I'm not privy to.

Sarah taps my foot with hers and says with a level of excitement that she can't control, "So, spill the beans! How was it? Does this mean Michael and Ryan are now out of the picture?"

I roll my eyes, but I can't help the grin that spreads across my face. "It was lovely." I pause, letting the suspense build before shrugging and saying, "There was this nice spread, and the salmon was great."

"Girl! You know I wasn't asking about the food!" Sarah scolds, looking positively flustered with my feigned coyness.

Mrs. Heart, never one to let gossip stay hanging for long, chimes in, "I saw Michael leaving her house the other morning, and Ryan leaving a few nights before. I doubt they're out of the picture."

"Mrs. Heart! Stop spreading my business!"

"Sorry, Celeste. You spread legs. I spread info. We each have our strengths," Mrs. Heart says, grabbing my knee and leaning into me.

"Nice one, Mrs. Heart," Andy chuckles, trying to give her a fist bump, but failing miserably. Mrs. Heart looks at their fist with confusion before lightly patting it with her fingers.

"You all are awful," I say with a bashful smile, loving the attention and having fun teasing them.

Andy groans, throwing their hands up in mock frustration. "You're killing us here, Celeste! Are you seeing all of them?"

"I'm...playing the field..." I respond, looking at Mrs. Heart, who gives me an approving nod.

"There's a little league pun in there somewhere, but my brain is too consumed with the details of your love life to come up with it," Andy replies.

"Sorry, we're so nosy, Celeste, but it's so boring around here. Your little love triangle...love square? Anyway, whatever it is you've got going on is the most interesting thing to happen around here in a long time. Until you moved back, all anyone could talk about was a ribbon-winning pumpkin. A fucking pumpkin, Celeste! That's what you're competing with. And now it looks like you might be locking down not one but three of this town's most elusive bachelors!"

I shrug, lean back, and kick my feet while playfully sealing my lips.

Mrs. Heart laughs at me, "Don't worry, you two, Sean and I will keep you updated. We see everything from our neighborly vantage points."

Sarah's expression grows more serious. "In all honesty, Celeste, we're just happy to see you smiling. You deserve some happiness after everything you've been through."

I nod, touched by their concern. "Thank you, both of you. Things haven't been easy since I came back, but you have all been so wonderful. I am enjoying myself."

Mrs. Heart gives my hand a gentle squeeze. "We're happy for you, dear. We hope that these boys are helping you heal."

"Thanks, Mrs. Heart," I respond, and I don't know if they are helping me heal so much as avoid.

"Speaking of…" Andy says, their eyes following a truck pulling into Mr. O'Connor's driveway.

Ryan hops out of his truck and retrieves a bunch of boxes and tape from the back. He leaves his truck in his dad's driveway and bounds toward us.

"Having a party, Celeste?" he asks, referencing the gaggle of gossips on my stoop.

"We were actually just heading out," Andy says, coldly to Ryan. *What the heck is that about? Does Andy dislike Ryan?*

"See ya, Celeste! Ryan. Mrs. Heart," Sarah says, as Andy practically drags her away.

Watson leaps from the stoop to ensure they give him a pet goodbye, which they both oblige.

"Sorry, Watson! Goodbye to you, too, boy," Sarah apologizes as they both pet him goodbye.

As the two walk away, Mrs. Heart turns to Ryan and says, "Ah, so it seems Andy's still mad at you for breaking up with Angela, huh, Ryan?"

"They'll get over it," Ryan shrugs.

"It's been years. It doesn't look like they will," Mrs. Heart says.

"Well, that's Andy for ya. They'll hold a grudge longer than a hair color," he says, feigning unconcern.

"I'm guessing you're here to get our girl on track? She's still living out of boxes with nothing in her fridge but a bunch of wine," Mrs. Heart says. I furrow my eyebrows at her and want to protest.

She gently scolds me, "Don't look at me like that, dear. There's no sense in denying it. I'm going to bet the only cabinets you've opened in that house have either held alcohol or glasses to put alcohol in."

It's true.

"Yep, I'm the impartial third party with arms built for tossing stuff," he says, wrapping them around me. With a kiss atop my head, he says, "Don't worry, Mrs. Heart, I'll get her mess all sorted out."

"You two are talking about me like I'm helpless," I pout.

Mrs. Heart pats my shoulder, "Sorry, dear, we both know exactly how hard it is for you to go through all those bad memories."

They nod at each other, sharing a knowing look. They seem to know better than I do why I've struggled to unpack my boxes.

"You really don't have to hold on to any of their stuff, dear," Mrs. Heart says, putting her hand on my arm.

I sigh and look back at the door. "I know…I just…it feels wrong. I'd regret not going through it more than I would regret going through it…if that makes sense."

"Well, Watson, how about you help out. I bet Celeste is going to need some cuddles that don't come with…strings," she says to Watson while giving Ryan the side eye.

"You wound me, Mrs. Heart," Ryan says, feigning offense. "I am capable of not taking advantage of a woman."

"Sure you are, dear. Just remember, sometimes the help you give isn't what someone actually needs." She points at Watson and commands. "Stay." He's lying on the porch, half asleep, and just looks at her like, "What makes you think I was going to move?"

We exchange goodbyes, and Mrs. Heart walks slowly to her home, holding her back.

Her back must really hurt. I hope she's okay.

Shit. I forgot to ask her about the unpaid bills.

I paid off my parents' house and debt years ago—despite everything. I should have helped Mrs. Heart, too.

Not only a bad daughter, but also a bad surrogate daughter.

"Let's get this over with," I sigh. "Watson," I say, waving to the dog to come with me. He and Ryan follow behind me dutifully.

33

"I'm going to leave my shoes on. Probably need to protect my feet if I'll be carrying stuff," Ryan says.

"Sure, honestly, the whole shoes-off thing was my mom's hang-up. I never really cared. I left them on in my home in California all the time."

"That's not very Minnesotan of you, Star Girl."

"I suppose."

He looks around the house, noting the piles of boxes that represent the untouched life I've tried to ignore. The clutter of living out of boxes on top of the ghosts of my past, becoming too chaotic.

"Quite the setup you've got yourself here. Building a sad girl fort?" he jokes, nodding at the jungle of boxes.

"Pretty much," I admit. I twist a strand of hair around my finger, a nervous habit that refuses to die.

"Have you gotten more stuff delivered since I was here last?" he asks, gesturing to the living room that is now overflowing with stuff.

"No, I've just kind of made a mess of it."

"No worries, Star Girl. Where do you want to start?" he asks, looking around at the towers of my procrastination. A flutter of relief mixed with dread rips through me at his decisiveness.

"How about the kitchen?" I say, fidgeting with hesitation."I've…I haven't been able to cook since I got here. I've just been eating at Sarah's cafe, or Mrs. Heart brings me food. I'm afraid that if I open a cabinet, a memory will jump out at me."

I sound ridiculous. What kind of grown woman is scared of cutlery? The kind who had cutlery thrown at her regularly, I guess.

Ryan nods and brings me into a half-hug, rubbing my shoulder.

"Kitchen sounds like a great place to begin. Let's get you a usable kitchen. Please tell me the fridge has been cleaned out, at least."

"Yes, thank God. Mrs. Heart did that before I arrived."

"Oh, good, that would be gross. We've got this, Celeste. Just one drawer, one cabinet at a time, yeah?"

"Yeah," I respond.

"If it gets too much, just say the word."

"Thanks, Ryan."

My heart begins to race. *Why is this so hard?*

Ryan stops at the door to the kitchen and must note my reluctance, because he says, "Celeste, you know, you could just sell the house and all the stuff. You don't have to stay here."

"I…I know," I say. Of course, I've thought of that. *My mom would turn in her grave if I were to get rid of her stuff without at least going through it. And my dad…I can't just throw him away, too.*

He simply nods. "Alright, let's do this!" he says with an unnecessary level of exuberance. He grabs a dining room chair and places it at the entrance of the kitchen. "Okay, Star Girl, here's how we're gonna do this. You're going to sit that cut little ass right here," he says, gently pushing me onto the chair. "And I'm going to hold stuff up. You tell me if it's storage, donate, or trash, ok?"

"Yep," I say, nervousness flooding me and tears threatening to fill my eyes.

He enters the kitchen and assembles two of the cardboard boxes he brought. He labels one "storage" and another "donate." He looks under the kitchen sink and grabs a trash bag.

"If it gets to be too much or you want me to just bull in a china shop the whole thing without your input, let me know, cool?"

"Cool," I say, steeling myself.

"I'm gonna start with one I know you've already opened," he says as he pulls open the cabinet that contains my mom's various teacups with a flourish, showboating and gesturing to it in a way that makes it seem like he's on a game show.

In a presenter voice, "In door number one, we have vintage tea sets. Gifted over the years by Mrs. Heart. What will it be, Celeste? Keep, Donate, or Toss?"

"Keep," I say with a decisive nod. He closes the cabinet.

"Keep, the girl chose keep, ladies and gentlemen, can you believe it?" he says, then pretends to make a cheering crowd noise.

"Alright, door number two," he says as he opens the second cabinet. "Old plates."

"Those were my grandmother's. We were only allowed to use them on special occasions."

"Oh, yeah, I remember these on the occasional Christmas or Thanksgiving. Keep, Donate, or Toss?"

"Keep. And I'm going to use them whenever the fuck I want."

"Atta girl," he says while shutting the door. Memories of all the holidays we used them start rushing in. Other, less pleasant memories come, too. Like the time my mom berated me for heating a Hot Pocket on one. She yelled at me for so long that I eventually snapped and called her a cunt. That was the first time she ever slapped me in the face. It made me drop the plate. That merited another slap. That was one of the few fights between us that Ryan actually saw. Usually she was so sweet around him.

"Actually…Keep. But storage. Too many bad memories," I say.

Ryan opens the door and peers at them. His face transforms as if the memory returns to him. "She was really protective of these things, huh?"

"Her mom…was kinda the same way. With my mom, not really with me. She was always kind to me. She was so proud of those damn plates. But when she gave them to my mom, they came with strings. God, I don't think they are even worth anything."

"Alright, storage it is," he says. "Shit. Do you have bubble wrap?"

"Yeah," I say and stand to go fetch it.

"Sit that cute little, emotionally damaged ass right back down," he says, rushing toward me and pushing me into the chair gently with a kiss to the head. "Where is it?" *This must be how Mrs. Heart felt with me fussing over her earlier.*

"Bedroom. By the bed. You'll find it next to a heap of broken trophies. Some crazy person went in there the other day and started breaking them all instead of wrapping them."

Ryan looks at me and wipes the tear rolling down my cheek, "Hey, you're doing great."

"No, I'm not. I broke all my mom's trophies."

"You mean your trophies?"

I ignore the question. "Who does something like that?"

"You do. And that's okay. They don't mean anything."

"They do, though. They represent her success. They represent her. I broke her. It was my fault she was always so cruel."

He's kneeling at my feet now, the smile wiped from his face. "No, it wasn't Celeste. It wasn't your fault. She was broken before you were born. She just refused to see it, and it was easier for her to blame you than admit she wasn't perfect. She tried to live through you."

I close my eyes, a wave of feelings overwhelming me. When I open them, tears blur my vision, but they don't yet fall. I grip the sides of the chair. "I was never good enough, Ryan! Everything I did was wrong. Even when I won, I did it wrong."

His hands are on my knees. "You were always good enough, Celeste."

"No, I wasn't! I was a bad kid."

"Celeste, that's not true. You were a good kid. You were kind. You never got in trouble."

"I was always in trouble! I was always grounded. Because I was always arguing with her."

"Because she was irrationa—"

"I should have just kept my mouth shut. Let her yell. Fighting back only made things worse. If I had just apologized…."

"Celeste, she yelled even after you apologized. I saw it. That's what she did. She just kept yelling. She always found other reasons to yell."

"I never did anything right."

"Celesete, you were so good at everything. Music. Art. Sports. You were valedictorian for fuck's sake."

The tears finally break from my eyes. "There were barely any kids in our class, Ryan. It doesn't count."

He rubs the outsides of my thighs. "It does."

"If I had just done things right the first time, she wouldn't have gotten so mad."

"You were a kid, Celeste. You were supposed to make mistakes. That's how kids learn. They aren't born knowing stuff. She was supposed to teach you, not expect you to do everything right the first time."

"All I ever did was make her miserable."

He chokes up. "Celeste…she was miserable and blamed you."

I dare to admit something even Ryan doesn't know."Then…why… why would my dad always take her side?"

Tears escape his eyes now. "I don't know, Celeste…"

"He…always agreed with her. 'Look how you upset your mother so, Ce-ce. You should just apologize to her.'"

"I don't know, Celeste. He…he enabled her. I don't know."

"And why would…why would he…she would send him…tell him to…teach me my lesson." I sob, looking at him. "'Just wait until your dad gets home, Celeste. Then you'll be sorry for treating me like this.'"

"Celeste. Listen. They were not good parents. But you were a good kid. None of that—none of it was your fault. I'm sorry, I didn't realize how she affected you back then. I'm sorry I stopped talking to you when you couldn't come back home. I didn't get it then, but I get it now. I'm sorry I wasn't there for you."

His eyes are soft with understanding and wet with tears. I can't meet them for long. The words bubble up before I can stop them. "I couldn't come back. I had to escape them."

"I know. I know."

"Nothing I ever did was ever good enough. If I made the slightest mistake, I'd be berated, I'd be reminded over and over and over how much of a failure I was. How worthless I was."

"I know."

"After I moved, when I tried to talk to her about it, she'd deny it ever happened. She'd say I was being too sensitive, that I was dramatic, that I was always so mean to her. That I was painting her out to be the villain."

Ryan pulls me close to his chest, "I'm sorry, Celeste."

"That's why I couldn't come back after college," I confess, the weight of the admission heavy and freeing all at once. "Every corner of this house reminds me of never being good enough."

"I didn't understand back then. You seemed to handle it so well. When you weren't fighting, the two of you seemed to get along well."

"I was pretending," I say, letting out a small, bitter laugh. "For her, and everyone else. If I didn't, it would be so much worse."

He looks at me with a seriousness in his eyes that I rarely see. "You don't have to pretend now, you know. I'm sorry you didn't feel like you could tell me back then."

"Ryan…I had to pretend for you, too. Whenever I get upset, you unfold. I…had to be strong for you, too."

"I know. I was…I'm sorry, Celeste."

"Is it going to still be like that, Ryan? Us pretending to be fine for each other? Because I don't think I can do it anymore?"

"No more pretending, Celeste," he says. The words hang between us, heavy with the promise of transformation. I brace myself, unsure of what he's about to say but feeling the magnitude of it. I look at him, anticipation in my eyes. *Will we finally admit how we feel about each other? Finally admit that we've loved each other our whole lives?*

"Celeste, when my mom left, you were there for me, and I'm going to be here for you now. I promise. Let's go get some food at the cafe and leave this for later, okay?"

"Okay…"

34

"So, Michael, what were you excited to talk to me about?" I ask. We're sitting in his usual spot: the table beside Mrs. Heart's favorite booth. Michael's sitting across from me, practically buzzing with excitement to tell me some information he's discovered. He's wearing a faded "Goose Grove Community Theatre" t-shirt with a cardigan and has his laptop and several notebooks sprawled out on the table in front of us. Paired with his glasses, he's got that hip, writing professor vibe. I didn't think I could find this man any sexier, but here I am, proven wrong.

Mrs. Heart sits next to us in her usual throne with a teacup balanced in one hand and the other idly stroking Watson's sleepy head. He sleeps peacefully beside her in the booth, his black-and-tan ears splayed out like he's melting.

Michael leans forward and beams, "I think I have some information about Richard's murder."

Watson lifts his head at the sound of Michael's excitement, tail thumping against the vinyl seat, but Mrs. Heart lets out a tiny "tsk" and gives me a meaningful look. "Well, I'm not one for morbid talk." She sets her teacup on the table, brushes imaginary crumbs from her skirt, and stands. "Have a good day, dear," she says, patting me on the back. Watson jumps from the table and follows her out the door.

We say our goodbyes to Mrs. Heart and Watson, and Michael returns his attention to me. "I've been combing through the town's public records concerning the revitalization effort."

"You mean gentrification efforts," I correct, since that seems to be the standard response of everyone in town, and a girl's gotta fit it.

He smirks with a slight chuckle, "Ha, yeah, anyway, all the budget files are online. The records show that they should have more than enough money to complete this project. But there are a few extremely large expenses that are missing. Whole sections are redacted. There are no details on where the money went."

"Redacted? For a town budget? Are they supposed to do that?"

"I don't know. I looked back five years, and it's literally the only information missing over the last five years."

Andy approaches with my coffee and my now-favorite turkey sandwich and says, "That's weird. The town budget has always been public record."

I ask Michael, "When do these redactions show up?"

Andy watches Michael intently, interested in his response. Michael says, "About three months ago—right when construction stopped."

"What are you all gossiping about?" Sarah asks, approaching Andy, placing her hand on their back and head on their shoulder. Her hair is braided back today, and she's wearing the cutest navy apron printed with little ducks. Her eyes are extra-bright even for someone who probably mainlines caffeine.

"Town budget," Andy replies.

"Gah, boring! I thought you would be talking about the murder," Sarah says with a yawn, the sparkle in her eyes seems to drain at the thought.

"We are," Michael replies, a bit flustered that we're no longer conspiring just the two of us.

"So, what does this have to do with Richard's murder?" I ask.

He turns his computer around to show me the documentation. "The initials RH pop up in the notes attached to one of those transactions."

Andy and Sarah sit in Mrs. Heart's vacated booth, leaning forward to peer at the computer with me.

"Richard Holbrook…" Sarah, Andy, and I all say quietly.

"Exactly!" Michael exclaims, and I kind of wish he had a pipe that he could point at us for his "ah ha" moment. *Where's Watson? I wanna tell him this is elementary.*

"Shit. Is there any way we can find out what those redacted files say?" I ask.

"It's supposed to be public record, so for it to be redacted like this seems extremely suspicious—possibly criminal," Michael responds.

Andy replies, "You can go to Town Hall. The clerk's office should have the unredacted files."

"What if they don't?" I ask.

Andy thinks for a moment before saying, "It's public record. It shouldn't have been redacted in the first place. If for some reason you run into trouble, you could always file a formal FOIA request."

"And this is where you lose me. I'm getting back to work before Andy puts me to sleep," Sarah says, leaving us.

"FOIA?" I ask.

"Freedom of Information Act," Andy replies.

I ask, "How do you know all this, Andy?"

"Ha, well, I was the mayor before Marcus. Two terms of that were enough for me, though."

My head whips toward Andy. "Wait! What?!"

"I'm an Astor," they say with a shrug. "Astors have dominated the mayoral seat since…forever."

"Oh, yeah. You're so nice, I keep forgetting that you're an Asshole-tor," I laugh, then immediately realize how insulting that sounds. "Oh, um, sorry."

"Nah, I get it. But, yeah, it was back before I came out. Dad wanted a kid who was a mayor. Now he's got a son-in-law mayor, so I'm off the hook. But enough about that, if you need help with the FOIA request, let me know."

I ask, "How long does that take? The FOIA request?"

"Well, that's…it depends. They're supposed to get back to you within twenty days…but there's wiggle room. The official rule is a 'reasonable amount of time.'"

Ryan breezes through the door, trailed by a swirl of fallen leaves. He spots me instantly, having a built-in Celeste-radar.

"Celeste!" He shouts like I'm halfway across a football field, and half the cafe turns to look. I brace myself as Ryan barrels over, almost colliding with Sarah, who sidesteps him with a practiced grace.

He pulls up a chair next to me, and Michael looks at him, dumbfounded, saying, "Hey, Ryan."

"Michael!" Ryan exclaims as if he is just now noticing him. "Andy," he says with less enthusiasm.

"Let me know how it goes. Feel free to call me if you need help, Celeste," Andy says, leaving without acknowledging Ryan. *Damn, Andy really doesn't like Ryan. Is this really just about Angela? I should look into this. That's a mystery that might be a bit easier to solve.*

"Help with what?" Ryan asks.

"Um, well, we're…" I don't know why I'm nervous to tell Ryan about the fact that Michael and I are not-so casually investigating this murder.

"We were talking about Richard Holbrook's murder," Michael says, staring Ryan down like he thinks Ryan killed him.

"What?! Why?" Ryan asks me, not Michael.

"It's just…it's just something that's been kind of nagging at me," I say, tracing the pattern of the tablecloth. "And, I think they suspect me, so I want to…I don't know…get ahead of it."

"And how's Andy gonna help? Talk to Angela?" Ryan asks.

"Right now, we're looking into some financial discrepancies with the town budget," Michael says, looking at me with a question in his eye. He's not sure why I'm clamming up, and I'm not either, really.

Ryan asks, "Oh, and Andy's gonna help with that?"

Michael responds, "They told us what we need to do if Town Hall won't give us the information we are looking for."

Ryan contemplates, "Oh, well, Celeste, why don't you just ask Marcus about it?"

"Huh? What?" I ask.

"Yeah, I bet he could speed things up for you," Ryan grins.

"I don't know…" I tense up. "He's been asking me to come to town hall…"

"There ya' go. Problem solved," Ryan says, snagging a fry from my plate and chewing it like he's Brad Pitt eating in a movie.

Michael tilts his head at me and lifts his glasses in that way he does when he's nervous about something. "Why does he want you to go to the town hall?"

"Probably because he's still in love with her," Ryan laughs, rubbing my leg under the table. I cut him a glance.

"He is not," I say matter-of-factly.

Ryan scoffs.

"He isn't! He said something about investment opportunities."

Ryan laughs, "That's a funny way to say 'fucking on the taxpayer's dime'."

"Ryan! He's not trying to sleep with me."

"Sure," Ryan laughs. "Everyone's trying to sleep with you, Celeste."

I sigh loudly, annoyed with him.

"Sorry, Star Girl, I'll stop picking on you."

Michael doesn't laugh at Ryan's jokes, but asks, "What does he want you to invest in?"

I shrug, because I have no idea, and worry Ryan may be right, but I'm not going to tell Ryan that.

Michael thinks for a moment, "Maybe he is hoping you can subsidize the missing money."

"Missing money?" Ryan asks.

"Um…" Michael tenses up, and now he's the one who doesn't want to talk. "Just some discrepancies we found when looking at the budget."

"Ooookay," Ryan says, side-eyeing Michael, obviously wondering why Michael is being so tight-lipped.

We all sit in non-companionable silence.

"Did you want something, Ryan?" I ask, just now realizing he rushed in here and inserted himself in our conversation.

"Oh, nah, I was just walking by and saw you through the window. Thought I'd stop in and check on you. You doing okay?" The last time Ryan saw me, I was a blubbering mess. He spent the whole night consoling me, telling me I wasn't a failure, and fucking me.

"Yeah, I'm good. Thanks. Michael and I are going to go to the haunted house in a bit."

"You're going to the house?" he asks with a laugh. "You?"

"Yes!" I say defensively.

"Alright, well, you two kids have fun," Ryan says, giving me a peck on the cheek and standing to leave. He smirks at Michael, "Take good care of her for me, Mikey."

Michael visibly stiffens and pulls at his shirt collar.

35

"Fair warning, if something jumps out at me, I might jump into your arms," Michael whispers, his breath warm against my ear.

I wrap my arms around his, "Same. So we might as well go ahead and cling to each other."

I'm not usually the type to willingly enter a haunted house, but here I am, standing before a Victorian monstrosity with Michael at my side. Somewhere in the distance, a recorded howl loops. The spookiness of it makes the leaf-bare trees feel like skeletal props.

I place my head on Michael's shoulder as we step toward the ticket booth, but a plastic skeleton drops from the awning above us, startling us both, but scaring the bejesus out of me. I'm so startled that I jump from Michael's arms with a yelp.

Realizing I am more easily startled than he is, Michael asks, "Are you sure you're up for this?" in that quiet, thoughtful way he does. "We can still grab coffee instead."

I straighten my shoulders. "Absolutely. I just wasn't expecting a jump scare outside." Despite my embarrassing tendency to scream at jump scares, I am looking forward to this. I'm eager to see how much it's changed since I was last here.

I've always found the Glendos Mansion fascinating, and unfortunately, the only time the public gets to peek inside is when it's open as a Haunted House every year. It was designated a historical site when I was a kid, and the proceeds from the haunted house are used to maintain its preservation. Its opening is one of the few tourist attractions of the town that brings people from all over the state to Goose Grove. But, I've always suspected most people come to see the house, not the haphazard attraction. So, this haunted house doesn't just keep the mansion from falling apart; it keeps at least two BNBs in business, as well. Unfortunately, keeping it open all year is just not sustainable.

The teenage ticket-taker hands us our wristbands with the enthusiasm of someone who'd rather be anywhere else. The kid's monotone "Enjoy your terror" makes Michael stifle a laugh. This kid must be one of the ones who did this in lieu of detention. Michael flicks the hair from his face and offers me his arm with all the charm of a Disney prince.

As we step into the dilapidated foyer, I marvel at the nostalgia the flickering amber sconces and peeling floral wallpaper stir within me. The floor beneath our feet creaks with every step: an effect that isn't staged. Portraits of stern-faced Victorian families line the walls, their eyes seemingly following our movements. If I didn't know the history behind these portraits, I'd think the artwork was designed specifically to make you think their eyes are following you. But I know they're just portraits of the Glendos family.

"I used to come here every year, so far, not much has changed. Well, I suppose the building seems a bit more dilapidated," I say, observing the walls and noting their familiarity.

We turn down a narrow hallway where fake cobwebs hang from a crystal chandelier. We squeeze closer in the confined space. Michael puts his arm around my waist and leads me forward.

"Its improvement was one of the things the revitalization effort was supposed to fund. They were going to open the place up for the whole year as a museum. It was supposed to be done before the season."

"It needs it. I'm surprised it's not condemned," I say as the floor beneath us gives an authentic groan that makes me think my feet may break through the floorboards. So far, the scariest thing about this haunted mansion has been the fear that the building might actually collapse. *Well, and that fucking skeleton outside.*

A hidden speaker emits a child's giggle that echoes through the foyer. I jump, and Michael's free hand cups mine that is gripping his arm.

I realize I'm squeezing his arm incredibly tight and loosen my grip, "Sorry, I'm probably cutting off your circulation."

"No, no. That's fine. I don't get to play the role of the big, strong protective male often, so I'm quite enjoying the fact that you're a bigger scaredy cat than I am."

"I'm not a scaredy cat," I say, pulling away from him a little and putting on an exaggerated pout. And, as if this mansion was designed specifically to prove me wrong, something touches my shoulder, driving me into Michael's arms. I turn to see a teenager slinking back behind a clothed table, a satisfied smirk on his face.

"Okay, you got me," I say, poking his arm lightly, "I'm a total wuss. This is so embarrassing."

Michael's laugh is low and warm. "Don't be embarrassed. This is quite endearing. It's nice to see the softer side of the all-powerful Celeste." *All-powerful? I suppose he does see me as a take-charge kind of person, both in business and in fucking.* I'm grateful for the dim lighting that hides my blush.

We navigate further into the manor, through a kitchen with mysterious red stains on the counters and plastic body parts stuffed into old-fashioned refrigerators. I'm actually starting to enjoy myself, the fabricated horror providing a strange comfort compared to the real-world mysteries I've stumbled into since returning to Goose Grove. Being embraced by Michael every time I jump into his arms isn't hurting either.

"Watch your—" Michael starts, but I've already tripped over a raised floorboard. His hand shoots out, catching me before I can fall. "—step."

His fingers wrap around my upper arm, steady and warm. "You okay?"

"My ego's bruised, but otherwise intact," I reply, hyperaware of his hand still on my arm. *God, I seem like one of those clumsy, helpless heroines. Am I a clumsy, helpless heroine?*

A sudden clanging sound erupts from somewhere behind the walls—pots and pans being struck together, if I had to guess. I startle again, wrapping my arms around Michael's neck and burying my face into his broad chest. He doesn't seem to mind, using the moment to pull me close and kiss the top of my head.

"I'm really happy I suggested this mansion," he says with a half-smile that makes my heart skip.

"You know, you didn't have to scare me to get me to hug you," I respond, my voice coming out more sultry and lustful than intended. The heat of his body pressed against mine, along with the jump scares, has my heart racing.

We continue through a hallway lined with mirrors that distort our reflections. Michael looks elongated and wavering in one, compressed and wide in another. I look ridiculous in all of them, but when I catch him watching me instead of his own reflection, I forget to be self-conscious.

"What exactly is the theme of this mansion? I'm so confused," I say, looking at the various decorations.

"I'm not sure," he laughs. "Usually it's a lot more thematic. It seems they really didn't plan to have it up this year."

"Let's see if we can get the story together," I say as we pass a particularly gruesome scene of a fake séance gone wrong, "A group hoping to summon a demon for nefarious sexual purposes, likely a book club that reads too much smut, actually summoned one, and instead of wanting to fuck them, he murdered them."

Michael shrugs, then wraps his arms around my waist, pulling me toward him so we can look at ourselves embracing in the mirror. "But not before he covered the walls with mirrors so he could watch himself do it. Joke's on them, it was sexual for him." He kisses my neck and we peer at ourselves in the mirror, wrapped in a casual embrace as if we've been together forever.

"We're cute together," I say, admiring our reflection. "Even all distorted." I sway back and forth to watch our reflection shift and morph.

"I think so, too," he replies, kissing my neck again before leading me further into the house.

We reach a heavy oak door at the end of a particularly dark corridor. A sign reading "The Forgotten Parlor" hangs crookedly from a rusty nail.

"This can't be safe. Maybe I should have read that waiver a little closer before signing it. I'm not sure if I'm up-to-date on my tetanus shots."

Michael grimaces. "Don't worry, I will protect you from the evil tetanus-causing bacterium."

He makes a real show of moving me out of the way so he can open the door for me, effectively saving me from the evil bacterium that may be on that doorknob. "After you," he says with a flourish.

I giggle and move in front of him, pausing to brush my body against his as he holds the door open for me. "Why, thank you." He moans slightly as I run my hand up his leg and down his outstretched arm before I step into what might be the most atmospheric room yet. It's designed like a Victorian parlor frozen in time—velvet furniture covered in dusty sheets, cobwebs hanging from a chandelier, and a player piano in the corner that starts a tinny melody as we enter. The wallpaper is faded, and sepia photographs of stern-faced strangers watch us from ornate frames.

"This is incredible," I whisper, genuinely impressed by the attention to detail. "It looks much more put together than the other rooms."

Michael moves closer to me, his presence solid and reassuring in the manufactured gloom. "The set designer runs the local community theater. They say he went a little overboard on this room."

A hidden fog machine releases a low-lying mist that curls around our ankles. Combined with the strategic lighting, it creates the illusion that we're walking through a dreamscape rather than a crumbling historic building.

"This place really should be better preserved. These books alone hold so much history," I say, running my finger along a bookshelf filled with leather-bound volumes—not daring to touch the actual books.

"Working to preserve this building and open it up all year was one part of the revitalization efforts everyone agreed on," Michael replies, as he steps closer.

"That's a shame. Maybe I can help."

"Thinking about actually taking Marcus up on investing?"

"What else am I going to do with all my money? I've been running from this place, this town, for so long. Trying to forget it. But maybe it's time to forgive it. Time to heal myself and heal the town," I say, surprising myself with my boldness.

"You know, I must say, this look on your face, this look of resolve and determination, is incredibly hot," he says, moving behind me and placing his hand on my shoulder.

A grandfather clock in the corner begins to chime, making me jump again. This time, when I startle backward, I bump directly into Michael's arms. His hands wrap around my waist, steadying me, as he breathes me in.

We stand like that for a moment that stretches into eternity, my back against his chest, his breath stirring the hair near my ear. The haunted house sound effects fade to white noise as my focus narrows to the points where his body touches mine. I press backward, causing him to grind onto me. He's now hard against my back.

I turn to face him and have to tilt my head up to meet his eyes. In the amber glow of the faux gas lamps, his expression is both tender and intense. I stand on my tiptoes and kiss him. He pulls me closer, and I want to fuck him right here, surrounded by fake cobwebs and motion-activated ghosts.

"Do you think they have cameras in here?" I ask.

"Why, Celeste, planning on doing something untoward with me?" he asks with a smirk. I pull back from him and consider getting on my knees in front of him, when a recorded scream pierces the moment, followed by the mechanical laughter of a hidden speaker. We both startle, then dissolve into laughter of our own.

"Perfect timing," Michael says wryly.

"Haunted cockblocking," I reply without thinking, then immediately flush at my own candor.

Instead of being embarrassed, Michael's eyes darken slightly. "Is that what was happening?"

"Well, I was seconds away from sucking your dick, cameras be damned," I say with a shrug.

The air between us grows charged again, and Michael pulls me back into a kiss. A group of giggling teenagers bursts through the door behind us, breaking the spell and pulling us apart again. One of them apologizes as they push past, their excitement over the haunted parlor radiating in their voices.

Michael and I share a look—half amused, half disappointed at the interruption. His hand finds mine in the dimness, fingers intertwining as if it's the most natural thing in the world.

"In that case. Let's get out of here," he says, tugging me gently toward the next door.

36

The night air hits my face like a welcome reprieve as we emerge from the mansion, both of us laughing at how the final scare (a teenager with a chainsaw) sent me practically climbing onto Michael's back. My heart's still racing, though now I can't tell if it's from the residual fear or the way Michael's body has felt against mine as we've clung to each other.

"Well," I say, trying to slow my breathing, "I think I fulfilled my quota of screaming for the year."

Michael's laugh is rich in the quiet street. "You know, for someone who claims to hate horror, you seemed to be enjoying yourself by the end."

"The company helped," I admit, then quickly add, "Plus, nothing in there was as terrifying as things I've seen in real life."

"You mean finding Richard?" Michael asks, his tone shifting slightly.

I nod.

"Do you want to talk about it, Celeste?" he asks, placing his hand gently on the small of my back.

Do I? I squeeze my eyes tight, reflecting on the sight of Richard's body, and shake my head, avoiding his gaze.

"Okay, we don't have to talk about it." He pauses for a moment, his face reflecting the multiple options of what to say next running through his head. He glances at his watch. "It's barely nine. Too early to call it a night." He pulls slightly at the collar of his shirt."Would you like to continue our evening with something less…chainsaw-oriented?" He adjusts his glasses. "At my place, perhaps?"

"I'd like that."

"It's just three blocks this way," he says, pointing in the direction opposite my house.

"Great," I say and begin to walk in the direction he is pointing.

He grabs my hand to walk with me, and the gesture is so sweet. He grabbed my hand a lot in the mansion, but I thought it was to guide me through it. It seems Michael just likes to touch me. I don't know if I've ever been with a guy who likes to hold hands.

Main Street is quiet tonight; most of the shops are closed except for the bar at the far end, where a few locals linger. Michael lives in the renovated Hartman Building—once a department store from the 1920s, now converted into upscale apartments. The brick exterior is softly lit by antique-style street lamps, giving it a timeless quality against the Minnesota night sky.

"Home sweet home," Michael says as he holds the main door open for me. The lobby has maintained its vintage charm with marble floors and brass fixtures, but modern security and lighting have been seamlessly integrated.

We take the elevator to the second floor, and Michael fidgets slightly with his keys as we approach his door. "Fair warning," he says with a self-deprecating smile, "I live alone and write for a living, so adjust your expectations accordingly."

But when he swings the door open, I'm immediately struck by how wrong his modest disclaimer was. The apartment is stunning with exposed brick walls, high ceilings with original wooden beams, and windows that span nearly the entire back wall, offering a view of the town square below. It's immaculately tidy, yet packed with a multitude of knick-knacks, colors, and textures. *So many pillows.* The lighting is low and ambient, coming from strategically placed floor lamps and a few dim lights on side tables.

"You just happened to have mood lighting ready to go?" I tease as I step inside, slipping off my jacket and shoes.

Michael takes my jacket. "Smart home system," he explains, hanging both our coats on a sleek rack by the door and removing his own shoes. "It's programmed to my schedule. When I come home after eight, it assumes I want evening ambiance."

"Fancy," I say, taking in the expansive open-concept space.

"Well, you know, after I turned thirty-five, as a man, I had a few options of things to become obsessed with, and since World War II and crypto are very much not my vibe, smart home systems were where I landed."

I giggle at the joke and appreciate how self-aware Michael tends to be.

"Make yourself at home, I'll get us some wine," Michael says, walking toward the kitchen. The living room flows seamlessly into a gourmet kitchen that, despite its gleaming counters, looks like it's used every day. Perfectly placed spices and utensils decorate the space. He's made every single item in the room look like it's an art piece rather than a functional item.

At the center of the living space sits a plush velvet sofa in deep navy, flanked by mid-century modern armchairs and a glass coffee table stacked with books and literary journals. Built-in bookshelves cover an entire wall, filled with what must be thousands of volumes arranged alphabetically by author.

But what truly captures my attention are the paintings—abstract pieces and moody landscapes hung throughout the space, all by artists whose work I don't recognize but whose talent is unmistakable. One particularly striking painting above the sofa depicts a forest scene at twilight, the trees rendered in deep blues and purples that somehow convey both menace and beauty.

"These are incredible," I say, moving closer to examine the forest painting.

Michael returns from the kitchen with two glasses of red wine. "That's one of Ryan's, actually."

I take a sip of wine—rich and complex, "Oh, really?"

"He and I have very similar tastes in beauty," he says quietly, his eyes holding mine over the rim of his glass.

Heat rushes to my face, and I turn to continue exploring his apartment to hide my reaction. The bookshelves reveal a Michael I'm still getting to know—fiction arranged alongside philosophy, science, and history. First editions sit next to well-worn paperbacks. I spot his own novels, their spines barely cracked as if he can't bear to read his own published work. He says he lives modestly, but I know from these books that he was being modest in that assessment of himself. Michael is obviously well off.

What strikes me most is how the space reflects success without ostentation. Nothing is showy, but everything is of quality—from the hand-knotted rug beneath my feet to the subtly expensive furnishings. Writing has clearly been good to Michael, more so than he's ever let on.

"Your place is beautiful," I say finally, turning back to him. "And not at all what I expected."

"What did you expect?" His smile is playful as he gestures to the sofa.

I sink into the velvet cushions. Michael sits beside me, placing his hand on my leg.

"Um, more…bachelory, I guess," I say, unsure how to indicate what I'm thinking. "When you said to set my expectations accordingly…I thought you meant I'd be walking into pizza boxes and mattresses on the floor."

"Ha, no. I just assumed it wouldn't line up with what you're used to."

"What do you mean?"

"Well, um…I just assumed your place in California was luxurious, given your…you know." He's obviously referencing my wealth. "And I'm assuming you've seen James's place." He clears his throat and adjusts his glasses before putting his hands on his own knees, obviously feeling some sort of way about accidentally bringing up James's home.

"I haven't seen James's place yet...we haven't spent much time together."

"Yeah, that checks out."

I cock my head at him. "What do you mean?"

"Oh, um, James is just a busy guy, is all."

We both sit, quietly waiting for the other to break the awkwardness that has fallen over us, given we've mentioned both the other guys I'm fucking in the last five minutes. *God, I really should read a book about how to navigate this stuff.*

I decide to change the subject by revealing something about myself I wouldn't reveal to anyone else. "To be honest...I am the pizza boxes and the mattress on the floor kind of person. Maybe I was more hoping that you'd live that way so I could feel less..." I trail off, wanting to say "like a pathetic fucking failure," but don't.

"Less perfect?" Michael asks, reaching for me, and I just laugh at the devotion of this guy. "If it makes you feel better, I can't take full credit for this place," he says, setting his wine on a coaster. "My ex-wife did some of the decorating."

"Ah, that explains all the pillows."

"Nope, the pillows were all me," he laughs. I recall the nest he made for us by the fireplace and giggle at his obvious affinity for soft things.

"So, um, how long have you been divorced?"

"She left a few years ago. She had moved here to open a clinic, but...she hated it here. Moved to Minneapolis and didn't take me with her."

"I'm sorry, Michael," I say, not knowing what else to say.

"Don't be. We didn't really work. It hurt at the time, but now, I realize it was really the best for both of us. We wanted different things." He pauses for a minute, then states. "Plus, if I had moved back to Minneapolis with her, I never would have met you—the woman who's held a piece of my heart for a long, long time."

The admission hangs in the air between us. Michael's expression softens, and he shifts slightly closer.

"You make it sound like you're in love with me," I say, feeling simultaneously bold and vulnerable.

"Celeste." The way he says my name makes my skin tingle. "I know that right now, I'm in love with the idea of you. But the real you is proving to be even more perfect than the idea."

I take another sip of wine, my insecurities pushing me to numb my feelings with alcohol. "Well, just wait, you'll find out I'm not all that great soon enough."

He reaches out, his hand taking my hand in both of his. "The fact that you think that saddens me. You're amazing, Celeste."

"How do you know I'm so amazing?" I ask, my voice barely above a whisper.

His eyes meet mine. "I might have downplayed exactly how much I've kept up with your career. To say I developed a parasocial relationship with you is a bit of an understatement. And, in real life, you're even more beautiful. And you're sweet, and funny, and have this self-deprecation that you wouldn't expect a woman like you to have. You're perfect, Celeste."

A shiver of anticipation runs down my spine. Not just from the compliment, but from the sincerity behind it.

"I'm definitely not perfect," I manage to say, though my voice sounds breathless even to my own ears. The voice of my mother raging in my head, telling me all the things I suck at.

"Perfect for me," he murmurs, his focus entirely on me, turning my wrist so our palms meet.

A perfect fucking failure. A slob. A slut. A weakling.

"Tell that to my mother," I say, laughing into my wine and surprising myself.

Michael's fingers intertwine with mine. "Your mother was wrong."

"But, I'm not that Celeste anymore, the one you're describing. I'm just a nobody living out of boxes. I don't even have any food in her fridge. I just prepaid a whole month's worth of meals at Sarah's because it's the only food I eat—I can't even take care of myself. I don't have a job. I don't have a hobby. I'm nothing."

"Celeste, you'll always be that Celeste. You're her, whether you are accomplishing anything or not."

My heart pounds so loudly I'm certain he can hear it. "Why are you so nice to me?"

"Because you deserve it. You deserve the world, Celeste." His free hand reaches up to tuck a strand of hair behind my ear, his touch feather-light. "You don't have to earn rest. You deserve love even when you're feeling weak. You don't have to earn love," he says, leaning closer until I can feel his breath on my cheek.

"How? How do you...how do you know to say these things? You always seem to know exactly what to say."

"My dad was a lot like your mom. I've been to enough therapy to recognize someone raised by a narcissist."

Narcissist? *Was my mother a narcissist?* The truth of the statement pierces through me like an arrow.

37

I don't want to think about it.

My hands rise to cup Michael's face. I trace the sharp angles of his cheekbones and look into those beautiful amber eyes. He looks back at me, confusion and concern etching across his face. I smile—hoping to ease his worry.

Show him you're fine, Celeste.

I kiss him with a gentleness that takes a significant amount of restraint. He rubs my shoulders.

He breaks away slightly. His breath dances across my lips when he says, "Celeste, we don't—" I kiss him again.

I stroke the area behind his jaw with my thumb and soften my gaze. *I am not sad, look. I'm happy.*

He doesn't buy it. "Celeste, are you okay? We can talk more."

"Michael, please. I don't want to talk about it."

I kiss him again. He returns the kiss tentatively. I deepen the kiss. Michael's hands slide from my shoulders down to my waist, tentative yet purposeful. He pulls me closer.

With my mouth locked on his, he asks through pressed lips, "Are you sure?"

"Yes, Michael. I promise. I'm okay. I was just having a little moment."

He wraps his arms around me and squeezes me tightly. His kiss no longer hesitates. As I melt into him, the noise in my head quiets. The voice of my mother: gone. The sight of Richard's corpse: gone. It's just me and Michael.

I am lovable. I am.

I want to reduce the space between us. I want to meld my body with him. Engulf him. Consume him. Love him until I am whole.

I grope at the edges of his shirt, ready to disrobe the pair of us. He pulls away from me to look into my eyes. His eyes are dark in this light, searching me.

"I can't believe I get to kiss you," he confesses. He takes my hand and stands, gently pulling me up from the sofa. "Come with me?"

I nod, allowing him to lead me to his bedroom. It's minimalist and calm with a large bed draped in soft-looking charcoal linens. But I pause at the threshold, his hand warm in mine. *Is this okay? I feel guilty. Is it okay for me to be with Michael when he feels so strongly for me, and I'm just jumping from one dick to the next whenever I get a little sad? I really, really like Michael. Is this fair to him?*

"Is something wrong?" he asks, ever attentive to my reactions.

"No, I'm just admiring your room," I say, lying.

His free hand comes up to trace my jawline with feather-light touches.

"Big fan of millennial grey, are you?" he asks with a quip.

"Women of my age are drawn to it," I tease, but my voice catches as his fingers trail down my neck to my collarbone.

Is this fair to him? Is this fair to Ryan? James?

"You're thinking about Ryan and James, aren't you?"

I look at him, surprised. "How do you read me so well?"

"I notice details," he murmurs. " Like how your pulse jumps when I touch you here." His thumb grazes the hollow of my throat, and sure enough, my heart races in response. "Or how you bite your lip when you're trying not to smile." He points at my mouth.

I hadn't realized I was doing exactly that until he pointed it out. "What else do you notice?" I challenge.

Instead of answering with words, Michael draws me into his bedroom. The space is minimal yet intimate—a large bed with a simple wooden frame, nightstands adorned with well-loved books, and a single painting above the headboard depicting a misty landscape at dawn. The light is softer here, coming from a lamp with a paper shade that casts a warm glow across the room.

Standing beside his bed, Michael lifts my hand to the side of his face, nuzzling into it and kissing my palm—a gesture that sends shivers through me. "I notice everything about you, Celeste. How you deflect compliments. How your eyes light up when you talk about your company. How you pretend to be tougher than you are. How you hide your pain with a smile."

How I run from feelings with sex.

His words strip me bare more effectively than hands could, leaving me feeling exposed in ways that have nothing to do with clothing. "I… I feel bad. Like I'm taking advantage of you. Like it's not fair to you that you have such strong feelings for me, yet I'm sleeping with Ryan and James."

"Celeste, I don't need to possess you," he says firmly. "I just need to be with you."

"But—" I begin to argue, but he places a kiss against my neck that cuts me off.

"Are you sure you want to be with me, Celeste?" he breathes against my neck, his own feelings of inadequacy revealing themselves now.

I pull back just enough to look at him, taking in his disheveled hair and the vulnerability in his expression. "Yes, I do, Michael," I assure him.

Something flickers in his eyes—relief, desire, and something deeper I can't quite name. "That's all I need from you, Celeste. I just want to be with you, and I want you to want to be with me when you are."

He removes his glasses and kisses me again. This time it's with renewed purpose. His hands slide up the hem of my sweater, warm against the skin of my lower back as he pulls it over my head. I respond by tugging at the edge of his sweater, our movements becoming more urgent, yet still measured.

I trace the lines of Michael's neck with my fingertips as his sweater falls to the floor, revealing smooth skin and lean muscle.

Michael runs his fingers through my hair, his touch reverent as he watches the strands slip through his fingers. "I still can't believe I get to do this," he admits. "Touch you. Taste you."

Our jeans join our sweaters on the floor.

"You're so beautiful," he says, his gaze traveling over me without hurry or presumption.

I should feel self-conscious, but there's something in his expression that banishes insecurity. Instead, I feel powerful, desired, alive.

"So are you," I tell him, allowing my hands to roam across his chest, learning the contours of him.

We move to the bed together. There's no rush now, just the slow build of desire as we trade languid kisses and explorative touches. His hand traces the curve of my hip, the dip of my waist, each contact sending sparks across my skin.

He's so slow with me. There's no rush in his touch. It's like he wants to savor me.

"I want you inside me," I whisper against his shoulder.

Michael's lips trail down my neck. His hands map the curves of my body. Each touch is deliberate and unhurried. I arch into him, craving more contact, but he takes his time, savoring every inch of exposed skin.

"Michael, please," I plead.

He chuckles against my collarbone. The vibration tickles and sends a warmth through my body. "Patience, sweetheart. I want to memorize every part of you."

I remove my bra. His eyes widen at the sight. His mouth descends to my breast, tongue flicking over my nipples until I'm writhing beneath him. The ache between my thighs grows more insistent with each measured caress.

I remove my panties. His fingers trail over my skin, softly brushing across my thighs, circling my belly button, approaching my pussy but never quite getting there.

Michael seems content to worship me with agonizing slowness, stoking the fire without giving me the friction I desperately need. I tug at his underwear, pulling them down. He kicks them off and resumes his exploration of my body, pressing his marvelous cock against my leg.

Unable to bear his leisurely pace any longer, I hook my leg over his hip and flip us so I'm straddling Michael. He looks up at me with a mix of surprise and delight, his hands coming to rest on my thighs.

"I need you now," I tell him, my voice husky with desire. "I can't wait any longer."

Understanding flashes in his eyes, followed by a wicked grin. "Then take what you need, Celeste."

Emboldened by his words, I reach between us to guide him inside me. We both gasp at the sensation as I sink onto him, taking him fully. For a moment, I'm overwhelmed by the intensity of our connection, physically and emotionally.

Then instinct takes over, and I start to move, rocking my hips in a steady rhythm. Michael's hands grip my waist, urging me on as he thrusts up to meet me.

I marvel at the way our bodies fit together. The way he reaches that spot deep within me. That perfect spot that sends a jolt through my whole body—making me gasp with each thrust.

He explores my body, igniting every nerve ending until I'm lost to sensation. His hands roam my back, my hips, my breasts. He worships me with a reverence that makes me buck faster and harder. The rhythmic creak of the bed frame, the pounding of the headboard, spurs me.

I lean down and suck his lower lip into a kiss, pouring all my desire, all my need into the connection. He responds with equal fervor, his tongue tangling with mine. His fingers dig into my hips, helping me to move faster, as he guides me along his length.

I oblige, riding him with abandon, chasing the pleasure that coils tighter with each thrust. The coil inside me winds tighter and tighter, my body straining towards the inevitable release.

"Celeste," Michael gasps, his voice strained with the effort of holding back. "I'm close…"

I can feel myself nearing the edge, my body tightening around him as the pressure builds to an exquisite breaking point. "Me, too," I manage, my words dissolving into a moan as he thrusts up hard, hitting that perfect spot inside me.

"Condom…we forgot a condom," Michael says into my breasts. I can feel his thighs tightening under me, as if he's trying to stop himself from coming.

"I don't care. I'm on the pill," I say, riding him harder, so close to coming undone and struck by my sheer irresponsibility. "Michael," I gasp, my voice strained with the effort of holding back. "I'm so close…please don't pull out. Don't leave me." The tightening of his legs creates the perfect leverage.

"Oh, Celeste, I'd stay inside you forever if I could," he says, leaning backward and closing his eyes.

His words are my undoing. A few more deep strokes, and I'm shattering, waves of ecstasy crashing over me as I clench around him. Through the haze of my own release, I feel Michael stiffen beneath me as he follows me over the edge with a moan. His hips jerk as we ride out our orgasms together.

Boneless and sated, I collapse onto his chest. For a long moment, we cling to each other, trembling and spent, chests heaving in unison.

Michael brushes damp strands of hair from my face with a tenderness that makes my heart clench.

"That was…" he begins, seeming at a loss for words.

"Incredible," I finish for him, my voice soft and sated.

A slow, satisfied smile spreads across his face. "You're incredible," he breathes, kissing my shoulder softly, and pulling me closer..

I lift my head to meet his gaze, seeing my own wonderment reflected back at me. As I look into his beautiful amber eyes, I have a strong desire to tell him I love him. But logic wins out.

We trade languid kisses as our heart rates gradually slow, basking in the afterglow of our lovemaking. Michael strokes my arm and back in a soothing pattern that threatens to put me to sleep. His touch is now comforting rather than igniting.

Eventually, I reluctantly disentangle myself from him and roll to the side, immediately missing his warmth. But Michael follows, gathering me into his arms so that my back is pressed to his chest.

"Please, let me hug you just a bit longer," he says, squeezing me tightly.

"Okay," I sigh out, because it's what I wanted, too. I'm so accustomed to not getting hugs after sex that I didn't even realize I wanted them. Tears well in my eyes as I feel a deep connection to him, hoping that I can lie like this with him forever.

For a moment, I consider breaking things off with Ryan and James, but I try not to think about them and just relish this moment. I turn to allow Michael to fully embrace me, burying my face in his chest and feeling safer than I ever have.

38

For long moments, we lie together without speaking. My head rests on his chest, and I listen to his heartbeat, gradually slowing. His arm is wrapped around my neck as he pets me and kisses the top of my head.

Michael's fingers shift to trace lazy circles on my bare shoulder. "Did I please you?" he asks, his voice gentle.

I nod against his chest, then realize he can't see me. "Yeah," I assure him, tilting my face up to his. "It was amazing."

"Yeah," he agrees. "It was."

Michael pulls the soft sheets over us, tucking them around my shoulders before drawing me closer again. There's something protective in the gesture that makes my throat tighten unexpectedly.

"What are you thinking?" he asks, brushing a strand of hair from my face when I look up to meet his eyes.

I consider deflecting with humor or changing the subject, but something about the way he looks at me is so raw and honest, I choose truth instead. "That I didn't expect to find this when I came back to Goose Grove. You. This. Any of it."

His smile is soft in the dim light. "I'm so happy you came back."

I settle against him, letting my body mold to his, savoring the warmth of his skin against mine.

I return my head to his chest and let it rise and fall with each breath. I smile to myself as his hand returns to my shoulder, tracing circles once again. *I feel so...happy. Why did I run from this kind of connection?*

"I've spent the last few years numbing my feelings with work. It's weird to start letting them back in again," I murmur.

Michael's hand pauses its lazy exploration of my skin. "I'm sure you've been feeling a lot of things. Good and bad."

"Yeah, I don't know if my obsession with this murder case is really about trying to clear my name, so much as it is another project to run from my feelings with, though," I say, reflecting on my actions since I've been here.

"What feelings are you running from?"

I trace a small circle on his chest, mimicking his strokes. "Processing my parents' death. Processing the loss of my company. And… processing my past with Ryan."

His arm tightens around me slightly. "I'm here if you need someone to, what's that phrase you coders use? Rubber duck?"

"Ha, you want me to just info dump my trauma on you so we can find the bug in my internal code?"

"Oh, so I did use the term correctly?"

I laugh and swallow, tracing the outline of his pecs. *Sure, why not?* "When my parents died, I…I tried to ignore it. I wouldn't think about it. I barely talked to them before they…so it was almost like they didn't die. Nothing had changed. Whenever I thought about it, all I could do was blame myself for not being here…for not…I felt so guilty about having avoided them that I just…That's why I didn't come to the funeral.

"Then one day, during a board meeting, someone said something that just…it sent me. I lost it. I fell to the ground crying. No one knew what to do. They'd obviously never seen me like that. I've always been so strong. I never cry. I never let my emotions break through. I hold them in.

"They all left, just left me there on the floor—losing my shit. All I wanted was a hug. But from whom? I had no one. No one to hug me. I was so embarrassed, so…ashamed.

"A company had been trying to get me to sell to them for years, and I'd always said no. When I finally stopped crying, I pulled out my phone and emailed them. Still on the floor. Told them I'd sell.

"Then I went home, put all my shit in boxes, and…that's when I came back to Goose Groove. I haven't stepped back in that office. I haven't looked at the emails from my team. I…" I trail off, letting the tears fall to his chest.

Michael takes the moment to console me, "Celeste, you lost both of your parents. Regardless of what your relationship with them was, that's hard. Really hard. You have every right to be sad about that."

"It's too late now. The deal's done, I can't get my company back. I'm such a fucking idiot. I threw it all away."

He pulls me in tighter. "No, Celeste, you're not. You're human and you're in pain."

I cry into his chest softly, "God, this is so not attractive, a woman who cries after sex."

"I'm just going to assume that my semen has magical defense-penetrating capabilities. Good thing you're on the pill, otherwise those eggs wouldn't stand a chance."

I laugh and kiss his cheek, "Thanks, Michael. This was…nice to talk about."

He brushes the hair from my face, slightly sticky from the tears and sweat. "And Ryan? Do you want to talk about that?" Michael asks.

I bite my lip and continue to trace his chest. "We…I don't know. We are both masters of pretending everything is fine when it's not. Honestly, I think I'm still hurt he ghosted me for so long. I'm sorry, I shouldn't talk about him with you…"

"You can talk about him with me. He's important to you."

"He is. It's weird. It's almost like he and Mrs. Heart are the only family I have, even though they're not really family. It's hard to trust him right now, after everything, though. I don't know how to talk to him about what happened between us."

"I think you're right not to trust him fully," he says. There's something in his tone—a subtle shift from contentment to something more serious—that makes me lift my head to look at him. His expression has changed, a shadow passing over features that moments ago were relaxed and open.

"Why do you say that?" I ask, suddenly alert despite the afterglow of orgasm still relaxing me.

Michael takes a deep breath, his chest expanding beneath my hand. "I don't want to ruin this moment."

"Don't do that. You obviously have something you want to tell me," I prompt, propping myself up on one elbow to better see his face.

He mirrors my position, our bodies still close but now facing each other on the pillow. The sheet pools around our waists, and in any other circumstance, I'd be distracted by how fucking hot he looks. Instead, I'm focused on the troubled look in his eyes.

"There's something I should tell you," he says finally. "About him. About Ryan."

The sudden change in tone feels jarring, like a splash of cold water.

"What about him?" I ask, confusion creeping into my voice.

Michael reaches out to brush a strand of hair from my face, his touch gentler than his serious expression would suggest. The same thing Ryan always does. "I care about you, Celeste. That's why I need to share this with you now, before..." He pauses. "Before things get even more complicated. I was going to tell you earlier, at the cafe, but then Ryan came in and..."

A knot forms in my stomach. "You're scaring me a little."

He takes a deep breath. "Celeste, I worry Ryan might have killed Richard." The words hang in the air between us, impossible and heavy.

"That's—that's not possible," I stammer, sitting up fully now, pulling the sheet around me. "Ryan wouldn't hurt anyone."

Michael sits up, too, his expression somber. "People change in twenty years, Celeste. He might not be the Ryan you remember anymore."

My heart pounds in my ears. "Why are you saying this?"

"The morning of Richard's murder...I saw Richard and Ryan arguing in the park. Ryan was screaming at him. I saw Ryan punch Richard."

"That doesn't prove anything," I say, though my voice lacks conviction.

"That's true. It doesn't."

My mind races, trying to consolidate the image I have of Ryan—the boy who was my best friend, the man who has always been there for me…except when he wasn't.

"But, why would he do that? Why did he punch Richard?" I ask, suspicion creeping in.

Michael has the grace to look uncomfortable. "I didn't hear everything they said, but I did hear Ryan say your name. That's what initially drew my attention."

"So, what are you saying? That Ryan killed him for me or something? That doesn't make any sense." A flare of anger cuts through my confusion.

"That's not what I'm saying," Michael says quickly.

"This was weeks ago. Why are you just now telling me?"

"I didn't know how to tell you."

I wrap the sheet tighter around myself, suddenly feeling exposed in more ways than one. "And you thought post-sex was the right moment? Right after you got me to open up to you?"

How could he do this to me?

He runs a hand through his disheveled hair. "I thought…I couldn't keep something this important from you any longer. You deserved to know."

I stare at a misty landscape painting above Michael's bed, trying to gather my thoughts. I recognize it now as another of Ryan's. Now that I look at it, it conveys a sadness…an anger…that I didn't recognize before. It doesn't match the Ryan I know. *Do I actually know him?*

I shake my head. "No…no, Ryan couldn't kill someone. I don't believe it."

Michael's expression grows more grave. "Years ago, Richard represented Ryan's father in some kind of legal dispute over his orchard. Richard might have deliberately tanked the case, causing Ryan's father to lose everything. His father never recovered from it."

Is this why Mr. O'Connor works at the grocery store now? Is this why he doesn't have the orchard anymore?

"You've been investigating Ryan…without me? I thought…I thought we were looking into this together. I thought we were a team…"

"Investigation is a strong word. It's a rumor I've known about for a while."

"Even…even if it's true…it doesn't make Ryan a murderer," I insist, though doubt has begun to creep in around the edges of my certainty.

"No, it doesn't," Michael agrees.

I reflect on Ryan's behavior since I've been back. *Had there been signs I missed because I was too focused on rekindling our friendship?* He got to me so quickly in the garden. He wouldn't let me talk about what I saw. I assumed he wouldn't let me text with James after I spoke with the cops because he wanted to console me. Or because he was horny or jealous. *But was it because he didn't want me thinking about the murder? Didn't want me suspecting him?*

"I'll ask him about it," I say, my voice cracking. "Talk to him face to face."

Michael's hand finds mine on top of the sheets. "That might not be wise, Celeste. If he is involved in Richard's death…"

"He wouldn't hurt me," I say with conviction, though a small voice in my head whispers: But would you have believed he could hurt Richard before tonight?

Michael pleads. "Let the police handle this. I already brought this to them."

The mention of the police makes this suddenly, terrifyingly real. "You went to the police with this? Before talking to me?"

"I had to," he says, his voice steady despite my rising anger.

Part of me wants to lash out, to accuse Michael of betrayal or overstepping. But another part—the part that remembers Richard's body—knows he might be right to be concerned.

"Ryan has been like family to me," I say quietly.

Michael's eyes soften with compassion. "I know. And I'm not saying he's guilty. I'm just saying it's a possibility."

I nod slowly, my mind replaying interactions with Ryan since my return. The way he tenses up whenever Richard's name is mentioned. *Does he actually do that? Am I…am I misremembering?*

I turn to Michael, my voice growing stern. "If you were so concerned about my safety, why have you just let me spend the last few weeks with him? Why are you suddenly trying to protect me from him?"

"Celeste, I've been grappling with how to tell you. I'm sorry. But after tonight…I feel…I feel like I couldn't keep it from you anymore."

Does he actually want to possess me? Is he lying about not caring that I'm also with Ryan and James? Is this a devious way to try to keep me all to himself?

I look at him, my face contorting as anger rages through me.

I can't believe I almost told him I loved him. I'm so stupid. All men are the same. They don't care about me. No one does. They just want to control me.

You're overreacting, Celeste. Calm down. Don't cry. Fucking stop it.

"I need time to process this," I say finally.

"Of course." Michael reaches for a t-shirt from his dresser and hands it to me—a peace offering of sorts. "You can stay here tonight, if you want. Or I can walk you home. Whatever you need."

I ignore the shirt and stand, gathering my own clothing. As I pull my shirt over my head, I catch a glimpse of us in the mirror across the room. Just a few hours ago, this image would have made me smile. Now it's complicated by shadows of doubt and betrayal.

"I'm going home," I decide. "I need space to think about all this."

Disappointment flickers across Michael's face, but he nods. "I understand. I'll walk you." He reaches for the nightstand, his hand slapping against the surface as he searches for his glasses.

"No. It's not far. I can walk myself."

"Celeste, it's late, I really should—"

"I said 'no.' I don't need your help," I say, voice raised.

He slumps in the bed, hair tousled, chest bare, and looks wounded. "Okay," he says, looking down at the sheets and adjusting his glasses.

As I dress in silence, the intimacy we shared earlier feels both recent and distant, like a dream that was interrupted by harsh reality. I catch Michael watching me with a mixture of concern and affection that makes my heart twist painfully in my chest.

When I begin to leave, he leaps from the bed and reaches for my hand. After a moment's hesitation, I let him take it. Our fingers intertwine, a physical connection that doesn't bridge the emotional distance that's opened between us.

"I'm sorry," he says quietly. "I didn't want to hurt you."

"I know." And I do know, which makes this all the more difficult. I give him a quick, tight smile and storm out. Leaving him standing there naked.

Who is Ryan really? Who is Michael, for that matter? And who am I in relation to both of them?

39

I'm still processing my feelings about the conversation I had with Michael a few days ago. I'm also grappling with my feelings about him. I haven't been avoiding his texts, exactly, but I've been replying with only single-word responses.

I recognize I'm being a bit immature and probably cruel, and I'm trying to work through it. He got to me, though, and I'm now afraid to talk to Ryan, too. So, I've been avoiding him, as well.

Luckily for me, James messaged me about going out to dinner. So, I still have one dick I can ride while I try to ignore my feelings.

It's been over a week since James and I hooked up after the Gala, and if it weren't for the random texts checking in on me every day or so, I would have thought he was ghosting me. I know he's a busy guy and has a lot going on—been there—but I'm not sure how I feel about being on the receiving end of someone's divided attention. *Hypocrite? Yes!*

I resolve to see how tonight goes before making any major decisions about whether I want to continue our relationship. *He is so smoking hot. And fuck, that was a good fuck.*

James and I enter Waddles and Wades, which, despite the silly name, is Goose Grove's most elegant restaurant. I've never been here before, it having been erected a few years ago during the start of Goose Grove's gentrification. I'm immediately taken by the ambiance.

It's fancy. Super fancy. Well, maybe the approximation of fancy. It seems like someone Googled "upscale restaurant" and threw the entire Pinterest board at it. It's quite ostentatious. It has more chandeliers than the lighting section of the Menards two towns over.

I look at James, and I must be making a judgmental face because he replies, "Yeah, it's a bit much, but the food is quite good."

"Do you eat here often?" I ask.

"Once. Brought a client here. I'm normally more of a cooks-at-home kind of guy. I'll make you an amazing breakfast tomorrow," he says, flashing a confident grin.

"Oh, we'll be having breakfast together?" I ask. I'm excited about the unabashed flirting that James and I are sure to engage in. He's been all hands and compliments since he picked me up. He's been flirty since I met him, but he's ramping it up hard tonight.

He responds, "Definitely," just as the host returns to his podium.

"Two for Montgomery," James says.

"I know who you are, James," the host responds with a scoff and a somewhat suggestive look.

James chuckles, and his smile falters slightly—as if this host has disarmed him. The host is incredibly handsome, his black hair slicked back neatly.

"Never thought I'd see you bringing a woman here," the host replies somewhat curtly, emphasizing the word woman, with a not-so-thinly veiled tone of jealousy.

James doesn't respond. Speechless. Something I didn't think was possible. However, he's doing his best to maintain his mask of self-assurance. "Our table?" he asks with a hint of annoyance.

"Yes, right this way," the host says and walks away.

James grins and offers me his arm. I take it with a smile, delighting in his chivalrous gesture, and we follow the host.

"This lighting is doing you all the favors, Celeste. You look gorgeous tonight," he says as we weave through the restaurant.

I look at him, and the light reflects softly off his golden brown locks.

"Honestly, same," I agree, "I suspect you already know that, though." My teasing earns me a chuckle from James and a repressed scoff from the host.

The host guides us through a door to a covered outdoor patio overlooking the lake. "Best seat in the house," he says. It's a corner booth, angled just right to see the water. There's no one else out here on the patio.

As we settle into the plush upholstered booth, the host says, "Enjoy," with absolutely no enthusiasm.

"I thought you said you don't come here often," I say, nodding toward the exiting host who obviously knows James.

"Oh, um, Jason and I are…um…acquaintances. I didn't know he worked here," he responds.

"Acquaintances?" I ask probingly, knowing there is more to it.

"We, um…saw each other. Briefly, a few months ago. Is that…is that a problem?" The confidence in James that is usually ever-present is now replaced with trepidation and fear. He's afraid of my reaction. I know some women have a problem with men being bisexual, but I am not such a woman.

"Is what a problem? That you've had past sexual partners or that at least one of them was a man?" I ask, trying to exude as much nonchalance as possible.

He looks at me like I'm being dense, cocking his head to the side and making a "come on," face.

"No. Neither thing is a problem for me." I soften my gaze and try to convey my sincerity as best I can.

The weight on his shoulders visibly lightens. He leans forward, his eyes sparkling mischievously as his confidence returns. "Well, that's good, because I had a whole thing planned for the night."

I smooth the napkin in my lap. "Oh, yeah? Blocked off your calendar for me, did you?"

"As a matter of fact, I did. I have my emails and phone autoresponding that I will be unreachable until tomorrow afternoon."

"Oh, wow, I must be something special," I tease.

"Celeste, you have no idea. Since the other night, all I can think about is when I can next have that tight pussy wrapped around my cock. I'd do almost anything to feel that again."

I sputter and blush. Spurred by my flabbergast, he smirks and stretches forward, putting his hand on my knee. He locks eyes with me as his hand teases at the hem of my dress's skirt. My legs instinctively spread for him, as the warmth of his touch feels like it lights up my loins.

He grips my thigh and slides me closer to him. I'm startled, and absolutely love being manhandled like this. I look around nervously, double-checking that no one else can see us.

He places his thumb on my chin and tilts my face to his—which I'm learning is his signature move.

He waits a moment, studying my face, searching for signs of protest, before he closes the distance, capturing my lips in a devouring kiss. The world around us fades away as he wraps his hand around the nape of my neck and engulfs me.

He brings his body even closer to mine, his hand leaves my chin, wraps around my waist, and pulls me so that there is next to no distance between us.

As my breath heaves, the hand on my thigh creeps higher up my leg. I spread my legs further, my dress hiking up my thighs as I desperately want him to plunge his fingers in me. He pulls back to look at me. I whimper at his absence, and my breasts heave toward him, wanting him closer.

A smile quirks at the corner of his mouth, and his hand rests at the topmost part of my leg, under my skirt. "Are you already wet for me, baby?"

His hand is flat against the inside of my thigh, fingers just outside my panties. A wave of fear rushes over me as I glance around to see who can see. We're alone. No other patrons are on this patio area, and the door between us and the inside of the restaurant provides further seclusion. If someone were on the lake, though, they'd see James's hand fully under my skirt.

Bravery and lust overcome me. The thrill of being discovered accentuates my arousal. I breathe out, "Why don't you find out?" I spread my legs further, inviting him.

James, needing no further signal, launches himself to my mouth, kissing me with such fervor the air leaves my lungs. His fingers now trace the edge of my panties, teasing me, making the anticipation of his fingers plunging into me unbearable. My kiss on him deepens when he finally slips his fingers inside my panties, gently tracing the line of my part.

Just as his fingers hit my clit and I gasp in pleasure, the door to the patio opens. James slowly backs away from me, trying to appear nonchalant. I miss the heat of his body and the taste of his mouth. My body vibrates with lust, and I squeeze my legs together, grinding against my own anatomy.

A waitress approaches and asks for our order. James chuckles and runs a hand through his hair, composing himself. "A few more minutes, please," he replies, flashing a charming smile. "We seem to have gotten a bit distracted. However, I would like a scotch."

"And you, miss, would you like a drink?" the waitress asks.

"Could I have a glass of Riesling, please?" I respond.

"Of course. I'll be right back with your drinks," the waitress responds.

"Hopefully not right back," James whispers into my ear as his hand floats back up my leg. The door swings open again, and the host from earlier escorts a couple to the table directly across from us, in perfect eyeshot of us. The host cuts James a glare as if he chose this table very specifically to stop James from fingering me.

"Well, fuck, I guess we'll have to actually look at the menu now," James laughs. I rub my neck, trying to calm my nerves and my arousal. *Maybe I should go to the bathroom and take care of myself.*

"I suppose so," I sigh out in disappointment and squeeze my legs together. I imagine taking him to the bathroom and fucking him in there. I'm not sure if I can wait until after dinner. Something about this man sets every single nerve of my body on fire, and I cannot wait to have him sink his dick so deep in me that I scream out his name.

We open our menus, and I bite my lip. "So, um, I feel like I should say it, but I'm not sure how to weave it in. I'm omnisexual. Since you told me about you…I figured I should tell you."

"Thanks for telling me, Celeste. I kind of already knew that, though."

"What, how?"

"Wikipedia."

"Oh," I laugh. "I forgot about that."

"Must be nice."

"What, having a Wikipedia page?"

"No, everyone already knowing."

"You're not—"

"Out? Not really. I don't tell many people. I don't date much, so it doesn't really matter."

"Oh…"

I want to ask him more about it, but before I can, he returns his gaze to the menu and says, "The chef's special is to die for."

To die for…the phrase reminds me of the murder, and I deflate slightly.

"James…" I choke.

"Celeste, what's wrong?" he puts down his menu and fully focuses on me. He scoots close to me again and places his hand on my thigh—but there's no lust in the touch, only comfort.

"I…I was with Michael last night…" I stutter. "Oh, I shouldn't talk about…"

"It's okay, Celeste. Please, talk to me."

"He…he told me he saw Ryan punch Richard the day of the murder. He worries Ryan killed Richard. I…I don't know what to think." Tears fall from my eyes.

James appears surprised for a moment, but he composes himself. He does that chin thing again, but this time he wipes the tear from my face with his thumb. "Celeste, that is circumstantial evidence, which, I'm sure you are aware."

I sniff and nod.

He continues, "They won't be arresting Ryan over something like that. And if they do, don't worry, I'll take care of him just like I take care of you."

He searches my face and continues, "But the thought of Ryan going to jail isn't really what's bothering you, is it? Why are you so upset about this?"

"I…I don't know if I really know Ryan anymore. What if he is a murderer? Am I safe with him? And Michael? Is he lying to me? Is he just trying to get the competition out of the way? I've been avoiding both of their calls."

James sighs and takes a sip of his scotch. He looks in the distance across the lake contemplating for a moment.

"Listen, Celeste. I…I can't say much, but…I don't think for even one second that it was Ryan who killed Richard. What I can say is, if Ryan were going to kill Richard…he would have done it a long, long time ago." *What does he mean? Does he know something about Richard's murder that he's not telling me?*

I furrow my brow and look at him. *What does he know?*

He carefully chooses his words, "And…I know Michael really well. He…can be anxious."

"He said Ryan was yelling about me, then he punched him…what if…what if Ryan killed him for me? But…why? Why would he do that? That doesn't make any sense."

"Would you like me to talk to Ryan for you?"

"What?! Why would you do that?"

"To find out what happened. Find out why he punched Richard."

"Would…would that be weird?"

"Weird for who?"

Ryan mostly. "No…no, um…I will talk to him."

"Are you sure? Do you feel safe speaking with him?"

"Yes, I don't think Ryan will hurt me."

"Okay," he says, kissing the last tear from my cheek. "If you want me to talk to him with you, just let me know."

The waitress arrives and requests our order again. It's probably obvious that I've been crying. James lightens the mood with a playful comment about the menu, drawing a laugh from the waitress and me, easing the tension that had settled over the table.

I still haven't looked at the menu, but when James orders the chef's special, I order it too. It sounds good, and if there's something else on the menu I might have enjoyed more, it doesn't really matter.

When the waitress finally leaves, I choke out, "James…you said you know Michael really well. Would he…would he make this up? He brought it up at a really weird time, and it just…it felt like he was saying it to…I don't know…turn me against Ryan."

He sighs again, "Celesete, Michael is one of the most honest people I know. Too honest, sometimes. It's a real problem for him. He fully wears his heart on his sleeve. He also has an incredibly steady moral compass. He did what he thought was right."

"Are the two of you close?"

"We were…once," he says, sipping his scotch. I look at his face, and I suspect that it is a loaded statement. "You should talk to him, too." He moves closer to me, putting his hand between my thighs again, against my bare skin. "Do you want to call them right now, get this cleared up?"

"No," I shake my head.

"I don't mind. If it's going to be weighing on you…"

"No, it's okay. I'll talk to them tomorrow…you cleared your whole calendar for me, after all," I say, my breath hitching as his fingers move up my thigh yet again.

"I bet there is a simple explanation for all of it," he says, kissing my exposed collarbone.

I hear the table across from us whisper, and James slinks away from me, respecting the rules of decency and the fact that we are in public. *Goddamn social norms.* I whimper slightly when his hand removes itself from me.

He whispers into my ear, "And don't be too hard on Michael, he's kind of a love-sick puppy when it comes to you. He can't think straight. Which I can empathize with."

We eat our dinner, chatting about all the things people on dates tend to do. The sexual tension never fully eases, but James at least stops trying to finger bang me in public. *I say that like I don't want him to finger bang me in public. I very much do.*

After a wonderful dinner and dessert, we're finally all paid up. When the waitress returns with the check, James gets his credit card and turns to me, saying, "Well, now that the check is taken care of, it's time to take care of you."

40

James's home is on the opposite side of town from mine. It's a relatively new house, and there is a distinct lack of trees in the neighborhood, as is often the case with most new developments. Each home is perfectly positioned around one of the larger lakes in the area, which was once a popular spot for spending the afternoon fishing. *I suppose you can't do that anymore unless you live here.*

His place is immaculate, perfectly cleaned—like he's never home, which I know is likely true. While it doesn't have a lot of color, with everything predominantly being white and millennial grey, there are splashes of vibrancy in the artwork. It resembles an art gallery.

Despite the coloring, sharp lines, and cleanliness, I wouldn't say it is sterile. It has a museum-like quality, and it is pretty comfortable. The lights are dimmed perfectly, as if he spent hours trying to find the precise position, wattage, and combination to elicit seduction. Michael was a master of lighting. I find it odd that they both are.

The furniture looks soft, plush, and inviting—no throw pillows, though. *Distinctly unlike Michael.* It's clear James has spared no expense in decorating the place, but it has a cultivated and curated feel to it. There is an unmistakable absence of personal items and a distinct lack of femininity. It exudes masculinity and wealth.

James removes his coat and shoes, placing them in the closet by the door. I follow his lead and remove my shoes and coat.

"Now this is a magazine-quality bachelor pad," I comment, taking in the sleek lines and modern decor. "Could use a feminine touch, though. Not a fluffy pillow or plant in sight."

James chuckles while taking my coat and shoes from me and meticulously placing them in the closet next to his. "Well, it's not just my home that could use a feminine touch," he quips, his voice low and suggestive. "But I'm hoping you'll help me remedy that." I smile at the flirtatious line and suspect he will jump me the moment he closes the closet door behind our clothing. He states, "Well, it's Minnesota tradition to give a tour."

"Oh, yeah, I'd like that," I say, craning my neck to see around a corner and spinning around on my bare feet, disappointed that he's not planning to fuck me right here by the door. I'm still amped up from the fingering in the restaurant despite it beginning over an hour ago.

"I know I've been forward with my intentions up to this point, but I am compelled to say this plainly: Celeste, I would like to fuck you on every surface of this house. I want to be able to walk through my home and know exactly which surfaces have received your feminine touch. Would you like that, Celeste? Would you like to tour my home while riding my cock?"

"I suppose that depends on the square footage," I quip. He laughs, but tilts his head at me, the lawyer in him obviously wanting a clear statement of consent. "Yes, yes, you may fuck me on every surface of this home," I say, waving my hand and absentmindedly walking toward his living room, eager to see the rest of the home.

With that clear statement of consent, James no longer holds back. He gently grasps my hand and pulls me toward him, spinning me so that our bodies collide. His mouth crashes onto mine, his lips parting and his tongue delving in, claiming me with a deep, passionate kiss. The force of it makes our teeth briefly knock, and I can feel his hard cock pressing insistently against my stomach. My interest in the layout of his home dissolves as I surrender to his embrace.

His strong hands grip my ass, squeezing and lifting me. He wraps my legs around his waist, my skirt hiking up to accommodate the new position. His fingers dig into my ass, kneading gently as he grinds his cock against me. I curse the thin fabric of my panties and the thicker fabric of his pants for the barrier they've created between us.

The wetness between my legs grows as his kiss deepens, his tongue exploring every corner of my mouth. A quiet moan escapes from deep within my throat. His body is hard against mine, his muscles taut as he holds me effortlessly.

He walks forward, while continuing to press his lips against mine, his tongue exploring my mouth as I grip his hair tightly in my hands. I remain latched to him as he navigates, eyes closed, gripping my ass to support me.

"This is the kitchen," he murmurs against my lips, and he lifts me to sit on the cold counter.

I gasp at the sudden chill against my bare thighs, bracing myself on the smooth surface. I run my hands along the surface and then peer down at it, distracted momentarily. I ask, "Oh, is this marble?" *This place is so fucking clean. I thought he said he cooked a lot.*

"Yes," he breathes, not breaking from his quest to kiss a trail down my neck. His hands slide down my body, lingering over my breasts before continuing their descent.

He leans me backward onto the counter, his breath hot on my stomach as he lowers himself in front of me. His hands run up my inner thighs, spreading them wide. He hikes up my dress and pulls me forward, so I hang slightly off the counter, then glides my panties off, tossing them to the side. I lift to see where he threw them, and he growls, gently placing me back down with the palm of his hand.

His tongue makes contact with my clit, a warm, wet sensation that sends a jolt of pleasure through me. I can't help but cry out softly, my eyes fluttering closed.

His large hands grasp my ass as he pulls me closer, further off the edge of the counter, positioning me perfectly for his mouth. He runs his tongue along my labia, parting them gently before flicking it against my clit once more. My body quivers in response.

"I've wanted to taste this sweet cunt all night," he says and plunges his fingers into me, "So, tight. You're going to feel so good wrapped around my cock."

"I want to feel it now," I say, grasping at his head and trying to pull him upward.

"Oh, how rude of me. There are other rooms in the house," he says, standing and pressing his mouth to mine. I can taste my own arousal on his tongue, and it sends a fresh wave of heat through me. The unmistakable crinkle of a condom wrapper being torn open is followed by his hands on my hips, lifting me. He positions me above his cock, the head pressing against my entrance only momentarily, before he pulls me down, filling me completely. He groans, his breath hot on my neck. "Holy fuck, you're so tight," he says, his voice a low growl.

He lifts me, his cock almost leaving me before he slams me down again, with a forceful thrust. He does this again and again, his grip on my hips tightening as he fucks me. I wrap my legs around his waist, my heels digging into his ass, urging him deeper, and hold onto his neck. He walks us to the living room, his cock still buried inside me, each step rubbing him against my inner walls, sending jolts of pleasure through me.

"This is the living room," he says, placing me on the back of the couch, and pumping harder into me now that the sofa is helping to hold me up. He unzips my dress and lifts it over my head, tossing it aside without a second glance.

"Your shirt off," I command, my hands already fumbling with the buttons.

He obliges, tearing it open and shrugging it off.

"Pants, too," I gasp as I suck on his collarbone.

Without removing himself from me, he drops his pants and underwear that had been pulled down at his hips to the floor. They pool at his ankles as he continues to drive into me. He grabs my ass, lifting me again as he steps out of the discarded fabric. He walks us to the couch and sits, so that I straddle him.

"Ride my dick, Celeste," he commands, his hands are on my hips, gently guiding me to move up and down on his shaft.

You don't have to tell me twice.

I lift myself until just the tip remains inside me before dropping back down onto him with all my weight and force with each undulation of my hips.

"Yes, baby, just like that. Oh, you feel so good," he moans as he takes my nipple into his mouth. His strong hand grips my hip, fingers digging into my flesh, as he guides me up and down on his thick, hard cock. He grunts and moans, "Shit, you feel so fucking good. I need to show you the rest of the house…"

He stands, lifting me once again as he walks with me latched on to him, grinding and kissing. *This man never skips leg day.*

We enter a room with a wall of books. "This is my office," he says, voice low and husky. He lies me on his desk, and the new angle allows him to go oh so deep. He moans out, "I'm going to make you come on my desk so the next time I work, I'll have the memory of your sweet moans to get me through the day."

My walls clench around his cock as he thrusts into me, deep and hard, filling me completely.

His thumb finds my swollen clit, rubbing it in rhythm with his powerful thrusts. I arch my back, reaching above my head, desperate for something to grasp as he rails into me. I hit something on the desk, and it scatters to the floor with the distinct sound of pens clattering on the ground. *Ah, a pen cup.*

His cock pistons in and out of me. His free hand explores my body, worshipping every square inch of it, before stopping to squeeze one of my bouncing breasts. The sensation sends electric shocks straight to my core, intensifying the pleasure building inside me.

My body tenses, the pleasure peaking. My toes curl, and my legs shake. I come hard, my pussy convulsing around his cock. My body jerks and twitches uncontrollably as waves of ecstasy crash over me. I cry out, "Holy fuck, James!" He groans, feeling my walls milk his cock, and continues to fuck me through the climax, drawing out every last shudder of pleasure.

"Unfortunately, I'm going to have to end the tour a bit early," he says, lifting me by the ass to walk with me yet again. My head lolls on his shoulder as I bask in the post orgasm bliss and the feeling of being carried.

He walks down the hall and enters a room that is unmistakably his bedroom. Still no throw pillows. "What's your beef with pillows, J-Money?" I ask.

"I like a tidy home," he says, and falls upon me on the bed.

He wraps his arms around me, pulling me so incredibly close, and pumps into me. He groans, "Oh my God, Celeste. You feel…too good." I run my hands through his hair, grasping tightly, and look at his strong shoulders. He has a deep scar on his left shoulder that I can feel under my fingertips as I bite along his neck.

James is forceful, dominant, and he takes what he wants from my body. He slides his cock almost all the way out before slamming back into me, filling me completely. He does it with a surprising gentleness, a rhythm that builds slowly, allowing me to feel every inch of him. He seems to savor each gasp of pleasure that escapes my lips as his cock pounds into me. I cling to him, my nails digging into his back, as he drives me closer and closer to the edge of oblivion.

"Come again for me, baby," he whispers into my ear. "I want to release while you tremble around me."

Our bodies tremble in unison, our hearts beat as one, and as his cock hits my G-spot, relentlessly driving me towards another orgasm.

I come yet again, screaming out, "Oh, God, James!" My saying his name seems to be what sends him over the edge.

He grunts and moans, his body tensing as he spills himself into me, before breathlessly whispering, "My name sounds so pretty on your mouth," into my ear. He holds me close, his breath hot against my skin as he twitches and writhes inside me. Locked together, we ride out the aftershocks of our joint climax.

We lie there, panting, his weight on top of me. My hand glides across his back, and I note the feeling of more scars across his back—something I didn't notice in my state of arousal.

"I'll be right back," he says, kissing me on the cheek and walking to the bathroom adjoining the bedroom, I presume, to remove the condom.

As he walks to the bathroom, I admire his tall, strong form, the muscles in his ass undulating with each step. The scars I could feel are now in full display. They cover his entire back and match the one on his shoulder. Deep, faint, and old. They appear to be lash scars, and I realize it wasn't just his mother that his father had been cruel to. He must have been cruel to him, too.

41

I awake in the middle of the night, my head nestled in James's shoulder, drooling on his pec. James's arm is slung carelessly across my shoulders like it belongs there. It's cold in here. I pull the comforter higher under my chin, letting the tip of my nose stick out, and pull my legs closer to him, hoping to soak up some of his warmth.

I don't even know how many orgasms I've had tonight, but the last one knocked me out. James is still awake, though, tapping furiously on his phone with his free hand. When he feels me move, he smiles down at me.

I lift my head from the crook of his shoulder and wipe my mouth. *So embarrassing.*

He shifts, removing his arm from under me so he can set his phone facedown on the nightstand. As he reaches, the comforter slips down, exposing the ladder of scars on his back.

He returns his attention to me and grins, dimples bracketing his smile. "Sorry, did I wake you?"

Maybe I should go home. But this bed is much better than my couch. I nuzzle back into his shoulder. His skin smells like faint soap and that musky man smell that soaks panties with a single whiff. He's so cozy and comfortable. If I close my eyes, I can almost trick myself into thinking this is normal. That James and I live happily ever after together.

"No, I think I woke from the cold," I say, shivering and pulling my body up.

"Oh, shit, I'm sorry, Celeste," he says, turning back to his nightstand to retrieve his phone.

I see the scars more clearly this time. Jagged white lines running from his shoulders down to the small of his back, parallel but not quite even, like someone tried and failed to make them symmetrical.

He pokes his phone before the sound of a heater clicks on. "I keep it kind of cold. Come here, let me warm you," he says, pulling me to him.

I bury my face in his chest and reach around him, tracing the faint scars on his back.

He asks, "You want to know about the scars, huh?"

"From your dad?" I ask because I can't help myself. Then immediately regret it.

But if James is bothered, he doesn't show it. He just brings his lips to my head. "Yeah. From my dad."

For a minute, neither of us says anything. His hand finds my waist under the covers.

"Sorry," I say. "I can be nosy. You don't have to talk about it." I pull away to look at him.

He tilts his head, considering me. His hair sticks up at odd angles, pressed flat where my fingers dug in when he was going down on me. He releases a long exhale. "It's okay. I figure you'd ask eventually."

I laugh, but it's more of an exhale. "You sound so resigned."

He flashes a crooked smile. "Resigned isn't quite the word. I want you to know me."

He props his chin on my shoulder, lips close enough to brush the shell of my ear. "The deepest ones: I was fifteen. I tried to stop him from hurting my mom. Called him a bastard." He says it matter-of-factly, like he's reciting a police report. "Got a good punch in, but…

well, you'll never see me wear a belt. It finally convinced her to leave, though. She thought he was going to kill me."

He falls silent. My heart thuds, aching for the boy he was and for his mother.

"You were so brave," I say, not because I want to fix it, but because I can't not say it.

James closes his eyes, long lashes flickering. "Brave or Stupid. Sometimes it's hard to tell."

I rest my head against his. "Brave."

His laugh is softer this time, but real. "Thanks."

We lie there for a while, tangled up, the space between our bodies quiet and safe.

I lean in and press my lips to the sharp edge of his jaw, the spot where the morning stubble is already trying to reclaim its territory.

James shifts, pulling me to him, resting my head on his shoulder. "He got away with it, though. So in the end, it didn't really matter."

He's holding me so tight, I can't look at him. I close my eyes and I whisper, "But it did. She left, James. That was because of you."

"He got everything. Left her with nothing. Even the scars on my back couldn't win that case for my mom." After a while, he says, "Sometimes I think—if I'd been older, stronger, smarter, had worked harder, already knew the law, maybe I could've protected her."

I press my lips to his shoulder, soft. "You were a kid, James."

He's silent before choking out, "Boys are supposed to protect their moms."

"No, they're not, James. Parents are supposed to protect their children." I kiss again. "But you did. You did. You convinced her to leave. You gave her the strength. That's more than most kids could do. That's more than any kid should have to do."

He loosens his grip on me so we can look at each other. He blinks, then laughs, a little choked. "You always know what to say?"

I shake my head against his skin. "Not even close. Normally, I just hand out oral sex when someone is crying. It's kinda how the whole Ryan and Celeste mess got started."

"Wait, you're telling me I could have gotten head instead of trauma dumping. Fuck. Ryan was lucky to have you around when his mom left."

"You know about that?"

"Small town, Celeste. Everyone knows everything."

"Yeah, I guess they do."

His phone buzzes on the nightstand, catching his attention. He doesn't reach for it, though.

I nod toward the phone. "Were you working?"

"Yeah, sorry. I know I told you I was going to have my out-of-office response."

"No, it's okay. I was asleep. Can't be mad at you for working while I sleep."

I look at the clock and it's 3 am. "Do you always stay up this late?"

He shrugs, his shoulder brushing my hair. "Not really a great sleeper. I've got a lot of people depending on me. I can't let what happened to my mom happen to them."

"Is that why you work so much?"

He laughs, but it's a dry sound. "I see the look in their eyes—women, kids—when they show up at my office. I can't leave them hanging. I can't be the guy who lets them down."

There's a moment where he seems to drift off, eyes unfocused. He returns, blinking at me. "I just want…" He trails off.

I nudge his cheek with my nose, smiling a little. "You just want everyone to be okay."

"Yeah."

I lift his chin with a finger. "You know, you're allowed to want things for yourself, too."

He gives me a wry look. "Like what?"

"Like this." I gesture at our tangle of limbs, the rumpled sheets. "Rest." I pause a moment, "Relationships."

He's silent for a long moment. "I'm sorry, Celeste."

"For what?"

"For not being able to spend as much time with you as you deserve. Work just—"

"You don't have to explain," I say, but he keeps going.

"I can barely keep a houseplant alive, let alone a relationship. But I can't let you slip away again."

"I don't want you to give up your work," I say, meaning it. "I get it. You're saving people, and that matters."

"It's not fair to you. I know it's not. I'd love nothing more than to have a spouse, a few kids, and a dog, but I work too much. And as much as I want those things, every time I've tried, I fail. I don't want you to think it's about you. It's me. I'm the one who's broken."

"You're not broken, James."

He gives a short, sharp laugh. "You're the only one who thinks that."

"Probably because I am too. You know, I used to pull all-nighters just to avoid going home. I was terrified of being alone with my thoughts. The office was safer. Less…haunted."

He softens. "Yeah?"

"Yeah. Workaholics are just sad people with a good cover story. It's socially acceptable self-harm."

He actually laughs this time, for real. "Ha! I never thought about it like that."

I grin. "See? I'm not just a pretty face."

"I noticed. The rest of you is pretty great, too."

I pretend to pout, but he kisses me, gently, then holds my hand against his cheek.

He's quiet for a moment. "You could do anything. Why come back here?"

I take a breath, the heat starting to settle on my bare arms. "I thought maybe if I came back, I could figure out what I actually wanted. Or at least what I'm supposed to do next. I thought if I faced my demons, I could finally…I dunno…forgive myself, maybe."

He nods. "Is it working?"

"I'll let you know."

After a while, he says, "So, what's it like, having all this time for yourself?"

"Honestly? Kind of terrifying. I spent so long with every second scheduled. I thought I'd be happier without the pressure, but now it's like…I'm just floating." I give him a wry grin. "And fucking, of course."

We laugh.

I continue, sighing at how pathetic I am, "And playing detective. Trying to solve a murder, like I'm still in control of something. I think I'm just finding new ways to run from my feelings."

James doesn't flinch. "You mean you and Michael looking into Richard's murder?"

My head snaps up. "You know about that?"

He grins, teeth white in the dim. "Come on, Celeste. Small town, remember? The whole town is watching you and Mikey. Everyone knows what you're up to."

I feel my cheeks burn. "Great. So I'm the town slut and the town busybody."

"No, that's Sean O'Connor."

"He's a slut?"

"No, a busybody."

So, you agree. I am the town slut."

"I said no such thing."

"Omission is permissible in a court of law, counselor."

"Okay, so you said words…but they don't…"

"Objection. Overruled. Leading the witness. You are liable for implying that your girlfriend is a slut."

"Girlfriend, huh?"

"Oh, um…well, I mean, there's Ryan and Michael, but I'm avoiding them and…well, I mean…fuck."

"Celeste." He laughs at me. "It's okay. You can call yourself my girlfriend. And you should talk to Ryan and Michael."

"But…"

"Listen. I wasn't lying when I said I'm okay with you being with them. It makes me feel a lot better knowing you've got someone to keep you company when I disappear for weeks at a time working."

"Seriously?"

"Yes. I'm not Ryan's biggest fan, but I'm near certain he didn't kill Richard. And Mikey's a good guy. Just talk to them."

"Not Ryan's biggest fan?"

"Ah, you latched onto that, huh?"

"Yeah…well, when we were kids, he was with the girl I loved, and we've just had unspoken animosity ever since."

Loved?

42

The walk to Hartman's Farm is a bit longer than I remember. Watson doesn't seem to mind and struts ahead of me like he knows exactly where we're going. His tail is held confidently high, as always, the hair swaying like feathers to the rhythm of his gait.

The faded red barn stands sentinel against the fall sky, the cloudless blue creating a perfect complement. Rows of corn stretch behind it, making a postcard-worthy landscape. A slight breeze picks up, and I pull my wool coat closed to button it. Hopefully, it doesn't start snowing soon. I really don't want to lose out on these times walking with Watson.

Instead of worrying about the future, I attempt to appreciate the present, breathing in the earthy autumn scents, accentuated by the approaching farm. The distinct scent brings back more memories than the sight of the place. It hasn't changed, even if everything else has.

Ryan's leaning against a weathered fence post, one foot propped up behind him, looking like he stepped right out of some magazine. His tousled blond hair catches the afternoon light, and when he spots us, his face breaks into that same smile that has made my heart skip since I was seven years old.

"Did you leave your watch in California?" he calls out as I approach, pushing himself away from the fence with a fluid motion.

"Nope, right here on my wrist," I say, checking my watch for effect.

He closes the distance between us in long strides, and I flinch slightly, distrusting him now. His arms wrap around me in a hug as he lifts me slightly off the ground. "Always worth the wait," he whispers into my ear, sending a lustful and fearful shiver through me. When he sets me down, his hands linger on my hips, and his chin rests on my shoulder. The familiar feeling of his touch and the way it lights me up like a horny Christmas tree disarms me. *I'm here to interrogate him, not fuck him.*

"I prefer this smell to the goat shit," he says, making a show of breathing me in.

My tension eases. "Saying I smell better than goat shit is not the compliment you think it is." I push against his chest playfully, but not hard enough to break contact. *How does he do this? How does he always break down my barriers?*

He looks at me with a mock surprised face, "You're saying my game hasn't improved with age?" He leans down to greet Watson who relishes the attention as the ever trusting boy he is.

He hasn't changed. He's still the Ryan I remember. There's no way he could have killed Richard.

"Some things never change. Like your inability to ever take anything seriously."

"What's to take seriously? We're just getting pumpkins."

I scrunch my face, considering a response. He doesn't know why I've asked to meet with him. I sent him flirty text messages under the guise of getting pumpkins. But really, I wanted to take him somewhere crowded enough that he couldn't hurt me, but private enough that we could talk without others hearing. *I need to find out if he killed Richard.*

"Wanna detour through the corn maze?" he asks me, thumbing toward the maze. The entrance looms before us, a tall archway of bundled stalks with a hand-painted sign proclaiming "Hartman's

Haunted Corn Maze" in faded red letters. *The answer is "absolutely not," but what plausible reason could I give? Should I blame Watson?*

"Let's just go straight to the pumpkin patch. I don't think you can take dogs through the maze."

"Oh, come on, you already know Watson can go wherever the fuck he wants," he laughs, leaning down to pet Watson. "Can't you, boy?" Watson does a full-force butt swing and a hop at the attention.

"But, like, what if he pees on the corn? That can't be good for it, right? Like unhygienic? Wouldn't it spoil the crop?"

"He just plants this for the maze, it's not his real crop. That's on the other side of the farm." He looks at me like I'm crazy, then ruffles Watson's ears and nuzzles him on the nose. "I think she's just scared she's gonna get lost." He stands and walks toward the maze.

"Um…" I say, holding back, not following him toward the maze entrance.

"Come on, I know this maze like I know the curves of your body," he says, catching my hand in his.

I squelch my reluctance. People are milling about. They've seen me with him. *There's no way he can kill me in this maze. Right?*

I stall further. "Um, it's just. I told Michael that I'd go with him in the corn maze."

Ryan turns and looks hurt for a moment. "Don't worry, I won't tell Michael that you did it with me first," he says, his eyes implying the innuendo.

"Okay, well, just a minute. Let me text him and tell him," I say, pulling out my phone. I need to tell someone where I am and who I am with, just in case he does kill me.

God. I am so stupid. Why am I about to go into a corn maze with a suspected killer? This has to be a plot of some movie, right? A dumb white woman walks into a maze, gets murdered, and no one is surprised.

Ryan seems annoyed, but doesn't protest. I hand Watson's leash to him, and he squats to play with the eager pup while he waits for me.

I've been avoiding Michael's messages for the last two days—my anger with him is still boiling hot. *But…if he's right.*

I text, "Michael, I'm sorry I haven't been responding to your messages. I've been a bitch. But I'm about to go into the corn maze with Ryan. I'm going to ask him about what you told me."

I watch the three dots immediately appear and reflect on what else to say.

Should I tell him to call the cops if I don't message him in a few hours? No. Right?

Should I text, "So, um, I almost told you I loved you the other night, but I don't know if it was just because your dick hits that special spot and I'm so oxytocin starved I just latch-the-fuck-on, but just in case I love you and just in case I die, I thought I should tell you: I might love you!" Double no. Right?

Should I message James?

"Please don't go in there with him," Michael responds. More dots.

"Okay, you've told him. Let's go," Ryan says, tugging me toward the maze before I can respond to Michael.

It's okay. I'll be okay. Ryan wouldn't hurt me.

I look to Watson. *Watson won't let him hurt me, right? Who am I kidding? That dog couldn't protect a milkbone. Gosh, I wish he were a Doberman right now. He wouldn't hurt Watson, would he?* As if Watson knows I'm thinking about him, he looks to me, with that doggy smile, and I feel like he's telling me, "Come on, Celeste, this will be fun!" *That dog has no sense of self-preservation. But who am I to judge right now?*

We stand at the entrance, and I can't think of another reason to say I can't go in. My phone rings, and I suspect it's Michael, so I silence it without looking. I shove it in my back pocket.

Ryan releases my hand only to place his palm against the small of my back. "Ladies first," he says, guiding me through the entrance.

"Why should I go in first?" I shoot back, glancing over my shoulder, suspicious of his intentions. "I thought you were going to lead the way?"

He just grins and winks. "Like you said, some things never change. And my appreciation of that ass is one of the things."

Disarmed by him yet again, I chuckle and blush with a flirtatious smile. "God, Ryan, must you always?" *I can't get distracted by our playfulness.*

I'll be fine, though. I try to ignore the flutter in my stomach that has nothing to do with his flirtation. *He won't hurt me. It's okay, Celeste.*

Inside, the world narrows to walls of corn, stalks reaching ten feet high on either side of us. The path of the maze is barely wide enough for the two of us, forcing us to walk pressed against each other. Watson, of course, leads the way.

Dogs have a good sense of direction, right? Like, he can smell his way out?

"Remember when we got lost in here as kids?" Ryan asks, his fingers finding mine again. The touch makes my heart race, and I still can't tell if it's from familiar lust or newfound fear.

"I recall you wailing about how we were going to starve to death," I laugh, the memory sharp and clear.

"I was expressing concern for your welfare," he protests, squeezing my hand. "Very manly concern."

He has always been concerned for my welfare. It's stupid of me to suspect him.

We reach the first fork in the path, and Watson pulls us left on instinct.

"Wrong way," Ryan whispers, his lips unnecessarily close to my ear. "Trust me, I've done this maze every year."

I think Watson is correct. Is Ryan trying to keep me in this maze longer than necessary?

"Since when do you have any sense of direction?" I challenge, but allow him to steer us right. "I also recall you getting lost on the way to my house…next door."

"I never got lost on the way to your house, that's just what I'd say when I got distracted."

"Sure," I say with a scoff.

"Celeste, I could always find my way to you," he says with a wistfulness that makes me look at him.

The path narrows further, twisting back on itself in a way that makes me lose my bearings completely. Ryan walks confidently, one hand still holding mine, the other occasionally touching my hip, my shoulder, the small of my back—each contact brief but deliberate.

"You're doing that on purpose," I accuse after his fingers trail across my lower back for the third time.

"Doing what?" His innocent face wouldn't fool anyone.

"Accidentally touching me."

He steps closer, our bodies almost flush. "Does it bother you?"

"I didn't say that." My voice comes out huskier than I intended. My suspicion of him is starting to take a back seat to my lust for him—like always.

His smile grows. "Good. Because I like touching you, Celeste."

43

When I stumble over an exposed root, Ryan catches me, his hands gripping my waist firmly.

"I see your tendency to get stuck in your head and ignore your surroundings hasn't changed," he says, eye fucking me. "Don't worry, I'll always be here to catch you."

Will he always be?

We come to another junction, and this time we follow Watson's lead as he pulls us down a path that feels promising. "This is the wrong way again," Ryan says, but doesn't insist on turning the other way.

"Let's see where Watson is taking us," I say, trusting the dog more than the man.

"Alright, but don't say I didn't warn you."

After we hit a dead end, Ryan gives me an "I told you so" look. His body presses against my back as I stop short. "Why are you letting him lead the way? I know where to go."

I look to Watson, and he just stares at me like he doesn't really give a fuck where we are; he's just excited to smell all the things.

I turn to face Ryan, finding myself trapped between the wall of corn and his chest. His looming body scares me in this moment. He could easily overpower me. *Let's not let on that I'm suspicious.* "I dunno. I just thought I'd let Watson have his fun."

"Are you sure you're not just trying to get me alone?" he asks, practically pinning me against the wall of corn and brushing the strand of hair from my face—his signature move. My knees weaken as I lock eyes with him.

"Ryan, I don't really have to try to get you alone. You're not exactly hard to get," I quip.

"Are you calling me a slut, Celeste?" he asks, placing his hand on his chest in mock offense.

"Kinda," I say, pushing past him and looking at him over my shoulder, swaying my hips enticingly. *If I just flirt with him, it'll be okay.*

He bites his lip and lunges toward me to follow me down the trail.

We backtrack and try another route, continuing our flirtatious conversation of gentle teasing and reminiscing.

I'll ask him about what Michael says, but after we get out of this maze and into the open.

Soon, the flirtatious comments and brushes against him to arouse him are no longer feigned; they're purposeful, and I'm lost in the joy of being with him. My suspicion is completely gone. We're having fun, and the last thing I want to think about right now is the murder of Richard Fucking Holbrook.

We continue through the maze, our progress slowed by our increasingly distracted state of flirting, brushing against each other, and stealing kisses.

When Ryan points out a fascinating cloud formation, his arm slides around my shoulders. When I spot a uniquely shaped corn stalk, my hand finds its way to his bicep, squeezing appreciatively.

"I do like these new arms of yours," I observe, not bothering to remove my hand.

"100 push-ups a day for the last five years," he says with a grin.

"That's all?" I ask.

"That's all!? How many can you do?"

"Um…none. What I mean is, it looks like you do more," I say boldly, squeezing his arm again. "It's working for you."

His eyes darken. "You know what's working for me? That little smile you get when you think you're being subtle about checking me out."

Heat rushes to my face. "I do not—"

"There it is," he interrupts, his finger touching the corner of my mouth. "That smile."

We turn another corner and find ourselves in a small clearing cut into the corn—a deliberate dead end with a wooden bench positioned for weary maze-goers.

"I think we're officially lost," I admit, looking around at the identical walls of corn surrounding us. My fear is returning to me.

Ryan shrugs, unconcerned. "Or maybe we've found exactly where we're supposed to be." He sits on the bench and pats the space beside him. "Take a break?"

I join him, our thighs touching. My heart is racing. The bench is smaller than it looked, forcing us to sit close.

"Won't the sun be setting soon?" I ask, trying to get us to move out of this maze as soon as possible, my fear returning to me. Watsons lies at our feet.

"Nah, we've got a while left," he says, draping his arm casually along the back of the bench behind me, "We should still have time to get the pumpkins."

I consider this, feeling the warmth of his body beside mine. "Are you sure? When is the winter solstice?"

"In winter, Celeste?" His fingers touch my hair lightly, and he looks at me, confused. "What's up with you? Why do you seem so distracted?"

I turn to look at him, finding his face closer than expected. "I…I don't know."

"Are you still trying to solve that murder in your head?" he asks softly. His gaze drops to my lips, then back to my eyes.

My heart pounds in my chest. *Does he know I suspect him?*

"Um…" I say, biting my lip.

When he leans in, I meet him halfway, instinct taking over. Our lips touch. His hand slides into my hair, cradling the back of my head as he deepens the kiss. I respond eagerly, my fingers gripping the front of his flannel shirt, pulling him closer. He tastes like cinnamon gum.

"You taste so good," he murmurs against my lips.

"So do you. Did you have gum?" I ask, breathless.

Instead of answering, he kisses me again, more urgently this time. His free hand finds my waist, then slides lower to my hip, fingers digging in gently. I shift closer, practically in his lap now, my body moving on instinct.

The corn rustles around us, creating a natural curtain that feels miles away from the rest of the world. Ryan's mouth leaves mine to trail along my jaw, down to the sensitive spot below my ear. I gasp, tilting my head to give him better access.

"Want me to eat your pussy on this bench, Celeste?" he asks, his voice rough.

"We probably shouldn't," I manage to say, guiding his face back to mine for another kiss.

"Why? I doubt anyone will come through here," he says.

Fuck. I want him. This fear is stupid. He won't hurt me. All he's ever wanted was to please me.

His hands wander boldly, skimming my sides, tracing the curve of my spine, cupping my face. I'm equally exploratory, marveling at how the boy I grew up with has become this man whose touch sets me on fire.

"I guess I'll just use my hands, then," he says, his fingers slipping into my pants.

It feels so good the moment his fingers reach between my folds, but I push his hand away.

"What's wrong?" he asks.

"I'm just not…in the mood," I say, closing my legs tightly and turning my body from him. *Lies. Such lies.*

"Since when are you not in the mood?" he laughs at me and moves away, respecting my request, and leaning back on the bench, arms splayed across the back.

"Not all of us have sex on the brain ALL the time." *Lies. More lies.*

"Sorry, you're just so…ravishing," he says, his smile slow and satisfied. "All I can think about when you're around is sinking my dick into you."

"I thought we were just friends, Ryan."

"Best friends." He shrugs. "It's not my fault, my best friend is so fuckable, though. I'm just a man."

"You know, friends don't think about fucking each other all the time, right? Sometimes they just go in a corn maze and don't fuck. Why can't you just spend time with me without trying to fuck me?"

"Wait, are you being serious right now? This isn't flirting?"

"Of course not! I'm being serious." Tears build in my eyes, and I'm not quite sure why.

He leans forward, tries to grab my hand, but I pull it away. "Hey, Celeste, I'm so sorry. I can be with you. Just be with you. No sex. It's just been our…our thing since…since you know."

I complete his sentence for him. "Your mom left."

He grimaces.

I say, "I'm sorry. I know you don't like to bring it up."

He leans forward with his elbows on his knees, his hands gripped tightly together as if he's about to pray. His head drops. "I found her. When I got cancer…I wanted to tell her."

"What!?"

"Yeah, she lives in Canada. I've got a little sister and a little brother. Well…they're adults now, so, not little…"

I don't know what to say. I just look at him and wait. I place my hand on his back.

He continues, "It's fine. She's…not the mother I remembered. Big surprise. Well, I got closure at least."

"Did you, really?"

He lets out a single laugh. "Ha, probably not. It's fine. They're not my family. Dad is. Mrs. Heart is. You…you are."

"Ryan…is that…is that when you finally started texting me again? After you found your mom?"

"Does it make me an asshole if I say yes?"

I shake my head."I don't know…does it?"

"Well, I've been an asshole. I'm sorry for running away from you all those years ago. Thank you for coming back home."

I place my head on his shoulder and, sensing a dog-pile of sorts, Watson jumps into his lap.

Ryan laughs. "Sorry, Watty. You're my family, too."

44

“Shit, I didn’t think this was the apple orchard exit,” Ryan says, looking around and rubbing the back of his neck nervously, as we exit the corn maze.

“I knew that whole ‘I know this maze like I know the curves of your body’ thing was bullshit,” I say to Watson. He just wags his tail, acknowledging he, too, knew Ryan was full of shit.

Ryan’s eyes gleam with mischief, and he tugs me toward him, pressing a quick kiss to my temple. “It was a shortcut,” he says, shrugging. “Had to take it since you were so late.”

“Whatever,” I laugh, bumping his shoulder with mine.

“Might as well get some apples while we’re here,” he says, and picks up a basket to put apples in.

The orchard stretches before us, perfect rows of apple trees. I pause and look toward the horizon, attempting to take in the surroundings. The air here smells different from the maze—sweeter, cleaner, with notes of ripening apples and rich earth. Something about the smell is instantly arousing. *Why is that?*

A few other visitors wander between the rows, making me feel a lot safer than I did in the maze. But the vastness of the orchard makes it feel like I can confront him without anyone overhearing.

"Okay, Watson, maybe don't pee on these trees? Alright?" I say as we walk forward. He looks at me like, "Whatever you say, Celesete." I resolve to just not let him get close to them.

Ryan leads me deeper into the trees, lazily swinging the basket at his side. He stops abruptly before a particularly vibrant tree, its branches bowing under the weight of the apples. Something about this tree looks particularly enticing, and I understand why he stopped at it.

"This one," he declares, reaching up to pluck a perfect apple just beyond my reach. "It's beautiful. Perfect." The way he says it, eyes darting to mine, suggests he's talking about more than just produce.

"Then maybe we should leave it," I tease, stepping closer to him. "Let it live out its life's purpose to fall and make new little baby apple trees."

"If we did that, chances are it would rot before it ever grew anything. Even if a seed takes, it won't make a tree like this one—apples don't grow true from seed. Each one's a genetic roll of the dice. That's why orchardists graft the ones they love—otherwise, every apple tree would be a surprise. Charming, but usually not that tasty.

"If you really want baby apple trees, you'd need to collect the seeds, stratify them over winter, and even then, you'd probably want to graft them onto rootstock to get consistent, healthy trees. So, this beauty, her purpose isn't to make baby apple trees, it's to be eaten. To be enjoyed," he says, wistfully plucking the apple from the tree.

He looks at the fruit, a thought crossing his eyes that seems sad and reflective.

"I forgot you were an apple nerd," I say, my voice breaking into his thoughts and causing him to snap his attention back to me, faking a smile.

He places his hand on the small of my back and kisses the top of my head. "You forgot all that time we used to spend at my dad's orchard?"

"No, I didn't forget…" I say, blushing and remembering what we used to do hidden amongst the trees, and now understanding why the familiar smell is so arousing.

"Um…speaking of your family's old orchard…"

Watson tries to tug me further into the orchard, but I reach up to pluck an apple, stretching deliberately so my shirt rides up slightly. Ryan's eyes immediately drop to the exposed strip of skin, precisely as I intended.

"What about it?" he murmurs, his fingers grazing my exposed midriff and his crotch jamming against my hip.

"What happened to the orchard?"

Watson gets impatient with us and lies at my feet, annoyed I won't let him approach a tree or move further down the path.

Ryan removes himself from me and puts his hands in his pockets. He looks to the side and bites the inside of his cheek before saying, "He sold it a while back."

"Why's he working at the grocery store? I'd have thought he would be set for life after selling it? What happened?"

"Why are you asking me about this, Celeste?"

"I'm…I'm just curious."

He sighs loudly. "Richard fucked him. That's all there is to it, really."

"What do you mean?"

"He…Someone got hurt and sued. Richard represented my dad. My dad lost. Bad. Had to sell the orchard to cover the costs." He kicks at the dirt. Watson snorts at him for doing something that dared to disturb his, somehow, deep sleep.

"How is that Richard's fault? Lawyers lose cases."

"Angela…she wasn't supposed to tell me, but…there was an investigation. They suspected he tanked the case on purpose and was working with the person who got hurt."

"Wow. That's…that's awful."

He looks far away. "Yeah, but I'm going to get it back. I'm close. If my gallery showing does well, I think I'll have the last bit for the down payment."

"How much do you need?"

He shakes his head. "No, Celeste."

"No, what?"

"I'm not going to let you pay for it."

"I wasn't—"

He places his hand on my shoulder. "Yes, you were."

He's right. I was.

Now's my chance. I steel myself and ask, "So, um…your dad's orchard. Is that why you punched Richard the day he was murdered?"

"What? How do you know about that?" His thumbs trace my collarbone, a distracting tactic that doesn't quite work.

"So it's true?"

He sighs, kicking the dirt and annoying Watson again. "Yeah, it was fucking stupid. But no, it was not about the orchard. Well, not entirely."

"Then what?"

"It doesn't matter..." Ryan shrugs, a too-casual gesture, and returns his grip to me, trying to distract me with kisses and touches.

"Ryan, please, for once in your life, just…"

He sighs, his hands stilling. "It was about you, Celeste. He called you, he called you…an ungrateful daughter and a slut. He was doing his usual thing, just being an ass. He came up to me in the park when I was painting and told me I was blocking the path. He insulted my work. I was just trying to ignore him, trying to keep painting, and turned my music up in my AirPods, but he said, 'I'll be seeing that old slut of yours. You know the one. The ungrateful Moon daughter.' I just…I just couldn't let him talk about you like that."

My heart pounds in my ears.

Ungrateful?

Worthless. A failure.

No...fuck that. Fuck him.

I steel myself and ask, "Ryan…did you kill Richard because of what he said about me?"

He startles backward. "What!? Absolutely not! Is that why you've been acting weird, because you think I killed Richard?" Watson jumps at the sound of his raised voice and barks.

"Well, I mean…kinda."

"Celeste, I went straight to Angela after he showed up dead and told her about it. I didn't know when he was murdered, but when she asked me about that night, I told her I had been live-streaming all night. I didn't kill him. I was painting. I have a beyond-solid alibi." His hands resume their gentle exploration of my body, sliding down my arms.

The pieces click together in my mind. "Oh, thank God."

"You really thought I killed Richard!?" His eyes meet mine, surprisingly earnest.

I repeat, "Well, I mean…kinda."

"Wow, Celeste…" Ryan's arm slides around my waist.

"I'm sorry! I just…It's been so long since we last saw each other; I didn't know how much you've changed. I didn't want to believe it."

His fingers find the belt loop of my jeans and hook through it possessively, as he guides me to walk through the orchard. Watson rises from his deep sleep, ready to continue sniffing stuff.

"Well, you couldn't have believed it too much, otherwise you wouldn't have let me make you come in the corn." Ryan grins, gathering a few apples into the basket.

"You're not mad?" I ask, raising my eyebrow to him.

Ryan's expression shifts to something more complicated, a blend of smugness and what might be guilt. "Nah. You've always been a bit… hypervigilant. But, I know you'll never be truly mad at me," he says, voice dropping to a conspiratorial whisper. "And if you ever are, I just gotta make you come." He grins, unrepentant.

I nearly choke. "God. You really haven't changed. I can't believe I suspected you had changed." My sarcasm earns me a playful squeeze at my waist.

Ryan snorts and hands me an apple. Our fingers linger together longer than necessary. "Let me guess, Michael told you about the punch?"

"Yeah…," I say. The feel of Ryan's fingers against my hip makes it hard to focus.

We stop beneath a particularly gnarled apple tree, whose twisted branches create a natural canopy. Ryan sets down the basket and turns to face me fully, his hands coming to rest on my shoulders.

"I figured he would. I wasn't sure if he saw us, though. I should have just told you, but I didn't want to tell you about what Richard called you…" Ryan trails off, his fingers begin a slow massage that makes it difficult to care about what Richard said. He leans in close, his lips brushing my ear with a kiss. "I'm sorry to have worried you, Star Girl."

As we collect our basket of apples and prepare to move on, Ryan's arm stays firmly around my waist. "I think we have enough apples. I'll make cider. The pumpkin patch is just up here. Let's go."

I nod, leaning into his side. "Lead the way, RyGuy." He kisses the top of my head, and we walk together, wrapped around each other, toward the pumpkins, Watson happily tagging along.

"Michael, I'm ok. And you were wrong about Ryan. It wasn't him. He was live-streaming all night. He's already talked to the police," I text quickly and put the phone back in my pocket without waiting for the three dots to finish. I don't want Ryan to see me texting Michael.

The sky has begun its slow transformation from afternoon blue to the first hints of evening gold. The temperature is dropping, but Ryan's hands feel warm against my back.

The pumpkin patch spreads before us. The chaotic, orange-speckled landscape feels like a completely different world from the one containing the ordered rows of the orchard. Watson weaves through pumpkins, threatening to twist his leash around them.

"Wanna see who can find the perfect pumpkin?" Ryan challenges, his breath tickling my ear as he leans close.

I turn my head, our noses nearly touching. "Gotta make a game out of everything, don't you?"

"I learned from the best," he says, his voice dropping to a register that makes my skin prickle with anticipation.

"Flattery will get you everywhere," I giggle, deliberately brushing my body against his as I step away to begin my search.

You're on, O'Connor.

"Let's beat him, Watty," I whisper to the pooch, who turns and marches onward. *Hopefully, he doesn't find another dead body.* I shake the thought away.

It's more crowded here than the orchard. Multiple families are scattered among the sprawling vines. Little kids run amok amongst the pumpkins, laughing, and attempting to lift pumpkins as big as themselves. I giggle at a particularly adorable toddler hugging a pumpkin and crying as her mother consoles her.

Most of the prime pumpkins have already been picked. What's left are mostly oddly shaped gourds that have a quirky charm. I wander amongst them, feeling Ryan's eyes on me as I bend to examine various candidates. Watson's speed slows, and I think maybe he's reaching his last leg of energy.

"The view just keeps getting better," he calls out, not bothering to hide his appreciation when I bend to inspect a particularly round specimen.

I glance over my shoulder, catching him staring unabashedly. "Eyes on the pumpkins, O'Connor."

"Can't help it if you're more appealing than the produce," he says, crossing the distance between us in a few long strides. He grabs my hips as I stand, turning me to face him.

"Oh, wait. Am I allowed to kiss you?" he asks and tucks a strand of hair behind my ear. "Or are we still just hanging out as friends?"

"Fine," I reply, rolling my eyes, unable to keep the smile from my face.

His kiss is confident, claiming, and I respond with equal enthusiasm, threading my fingers through his hair.

We continue our hunt for the perfect pumpkin, our search punctuated by stolen kisses and lingering touches.

Ryan trails his fingers along my arm when I point out an interestingly shaped gourd.

I "accidentally" brush my ass against him when reaching for a pumpkin in front of him, and he discreetly digs his crotch into me.

A thought suddenly strikes me. "Ryan, earlier, you said you spoke to Angela. Not the police. Angela."

"Yeah," Ryan balks, and his body tenses slightly against mine.

"Why did you go to Angela?"

"Angela and I…have a history. It's complicated."

"Complicated how?" I ask, turning to face him fully.

He sighs, obviously frustrated that I keep asking him about things he doesn't want to talk about. I know he'd rather just dry hump and play around. "She and I were engaged. We didn't end amicably. Maybe…maybe when you talk to the police, talk to Detective Kim, not her."

"What, why?"

"I just…don't know if she can speak to you…impartially."

She seemed perfectly amiable when I spoke to her. "Why? Is she still harboring intense feelings for you and will scratch my eyes out if she sees me?" I tease, trying to lighten the sudden heaviness.

"I mean…maybe," he says, his eyes meeting mine with unexpected intensity.

"What!? Why!?"

"Well, she always blamed you for our breakup."

"What? What did I have to do with your breakup? You and I haven't even spoken in years."

"Well, she always thought I didn't want to marry her because I was holding out for you."

I dig my heels into the ground. "Why would she think that, Ryan?"

"I dunno."

"Ryan…please, just be honest with me. You're holding something back from me. Did you break up with her because of me?"

"No! I broke up with her because I got cancer."

"That doesn't make any sense, Ryan. Why would you break up with her because of that?"

"Because she wanted kids. That's all she ever talked about. When I got cancer…I just couldn't…I knew she'd stay with me out of obligation, and I just couldn't do that to her."

"Ryan, if she loved you, she would have—"

"That was the point, Celeste, she would have, but I didn't want her to do that. I couldn't be the guy she stayed with out of pity."

"But, that's not how love works, Ryan."

He shrugs. “We weren’t a good fit. It was for the best.”

The phrase strikes through me, loaded with so many memories. He always said that: “It was for the best.” He makes decisions and assumes he knows what is best for everyone involved. But he doesn’t discuss it with them. It’s fucking annoying. *Is that why he stopped talking to me? Was it ‘for the best’? Best for who, Ryan!?*

He continues, “You’ve seen her. The fact that she’s pregnant isn’t exactly a secret. She’s better off now. Got exactly what she wanted.”

“Ryan…”

“I…I realized I might have been staying with her out of obligation. I thought I was gonna die. I didn’t want to live the last bit of my life with regrets.”

“Do you have regrets now?”

The afternoon is fading, shadows lengthening across the pumpkin patch as other visitors begin to drift toward the parking lot.

“Well, I regret that we didn’t find that perfect pumpkin,” he says, putting his hands in his pockets and looking around.

I laugh.

He’s at the point where he is deflecting my questions with jokes, so I know there’s no point in trying to push anything else out of him. I’m surprised I’ve gotten as much out of him as I have.

Ryan pulls me against him, his arms encircling my waist. “There’s a hayride starting soon. Wanna’ go?” he asks, dropping a kiss on the top of my head.

I glance at my watch. “I should probably take Watson home. He looks tired.” A drop of rain splashes on my wrist. “And, it looks like it’s starting to rain.”

He grabs two gnarled, but charming pumpkins, holding one under each arm. “Alright, let’s take him home and carve these pumpkins at my place. I’ve got all the tools. I’ll drive you.”

45

Ryan's studio apartment occupies the top floor of a converted warehouse at the edge of town, all exposed brick and iron-framed windows that stretch from floor to ceiling. It's exactly the kind of space I'd expect him to inhabit—chaotic yet intentional, with canvases in various states of completion leaning against walls and dried paint splattered across the concrete floor. The light from a streetlight filters through rain-speckled windows, casting long shadows across the open floor plan where a king-sized bed occupies one corner, a kitchenette another, and the central space serves as both a living room and art studio.

"Home sweet home," Ryan says, shrugging off his jacket and hanging it on a repurposed ladder that serves as a coat rack.

I wander toward a half-finished landscape, recognizing the bend in the river I've visited many times. "It's perfect. Very you."

He moves to the kitchenette and places the basket of apples in the sink."That could be an insult or a compliment, depending on your definition of 'very me.'"

"Definitely a compliment," I assure him, continuing my exploration. Vintage lighting fixtures cast warm pools of amber across the space, softening the industrial edges. A massive wooden table dominates the center of the room; it, too, has paint stains upon it.

"I'm hoping to move, actually. Have some more space. Get a dog. Or maybe a cat. I've been here…forever. I'm so close to having enough to buy the orchard, though." He pauses, removing a pot from a lower cabinet. "I was hoping to make cider. To continue the autumn theme. How's that sound?"

"Awesome." I settle onto a weathered leather couch positioned to catch the best light from the windows.

He grins, retrieving cinnamon sticks and brown sugar. "Just so you know, my oral sex skills aren't the only thing that have improved with time. My homemade cider also has."

My body still hums from the foreplay that has been the entire day, making me hyperaware of his movements as he crosses the room to hand me a steaming mug.

"Did someone tell you your oral sex skills have improved? It certainly wasn't me," I laugh.

"You wound me, Star Girl," he says, washing the apples.

"Thanks for today," I say, breathing in the aroma of the apple as he begins to peel and cut them. "I needed this more than I realized."

Ryan turns from his apple cutting to look at me. "The farm, or…" he trails off, the question evident.

"All of it," I admit. "And…Michael really got in my head. The idea of you killing Richard…I don't know. It just…threw me."

He fills the pot with water and says, "Well, I'm happy to have cleared my name."

Outside, rain begins to fall in earnest, fat droplets tapping against the windows in an irregular rhythm. The sound creates a cocoon of intimacy around us, as if the world beyond the loft has ceased to exist.

While we wait for the few hours that the apples need to boil, we chat, and he tells me about the various unfinished art pieces he has scattered around his home. Primarily, he creates paintings, but he also has a few pieces in other media, including clay sculptures and stained glass are also placed among his work. He even has a massive computer with a drawing tablet attached. He shows me pictures of the ones already in Minneapolis, ready for the art gallery opening. His work is beautiful, and I love to see how excited he gets when he talks about it. It's nice. Like old times: the two of us just chatting and sharing with each other.

"So," Ryan says after we've savored the cider, "still up for pumpkin carving? Or would you prefer more…creative activities?" His eyebrow raises suggestively, and I can't help but laugh.

"Let's carve the pumpkins," I decide. "I haven't done it since we were kids."

"Alright." He stands, collecting newspapers from a stack near his painting supplies. "I want to see if you're still as terrible at it as you were when we were kids."

"I was not terrible," I protest, helping him spread newspaper across the wooden table. "I was…innovative."

"Is that what we're calling it now?" He retrieves the two pumpkins from a canvas bag by the door. "Because I distinctly remember your last jack-o'-lantern looking like it had been attacked by a rabid animal."

I throw a crumpled piece of newspaper at him, which he dodges effortlessly. "At least I carved mine! You would spend so long drawing the design that you almost never got around to carving it."

"Precision is an art form," he defends, setting the pumpkins on the table with an exaggerated formality that makes me smile.

Ryan lays out an impressive array of carving tools and sculpting implements. He catches my raised eyebrow and shrugs. "Artist," he reminds me. He chuckles to himself, then says, "These pumpkins aren't the only things getting carved tonight."

"I know that's meant to sound seductive, but I can't for the life of me figure out what it actually means."

He laughs, "I don't know. It definitely sounded sexier in my head."

"It sounds menacing, actually," I laugh. And I'm thankful he gave me his alibi before he said a line like that. "Good thing I don't still suspect you're a murderer. To confirm, you haven't murdered anyone who's not Richard, have you, Ry Guy?"

He just laughs, "No, Star Girl, you haven't murdered anyone, have you?"

"Nope."

"Well, good. I'm glad we got that out of the way."

We work side by side, cutting lids from our respective pumpkins. The smell of pumpkin innards fills the space as we scoop out the stringy guts and seeds. Ryan's methodical approach contrasts with my more haphazard technique.

"You've got some..." Ryan gestures to my cheek, where I've apparently smeared pumpkin goop. Before I can wipe it away, he leans across the table and runs his thumb along my skin, removing the offending substance with a gentleness that contradicts his mischievous expression.

"Thanks," I murmur, capturing his wrist before he can pull away. On impulse, I turn my head and press a kiss to his palm, tasting the bitterness of pumpkin and the salt of his skin.

His eyes darken, pupils expanding in the dim light. "Careful, Celeste. We'll never finish these masterpieces if you keep looking at me like that."

"Like what?" I ask innocently, releasing his hand.

"Like you want me to fuck you on this counter."

I laugh, returning to my pumpkin. "Well, there's no room. These are really big pumpkins."

His eyebrows shoot up. "Say the word and I'll throw these fuckers right on the ground."

I tease. "I know you're jealous of my artistic skills, but destroying my work isn't called for."

"So, jealous," he laughs. He begins carving with precise, confident strokes, transforming his pumpkin with apparent effortlessness.

I focus on my own creation, which is already taking a more abstract form than I intended. I marvel at his. He's always been a talented artist, but the years have only improved his skills. "You've become quite the artist in every sense of the word. Very...skilled with your hands."

The double entendre isn't lost on him. "I've had plenty of practice," he says, his voice dropping to that lower register that indicates he's trying to seduce me.

Our banter continues as we carve, each comment more suggestive than the last, building a tension that crackles between us. When Ryan stands to retrieve candles from a drawer, he deliberately brushes against me from behind, his hands settling briefly on my hips.

"Just reaching past you," he murmurs, his breath warm against my neck.

"No, you're not," I counter, leaning back into him slightly. "You're trying to distract me from my masterpiece."

His chuckle vibrates through my body. "Is it working?"

In answer, I turn in his arms, abandoning my half-carved pumpkin to face him. "It always has."

Our lips meet in a kiss that's significantly less gentle than our earlier exchanges. There's an urgency now, a hunger that's been building all day. Ryan's hands slide beneath my sweater, fingers splaying across the bare skin of my back, pulling me flush against him.

I taste apple cider and desire on his tongue and feel the solid strength of his body aligning with mine. My own hands aren't idle, exploring the contours of his chest through his shirt before working at the buttons with determined fingers.

"The pumpkins—" he starts to say against my lips.

"—can wait," I finish, pushing his shirt from his shoulders to reveal skin I've been wanting to touch all day.

He groans as I palm his chest. With surprising strength, he lifts me onto the edge of the table, positioning himself between my thighs. My legs wrap around his waist instinctively, drawing him closer.

"Want me to fuck you on this table now?" he asks, his voice rough with want but his eyes searching mine for confirmation.

"Maybe let's go to the bed. I don't want pumpkin goop to get all over me," I tell him.

That's all the permission he needs. With swift movements, he helps me out of my sweater, his appreciative gaze making me feel beautiful despite my practical cotton bra. His lips find my collarbone, trailing kisses down to the swell of my breasts as his hands support my back.

"You're still so perfect," he murmurs against my skin.

We abandon the pumpkins entirely, leaving them hollow-eyed witnesses as Ryan leads me toward his bed. The rain has intensified, drumming against the windows and painting streaks of silver across the darkening loft. *It'll start snowing soon. I bet these windows give a beautiful view of it.*

Our remaining clothes fall away piece by piece. Ryan lowers me to the bed with a tenderness that makes my heart ache. "I've never seen anything as beautiful as you naked," he confesses, hovering above me, his eyes drinking in every detail as if committing me to memory.

"That can't be true," I whisper, reaching up to trace the contours of his face.

"It is," he says, running his hands down my body. Knowing exactly where to touch, how much pressure to apply, when to be gentle, and when to be firm. Years of experience are not forgotten after years of separation. His mouth follows paths that his fingers blaze, drawing sounds from me I didn't know I could make. When he settles between my thighs, looking up with a question in his eyes, I nod wordlessly, threading my fingers through his hair in encouragement.

The sensation of his mouth against me is almost too much after the anticipation we've built throughout the day. My back arches, my body seeking more of what he's offering so skillfully. He steadies me with a strong arm across my hips, taking his time as if we have forever, as if pleasing me is the only goal that matters.

When I'm trembling on the edge, he rises to kiss me deeply.

"Okay, so you have improved," I whisper.

"I know," he chuckles.

Our eyes lock as he positions himself. In this moment of connection, I'm overwhelmed with how much I love him. Always have. I wish he loved me in the same way.

"Ryan," I breathe as he pushes forward, filling me in a way that feels like completion.

"Star Girl," he answers.

We move together with increasing urgency, my nails scoring his back as he drives deeper. What begins as controlled passion soon dissolves into something more primal, more necessary. The sound of rain and our mingled breathing creates a mesmerizing soundtrack.

"Look at me," he urges as I feel myself approaching the precipice again. "I want to see you."

I open eyes I hadn't realized I'd closed. His gaze burns into me with an intensity that pushes me over the edge.

My release washes through me in waves. He follows soon after, his rhythm faltering, his arms shaking as he collapses beside me, careful not to crush me with his weight.

For several minutes, we lie tangled together, our breath slowing and heartbeats gradually returning to normal. Ryan's fingers trace my thighs, his touch now soothing rather than arousing.

"Celeste, I missed you so much," he says finally, pressing a kiss to my temple.

I say softly, curling into his side, "I wish we hadn't lost so much time."

"Me, too," he murmurs, pulling a soft blanket over us. Outside, thunder rumbles, a distant accompaniment to the persistent rain.

We lie in comfortable silence, listening to the storm and exchanging gentle touches. Thoughts of Michael and James flit through my mind.

Really, what am I doing? Running from my feelings by having sex with these guys? Instead of facing reality, I just spend all my energy thinking about hooking up or solving this murder I'm not qualified to solve.

"What are you thinking about?" he asks, his voice thick with approaching sleep. *That I need to apologize to Michael.* I don't want to tell him that, though.

I prop myself up on one elbow to look at him properly, taking in his tousled hair and satisfied expression. "That we never finished our pumpkins."

His laugh is deep and genuine. "Tomorrow," he promises, pulling me back down against his chest.

46

Ryan whistles a tune I can't place, something swingy and old, as he hovers behind me on my porch. His hands find my waist, and he grinds against my backside as I fumble with the keys. My neck is stiff from falling asleep on his chest last night, but it's probably better than the couch I've insisted on sleeping on for the last few weeks. It's early and we've come to get a change of clothes so we can go to the cafe and eat breakfast. *Maybe have some shower sex first.*

Just as I turn the key in the latch, we hear, "Oye, Duck, Son! Hold up!" from Ryan's father's house. I see a flash of flannel and silvered-blond hair disappearing into the house for only a second.

"Fuck," Ryan whispers, pulling away from me.

"Where'd he go?" I ask arching to see him.

"I think he went inside to get something."

Mr. O'Connor pops out of his house and bounds toward us, looking so remarkably like Ryan it's almost disarming. He's holding two large brown paper bags.

Ryan closes his eyes and groans. "Morning, Dad."

"Mornin', Son. Happy to see I raised a gentleman who doesn't make young ladies walk home by themselves in the morning."

"Dad…we're almost forty."

"Young to me! Morning, Duck." He walks past Ryan and gives me a fatherly peck on the head.

"What's with the bags, Dad?" Ryan asks.

Mr. O'Connor ignores him, focusing instead on me. "Figured you might not have much in the way of groceries."

I feel my cheeks color. "Oh, Mr. O'Connor, you didn't have to do that."

He leans forward. "Aye, I know. But if I waited for you to ask for help, I'd be waitin' forever. So here." He says, shoving the bags into Ryan's arms. "Take those in for her, Son."

I peek inside and spot a loaf of bakery bread, a stick of butter, a pint of milk, and a box of tea. I blink. "Thank you, Mr. O'Connor."

He shrugs, but there's a proud set to his shoulders. "Think nothing of it, girly—just the essentials. Regina tells me you haven't been feeding yourself. I couldn't have that."

"Thank you," I say, voice wavering. "Really. How much do I owe you?"

He waves off my gratitude. "Not a cent, Duck. You may be a millionaire, but I'm the adult here. I will not take money from you." *Billionaire, actually.*

Ryan protests. "Dad…we're almost forty."

Mr. O'Connor waves him off, "Stop saying that, you're making me feel old. And don't you dare say that I'm old." He returns his attention to me. "So what have you been up to? You sold that company. What's the plan now?"

"Dad! Stop interrogating her."

"I'm not interrogating her, Son. I just wanna know about her."

"Why, so you can tell everyone what she's up to?"

"I don't need to tell them, Son, she's always at the cafe, everyone already knows."

I break in, "I'm not sure, Mr. O'Connor. I've been thinking about, I don't know, settling down. Maybe starting a garden. Starting a family. Maybe getting a dog. I've been enjoying my time with Watson."

Mr. O'Connor nods at me. "That sounds wonderful, Duck."

I look down at my feet, frowning. *What the fuck am I doing?*

Mr. O'Connor must note my change in mood, because he asks, "You sure you're doing okay, Duck? I…worry about you in this house all by yourself."

I respond, "I'm okay, I've always lived alone."

Mr. O'Connor fixes me with a look; there's no longer a teasing O'Connor joviality to it. He says with mournful concern, "Yeah, but this house has all those memories."

I sigh. Realizing in this moment the truth of what he's saying. "It's been a bit difficult," I say. "Some days I'm fine. Some days, I can't breathe in there. But it's getting easier. I've got Ryan helping me."

Mr. O'Connor shakes his head, lips twitching. "You two: always the same." He looks at Ryan, then back at me. His gaze lands on Ryan, and his whole demeanor shifts—becomes sly, a little challenging. "I just hope my boy doesn't pull the same stunt as he did with Angela." He lets the implication hang.

Ryan bristles, and for once, his joking shields are down. "It wasn't a stunt, Dad. I wanted her to have what she needed. I couldn't give it to her."

"I just don't want you chasing Duck off again, Ry." It's such a dad thing to say, and so completely out of left field, that my heart aches.

"I didn't chase her off, Dad, she left, and you know why she left." The tension zings, then flattens.

"Sure, but if you had proposed like you planned, maybe it wouldn't have taken her twenty years to come home," Mr. O'Connor says, so quietly I almost miss it.

My heart pounds in my chest. *Propose?*

Ryan's jaw works. "Dad, I wasn't the reason she didn't come back."

"Well, you certainly didn't help, pushing her away like you always do. And now she's got all those other guys. Just like with Marcus. You've been like this ever since your moth—"

"Dad, enough. I'm not going to push her away this time," Ryan says, plain as day. It knocks the wind out of me.

Mr. O'Connor crows, claps his hands together. "That's what I like to hear! See, Celeste? He's a slow starter, but he gets there. Well, I'll leave you two love birds to it. There's eggs in there. Make her breakfast, Son."

"Sure, Dad." Ryan rolls his eyes, likely for the hundredth time in the last five minutes.

My door barely clicks shut behind us before Ryan heads straight for my kitchen. I trail after him, my head buzzing from the collision of emotions.

Ryan pulls open a cabinet and lets out a little "Ha!" marveling at remembering where my parents kept their plates.

He holds up the loaf of bread. "How long do you think Dad's been planning this rescue mission?"

I don't answer.

He pops the bags open. "You want some tea? Or are you sticking with coffee? He got some of that, too."

I hesitate. "Tea."

He slices the bread like he's done it a thousand times, which he probably has. Ryan's hands are quick and competent, making short work of the little kitchen, remembering where everything is placed like he's lived here his whole life.

I just watch him in silence, elbows on the counter.

When the kettle hisses, he opens the cabinet with mugs, grabs the first, and places it in front of me. My eyes lock on it—one of my mother's old "World's Best Mom" mugs. The irony is suffocating. He follows my gaze, then realization crosses his face. He grabs the mug, walks to the trash can, pops it open with his foot, then drops it in, before retrieving a less emotionally loaded mug.

He watches me, like he's waiting for a confrontation as he pours us tea. The silence stretches.

Ryan butters a slice of bread for me and slides it across the counter. "Eat," he says, like I'm a stray cat he's decided to keep.

I chew, slow and deliberate, then hold the warm cup against myself.

"Care to explain?" I finally ask.

Ryan's face flames red. I expect him to deflect, to change the subject, but he doesn't. Instead, he glances at me, and for the first time, I see the truth in his eyes—raw, unfiltered, nothing held back.

"You were my girl…" he says, his voice cracking.

"I was your best friend, you mean…" I say, watching his face, waiting for him to admit what I've been suspecting since I've returned.

"Nah, you were my girl. You just didn't know it. I didn't either," he says with a laugh. "Well, not until you dumped me for the golden boy quarterback. That's when I figured it out."

I blink, genuinely confused. "What are you talking about? I never dumped you, Ryan. We were never together."

A shadow crosses his face. "I know. But…we might as well have been. We spent every moment together. We did everything together. Everything. Then Marcus decided he wanted you, and suddenly I was just your buddy again. No more benefits for this friend."

I stare at him, trying to reconcile his version of our past with my memories. "Ryan, we were best friends. You always introduced me as your 'practically sister.' You never once hinted that you wanted anything more. You always said the sex was just…what was it you used to say? 'A way for us to get off without having to worry about all those feelings that come along with dating.'And if I ever asked about our relationship, you'd be like, 'Why ruin a beautiful friendship, Star Girl?'" I say that last bit in a deep mocking voice.

"Because I was terrified of ruining our friendship," he says, frustration edging his voice. "And then when I finally worked up the courage to tell you how I felt, you started dating Marcus."

My mind races back through our shared history, reassessing moments I'd taken at face value. The way he'd look at me sometimes when he thought I wasn't paying attention. His sullenness when I started dating Marcus. The distance that grew between us during that final year of high school. The way he never went anywhere without me in college.

"You never said anything," I say softly. "Not once, Ryan."

"I tried," he counters. "So many times."

"And you…You were going to propose?" I ask. Unable to believe it.

He winces. "When we graduated from college, I asked you to come back to Goose Grove with me instead of going to California. I'm sure you remember that."

I do remember—it was the last time I saw my best friend. The night he listed the reasons why he and I should return to Goose Grove. He got unusually serious. I thought he was just sad he wouldn't be living with me anymore. That he'd miss me. If I had known it was going to be the last time I saw him for twenty years. If I had known he was going to ask me to marry him…

"I had no idea that was a romantic declaration," I tell him honestly and rise to stand beside him.

He laughs, but there's no humor in it. "Yeah, well, I wasn't exactly smooth back then."

"And you think you're smooth now?" I bump his arm with my shoulder, trying to recapture our earlier lightness.

His smile returns slowly. "I mean, ladies on the internet tell me I'm a real catch." His hand finds mine, our fingers intertwining naturally.

I feel a flush creeping up my neck. "They're not wrong."

"Are you saying you think I'm a catch, Celeste?" His eyes search mine, vulnerability peeking through his confident exterior.

Instead of answering with words, I lean forward and press my lips to his, a soft kiss that quickly deepens as his free hand comes up to cradle my cheek. When we part, he remains at my eye level, and I rest my forehead against his.

"Does that answer your question?" I whisper.

He nods, his thumb stroking my cheekbone. "For the record, I'm glad you didn't stay for me back then. You needed to go live your life."

"And now I'm back where I started," I say, a trace of irony in my voice.

"Not where you started," he corrects me. "Just back to where you belong. With much better kissing this time around."

"I dunno, the kissing was always pretty good," I say lightly, though the words hold new meaning now that I understand the depth of his feelings back then.

"It wasn't the only thing that was pretty good," he says simply.

47

The autumn wind at the edge of Goose Grove Park smacks the tip of my nose, which is already pink from the walk. *It's not the cold that will getcha', but the wind.* The sound of the Fall Festival carries on the painful breeze, a delightful ribbon through the trees: music, laughter, the din of carnival rides.

Watson flings himself forward and immediately buries his face in a mound of leaves. He emerges seconds later looking triumphant, his muzzle freckled with bits of maple and a dead beetle lodged squarely in the middle of his forehead. I squat and flick it off before Mrs. Heart notices.

"Nice work," I say to Watson as we start the slow parade down the path, "you've thoroughly scattered that perfect pile of leaves."

He blinks at me, then resumes his prancing. Mrs. Heart is right behind us, clutching her prized apple pie to her chest with both hands; her knitted cardigan is buttoned all the way to the chin, and I wish she had brought a coat.

Rows of vendor tents stretch across the baseball diamond, their striped roofs staked down with cinder blocks and hope. Kids in face paint zigzag between hay bales stacked into a makeshift maze.

Mrs. Heart pauses for a moment. "Celeste, dear, just a moment." I turn to wait for her. She edges open the pie box just enough to check the lattice.

She's made eight pies this week, but this is her "show winner." It's the kind with a golden top crust and precisely braided edges. I personally prefer her crumble top, but I'd die before telling her. She keeps pausing to make sure it hasn't shifted. I offered to hold it for her, but she's protecting that thing as if her life depended on it. She acquiesced and let me hold Watson, though—her other prized possession.

It's fine that she keeps pausing to check, because Watson and I aren't moving particularly fast. Watson stops every twenty feet to sniff a suspicious clump of grass or to flirt with a passing townsperson. I don't mind. It's hard to be impatient when the whole park is frosted in orange light and the air smells like apple cider and wood smoke—*fall as fuck.*

Mrs. Heart peers at the pie, her face scrunching as she scrutinizes it. She snaps the lid closed and says, "I really need a win this year. This might be my last chance."

"You'll win," I say, scratching behind Watson's ears. When I look up to meet Mrs. Heart's eyes, Angela and Sheriff Kim appear in my periphery. They're staring at me and whispering to each other.

"Mrs. Heart…" I choke.

"Yes, dear?"

"I think the cops…are watching me."

"Where?" she asks, her voice rising in pitch slightly, as her head whips around to find them.

I look back at Watson, trying not to call attention to the fact that I can see them, and nod my head discreetly in their direction.

She looks casually and then more blatantly. "Hmm…I don't see them, dear. Are you sure you saw them?"

I whip my gaze back to where I had spotted them, and they are no longer there. "Oh…I…don't see them anymore."

"They're probably just here patrolling. Don't let it ruin your day, dear."

I stand slowly, feeling the eyes of cops on me. But, no matter how much I look around, I don't see them again. *Mrs. Heart is right. The whole town is here. Of course, they're here, too.*

The contest tent looms at the center of the festival area, striped in white and red so bright it burns into your retina. The entrance is flanked by two scarecrows in matching Vikings football jerseys.

Mrs. Heart inhales, squares her shoulders, and marches inside as if she's entering a gauntlet. I follow with Watson, who instantly zeroes in on a booth labeled "Homemade Jerky" and tries to drag me off course. I pull his dead weight through the dirt.

Inside, I spot Gus, this year's master of ceremonies. His outfit is ridiculous: red suspenders covered in apple appliques and a hat shaped like a pumpkin. Mrs. Heart smiles at him, and her tension relaxes when he winks at her.

"Watson and I will wait over there," I whisper, giving Mrs. Heart's shoulder a quick squeeze, and pointing near the entrance.

She gives me a nod. "Thanks, dear."

She moves to the check-in table, where two tweens in matching sashes jot her info on clipboards and try not to look bored. The rest of the room is a low-grade chaos of nervous bakers.

Watson sits obediently, then slowly slides into a lying position, head on paws, his nose twitching in time with each pie that passes us. His patience amazes me, though it might just be resignation; he's learned that if he waits long enough, someone will inevitably drop food within range.

Mrs. Heart is making the rounds, greeting old friends and frenemies alike. There's a performative element to the whole affair, a gentle ribbing disguised as rivalry.

Watson lets out a huff and presses his head into my knee. "I know, buddy," I say. "It's a lot." I scratch under his collar and watch as the line for judging grows longer.

Out in the field, the lights on the Ferris wheel flicker to life, and the sun sinks behind the tree line in a last burst of gold.

Mrs. Heart waves from the table she'll be stationed at, her face flush with excitement and exertion. "All checked in!" she calls.

I head over, Watson at heel. "Well, I'm going to go find Michael. I'll be back for the judging. Do you want me to take Watson?"

"Yes, we're still going to be setting up, and the smells will be a bit too tempting for him," she says.

Watson wags his tail in solemn approval.

By the time I slip out of the contest tent, the sky is the color of blueberry jam, and the evening lights of the festival begin to light. Watson weaves between my legs, which is a trick he only pulls when he's particularly excited.

48

The Ferris wheel is our goal. Its lights blink through the dusk, a slow hypnotic spin against the darkening blue, drawing a steady line of people to the ticket booth.

I spot Michael near a display of jack-o'-lanterns. He's got his hands jammed in his jacket pockets, and his eyes are scanning for me.

He sees me, adjusts his glasses, and manages a small smile. When we approach him, he lets out a "Hey," that's almost a sigh.

"Hey," I reply.

"Celeste, I'm so sorry, I—"

My stomach twists. This is what I came for, so I need to say it. I cut him off. "No, don't be sorry. I was being stupid." And then, because it's been festering, "I'm sorry I was so mad at you. And I'm sorry I was being short with you via text. I'll be more communicative in the future."

He lifts one shoulder, a slow, careful shrug. "I would've been mad at me, too. I wasn't exactly…tactful."

I shake my head. "No, I just—I don't like surprises. And it's been a weird few weeks. Of course, you should have told the police what you saw. I'm so sorry, Michael."

Michael looks at me. "You don't have to apologize. I understand why you were upset. I know Ryan is important to you."

Watson noses at his shoes, tail wagging like a perfect metronome. Michael bends and scratches the dog behind the ears. He smiles at me, but the tension between us is still there.

"Still, I'm sorry…um…I'd like to make it up to you," I say, batting my eyelashes at him in a way I hope is obviously a sexual proposition.

Michael's smile turns sideways, wry. "What exactly did you have in mind?"

I look toward the Ferris wheel. "How do you feel about heights?"

Michael's eyebrow shoots up, and his gaze turns to the Ferris wheel. "You want to ride the Ferris wheel?"

I say yes, before my anxiety can say otherwise. I don't actually like heights, but if my eyes are pointed toward the ground of the gondola, I won't even know I'm in the air. *Right?*

We step into line, surrounded by sparkling lights and the scent of machine grease. Michael's hands are jammed in his pockets—protection against the cold.

I thread my arm around his, recalling how much he likes cuddles. He smiles at me and hugs my arm with his opposite hand. The twinkling lights of the wheel reflect on those slutty little glasses that drive me crazy, and his kind eyes soften when they catch mine. *He is so beautiful.* I swoon, "You look nice tonight, Michael."

He grins, the small and private kind. "Thanks. You look gorgeous." We kiss in that comfortable way two people who appreciate each other do, and the tension of the fight we had seems to have melted between us.

Our turn comes, and the Ferris wheel operator waves us forward. "Michael, you can't bring Watson on this thing! It's not safe," the operator chides.

If it's not safe for the dog, is it safe for us? Fuck, am I really going to get on that thing?

The man reaches for Watson's leash and says, "Here, give me his leash, I'll watch him."

I don't hand it over and look at Michael for an explanation. He replies, "Celeste, this is Dr. Vance. He's the local vet. He'll take good care of Watson."

Still unsure about handing over woman's best friend, I stutter, "Oh, okay, if you say so." I reluctantly give the man the leash.

"Want some peanut butter, Watty?" Dr. Vance asks Watson.

Peanut butter must be on the list of phrases Watson knows, because he immediately forgets I exist and accepts the transfer of power without hesitation. I laugh at his opportunist nature.

Dr. Vance ushers us into a rattling blue carriage. It's top-half is fully glassed with benches on both sides. I'm grateful for the protection from the cold, and I'm sure Michael will be, too, given his dislike for it. We get comfortable, and I hope no one else gets in with us, because this is the kind of privacy a girl can use to her slutty, apologetic advantage.

Dr. Vance approaches the gondola and says, "I'll let you two have this one to yourselves," with a wink.

Michael laughs and thanks him as he closes the door.

The wheel turns slightly to queue up the next carriage, and my heart lurches into my stomach.

I grab the safety bar, pulse hammering, but Michael just sits, legs crossed, utterly at ease.

I wish this thing had a lap bar. Or fucking seatbelts. Shit. This was dumb. I saw an enclosed space, and my horniness got the better of me.

The wheel jerks to life, spinning consistently now, and the town drops away beneath us in a quilt of lights and shadows. From up here, Goose Grove looks small and gentle. I close my eyes, just for a second, and try to push the terrified thoughts out of my head.

The carriage rocks back and forth under us, and the sound of the fair drops away as we rise. I grip the safety bar at my left tighter, like I might float off if I let go.

Michael notices I'm freaking the fuck out and asks, "So, jump scares aren't the only thing that frightens you, huh?"

"What? What do you mean?" I ask, gripping the rail harder, fooling absolutely no one.

"Celeste, sweetheart, why did you bring me to this thing if you're so scared?"

"I…I had a dumb idea of blowing you up here," I laugh.

"Ah, Celeste, you don't have to do that. Come here," he says, scooting toward me and pulling me into his chest. "Don't worry, sweetheart. I got you."

His touch comforts me, relaxing my shoulders. I let go of the bar and lean into him.

The cart shakes as he pulls me tighter. I squeal, close my eyes, and nuzzle into his neck. His pulse jumps against my nose.

For a while, neither of us speaks. He just hugs me, rubbing my back, and I take him in his warm scent.

When we reach the apex of the wheel, it comes to a screeching halt, making a noise similar to the one I make in the exact moment. The carriage tilting forward in a slow, stomach-churning arc, at the loss of momentum.

"God, you're fucking adorable," Michael says, petting my head as I nuzzle deeper into him.

I open my eyes and peek out from his neck, getting an eyeful of his jaw. "Did…did we stop?"

"Yep."

"Why!?"

"That's what Ferris wheels do," he says with a chuckle. "This is when you appreciate the scenery.

"I like your neck just fine," I reply, returning to the safety of his neck.

He chuckles, "Okay, sweetheart."

After a few moments, I open one eye and peer out, craning my neck slightly to see over the rim without letting go of Michael. Below, the festival glows in pools of blue and amber. The amber reminds me of Michael's eyes. The air is full of music, but up here it's just a vague tremor. We're in our own world.

Michael leans slightly to the side, trying not to shake the cart, and looks down. He keeps his arms wrapped around me, protecting me.

The way the muscles in his neck pull taut and his hair brushes against it, paired with how the light reflects off his slutty little glasses—*Jesus, he is so handsome. I should tell him.*

"You're so handsome," I say, and his eyes flicker to mine. He smiles, like he wasn't expecting me to say that.

There's a heat now, not from the air—my hands are still numb from the October wind—but from the way he looks at me. Even with the town spinning below and the carriages creaking like they're made of nothing but rust, I feel still. Maybe even brave.

I shift closer and put my hand on his. "You know," I say, "I really like you, Michael." He simply smiles in return, before nervously adjusting his glasses.

My hand moves to his lap, and even though I know exactly what I'm doing, my heart is doing backflips. I don't ask; I just brush the inside of his knee, slow enough to give him a chance to move away if he wants. He doesn't. His leg tenses, then relaxes, and I can feel the pulse in his thigh.

I unzip his jeans, careful, like unwrapping something breakable. Michael inhales, his hand not wrapped around my shoulder, moving to his knee, gripping hard. I release his beautiful dick and admire it only momentarily, before cupping the tip with my fist. I glance up—his eyes are closed, his mouth in a straight line, and he pulls at the collar of his shirt.

Be brave, Celeste.

I slowly lift from the seat so I can kneel on the floor of the carriage. It's cold and gritty with sand that I can feel through my jeans. The carriage rocks again, just enough to throw off my balance. Michael grips me, stopping me from freaking the fuck out. I plant one hand on the bench to steady myself, and shriek again.

"Celeste, I appreciate the gesture, but, seriously, you do not—"

He cuts off when I take him into my mouth, and lets out a sound that's almost a word. My hair slips over his thighs, and he tenses under me, hands now braced against the seat.

I go slow, letting him get used to it, and there's something so intimate about the small space and the chill in the air and the way his hand moves—tentative at first, then steady—into my hair. He's never rough, not with me, and even now he only guides, doesn't pull.

The wheel resumes, turning. Every so often, it halts, and we hang in space. I hear a voice from below, the operator shouting something, but it might as well be in another world. I glance up, and now, the glass of the gondola is so fogged that Michael probably can't see out of it anymore. Which means others can't see in. Not that they could see me down here anyway.

Michael's hips roll up, subtle, a rhythm that matches the slow turn of the Ferris wheel. The cart shakes with his gentle thrusts. I can hear the sharpness of his breath, the way it stutters when I take him deeper, the tiny gasps that he'd probably be embarrassed to know he makes.

"Celeste," he says, a whisper, and I pull back just enough to look up. His eyes are open now, fixed on me. "Can I? Can I come…in your mouth?"

I give him a small thumbs up, and I press my tongue under the head of his cock, feeling the tremble go through his whole body. I take him in again, working a steady rhythm. The carriage lurches, but this time I'm ready, one hand cupped around him, the other steadying myself.

He's close; I can tell by the way his legs lock. I reach up his shirt and feel his chest. I keep going, a little faster, sucking a little harder, and when he comes, it's quiet but intense. He bites back a sound, but I can feel it everywhere—in his thighs, in his hand tightening in my hair, in the way his whole body shudders against me. I hear a slapping sound, and I suspect he slapped the glass.

I swallow, then wipe my mouth with the back of my hand and grin up at him.

"You okay?" I ask, voice low.

He's breathing hard, but he laughs. "I'm amazing."

I tuck him back into his jeans, careful with the zipper, then slide onto the bench beside him. My knees ache from the metal floor, but I don't care. There's a handprint streaked against the fog of the window. When I spot it, we laugh, and Michael wipes it away with his sleeve.

He returns me to his neck in a hug, and we finish the ride in comfortable silence.

We step off the ride together, and I try not to look too pleased with myself when we collect Watson. As we walk away, Michael whispers, "Don't think I'm going to let you get through this night without coming, too."

49

We walk away from the Ferris wheel, fingers interlaced like we're teenagers who just discovered holding hands. I'm smiling like a fool and leaning into Michael as we walk lazily through the festival grounds. Watson walks beside us, enjoying our languid pace as it allows him the opportunity to sniff everything, and everything here is sniffable.

We wander past game booths, and I'm tempted to get a funnel cake, then remember I need to save room for apple pie.

I spot the "Mysterious Mirror Maze" set up at the edge of the midway. Purple lights flicker through its translucent walls, casting violet shadows across the trampled grass. The entrance is a black mouth ringed with bulbs that buzz and sputter.

"Want to get lost?" I ask, nodding toward it.

Michael's eyes catch the neon light. "With you? Always."

"Wait a minute, is that Andy?" I ask when I see the bright red hair of the person standing at the podium outside the hall.

I rush toward them. "Hey, Andy! What are you doing here?" I ask.

"I'm working here."

"Why?"

"Oh, all the downtown businesses are volunteering their time.

We're trying to raise money to help finish the street repairs," Andy replies.

The street needs repairs? Was that part of the revitalization effort that got postponed?

Andy sighs. "It's been so boring tonight. No one wants to go into this thing. It's kinda cool, though. Why don't you two go in? I can watch Watson."

We pass off Watson once again, and we're barely inside before the world splinters. Mirrors line every surface—walls, ceiling, even sections of the floor—creating an infinite regression of Celestes and Michaels. The purple light makes everything dreamlike, turning my skin lavender and Michael's eyes to dark pools. Music filters in from outside, distorted and watery.

"This way," I say, tugging him down a narrow corridor. Our reflections follow, a hundred Celestes leading a hundred Michaels deeper into the maze.

We bump into dead ends, laugh, and double back. I lose track of which way is out. The pathways are tight, forcing us to walk single file in places, my back brushing against his chest.

"I think we're going in circles," Michael says, his voice bouncing off the glass.

"I think that's the point," I reply, turning to face him.

I press my back against one of the mirror panels. The glass is cool through my sweater. Our reflections multiply around us—me leaning back, him standing close, the space between us electric. I reach out, hook one finger through his belt loop, and pull him toward me.

His hands find my waist. I drape one leg over his hip, and he steps closer until we're flush against each other. The mirrors show us from every angle—the curve of my back, the tense line of his shoulders, the place where our bodies meet.

"I was just thinking about that comment you made," I say, my voice dropping to a whisper. "About the sexual demon at the mansion."

His eyes widen a fraction, then crinkle at the corners. "The one who murdered everyone for sexual gratification?"

"Oh, I forgot about the murder part…" I laugh. "I was mostly just thinking about how I wanted to fuck you in front of all those mirrors."

"Oh, you did?"

I flick open the button of his jeans, with a desperation that betrays my eagerness. His breath hitches. I watch his reflection over his shoulder and enjoy the way his head tips back, just slightly, as I slide my hand down and cup his growing bulge.

"Celeste," he murmurs, his voice a mix of warning and plea. "Someone could—"

"Could what?" I shift against him, feeling his cock harden. "Could see? Could hear?"

His answer is to spin me around, pressing my ass firmly against his crotch. He kisses my neck as he grinds his cock against me, sending waves of heat through my body.

"You're not as shy as you pretend to be," I gasp, as his hands roam over my hips.

"Well, I did say I owed you an orgasm," he whispers into my ear.

He leans me forward, one hand firmly pressed against my back until I'm bent over, my hands braced on the mirror. He unbuttons my jeans and pulls them down, along with my soaked underwear, to my ankles.

I bite my lip to stifle a moan as he runs his fingers over my exposed pussy, spreading the wetness from my entrance up to my clit. He's never been this forceful with me, and I am fucking into it.

He unzips his pants, pulling out his thick cock and sliding it between my slick folds, coating himself in my wetness.

"Oh, God. The things I'd do to be inside you," he says, reaching around and grasping my breasts and pressing his chest against my back. He slides his cock further through my folds, tapping my clit with its head.

I want him inside me. NOW.

"Please fuck me, Michael," I beg, my voice trembling with desperation. "I need you inside me."

He stands upright, shifts, and grips my hips tightly. The head of his cock notches against my entrance for only a moment before he thrusts forward, driving his length into me inch by inch.

He moves slowly at first, but when he finally sheaths himself fully, I can't help but cry out, my body stretching to accommodate his size.

"You okay?" he whispers, holding still, his breath hot on my neck, electrifying me further.

I nod, unable to form coherent words, my senses overwhelmed by the sensation of his body melding with mine. He moves again, drawing his cock back slowly before plunging back in. I arch my back, angling my hips to allow him even deeper access. Another fierce cry escapes my lips as he hits a spot that sends waves of pleasure coursing through me.

"Oh, fuck that sound is hot," he groans, biting his lip as he starts to pound into me more forcefully.

Our reflections surround us in the mirrored room, creating a kaleidoscope of our entwined bodies. The purple light cuts across his face in slices, making him look otherworldly. I watch the reflection of his neck muscles flexing as he drives into me. He lifts my sweater and bra, exposing my breasts so that he can watch them bounce with each powerful thrust.

Everything narrows to this—the pressure of the mirror against my palms, the heat of him inside me, the strange doubling effect of watching ourselves while being lost in sensation.

His pace quickens, his hips thrusting faster and deeper, his cock sliding in and out of me with increasing urgency. My fingers curl against the mirror, leaving foggy prints on the cool surface. My legs start to tremble, my thighs quivering with each powerful stroke he delivers. He shifts his angle, and suddenly his cock is hitting a new spot—one that sends sparks shooting up my spine.

"Look," he whispers. "Look how perfect you are, taking my cock like this."

"Look how perfect you are, fucking me like this," I parrot back, my voice breathy and desperate.

I come, waves of pleasure crashing through me, my pussy clenching around his cock. I reach back to cling to him, my nails digging into his thighs. He comes seconds later, with a shudder and a groan that he buries in my hair, his cock pulsing as he spills into me.

For a moment, we stay locked together, his cock still inside me. We're breathing hard, but I turn so that I can place my forehead against his jaw. Our eyes lock in the mirror's reflection.

Before we can fully recover, voices and laughter from somewhere deeper in the maze indicate others are now in the maze with us—getting closer.

"Shit, Andy said that no one ever comes in here," Michael says with a slight panic, breaking away from me and adjusting his clothes.

"Well, two people just came," I laugh, pulling up my pants.

His anxiety softens, and he laughs at my joke, shaking his head and adjusting his glasses.

We look at each other, both a little wild-eyed, and I can't help but grin. His hair is a mess, somehow, so I run my fingers through it, combing it for him. He adjusts my sweater for me.

"Well, now we need to find the exit," I say.

He tucks a strand of hair behind my ear and points his finger above his head, "Found it."

We follow a glowing exit sign, navigating the last few turns of the maze. When we stumble out into the night air, the sudden space feels vast after the close confines of the mirrors. The festival swirls around us. I glance at my watch. "I should probably get back to Mrs. Heart. The judging will be happening soon."

Michael takes my hand again. His palm is warm against mine, a small intimacy that feels almost as profound as what we just shared. He looks around, "Damn it. We're at the back of the maze."

"Well, that was fun," I say, smiling like a maniac at him.

A look crosses his face, and he pulls me toward him, pulling me into a deep kiss that is more aggressive than he usually is. "You're amazing, Celeste."

"So are you, Michael." I brush his hair out of his face, and he adjusts his glasses in that way he does when he wants to say something.

"What?" I ask, giggling at him.

"Nothing. You're just…so beautiful."

"Thank you, Michael, you are, too."

"Celeste, I lo—"

He's cut off when a gruff, "Hey, you two," startles us from our post-orgasm glow.

We break apart at the sight of James, dressed in his usual suit and sticking out like a sore thumb. He and a few other lawyerly-looking people stand behind a booth with the sign "Ask a Lawyer" overhead.

James laughs and says while looking the two of us up and down, "You look like you've been doing something that might require legal representation." He walks from behind the booth and approaches us.

"We were just in the hall of mirrors. Just walking around," I say as Michael stands tall at my side.

"Mikey, your fly," James whispers, pointing at Michael's crotch.

Michael looks more embarrassed than I've ever seen him when he zips his fly with a "Oh, um, thanks."

"Hey, baby," James says, reaching for my shoulder.

The lawyerly-looking people behind him whisper, and as if reacting to it, he stops his hand, apparently thinking better of displaying affection to me publicly.

Michael glares at him.

James turns to Michael and says, "Never expected to see you at the Harvest Festival, Mikey. It seems Celeste has you coming out of your shell."

"Well, she's worth it," Michael says matter-of-factly.

"That's true. She is," James smiles, and the two just stare at each other, a silent argument brewing between them.

"Well, we have a pie contest to get to. We'll let you get back to work," Michael says, coating the word work with a bit of venom "Let's go get Watson, Celeste."

James smiles almost sadly, "Alright. Goodnight, Celeste. Goodnight, Mikey. Wish Mrs. Heart good luck for me."

"Bye," I say, waving to James as Michael all but pulls me away.

After we are a sufficient distance, I ask Michael, "What was that about?"

His demeanor softens, and he loops his arm around me. "Oh, um, I've always been a bit of an indoor cat. Going to the cafe to write or for a jog outside was about as adventurous as I used to get."

Of all the things that just went down, the comment about Michael coming to the Harvest Festival was the least of my curiosity. *Did you almost tell me you love me? What's with you and James?* I think Michael might be deliberately deflecting, so I don't push. I don't want to splinter our newly healed truce.

"Oh, so you didn't do a lot of public indecency before meeting me?" I ask with a laugh.

He laughs, pulling me closer, "No, I did not."

"Wanna do more?"

He laughs again. "Maybe let's get the dog and some pie first?"

"Sounds good."

50

Principal Gandy's, I mean Gus's, voice booms tinny through ancient speakers, "And now, ladies and gentlemen, we'll be judging Best Pie!"

We slip in through a gap in the crowd, murmuring apologies as we navigate around elbows and purses. Straining on tiptoes, I scan the room for Mrs. Heart.

"There," Michael says, pointing. Mrs. Heart stands at the edge of the crowd, one hand pressed to her collar, the other clutching her pie plate like a shield. She's looking around, likely for me and Watson.

We rush toward her, "I'm so sorry I'm late, Mrs. Heart!"

The relief on her face is palpable. "Oh, no, dear, you made it just in time. I definitely needed my good luck boy with me, though." I hand her Watson's leash, and she loops her arm through it.

"Sit, boy, and turn up the charm. Sway those judges in our favor," she says.

Watson obeys and perches regally on a straw bale at her feet, his tri-color coat gleaming under the fluorescent lights. He sits with perfect posture, as if he knows this is an important occasion deserving of his best behavior. His eyes are fixed on Mrs. Heart—or perhaps on her pie.

The judging is painfully slow. There are five judges, moving as a group down the line of pies. They stop at each of the dozen or so contestants, take a bite of their submission, ask questions, murmur appreciations, and write things down on little clipboards. The crowd is enraptured, acting as if this is some baker reality show. Unfortunately, I'm not too interested in the composition of their pies or the various ways in which these judges can say "this tastes good." Mrs. Heart is nearly last and the only pie I am interested in hearing about, so my attention wanes—hard.

Michael, on the other hand, is on the edge of his seat, hand on chin, listening with rapt attention.

I ask, "Watch a lot of bake-offs, Michael?"

He leans back and whispers to me. "Yeah, they make great background noise when I'm working out."

"Really?"

"Yeah, not sure what it is. But if I watch anything else, I lose count of my reps," he says as his attention returns to the contest. Judging by the way his attention is so laser-focused on this, I think maybe he loses count of reps watching bake-offs, too. *Maybe that's why he's so jacked—doing more reps than he realizes.* I giggle to myself and try to refocus on the contest.

My attention drifts to other things.

I try desperately to focus on what the judges say, but they've been talking about this rando's raspberry pie for what feels like an eternity. *Come on, I just want to hear about Mrs. Heart's pie.*

Mrs. Heart looks like she might die of anticipation, too, but her beauty queen training has not worn off. *I wish I could project that level of poise.*

I ask Michael, "Did you know that Mrs. Heart used to be a model?"

He laughs, "Yeah, my dad had one of her old calendars in the garage. Used to piss my mom off." He doesn't break his gaze from the contest.

I probably should just let him watch. I look around, trying to find something less mind-numbingly boring to focus on, when I see Angela and Sheriff Kim outside the tent. Once again, it seems as if they're looking at me—both standing arms crossed, facing me, talking with their heads close to each other conspiratorily.

They approach the tent.

I place my hand on Michael's shoulder. "Michael…"

"Hmm?" he asks, not breaking his focus.

"I think the cops are coming over here."

"Huh?" his focus snaps to me.

"There," I say, motioning my head toward the approaching police that I'm watching out of the corner of my eye.

He cranes his neck, looking toward them.

"Don't look directly at them!" I whisper yell. The panic in my voice cracks. "They keep watching me. Should I call, James?"

His eyes return to me, "I think they're just watching the contest."

I steal a glance at them. They're both at the entrance to the tent, arms still crossed, looking menacing as hell.

My heart pounds in my chest.

Michael leans in close and discreetly points at the man standing next to Mrs. Heart. "See that guy next to Mrs. Heart."

"Yeah," I nod.

"That's Angela's husband. They're probably just watching him."

A blond man with a smile that could rival Ryan's beams next to Mrs. Heart, his hands folded behind his back. He leans toward Mrs. Heart and whispers something to her, making her giggle. *Seems like Angela has a type.*

"Oh," I say, feeling silly. Of course, the cops aren't watching me.

God, Celeste, not everything is about you.

Michael puts his hand on my leg reassuringly and says, "It's okay. If they bother you, I'll get James. Don't worry."

"Michael, I can't take this paranoia anymore. We have to figure out who killed Richard."

He squeezes my leg. "Of course. Let's go to the town hall on Monday and get those financial documents."

I nod, deciding to step this investigation up a notch. "Yes, let's do that."

Michael gives me one more leg squeeze before his attention returns to the contest. He puts his arm around my shoulder and doesn't return to his edge-of-the-seat position, obviously trying to comfort me.

I'm able to maintain focus now that I feel like two pairs of law-enforcing eyes are boring into the back of my head. The judges finally taste Mrs. Heart's pie and ask her a ton of questions. She and Watson look photogenic, so I snap a ton of pics. *I should get these printed for her. She'd like that. Especially if she wins.*

The judges return to their tables, tallying and discussing in a quiet argument. It doesn't take them long to decide, and I wonder what their scoring system is like.

One of the judges hands a slip of paper to Gus. He unfolds it, reads the results, and smiles so big I can see all his teeth. "And this year's blue ribbon for Best Pie goes to…" he pauses for dramatic effect, and I swear I can hear Mrs. Heart's inhale from across the tent. Watson's tail thumps against the straw bale, but he doesn't move from his post. *Good boy.* "Regina Heart, for her Classic Apple with Rosemary Crust!"

The tent erupts in applause—some genuine, some politely concealing disappointment. Mrs. Heart's hands fly to her mouth, and for a second, I think she might cry. Instead, she squares her shoulders and moves toward the stage with the dignified grace of someone used to win beauty pageants. Watson jumps from his straw bale perch to follow, dodging the other contestants to stay at her side.

Watson barks once, sharp and clear, as if adding his own congratulations. A few people laugh. A few say, "Good boy."

"She did it," I whisper to Michael, squeezing his shoulder and taking a billion pictures.

He nods and claps.

Mrs. Heart steps onto the small platform, accepting the blue ribbon with both hands as if it's made of spun gold. Watson sits next to her, looking as if he thinks he won something, too.

Gus says something about "carrying on a tradition of excellence," but I'm focused on Mrs. Heart's face—the flush of pleasure across her cheeks, the sparkle in her eyes that makes her look decades younger.

She leans into the microphone. "Thank you all so much."

Gus says, "Congrats, Regina," into the mic and gives her a peck on the cheek.

"Nepotism!" someone yells from the crowd with a laugh.

"She's not my wife. Plus, I didn't vote!" Gus chuckles.

Watson barks again, and Mrs. Heart beams in his direction. More laughter. *That dog is trying to steal the show.*

Mrs. Heart continues her speech, thanking the judges and her friends, but I can tell she's overwhelmed by the moment. Her fingers keep touching the ribbon, tracing its satin edge as if to convince herself it's real.

Michael's arm slips around my waist, pulling me closer. "You're proud of her," he says. It's not a question.

"Yeah, she's…she's like the mother I never had. Well, the mother I wish I had," I reply simply, and it feels true in a way I hadn't fully recognized until this moment. "I'm so happy I got to see this."

When Mrs. Heart finishes her speech, there's another round of applause. She steps carefully down from the platform, immediately surrounded by well-wishers.

"Let's go congratulate her," Michael says.

We press forward through the crowd. Mrs. Heart spots us and waves, her face lighting up even more. Watson bounds toward us, testing the limits of his leash and nearly tripping a man in his enthusiasm.

Stoic Stationary Spaniel has evolved to Wiggle Worm Watty.

"Careful, buddy," I laugh, kneeling to receive his wiggling body. He licks my face, tail whipping back faster than I've ever seen it. "I know you're proud of her, but not the face, boy."

Mrs. Heart follows in his wake walking up to me, the blue ribbon pinned proudly to her cardigan. "I'm happy you got off in time."

Michael coughs, and a blush creeps up my neck. "You mean got here?"

Mrs. Heart's eyes twinkle knowingly. "I said what I said."

Michael tugs at his shirt and adjusts his glasses, thoroughly disarmed. "We were just exploring the fair."

She smirks. "Of course you were, dear." She holds up her ribbon to me. "What do you think?"

"Excellent work," I exclaim, hugging her and taking a bunch of selfies.

51

Watson and I stand outside Town Hall as I rehearse what I plan to say. "Excuse me, I'd like to review the budget files for the Goose Grove Revitalization Effort for the past five fiscal years, please. I'm particularly interested in files related to the Riverside Development Project. Um, please. Thank you." *Ugh. I sound like a shitty AI.*

Watson looks up at me, possibly sensing my nerves, possibly just hoping for a dropped treat.

The wind picks up, and I button my peacoat, a feeble attempt at protection from the cold. *I should just go in.*

"Okay, I can do this. This is a standard request," I say to Watson. He waits for me to open the door, and I swear he rolls his eyes at me. "Some emotional support animal you are."

The main doors squeak as we enter, and the faint aroma of burnt coffee and over-waxed tile washes over me. There's a weird, low-level hum—old fluorescent bulbs and quiet municipal desperation. *Is this what bureaucracy sounds like?*

I follow the signs to the clerk's office and pass a hallway in which the walls are lined with faded photos of Goose Grove's past mayors. *Oh, look, there's Andy. They look so different—sadder.*

The clerk's office is located at the end of the main hall, behind a window designed for maximum opacity and minimal human interaction.

I text Michael that I'm here, and then press the little silver bell on the counter. Watson chuffs. His good boy training outweighs his desire to bark at it.

Michael was going to come with me, but we decided that Ryan's idea of using Marcus's supposed feelings for me to my advantage would be more easily executed if I were alone.

After an appropriate amount of shuffling, a woman emerges from the back room. She's an attractive woman, about my age. I think maybe I've seen her before, but I can't place her.

"Watson! Hey, boy. Oh, and Celeste Moon," she says, taking in Watson first, then me.

"Oh, um, hi, yes," I say.

"It's me. Clara!"

"Oh, Clara!" I say pretending to know who the fuck she is. *God, I suck at remembering people.* "How have you been?"

"Oh, I've been great! I married Tom!"

"That's wonderful." *I have no idea who the fuck Tom is.*

"Yeah, we have two kids. Wanna see?"

Of course not. "Sure!"

"Oh, they're cute!" I say, and at least this time I'm not lying.

"How about you, Celeste! Any kids?"

"Oh, no, not yet."

"Well, there's still time…" she says with that semi-judgmental tone you always get when you reveal you're a woman past the age of thirty who has yet to procreate.

"What can I help you with?"

Fuck. Why did I come here? This is why I practiced.

"I'd like to review the budget files for the Goose Grove Revitalization Effort for the past five fiscal years, please. Full copies, not the redacted ones from the website. Oh, especially the ones related to the Riverside Development Project."

Clara nods, tapping her acrylic nails on the computer mouse.

"Nice nails," I say, noticing the cute patterns on them and once again not lying.

"Oh, really!? Thank you! I did them myself."

"Wow, really!?"

"Yeah," she says, holding her hand out to me. I lean down closer and peer at them. Cute little teddy bears and hearts are hand-painted with diamond bowties. *Oh, I remember, Clara! She was in the Art Club with Ryan.*

I gush, "Wow, I wish I could do that!"

"Oh, um, I'm not supposed to do this here, but Marcus won't care." She looks around, ensuring no one is watching her, and pulls something out of her purse. "Here's my card. I don't have a shop yet, but I do house calls."

"I will definitely call you," I say, looking at my sad excuse for a manicure. She beams at me.

"Anyway," she says, returning to the computer. "Those records should be digitized, so just give me a sec. Let me see here…always something with that department." Her typing is forceful, more Morse code than data entry.

I pass the time squatting down to pet Watson.

Clara makes a low "hmmph" noise. "That's odd. The folders are there, but every file inside is just labeled 'See Clerk.' Which is me, I guess. Let me check the server."

I can practically see her soul leave her body as she seems to encounter another digital roadblock. "Weird." She shakes her head and whispers to herself, "Never seen this before." She stands abruptly. "Sorry, Celeste, it'll be just a moment."

She disappears behind a door marked "AUTHORIZED PERSONNEL ONLY—NO EXCEPTIONS." I hear the rattle of paper, a distant muttering, and the repeated thump of a file cabinet resisting its purpose in life.

Watson is now fully lying down, snoring, completely bored with bureaucracy.

Clara returns, balancing a precarious tower of manila folders and a single, slightly dusty three-ring binder. She sets it down with a grunt. "I found the print copies. Budget Committee should have digitized these, but…" She flips the first binder open, running a finger down the index. "What is…Who did this?" She shows me the binder, flipping through the pages and indicating where they should be.

The pages are torn out, which seems silly—it's a three-ring binder. *Did someone pull them out in a rush? In too much of a hurry to actually open the ring?*

She looks up from the binder. "Celeste, I…they should be here."

I suspected this would happen, actually. "Um, is there anywhere else they could be?" I ask.

Clara looks dumbfounded, "I'll have to get back to you, Celeste. I'll reach out to IT and see if they can help, maybe…I dunno…find old versions of the files. I don't know what those guys can do. I've never seen this before. Maybe the mayor's office can help."

It's almost too obvious, like a finger pointing in all caps to my next destination. *Looks like I will have to put Ryan's plan to the test.*

I smile at her and say, "Thank you, Clara. I'll go meet with Marcus."

"Sorry, I couldn't be more helpful!"

"No, you were great! Thank you. I'll message you about the nails."

She nearly jumps for joy at the idea of doing my nails, as Watson and I duck out of her office.

In the lobby, I crouch to Watson's level and give him an ear-scratch, while I pull out my phone. I text Michael, "Budget files are all missing or redacted."

Michael replies, "Well, fuck," with a groaning emoji.

I reply, "She suggested I go to Marcus."

"You ready to talk to him?"

"Yep. I've got my secret weapons."

"What's that?"

"Watson and a low-cut shirt."

"Our Mayor is a tit guy?"

"And a dog guy."

"Sexually?"

"No gross, Michael!"

He replies with a smirking emoji.

I'm still smiling at the phone when I hear a voice behind me, smooth and a little too loud. "Celeste," it booms. "I didn't expect to see you today."

I turn and almost ram into the broad chest of Marcus. He still wears his old letterman charm; now it's under a layer of mayoral polish. His suit is designer, his shoes absurdly shiny. He moves like someone who expects doors to open on approach, which, in his defense, they usually do. The proximity to him sends sensations through my body I'd prefer were not present.

Watson makes a beeline, tail going hyperdrive. Marcus kneels, unbothered by the expensive pants, and gives Watson a thorough greeting.

"Hey, buddy." He looks to me and grins, his teeth almost a little too white, a little too perfect. Then he returns his gaze to Watson, "Such a good boy. Thank God you can't run for Mayor."

"Aren't there a few towns with dog mayors? This one's already allowed everywhere. I think precedent indicates he could run for Mayor."

"Well, I guess I wouldn't mind losing to him."

I consider saying something snarky, but the memory of our breakup is like an old injury—painful, pointless, and best left in the past. I opt for a polite joke instead. "Watson's not ready for the hard choices. He's strictly a bipartisan treat guy."

Marcus straightens and runs a hand through his hair, more self-conscious than I remember. "What brings you to Town Hall? Did you want to talk to me about those investments I mentioned?"

I pocket my phone and try not to sound like I'm accusing him of anything. "I was just here looking into some budget files. Clara suggested I speak with you."

He arches an eyebrow, "Oh, yeah? Well, let's go to my office." He gestures and we follow. Watson tugs me forward, instantly trusting Marcus a little too wholeheartedly.

We follow him past a taxidermied goose in a glass case (Goose Grove's original mascot: "Jefferson") and into the administrative wing. Marcus's office is at the very end, where the windows get the best sunlight and the walls are lined with certificates of civic virtue.

52

"Come in, come in," he says, leading me inward, closing the door behind me.

I turn, unsure if I like the door being closed.

"You can let him loose," Marcus says, gesturing to Watson. "He can't go far now."

Is he trying to imply he shut the door so I could let Watson walk around?

"Oh, um, okay." I unbuckle Watson's leash, and he immediately begins smelling around. I've known Watson long enough now to know he won't pee on anything, but he certainly looks like he wants to. He growls at a large stuffed bear.

Marcus laughs, a little too loudly, then abruptly shushes himself, as if realizing this is a government building and joy is strictly rationed. "Yeah, I don't like it either, buddy."

He motions to a chair in front of his desk, and I sit in it. He drops into his own chair, elbows on the desk, face suddenly serious. "I wanted to catch up. See how you're settling in."

"I'm fine," I say. "Really." This is not the direction I expected.

Marcus looks down at the dog, who has already wedged himself under his desk. "I'm glad you're back, Celeste. The town needs more people who care."

He flashes another smile, then seems to remember what smiles are for and tries to reabsorb it. He opens his mouth, but coughs, looking down, as if trying to decide what to say. He does this again, then just smiles at me with hands folded on the table, as if he's waiting for me to speak—or waiting for me to take his mayoral portrait.

What is with him?

I raise my eyebrows. "Soooo, Marcus," I start, "I'm here about the Goose Grove Revitalization Effort budget—especially those related to the Riverside Development Project. I requested the files, and—long story short—they're all missing. Even the backups."

His face does something peculiar. Not the poker-faced denial I expected, but a twitch, a stutter, like someone learning bad news about a distant relative. "Really?" he says, dragging the syllables out like they're heavy. "That's…concerning."

"Is it?" I ask. "Because it looks a lot like someone wants the revitalization fund to disappear, along with every paper trail."

He steeples his fingers. "I—Celeste, these things are complicated. We get a lot of eyes on the budget, and sometimes mistakes happen. I'll look into it, I promise."

Ah, so he's just going to dismiss me?

I try a different approach. "You know, Marcus. I really am interested in helping to fund some progress for the town. I'd love to help you out with this initiative. We've made a good team in the past." I open my coat, revealing my low-cut shirt.

He clears his throat, his composure further leaving his body, and his eyes can't help themselves but land on my breasts. "Oh, yeah! That's great, Celeste."

He clears his throat again and shifts in his seat. *Gotcha.*

I lean forward, elbows on knees, emphasizing my assets that aren't financial. "But, before I can invest my money in this. I'd need to know I could trust you, Marcus."

"Of course," he says. Now he's visibly sweating. I half expect him to lunge for my tits across the desk.

"Before I can invest, I'd like to know why the Revitalization Effort is stalled. And where those files are." I pause for effect. "Does their disappearance have to do with Richard Holbrook?"

"Holbrook?" His voice rises almost an octave. "No, I mean—he's dead, so…" He clears his throat and glances at Watson, as if expecting backup.

The silence builds.

I stand and lean in, hands on the desk, tits fully in face. "Marcus. This isn't a deposition. I'm just trying to understand why all the files are suddenly top secret, or in some cases, just gone. If you know something, you can tell me." I bat my eyes and lean down even further.

He opens his mouth, closes it, then takes a long, measured breath. "Look, there's a lot going on. The town's in a tough spot. Grants are getting cut, state's breathing down our necks, and—" he stops talking when I peel my knee-length wool coat off to reveal how tight my shirt and skirt are.

I non-discreetly bend to fold it onto my chair. Ass in face now.

He swallows hard and continues. "The town could really use your help with the revitalization. There are quite a few things that could really improve the quality of life for everyone. If you're not interested in funding, I thought maybe you could lead a project committee or be the face of the fundraising campaign. You were always good at bringing people together. People are…" he pauses as I sit and cross my leg high up my knee, turning to reveal more leg, "drawn to you, Celeste."

I smile. "That's flattering, Marcus. But I need to know that any money I put in or help raise will be safe in your hands. The line items are just…missing. There's nothing for us to promote if the money's been rerouted or—" I stop short, seeing the panic in his eyes.

He stands, suddenly energized, and begins pacing in front of the window. "I can't say anything official yet. Legal reasons. But the truth is, some of the money might have been…misallocated. We're still looking into it."

He gives me a look that says, "Please don't ask."

So I do the opposite. "Who would have access to make that

happen? The clerk's office is locked down. I assume it goes through your desk."

He stops, turns, and leans against the file cabinet, arms crossed. "Celeste, I'm not a crook. I promise you. I'm not even that organized." His voice cracks on the last syllable, and his stance is pure defensive lineman.

I almost believe him.

The mayor of Goose Grove is hiding something. I'm not sure what it is, but it's poorly disguised.

"Okay," I say, shifting gears again. "Maybe it's just a paperwork thing."

He nods vigorously. "That's gotta be it. I promise I will look into it." He's smiling, desperate to change the subject.

"Okay," I say, standing and putting my coat back on. He seems visibly relieved I've covered myself. "Well, thank you for your time. I'll stop bothering you and let you get back to work, Marcus."

Marcus laughs, and the tension breaks, just a bit. He steps closer, leaning in like he wants to share a secret. "You're not bothering me, Celeste. I'll always have time for you."

I look at him, incredulously. I know I turned up the seduction, but that seems a bit forward. "Is that so, Marcus?"

"Of course! Anything you need, I'm your guy." He grimaces realizing that he's coming off a bit simpy.

God, I've always loved a simp.

A flash of the first time we had sex enters my mind.

I stare at him, and the silence is not awkward this time. It's almost…nostalgic.

"You haven't changed, have you?" I ask, almost rhetorically.

"Nope. Neither have you," he says. His voice is low, and there's a flicker of something sad behind the bravado. "Just like I remember."

I smile warmly and genuinely.

Fuck, he's still hot. But married.

I remember the reason I came, and I straighten up. "Oh, well, thanks, Marcus. I appreciate you hearing me out. I'll consider your proposal, but please let me know about those files when you find out."

He grins again, but there's a melancholy edge to it. "It's a deal. If you ever need anything. Anything. You know where to find me."

The universe must be in a generous mood today, because as soon as I'm out of Marcus's office, I hear the click of high heels echoing toward me, sharp as hail on a tin roof.

Fuck.

Nicole.

She's dressed in a cream-colored coat that, despite my knowing better, feels like I couldn't afford it. She spots me instantly, blue eyes narrowing to sniper focus.

"Celeste!" Nicole trills, obviously wondering why I'm walking away from the one door down this hall—the one belonging to her husband. "Look what the cat dragged in. I didn't expect to see you, of all people, here," she says, as if I literally resemble a dead animal.

I button my coat, trying to hide my revealing outfit.

Watson, ever the diplomat, sits at attention and offers a paw. Nicole, to her credit, takes it. He doesn't quite melt the ice queen, but he comes close.

"Nicole," I say, "nice to see you." *Back to lying.*

She cocks her head, all innocence, and obviously wants to ask what the fuck I'm doing here. "Lunch date! Marcus always makes time, you know. It's so important to spend quality time with the one you love," she says, emphasizing the word one. She leans in. "I presume you just had a little…meeting with my husband. How did that go?" she asks, emphasizing the word husband.

"Productive," I say. "I think we really got to the bottom of some things," I smirk, trying to imply some sexual innuendo in my words.

Her laugh is airy. "Oh, Celeste, always so thorough. You just cover all bases…even on a first date." I blink. The compliment is so backhanded it might as well be a tennis serve.

"What can I say? He comes easy for me. Ha. Sorry, I misspoke. It comes easy to me." Her cheeks flush so red you can see the blush through her perfectly airbrushed contouring.

God, I wish I knew how to do my makeup like that.

Focus, Celeste.

Her smile slips, then snaps right back into place. "Well, I guess it's lucky for me that Marcus prefers someone who's less run through. Oh, sorry. I misspoke. I mean thorough. Ha! What a slip!" She waves her hand, folding it to her chest like she's just so pleased with herself.

God, I really don't feel like fighting with her right now. I gain nothing by doing it.

"Yes, I guess it is lucky for you," I say, "you got everything you ever wanted. Well, it was nice to see you, Nicole."

I attempt to side-step her, but she stops me, putting her shoulder in my way.

She sneers at me. "I swear to God, if you fucked my husband, I will kill you."

Shit. She's actually going for it.

I sigh, "I did not sleep with him. Recently, anyway." I shrug.

She flinches again. "And am I supposed to believe you? You're sleeping with everyone else in this town?"

"I'm not interested in sleeping with someone's husband."

She stops and stares at me, huffing, ready to claw my eyes out. I've never seen her like this before, but I guess time really can change people. "Fidelity has never been a word in your vocabulary."

I sigh, tired of this game. "And what exactly does that mean, Nicole?"

She pulls back, her mask returned. "Oh, sweetie, we were all rooting for you two. Still, I guess things work out as they're meant to." She glances at the closed office door, eyes briefly darting with calculation. "Marcus was so devastated when he found out you were sleeping with Ryan while you two were together. I hated to be the one to tell him, but I didn't mind being the one to console him."

A slow realization crawls across my brain. "Wait, you told him that?"

She shrugs, the picture of plausible deniability. "I only wanted to protect him. You know Marcus—so sensitive. So trusting."

A loud hum buzzes in my ears as my brain realizes what she's saying.

So...Nicole is the reason Marcus and I broke up?

I want to punch her.

I want to go in there and actually fuck her husband.

She looks so fucking smug right now—moreso than usual.

She thinks she's got the upper hand, and she kinda does.

Alright, bitch. Time to meet Celeste Fucking Moon, CEO...Ex-CEO...

Instead of letting her send me into an emotional frenzy, I lock all my feelings away and decide to ask her about what I overheard at the gala. Maybe I can get her to admit something that I don't even know.

I open my jacket, just so she can see what was in her husband's office. Her eyes widen.

Yeah, bitch, I can afford designer, too.

I run my fingers through my hair. "Speaking of trust, I heard you and Daniel Stevens are working together on the revitalization committee. How's that going?"

Her eyes flicker. "Daniel's…fine. He's just…so passionate about the town. Always has a new idea. Sometimes it's hard to keep up, but we manage." She's rambling. *Is this working?*

I let the silence dangle for a second, then lean in, conspiratorial. Her eyes flicker to my tits. Still got it. I whisper, "Funny, I thought I heard you two talking about some kind of side project. Something that Marcus would be devastated to hear about."

Nicole's veneer cracks, just a microsecond. "You must have misheard. Daniel and I barely see each other outside meetings."

I nod, and run my finger from my lip down my neck, feigning thinking—but sexily. "Of course. But, you know, Marcus is so trusting. And I just want to protect him."

She steps closer, voice dropping to a hiss. "Listen. I don't know what you think you heard, but if you spread rumors, it will not go well for you. Goose Grove may be small, but it has a very long memory."

The threat is thinly veiled, but the venom is real. I feel the urge to poke at it, just a little.

I shrug. "Relax, Nicole. I'm just trying to help the community. If there's something off with the budget or the project, it's better to get ahead of it now before it turns into a real mess. No one wants another Holbrook situation."

Nicole's face goes pale. For a second, I wonder if she's about to faint, but she rallies like only a pageant veteran can. "You have no idea what you're talking about, Celeste. Some of us are just trying to keep our lives from falling apart. Maybe you should do the same." She jabs a French-manicured finger at my chest. "Stay out of it, or I'll make sure you regret coming back here."

She stalks past me, heels clicking with renewed fury, and disappears into Marcus's office without knocking.

The door slams behind her.

I hear her bright, brittle laughter moments later, followed by the rumble of Marcus's voice, awkward and unsure, then her voice sharp and raspy as a harpy.

He's obviously getting an earful.

Watson and I stand in the hallway, a little stunned. I kneel to scratch his ears, and he licks my hand, as if to say, "We survived. Let's go home."

I fish my phone out of my pocket and text Michael, "Marcus wasn't much help. He said he'll look into it."

He replies, "I'll start the FOIA process."

"Damnit. This was a waste of time," I tap into my phone.

"You did your best."

"I had a run-in with Nicole. She told me something that really frazzled me. But also, pretty sure she's hiding something big."

"Watson with you still?"

"Yeah."

"Bring the dog. Let's chat. I'll make you both steak."

"K. Be there soon."

I put the phone in my pocket. Then bend to pet Watson. "Well, looks like we earned ourselves a steak, though I'm not sure exactly what you did. I don't know if I achieved anything either."

53

The farmers' market sprawls in front of us, all color and movement and chatter. It's the last day it'll be outside, and I'm happy we found the time to come together. Mrs. Heart has been searching for a secret ingredient that she refuses to reveal, not even to me, for a pie she plans to make for Thanksgiving. But when she's not anxiously searching, we've been casually browsing and chatting.

Watson tugs at his leash, nose twitching at the symphony of scents—fresh bread, flower bouquets, homemade soaps, and at least three different kinds of artisanal cheeses. I let him lead us through the crowd, his doggy confidence parting the sea of weekend shoppers better than any excuse or pardon me I could muster.

"You're not exactly subtle about your priorities," I tell him as he makes a beeline for a stall selling organic dog treats. His tail wags with such enthusiasm that it seems to power his entire back half. "Can he have one?" I ask, Mrs. Heart, who's anxiously looking around for her secret ingredient.

"That'd be fine, dear," she says, distracted.

"You okay?" I ask, as I fish out my wallet to pay for the doggy treat.

"Oh, yes, dear, I'm just worried I won't be able to find it."

"You know…I could just buy it online for you."

"So you can learn my secret ingredient? Absolutely not!"

I know that this is only partially the reason. She's never accepted any money from me, and I'm honestly surprised she's letting me buy this treat for Watson.

I decide to try to broach the subject. "Mrs. Heart, I wasn't trying to snoop, but…" I look around to make sure no one can hear me. "I saw the unpaid bills. Will you please let me help you?"

"Absolutely not, dear."

"But…why not?"

"Because my mistakes are not your responsibility, dear."

"Mrs. Heart, please, I want to help you."

She fixes me with a determined gaze, "Dear, you don't have to buy my love."

I know her meaning. In the last few years, the only real communication I had with my parents was related to the allowance I sent them or extra money I gave them. They were on their way to the airport for a vacation I paid for when they…when they…

I shake my head, trying to remove the thought. She must notice my change in mood, because she places her hand on my arm. She's always allowed to help me, but I'm unable to help her. I feel bad about our one-sided relationship.

She says, "I'm okay, dear, truly. I've got it all worked out."

A familiar voice rings out above the market's gentle hum. "Celeste! Mrs. Heart!"

I turn to see Sarah waving at us and smiling brightly. She's wearing a yellow plaid A-line dress and a purple sweater, looking like she fell out of a Goose Grove Grease Musical adaptation. Andy stands beside her, their red hair catching the light like copper wire, wearing all black.

"Morning," Sarah says, pulling me into a quick hug. She smells like coffee beans and vanilla. "No boys with you today?"

"Just the best one of them all—Watson," I joke, tucking my hair behind my ear.

Andy crouches down to let Watson sniff their hand. "He is best boy," their voice carries that familiar sarcastic edge, but it softens when addressing the dog.

"How about we walk together?" Andy suggests straightening up. Now that we're closer, I can see that their black button-up shirt has little embroidered flowers—clearly Sarah's influence.

Mrs. Heart smiles warmly at them before looking around again for her secret ingredient.

We stroll through the market together, enjoying the beautiful weather. The October air carries a certain refreshing crispness. Watson trots alongside us, as if this whole excursion is purely for his benefit. Mrs. Heart trails quietly beside us, anxiously scanning for this secret ingredient—her anxiety mounting as we run out of market to peruse.

"So how are things with you two?" I ask as we pause at a stall selling homemade jams.

Sarah picks up a jar of blackberry preserves, studying the label. "Busy," she says. "Technically, we're working now."

Andy snorts. "Yeah, when you own a business, everything is work."

Sarah playfully bumps Andy's shoulder and bats her eyes at them. "Well, not everything…"

Andy kisses her cheek and says wistfully, "Yes, not everything."

This easy back-and-forth they have is so adorable. They obviously love each other a lot. It makes something twist in my chest. *Jealousy? Not exactly. More like longing. Loneliness. A recognition of what I don't have.*

"How long have you owned the cafe?" I ask, selecting a jar of apple butter.

Sarah hands some cash to the vendor before answering. "Seven years now. I bought it when old Mr. Harrington retired."

"It was falling apart. She did a great job converting it," Andy interjects, taking the bag of jam jars from Sarah automatically.

"And how long have you two been together?" I guide Watson away from a particularly enticing cheese sample that's too close to his eye level.

Sarah nods. "Six years. Andy came in every morning for—"

"A large black coffee," they say in unison, then laugh.

"Most boring order in the world," Sarah continues.

Andy laughs, "Thanks to Sarah, my taste in coffee has become much more refined now."

Sarah continues the story, "They came in all smiles every day. I thought they were just being mayoral—trying to support local businesses."

Andy's face flushes slightly, almost matching their hair. "I've never been great at flirting. I thought I was being obvious, and Sarah was politely rejecting me."

They both laugh.

"So how did you go from badly flirting to getting married and running the cafe together?" I inquire as we move through the market.

Andy looks at Sarah, one eyebrow raised as if in question. "When I resigned as mayor, I came to the cafe every day. Spent all my time there. I'd absentmindedly help Sarah out while I hung around her like a lost puppy."

Sarah's face lights up. "Hey, I enjoyed the company! It was just me running it back then, so it was nice to have you around."

"The whole town thought I was going through some kind of existential crisis...which, maybe I was," Andy says dryly, but there's real tenderness underneath.

Sarah brushes their arm. "I joked that they should get paid for all the work they were doing."

Andy shrugs. "I was looking for something to do with myself, so I took her up on it. Being with her forty plus hours a week sounded like as good a plan as any."

We stop at a flower stall, and I watch as Sarah absently reaches for Andy's hand. Their fingers intertwine without either of them seeming to notice they've done it.

"Then, one night while doing inventory..." Sarah says, leaning into Andy slightly.

They both blush and share a coy look before Andy finishes, "Well, you can guess what happened."

I sigh loudly. "Seriously! You two nosies always asking me for details about my love life are gonna be vague about the best part?"

Sarah and Andy exchange a look loaded with meaning.

"Let's just say we joined forces and haven't separated since," Sarah laughs.

I roll my eyes at them.

I pout. "Fine, but don't expect any more deets from me about my dates."

Sarah laughs and adds, "We got married about five years ago."

Mrs. Heart wanders between stalls, eyes scanning the wears with extreme precision, but adds, "It was a lovely service. Unforgettable," before heading to the next secret ingredient candidate.

I smile, but I feel that twist again.

Andy interjects, "After quitting as mayor, hyphenating my name was the last straw for my dad. He pretty much disowned me after that." There's no sadness in their voice—just a statement of fact.

I think for a moment: *Andy Astor and Sarah Gandy.*

I roll the hyphenated name around in my head before asking, "Wait a minute. Is your name…Andy Astor-Gandy?"

"No," Andy laughs and pauses for effect, raising their eyebrows, "Andy Gandy-Astor. Fuck my dad. His name went second."

I begin to ask, "So, you and your family—"

Andy replies, predicting the rest of my question, "Mostly. Nicole can be…well, Nicole…but she refused to cut me off. Told my dad he could get over it or lose his entire bloodline. She and Marcus are the only family I have now, as far as I'm concerned. Well, and my nieces."

I add, "Speaking of Nicole and Marcus…I went to the town hall the other day."

Andy's eyebrows raise in curiosity. "Oh, yeah? Were you able to get those budget files?"

"Nope. The files are all missing. The hard copies were literally torn out of the binder."

Andy pulls at their lip in contemplation, asking themselves, "Who would have done that?"

"Michael and I sent in a FOIA request. Thanks for the info on that, by the way."

Andy remains lost in contemplation, "…that's good…"

Maybe Andy knows something, and I can get information out of them. "I spoke to Marcus and he was no help, either. It seemed like he knew they were missing…like I wasn't the one to tell him."

Andy looks up at the sky, fully lost in thought, and says to themselves, "I wonder if this is why they've been…"

"Been what?"

Andy startles. "Oh, it's nothing. Nicole and Marcus have just been…weird the last few months. It's hard to explain…" They don't elaborate.

I bite the inside of my lip, "I had a run-in with her, Nicole…she was extra hostile."

Andy laughs, "Well, yeah, she's been extra on edge since you came into town."

"And…I had just come out of Marcus's office…"

Sarah laughs, having been paying only slight attention since the budget info came up, "Oh, boy. I bet she lost her shit at that."

I reply, "Yeah…she thought I slept with Marcus."

Andy and Sarah share another loaded look.

54

We're passing a stand selling fresh apple cider donuts when Watson suddenly lunges forward, tangling his leash around my legs. I stumble, windmilling my arms in a desperate attempt to stay upright.

"Whoa!" Andy says while reaching out to steady me, but it's too late. I'm already falling.

I graze against the stand's table as I fall and land with an ungraceful thud. The older woman running it peers down at me with surprise, while Watson takes advantage of the chaos to snatch a donut that's rolled off the edge of the table.

"Watson!" I lightly chastise with a mortified giggle and rub my bruised ass.

Mrs. Heart rushes to my side, panic contorting her face. She embraces me, hands searching me for injury. "Celeste! Celeste! Are you okay?!"

"I'm okay, Mrs. Heart. I'm okay," I say, attempting to ease her anxiety, while Andy helps me up and Sarah untangles Watson's leash from my legs.

Watson looks entirely unrepentant, crumbs on his muzzle the only evidence of his crime.

Mrs. Heart scolds Watson, with a harshness I've never heard from her before, "Watson! Bad boy. You could have killed Celeste. You always do this!" Tears well in her eyes.

Watson now does look a bit ashamed of his actions, but his eyes flick to the donut stand while he licks his chops–probably wondering if he can get another for his attempt at contriteness.

"I am so sorry," I tell the donut vendor, brushing dirt from my jeans. "Please let me pay for that."

The woman waves away my wallet. "I wouldn't dream of it," she says, amused. "Watson always eats for free."

Andy laughs. "He planned that. Look at him—so smug."

Indeed, Watson sits, wearing an expression of doggy innocence that fools absolutely no one. He looks up at me with pleading eyes that clearly communicate his desire for another treat.

My attention turns to Mrs. Heart and she is griping at her chest, breathing in a way that is concerning and staring at the ground.

I reach for her, "Mrs. Heart, are you okay?"

Her eyes meet mine and soften slightly, "That just…it really scared me. I was worried you got really hurt."

I hug her and attempt to reassure her. "Oh, no, I'm okay, Mrs. Heart. I just bruised my butt a bit."

She looks at Watson, sadness etching across her face. "Well, I'm going to take that as my cue to take Watson home, before he causes more trouble."

I say, "You sure? You didn't find what you were looking for, though."

She just sighs and looks around, "It's fine. I'll do something else."

We say our goodbye, and I remain with Sarah and Andy. We browse for a little longer before we pause at the edge of the market, our circuit nearly complete. The morning has warmed, and the crowd has thickened. I look at my watch and consider going home.

Angela's unmistakable silhouette, nearly ready to tip into full maternal waddle, appears at the end of the aisle. She's flanked by Detective Kim, whose expression makes it clear he'd rather be anywhere else. Both are in uniform, which implies they're at work and not just browsing.

Angela catches my eye and gives the world's tiniest nod. Detective Kim's gaze flicks over the crowd, then lands on me and stays there, unblinking. For a split second, I consider hiding behind a rutabaga display, but instead I straighten my spine and walk directly toward them.

Andy sees them too and, not sensing my discomfort, beelines to their friend, with a "Yo, Angela!" that feels much lighter than the mood had just been.

Angela's smile is tired but genuine. "Hey."

Sarah, Watson, and I slowly follow Andy as they rush toward Angela.

Andy and Angela chatter like two best friends would: all hugs and exuberant gestures. Sheriff Kim just stands behind, not participating in the conversation but watching the surroundings in a way that indicates he is on duty.

Sarah leans in and whispers to me, "Are you still a suspect?"

"I don't know. I think so," I reply, not really knowing if I ever actually was to begin with.

"We don't have to go over there; we can just wait here and stare at these vegetables."

"No, it's ok…"

As we approach, Sheriff Kim gives me a look that makes me feel like I very much am a suspect. "Enjoying the market?" he asks.

"Yes, it's a nice day today," I say.

Andy and Angela continue to chatter as if they've forgotten the rest of us are here, standing awkwardly by.

I try to act natural, which in my case means picking dog hair off my leggings.

Angela pats her stomach and says, "I'm ready for my maternity leave to kick in."

"When are you due?" I ask, my curiosity getting the best of me.

Angela looks surprised I've spoken, but she obviously likes talking about her baby, because she says, "A couple of weeks, give or take. I'm hoping before Thanksgiving so I can enjoy the holiday without getting called into work."

There's a soft lull in the conversation, just awkward enough to make me want to fill it. "So, are you two working today, or is this strictly a produce run?"

Kim answers sternly, reducing the levity, "Always working, Moon."

I take a risk. "How's the investigation into Richard Holbrook's murder going?"

Everyone looks at me like I've lost my damn mind, and perhaps I have.

Kim replies with a non-answer, "We cannot comment on an ongoing investigation."

I fidget with the buttons on my jacket, "Oh, okay. Michael Nguyen and I have been reviewing the budget files for the revitalization effort, and I believe they may be related. Whole sections are redacted… budgets are missing huge chunks of money. Richard Hollbrook's initials are all over it."

Kim's eyebrows rise, and for the first time, he actually looks at me, not through me. "We're already aware," he says, deadpan. "And if you or your boyfriend uncover anything else, next time you should report it, not go snooping, possibly corrupting evidence."

"Michael's not my boyfriend," I say, and instantly regret it. "And we weren't snooping. We were…investigating. Like concerned citizens."

There's another pause. Without warning she hands me a slip of paper. "If you think of anything else, call this number," she says. "Direct line."

Kim shifts his weight, then folds his arms. "Out of curiosity, why do you care so much about this, Moon?"

I bristle, surprised by my own reaction. "Um, well, I have been interested in the financials of the town."

"Why would you be so concerned with the financials of this town?"

"Well, I am a citizen of this town."

He doesn't smile, but his eyes glint. "Who just happened to move here after a bunch of money went missing from the town budget as well as her parents' account, and right before the first murder we've had in Goose Grove in decades."

Andy is instantly at my side, voice sharp. "You think Celeste killed him?"

Kim holds up his hands. "Didn't say that. But she is very… involved."

"I'm considering investing in the town's success. I want to make sure things are on the up and up," I say, which is true, though I suddenly can't remember why I thought opening my mouth would make things better. "Have you been looking into the Mayor's involvement with all this? And Daniel Stevens and Nicole Adams are certainly up to something."

Andy bristles at their sister's and brother-in-law's name. Sarah's mouth gapes open.

Angela senses the shift and intervenes. "We are following all leads, Celeste," she says gently.

"I'm just a concerned citizen asking questions that anyone would ask…"

Kim doesn't smile. He leans in, just enough that I can smell his aftershave. "How about we head to the station and you tell me more about exactly what you and Mr. Nguyen have been up to."

That does it. My cheeks flush, and for a second I can't breathe. Andy puts a hand on my shoulder, steadying me, but it takes a few seconds before I can speak without trembling.

"I think I need to call my lawyer before I do that," I say.

Kim's eyes widen, just a touch. "Suit yourself," he says. "We'll wait."

I walk away from the cops and pull out my phone. Andy hangs back with Angela, both of them looking particularly uncomfortable. Sheriff Kim stares at me like a smug statue.

Sarah follows and whispers, "You okay?"

"I'm fine," I lie. My hands are shaking, so I clutch my phone like a lifeline. "I just need to call James."

I break away from Sarah to step behind a stand of pumpkins.

Sheriff Kim shouts, "Stay within eyesight, Ms. Moon." Everyone looks at him and at me. I feel the eyes of the entire town on me.

I stop beside the pumpkin stand, within his eyesight, and dial James's number. As it rings, I try to breathe. He picks up on the first ring. "Hey, baby. I was just thinking of you. I'm a bit busy, but—"

"Can you meet me at the market?" I whisper, voice barely audible, cutting him off.

He must sense something is wrong, because no questions asked, he replies, "Be there in five," and hangs up.

My heart races, and I wish Mrs. Heart was still here with me. I hang back, not rejoining the group, as I wait for James.

James arrives exactly four minutes later, impeccably dressed, even in jeans and a sweater; his hair refuses to move in the wind. This must be how he dresses when he works on the weekend. He spots me instantly and beelines over. He looks toward the Sheriff and Deputy and immediately assesses the situation.

He puts a protective hand on my back and walks me toward the cops. "Sheriff Kim," he says, tone friendly but lethal, "do you have official business with my client?"

Kim's mouth opens, then closes. He shakes his head. "Just chatting."

"Unless you're prepared to formally arrest or charge my client, she will not be answering any further questions, and we shall be leaving."

Sheriff Kim replies nonchalantly, "Like I said, just chatting."

"Then you'll excuse us," James says. Without waiting for a reply, he steers me away.

Andy and Sarah look dumbfounded before rushing toward us. Andy waves and says, "See ya, Angie!" as they trot toward us.

The cops stand stone still before sharing a knowing look and turning away to go do some other cop-like thing.

"Are you okay?" James asks, quietly, his hand still on my back, walking purposefully away at a speed I can barely keep up with.

"I don't know," I say.

He grins. "Don't worry, baby. I got you. Thanks for calling me this time."

Andy and Sarah catch up.

"Dang, James, that was kind of hot," Andy says.

Sarah replies, "Yeah, remind me to call you if I'm ever a murder suspect."

I lean into him, "Thanks, James. I'm sorry, I know you said you were busy."

"Anything for you, baby. Besides, I needed to get some food anyway. Is the cafe open?" he asks Sarah and Andy.

Sarah looks at her watch, "Yeah, we actually should get back and relieve Jessica anyway."

"Great," James grins in response, then says to me, squeezing me tightly, "Now, let's get lunch before you get yourself arrested."

55

"You feeling better now, baby?" James asks, wiping my lip with his thumb.

"Yeah, the turkey sandwich and lavender coffee are really calming," I say with a smirk.

"Well, I guess it was good I thought to bring you here."

"It's nice. Being able to eat like this together. We don't get a lot of uninterrupted time. I appreciate you stepping away from work."

"You were right the other night. I should try to take more time to just…relax."

We snuggle against each other in the booth, and James hasn't looked at his phone or watch once since we've been here. However, as if I summoned him with my uninterrupted comment, the chime on the door turns all our attention to Michael entering.

Sarah and Andy instinctively say, "Welcome," before they even look up. When Andy and Sarah's eyes land on Michael, they both go wide-eyed and look at each other, sharing a knowing glance, then turn to me and James, smiling. *God, these two love drama.*

Michael strides in, his hair windblown, as if he's been running his fingers through it, and his eyes immediately find James and me.

Michael's wearing a sexy sweater and his glasses, and God do I love the fall.

He pauses at the door, pulls at the neck of his sweater, and grips the handle of his bag tighter. It's as if he's having a silent argument with himself about whether he should sit with us, sit in his usual seat, or just leave. He turns slightly, and I think he will leave. But then, after adjusting his glasses, he turns and approaches us purposefully, bypassing the counter. I brace myself for the confrontation.

"Hey, Celeste," Michael says, followed by "Jamie," when he stops in front of our booth.

"Hey," I say and look at James, whose arm is around my waist.

"Join us?" James says, gesturing to the seat in front of us.

What?

"Sure," Michael says, dropping into the seat on the other side of the table and sliding in, pushing his laptop bag to the side.

What?

"Not working?" Michael asks James with a level of venom I don't usually hear from him.

"I guess you can say I am," James smirks, squeezing my leg.

Michael looks to me for clarification.

"I stupidly tried to get info from Sheriff Kim and Deputy Martinez," I say, putting my face in my hands. "James had to come save me."

"The two of you are going to get arrested for obstruction if you keep trying to solve this murder," James adds, giving Michael a look I don't understand. "Luckily, you both have a good lawyer."

"You're Michael's lawyer, too?" I ask.

"If he needs one," James replies flatly and looks away.

Michael looks down at the table, before saying, "James has a thing for damsels in distress" with a smirk. "It's why he became a lawyer. That white knight complex needed an outlet." And, I'm not sure which of us is the supposed damsel in distress: Michael or me.

"I prefer to think of it as a strong sense of justice," James counters, putting his arm on the back of the booth behind me, confidently.

Michael retorts, "Call it what you like. You've always been the one rushing in to save the day." There's something in Michael's tone—affection mixed with something deeper.

"Not always," James says quietly, his confident posture softening.

"Yeah, not after three months," Michael says flatly. "That's the cutoff. But, usually it's three dates, right?" Their eyes meet in a way that suddenly makes me feel like I'm intruding on a private moment.

"Am I missing something here?" I ask, curiosity finally getting the better of me.

Michael's expression shifts to one of amusement. "Oh, just commenting on James's inability to maintain a long-term relationship. Have the two of you had three dates yet?" Michael says with a bit of disdain.

James's mouth purses at Michael, who defiantly smirks at him.

This is technically our third date, actually.

I watch this exchange with growing curiosity. There's an ease between them, a familiarity that goes beyond casual acquaintance. Their back-and-forth has the rhythm of long practice.

"Are you two always like this?" I ask, glancing between them.

They exchange a look, something passing between them that I can't quite decipher.

"Like what?" Michael asks, accepting his coffee from Sarah with a grateful nod. *I guess he's here enough to have a usual order and a tab, too.*

I bite my lip, "Umm…I'm not sure how to explain it. Like, you're always on the verge of fighting, but…not…"

They give each other a look that's charged with electricity.

"Tell her, Mikey," James says.

"Celeste. I have something I should tell you," Michael spits out.

"What, do you suspect Mrs. Heart now?" I say with a laugh.

He doesn't find my joke funny. "Of course not…"

He looks deathly serious, and I worry about what he has to tell me. "Michael, what is it?"

"I've been struggling to decide how to tell you…"

"Michael, you're scaring me."

"Oh, gosh, I'm sorry. It's not…it's not bad really. It's just a complication…a coincidence, more like it, just a little thing I feel I should tell you."

"Mikey, you're rambling," James interjects.

"Sorry. Um, well, I've been trying to think of a way to tell you, and I spoke to James—"

He pauses, looking to James, who nods.

"I wanted to make sure he was okay with me telling you this. He said he hadn't told you because he also wanted to check with me—"

"Michael, please spit it out, you're killing me," I say.

He looks around to make sure no one is listening and leans in slightly. He closes his eyes and exhales, still not actually saying what he wants to say.

James sighs, but there's no real annoyance behind it. "Michael and I…" he begins, then pauses, seeming to search for the right words.

Without opening his eyes, Michael finally blurts out, "We dated."

James continues, "'dated' is a generous term for what was essentially—fucking interspersed with heated arguments about books and video games."

I nearly choke on air, not expecting such frankness. James runs a hand through his perfectly styled hair, messing it up slightly in a way that only makes him more attractive.

Michael scoffs, "Jeeze, thanks, Jamie. Happy to hear it meant so much to you."

"Mikey, that's not…," James stops and sighs, obviously exasperated by this conversation they've likely had many times.

Michael continues, "I would maybe describe it more as 'a passionate but ultimately incompatible relationship,' but, fine, fucking and discussing books and video games works, too."

They look at me, awaiting a reaction.

"Oh…," I trail off, reflecting on their interactions up till now. I guess it makes sense. "So, you used to be a thing?" I say, emphasizing "used to."

Michael begins to ramble again, "Yes, just a little thing. It wasn't long. It was just…" he opens his eyes, "sexual. Mostly. Friends with benefits, kinda like you and Ryan. And…now that we're both with you, we thought it was relevant for you to know about our…history." He doesn't seem to have caught the implied question. I'm wondering if they're still a thing.

Is it my place to actually ask that?

Michael continues to ramble, "It was right after my divorce. It didn't last long. We were just hooking up, really. We didn't really date per se, not that it matters. Does it matter? But he helped me get over my ex, and he told me you knew he was bi, but a lot of people don't. It's hard for him with his job to be out. And I don't really talk a lot about myself. Except with you, that is. Sarah and Andy know, but that's—"

I hold up a hand. "Michael, it's okay. You don't have to explain yourself to me."

Michael's shoulders relax, just a millimeter.

I look between them, "And now you're what? Friends?" So, they're not lovers anymore, but are they friends? It's hard to tell with these two.

"Friends is accurate," James nods.

"Friends who occasionally still argue about books and video games," Michael adds.

There's a weight to his words that makes my skin tingle. The atmosphere shifts, charged with something I can't quite name but can definitely feel.

"To be clear. The sex stopped a while ago," James adds.

"Why?" I ask, "Why did you break up?"

Oh, should I have asked that?

"Well, you'd have to be officially dating to break up," James says.

"And James doesn't date anyone," Michael says, obviously still annoyed at the way he and James ended it.

James smirks at him, replying, "Married to the job."

"Is that so…" I say, sipping my coffee and contemplating what this means. "Is this our third date, James, or does it not count since you're technically working?"

James looks at me, and a moment of panic crosses his face, realizing the implication for me, "Celeste, if I were ever to settle down, it would be with you. You must realize that."

"Ah, so you'll let her spend every Friday night alone while you go and save all the other damsels?" Michael snarks.

"Well, that's why I'm happy she'll have you to keep her company, Michael," James says flatly.

Michael's face contorts in anger. "Ah, so I'm your bed warmer?" Michael asks. "The James substitute for when you work. I get to do all the relationship stuff, and you get to do the fucking? Is that how it works?"

"No, I was hoping that the three of us could eventually…" he looks at Michael and smirks, "Well, you can guess what I was hoping, Mikey."

Michael immediately backs off the offensive, blushes, and looks down, pulling at the collar of his sweater.

"What?" I ask, thinking I suspect what he's referring to.

James remains coy, trying to get Michael to tell me, "Do something Michael and I fantasized about when we were a thing."

"What?" I ask, looking between them, curiosity overwhelming me.

James waits for Michael, but Michael doesn't speak up. So, he says, "Well, I've told you how obsessed with you I've been. Has Michael told you of his obsession?"

"I've mentioned it…" Michael says. *Mentioned is an understatement, Mikey.* "When we found out about our mutual…pining…we talked about how great it would be to…be with you…at the same time."

"You don't have to be coy, Mikey," James says. A switch flips in James, and he places his hand on Michael's, that are currently twisting his napkin on the table. Michael looks down at James's hand, who then leans into me and strokes my chin saying, "We've always wanted to fuck you together."

I spurt, stunned.

Michael's Adam's apple bobs.

James asks, "What do you say, Celeste? Mikey? Down for a threesome?"

56

A hush falls over our table. No, it's the sharp, spark-laced silence of three people realizing the conversation has veered into uncharted territory. Territory that has inexplicably changed everything between us, regardless of what is said next.

James and Michael are looking at me with distinctly different expressions. James sits beside me, arm still draped behind me, and watches me with the self-satisfied patience of a man who knows the answer before you do. He's almost smug in his cockiness. Michael, meanwhile, tries to look casual, but he's got that nervous energy he displays occasionally. He obviously wants to do this, but is scared I'll say no. Probably scared, I'll say yes, too.

"So," I say, because someone has to break the tension, "I just want to make sure I'm reading this right. You're asking me to—"

"Have sex with us," James says, and it's not even a question. It's almost a command. He leans forward and grins at me before placing a kiss under my ear.

Michael snorts, eyes flicking up from his coffee. I'm having trouble reading him. I squint at him. "Michael, you want this, too?"

He twists his napkin. "I would be amenable to it."

"Well, now, Mikey, that's not enthusiastic consent," James says with a firmness that seems to embolden Michael.

"I very much would like to, yes…" he says with more confidence, but then balks and adds, "as long as you're okay with it, Celeste."

The most alarming part of this entire situation isn't the proposition; it's how quickly my mind is leapfrogging past logistics and right into anticipation. These men are both impossibly attractive in totally different ways. The idea of both of them? My nervous system might short out.

But there's a part of me that's always looking for the angle, the scam, the dramatic twist. Old habits, I guess. So I try to keep my voice steady, letting it slide into mock disapproval. "What exactly would I get out of this arrangement, other than sore muscles and dehydration?"

Michael laughs, dropping the napkin and placing his hands in his lap, watching me intently now. He must understand that this question means I'm likely going to say yes; he always seems to read me well.

James strokes my chin again, "Orgasms, obviously."

"I mean, I get those all the time already," I laugh.

Michael props his elbow on the table and his chin on his fist, "You'd be the center of attention of two men who worship the ground you walk on," he says.

Here's the thing about me: I've got a bit of a praise kink. I can't take a compliment when I've got my clothes on, in my civilian life if you will, but once I'm in "horny Celeste mode," I love being worshiped.

Sarah walks past our table and cuts me a smirked glance that makes me suspect she knows what we're talking about. Her eyes widen in question. I smile at her, and she makes another face that seems to say, "Girl, go fuck them!"

"So…" I say, tracing the pattern on the tablecloth with my finger, "if I say yes, am I agreeing to, like, a one-time event? Or is this more of a…recurring calendar invite?"

James opens his mouth, but Michael answers first, scoffing, "Good luck getting a recurring calendar invite with James." This is obviously a sore subject with him, and it seems to have played a significant role in their no longer having a sexual relationship.

James shoots him a look. "I am open to whatever the two of you are interested in. It can be a one-time thing, but I'd also be thrilled to do it again."

"So, is this your way of asking me back out, James? To start back up our canceled dinner dates, paid back in blowjobs?" Michael asks, and I see the rarest thing: a flush creeping up James's neck. *Huh. He can dish it, but he can't always take it.* Filing that away for later.

"Mikey, you know as well as I do I was not the one to call off our arrangement and would have been perfectly happy to continue it," James says.

Michael purses his lips, and I wonder if this is a good idea given Michael is obviously still hurt by the way their relationship ended.

But, instead of continuing their slightly antagonistic banter, they look back at me with expectation. They're willing to put whatever this squabble is aside and are waiting on me.

There's a beat where the world could tip either way. I could laugh it off, make an excuse, and things could continue the way they have been. Or I could take the leap and see what happens.

I look at James, then Michael, and I let myself imagine it—the three of us, intertwined, both of them inside me. I want that. I want it so badly that the sheer thought of it sends sparkles throughout my body.

"So, are we talking about doing this now?" I ask.

"Now works for me," James says. "How about you, Mikey?"

Michael just nods.

"Let's go," I say as calmly as I can muster. I have to actively stifle the urge to lie across this table with my ass in the air and beg them to, "Just go ahead and get to fucking."

James is up so fast I didn't even see him move. Michael smiles and slides out of his side of the booth. James offers me his hand, helping me slide out.

Andy and Sarah, now both behind the counter, whisper to each other and give me encouraging giggles and sly thumbs up. The rest of the cafe patrons don't pay much attention to us. Goose Grove is a tiny town, and the idea of anyone seeing us leave together should mortify me, but instead, it feels like a dare.

We exit the cafe, and the autumn air outside snaps around us, charged and expectant. We stand on the sidewalk for a moment, indecisive, realizing we didn't really discuss where we should do this thing. But James turns and walks purposefully. I follow James's lead, and Michael falls in step beside me, hands in his coat pockets, a small, boyish, anticipatory smile on his face.

"Where are we going?" I ask.

James slows so that we can catch up with him. He places his hand on my lower back and says, "My office. It's close, and I can't wait any longer to fuck you two." Michael and I both give off a nervous giggle, equally enjoying the praise.

The sidewalk is covered in leaves, the color of warning signs. My shoes crunch through them as we pick up speed. Part of me wonders if I'm walking toward disaster, but a bigger, louder part just wants to see what happens next.

57

James unlocks the door to his office, and it's what you'd expect if you only saw him in a suit at fundraisers: bookcases, heavy wood, the faint scent of expensive aftershave. There's a leather couch under the window, and for a split second, I imagine how many people have been bent over its arm. I immediately have to look at my shoes to hide the blush.

James doesn't flick on the harsh overheads; instead, he taps on two lamps on opposite sides of the room, so the whole place glows amber. It's so warm, I suspect this is all part of his seduction tactic. I wonder if these two taught each other how to use lighting to seduce, because it's a bit weird that they both seem to be pros at it.

Michael hovers near the window, running a finger along the bookshelf. James turns from the lamp with the dazzling confidence of a man who enjoys every second of what comes next.

"Should we sit? Or do you prefer to negotiate standing?" He makes air quotes around "negotiate" and flops onto the couch, one arm stretched along the back like he's hosting a talk show.

Michael sits beside him, his ankles crossed, hands clasped. Instead of joining them on the couch, I perch on the coffee table across from them, knees almost touching theirs. They seem almost disappointed

I'm not sitting with them. It feels like a bizarre interview panel—two wildly overqualified candidates, both intent on impressing me.

"So," I ask, "what exactly are we negotiating?"

James's posture shifts to a professional, lawyerly one. "Well, I know we've all been together, but the addition of another person adds a layer of complication. We all should discuss what we'd like out of this, since it will be harder to judge in the moment. As you are both well aware, I am strongly committed to consent, and not just for legal reasons. But if at any point either of you is not having fun, we stop, no questions asked. Cool?"

"Cool," I say, sounding steadier than I feel.

"What if you aren't having fun?" Michael asks, with a smirk.

"Oh, I'll have fun," James says in that reassuring way. Then he returns his attention to me, tipping his head, "So, Celeste, anything off-limits? Choking, hair-pulling, spanking—"

Michael groans. "Jesus, James, give her a second."

I grin at James. "I'm not really into pain…Well, I kinda like it when penetration is rough enough to hurt. And, I'm okay with a little hair-pulling if it's light and kind of…to direct me, if that makes sense. I'm really not into spanking. I do like to bite, though. Not to be bitten. But to bite. Choking…once again, light grips…Sorry, no one's ever asked me this stuff before, so I don't really know how to explain."

James lifts a hand, reassuring me that it's okay. "I get it, Celeste, we'll keep it gentle. But when you're ready for that rough dicking, let us know."

I blush, squeeze my legs together, and grip the edge of the coffee table.

James turns to Michael. "Mikey?"

Michael glances at me, then James. "I like making out. I like taking my time. My favorite part is the anticipation. I don't mind a little pain, but nothing that draws blood. I need cuddles after—especially if it gets rough. Sometimes I get too in my head. So, I like it when my partners explicitly tell me what they want."

James's mouth quirks and looks at Michael in a way that seems to convey, "Why hadn't you told me this before? I could have worked with that," but instead he just says, "Noted."

"And you?" I ask James. He seems surprised I've asked.

"I like to be in charge," he says, and honestly, I kinda already knew that. "Other than that, I'm really down for almost anything. Based on what the two of you just said, none of my lines are going to get crossed."

"And, well, Mikey and I already know each other's preferences on this, but, Celeste, how do you feel about anal?"

I look between the two of them and consider the idea of them both inside me. *Fuck that would be so hot.* "Never done it. But I'd be interested in trying."

"Got lube just lying around the office, James?" Michael asks.

"Oh…ha. No. Never mind then," James says with a chuckle.

There's a pause, long enough for me to hear the distant traffic and the gentle tick of the wall clock.

James clears his throat, suddenly a little more earnest. "So. The last time you were tested?" he asks, looking at us both. "I was tested about three months ago, all clear. The only person I've been with since then is Celeste. We've also used protection both times."

Michael replies, "Oh, um, I was tested about a year ago, all negative. I've only been with Celeste since. We, uh, didn't use a condom the last two times, though." I cringe, worried James is going to be mad about our irresponsibility.

James's eyes flick to mine, and he looks at me the same way he did when we ran into each other on the street a few weeks ago. It's hunger, but it's also delight. He's not mad, he's…excited.

James looks at me, waiting for my answer. I say, "I was tested before I got here. Negative. Um…I've also been with Ryan. We haven't been using protection. He said he had been tested and didn't have anything."

James looks incredibly pleased when he leans in. "So, I have a confession." He drums his fingers on his knee, like he's giving himself a countdown. "I ask all this because I have a bit of a kink about, um—"

Michael saves him the trouble. "He likes the idea of filling you up with his seed," he says, deadpan. "It's like a whole thing for him."

James groans. "Thanks, Mikey. Really appreciate you cutting to the chase for me."

I'm glad I'm already sitting, because my legs do a little jellyfish impression. "Wait, like, actually—"

"Yeah," James says, sheepish but not apologetic. "I've got a bit of a breeding kink. It's stupid, but it's so fucking hot to me. I like thinking about knocking you up…but not really, if that makes sense. Don't get me wrong, I really want children, but I'm not actually trying to impregnate you."

It's not stupid, and it's not un-hot. I feel my face go bright red, which is how I know I'm into it.

"Well," I say, "lucky for you, I'm on the pill."

James's smile is the human equivalent of a sunrise, and he asks hopefully, "So, are we all comfortable with—"

I cut James off, "Going raw? Yes."

Michael chortles softly, and James smiles bigger than he has yet, which is saying something.

"Mikey?" James asks.

Michael adjusts his glasses. "Yeah, I'm okay with it."

"Good…good," he says, leaning back further. "If it wasn't clear, I'm more than okay with it."

"You're just going to trust us? And Ryan?" I ask.

"Yeah, I am," James says without any hint of a joke in his voice.

"Okay then…" I say, trailing off.

"Okay then…" Michael and James say in unison.

Another silence, warmer this time. Michael nudges my ankle with his. "You good with all this, Celeste?"

I nod. "Yeah. I like this. I like you guys. I want this."

"What about you, Mikey?" James asks. "Still mad at me?"

Michael sighs loudly and leans back a bit. "What's to be mad about? It was just fucking and arguing, right? We never stopped arguing. So, I guess now we're just adding the fucking back in."

James turns to Michael. "I'm sorry. That was a shitty way for me to describe it."

Michael pulls at the throat of his sweater. "Oh, so now that you want to fuck me again, it was more than that, huh?"

"Mikey, I never stopped wanting to fuck you. You broke it off, not me."

Michael's face scrunches a bit while he recalls their past. I keep quiet, not wanting to sway this conversation or pressure him in any way. James does the same.

Michael looks between the two of us. "Yeah, I want to do this." Then, looking at just James. "But…stick to showering Celeste with your affections…for now."

James takes a breath, his whole demeanor shifting, like he's just remembered he can have exactly what he wants. He stands, offers me his hand, and when I take it, he pulls me gently to my feet.

"Then let's get started," he says, voice low and certain.

I don't know what I was expecting, but the way he leans down and kisses me is as much a promise as it is a prelude—a soft, careful brush of lips, the tiniest bit of tongue, enough to make my heart stutter. Michael watches, lips parted, hands gripping his knees.

58

James breaks our kiss and grins at me. Then nods over my shoulder to Michael. "Care to join us, Mikey?" he asks.

Michael doesn't answer. He simply takes off his glasses, placing them on a side table, and stands. He positions himself behind me, places his hands on my waist, and kisses my neck.

James takes my face in both hands, thumbs running along my cheeks. He's gentler than his demeanor suggests, but there's nothing uncertain about him. "You're gorgeous," he says, then looks past me to Michael. "Don't you think?"

Michael's answer is a low, pleased sound, his lips grazing my ear. "She's perfect."

They keep saying this to me. Maybe I'll believe them one day, but despite not being able to internalize the message, it feels good to be the center of attention. Really, really good.

James pulls me in for another kiss, but this time he's more forceful, tongue pushing its way in. Michael takes his place at my mouth, and James watches us intently.

Michael grips my ass, slowly descending to the couch. I follow, straddling him, knee on the sofa.

Michael and I continue to kiss. James sits beside us and continues to watch, just enjoying the show, apparently.

James kisses me again, hard and deep, while Michael's hands work my hips, sliding beneath the hem of my sweater. His fingers are warm and sure, kneading the flesh of my back.

"Mikey, take her shirt off," James says, and Michael immediately peels my top up and over my head, careful not to tangle my hair. He tosses it to the side, and for a second, both men just look at me, their faces lit by the amber lamps, eyes dark with want.

"You're so fucking beautiful," Michael says, voice hushed.

James grins. "You both are so fucking hot."

They make quick work of my bra, and then Michael is kissing my neck, my shoulder, his teeth just grazing. James's hand runs through my hair, and, more tentatively, reaches for Michael's. When James's hand runs through Michael's hair, I can feel the electricity of this touch and can tell it's something they've both wanted for a long time. James leans forward, taking both our mouths with his, and soon, I can't tell whose tongue is whose. Whose lips are whose.

My hands grip the edges of their shirts, attempting to tug them upward. James shrugs out of his sweater one-handed, barely breaking the kiss. Michael, on the other hand, pulls back, leaning against the back of the couch, and I pull it over his head. I admire his chest, placing both my hands on his pecs.

James looks at Michael, admiring his body. "You got buffer," he says to Michael.

"Thanks for noticing," Michael says with a smirk, and a flick of his head to remove the hair from his eyes. He doesn't compliment James back.

They both look at me, then at each other, and something passes between them—an old joke, a promise, I don't know—but it makes them both smile.

James turns to Michael, strokes his face, and kisses his cheek before he says, "You first." He stands and removes his marvelous cock from his pants, rolling his thumb over the tip. "I just want to watch you two for a bit," he says, looming over us.

Michael and I continue to make out, the passion between the two of us increasing as I grind on his lap. He unbuttons my pants, and I stand to kick them off along with my underwear. He removes both his pants and underwear in one movement, throwing them to the side.

Fuck he is so hot.

Never able to resist the urge to jump on Michael's cock, I leap to return to my perch on his lap. He pulls me onto his lap, and I appreciate the delight on his face as I sink slowly down onto his cock. His hands slide over my ribs, my breasts, down to my thighs.

He's careful, almost reverent, kissing my neck and shoulder, whispering things I can't quite catch, but make me flush all the way down.

James pumps harder at his cock, "Fuck, that's so hot." He bends forward, kissing my back and my shoulders.

He whispers into my ear, "Can you turn around for me, baby?"

I turn around so my back is to Michael, and sink back down on his dick.

"Spread her for me, Mikey, let me see that perfect cock in that perfect pussy," James says, eagerly.

Michael's hands spread my thighs further apart as he kisses my neck. Michael's hands glide up my legs until they stop at my pussy. With one hand, he spreads my lips open with two fingers, somehow slightly stroking my clit at the same time. I moan and lean back, kissing Michael's ear, causing him to twitch under me and moan, as well. With his other hand, he presses against my clit.

"Fuck, you look so pretty wrapped around his cock, baby," James says, and I want to be embarrassed, but instead I just feel proud, like I'm passing some secret test.

James pushes the coffee table out of the way and gets on his knees in front of us. We freeze. James kisses up my and Michael's legs, causing us to twitch. When he gets between our legs, his tongue reaches out and licks Michael's balls, causing a deep guttural groan and twitch from Michael. James runs his tongue up the shaft of Michael's cock until he reaches my clit. He takes it into his mouth with a deep suck.

It's almost too much—all this attention focused on me. I want to hold on, make it last, but I can't. I come fast and hard, shuddering around Michael's cock, clutching at his forearms, my voice crying out so loud I bet passersby outside can hear me. "Oh, Michael. Oh, James. Yes. Yes!" They don't relent until I'm pushing them away.

James pulls back, wiping his mouth with the back of his hand, then kisses my inner thigh with something like affection. "You taste so fucking good, baby," he says, and I don't even care if it's a line. "And the sound of you coming is the best thing I've ever heard."

Michael strokes my hair, pressing kisses to my temple, and for a moment, I just bask in the feeling of being held. I might fall asleep.

But it's not over. James stands and kisses Michael on the mouth, sharing the taste of me with him. Then whispers to Michael over my head, "You know what I want to see."

Michael smiles, a little sheepish, but he's game. He nods.

James pulls me to my feet, off Michael's cock, a little boneless. And hugs me.

James grins, holding my gaze, and says, "You're going to let him fuck you while you suck my cock, right?"

I nod, not trusting my voice.

"Good girl," he says, and the praise sends another shiver through me.

Michael moves behind me, hands on my hips, kissing down my spine. James steps in close, cupping my face, kissing me hard. I taste myself on his tongue, and it makes me dizzy.

Michael presses against my back, his cock hard and insistent. He slides a hand between my legs, spreading me open, and I gasp at the sensation.

James guides my head downward, bending me at my waist with a gentle hair pull. "Open up for me, baby."

I take James in my mouth, savoring the weight, the taste, the way he groans and threads his fingers through my hair.

Michael, still behind me, enters me in one slow, steady push. I moan around James, the sensation overwhelming. Perfect.

James sets the pace, thrusting gently into my mouth, one hand in my hair, the other stroking my cheek. Michael moves behind me, each thrust sending a jolt up my spine. Every nerve ending alive.

James pulls out occasionally to let me breathe, wiping tears from my cheeks with surprising tenderness. "You look so fucking hot like this, baby," he says.

Michael's hands dig into my hips, holding me steady, and I can feel him getting close.

James seems to be close, too. He pulls out of my mouth. "Oh, baby, you're too good at that. I can't let you swallow my seed, though. I need to fill that perfect pussy."

James stands there cock in my face, and strokes it, slow and deliberate, watching as Michael thrusts into me.

After he composes himself, James says, "Open up," his voice softer, and I do, letting him slide into my mouth again. He doesn't move this time, just lets me bob on his cock to the rhythm of Michael pumping behind me. Perhaps, not wanting to come.

"Fill her up for me, Mikey. I want to feel her tight cunt lubed with your warm cum," he reaches forward, stroking Michael's hair above.

Michael thrusts within me, his pace quickening, "Say, 'please,' or I'm spilling it on the floor."

James chuckles. "Please, Mikey. Please fill her up for me."

I feel Michael tense, his breath hitching, and then he's coming, hard, holding me tight. The sensation pushes me over the edge again, and I moan, James's cock deep in my throat, the sound vibrating through both of us.

"That's my good girl, come for us," James whispers. James waits until Michael is done, then pulls out, before sliding his cock across my tongue and lips. He looks at me, eyes wide with pleasure, then bends down and kisses me.

"My turn," James says, helping me stand and kissing me fiercely before guiding me onto the couch. "Lie back," he says, and I do. He joins me on the couch, hovering over me, "Can I be rough with you, baby?"

"Yes," I say, fully jelly as he lies on top of me. He lifts my legs above my head slightly, looking down at my pussy and rubbing his cock at my entrance.

"You're spilling out of her, Mikey. We can't have that. Hold her legs up for me," he says, as Michael comes to the side of the couch over my head, gripping my ankles. Michael looks me in the eye, asking if it's okay, and I nod.

James slides his cock up my entrance, catching Michael's semen with his head, "I'm gonna pump you so full you'll be spilling us for days."

James enters me with a deep thrust, hitting the spot deep inside of me that makes me scream with each thrust.

"That's it, baby, take me, take all of me," James says, pumping harder and faster into me.

Michael kisses my forehead, "You take him so good, sweetheart. So pretty as he fills you up."

"Oh, Mikey, she feels so good filled with you," James says as he pumps one final time, twitching and groaning on top of me.

"Perfect," James says, collapsing onto the couch beside me.

Michael joins us, still breathing hard, his arms wrapping around my waist as he snuggles against me, nuzzling into my breasts. I stroke his head and hug him close to me, knowing cuddling is important to him.

Fuck. I think I love both of them, and I don't know if it's the dopamine and oxytocin rush or the fact that they're both spilling out of me right now.

For a while, none of us speak. There's just the sound of our breathing, the soft tick of the clock, and the warmth of our bodies pressed together.

Finally, James says, "You two are so fucking perfect. Mikey, please stop being mad at me so we can keep doing this."

I laugh, my whole body shaking with it.

"I suppose I can forgive you, Jamie," Michael says, kissing my shoulder. "But, only if you shut the fuck up and give us some cuddles."

59

I awake to the late afternoon sun filtering through the blinds of James's office, painting stripes across our still-entangled bodies, and piercing my eyelids. We fell asleep in a cramped but comfortable arrangement that had me sandwiched between James's solid warmth at my back and Michael's lean frame at my front.

Michael stirs first, his eyes blinking open to meet mine. For a moment, he just looks at me, his expression open and unguarded in a way I haven't seen before. Then his lips curve into a smile that crinkles the corners of his eyes.

"Hi," he murmurs, voice rough with sleep. "Any regrets?"

It's a brave question, direct in a way that's becoming familiar from him. I consider it seriously, taking stock of my feelings, the weight of James's arm around my waist, the warmth of Michael's breath against my cheek.

"No," I answer honestly. "You?"

"No," he says, reaching up to brush a strand of hair from my face.

Behind me, James stirs, his arm tightening briefly around me before relaxing. "Was that enough cuddling to merit forgiveness?" he asks Michael, his voice a rumble I can feel against my back.

Michael laughs softly. "You're forgiven."

I shift slightly, turning so I can see both of them. It's a tight fit on the couch. They're beautiful, and the fact that I'm here with both of them still seems surreal.

"I should probably…" I gesture vaguely at my scattered clothes, suddenly aware of our state of undress.

"Probably," James agrees, but makes no move to let me go. Instead, he props himself up on one elbow, looking down at me with an expression that's both tender and serious. "I think we should talk about what happened…about what happens next."

Michael sits up too, creating a little more space on the couch but keeping one hand on my knee, as if reluctant to break contact completely. "I'd like to do it again," he says.

"I feel the same way," James agrees quietly. "If my near declaration of love while coming wasn't clear enough."

Near declaration of love?

They both look at me, waiting.

I sit up too. "Me, too," I admit. "But I'm not sure what that means."

Michael takes a deep breath. "It could mean whatever we want it to mean. Including…something ongoing. Between the three of us."

The suggestion hangs in the air, both terrifying and exhilarating. James watches me carefully, his expression giving nothing away.

"You mean…a relationship?" I ask, wanting to be clear.

"A polyamorous relationship," James clarifies. "All three of us, together. And not separate like we are now."

I look between them, these two men who were already connected before I entered the picture. "Have you ever done something like that before? Either of you?"

They exchange a glance that speaks to their history, then both shake their heads.

"We discussed it," James says. "Back when we were together."

"It's not something to take lightly," Michael adds. "It requires communication, trust, boundaries."

James smiles. "I think…" he glances at Michael, who nods slightly, "that the chemistry between the three of us is worth exploring. If you're interested."

I consider their proposal, turning it over in my mind. There's an undeniable attraction, a connection that goes beyond the physical. But there are complications, too, practical considerations.

"Would it just be physical?" I ask. "Or are we talking about something more…emotional?"

"I don't think we can separate those things so neatly," James says thoughtfully. "What we share already has an emotional component. The question is whether we want to nurture that, let it grow into something deeper."

"I'm open to that," Michael says simply. "More than open. Interested. Invested. Hopeful, even."

James nods in agreement. "As am I."

"I thought you were 'married to your job,'" I quip at James, challenging him. "How do you go from being married to being locked down by not one, but two people?"

James sighs. "I do want to be in a committed relationship. I just know that my work is really important to me and takes a lot of my time. It makes me unavailable in a way that someone…especially someone who likes a lot of cuddles…," he pauses and smirks at Michael, who looks down, his hair covering his eyes while he smiles, "it just isn't fair to a partner. But if that partner had someone else to… cuddle in my absence. I'd feel a lot better about committing to that."

Michael asks, "What about you, Celeste? What do you think? I understand if you need time to think about it."

I fiddle with the edge of the couch, organizing my thoughts. "I'm falling for both of you," I admit. I think I'm in love with them both, but not quite ready to say I love them. "And this was…incredible. But I have reservations."

"Such as?" James prompts softly.

I respond, "For one thing, we live in a small town where everyone knows everyone else's business. How would this even work in practice?"

"Discretion," Michael suggests. "At least initially. Not because we're ashamed, but because it would give us space to figure things out without the entire town weighing in."

I nod, "And then there's Ryan," I say, knowing that Ryan is my primary point of conflict.

They both straighten slightly at the mention of his name.

"You're in love with him," James states rather than asks. I can see in their eyes that they want to ask if I love them, but they don't.

"Yes," I sigh. "I've tried to deny it, but I can't any longer."

"Does he love you?" Michael asks.

"Sometimes I think he does, and others, I think he really does just want to be friends," I explain. "But, I can't help but think that all of this is just another example of him hiding his feelings to protect me somehow."

"Have you asked him directly?" Michael asks.

"Yes. But he's a master of deflection. I'm not sure why he's so guarded. But I know that if I were to start dating the two of you seriously and break off things with him, he'd be devastated. Probably not talk to me again for another 20 years. And I can't lose him again."

James considers this. "So, your main concern about making this thing official with us is losing Ryan?"

"Yes," I admit.

"What if…what if he joined us?" James asks.

"Wait, you're suggesting all four of us enter a relationship?" I ask, confused.

James responds, "Yes."

I look at him, dumbfounded. Then look to Michael.

Michael runs a hand through his already disheveled hair. "I can't say I would mind seeing Ryan naked…if, you know, it came to that."

"I don't know if he'd be okay with that," I say, hugging myself.

Michael says, "Well…if we did this. Like, really did this. I'd be okay with you having a plus one, as long as it's just Ryan." Michael looks to James to see his reaction.

"I'm fine with that. It wouldn't be much different than how things have been," James responds with a shrug. Then he cuts Michael a glance and smiles when he says, "Except this lets me be with you again."

Michael blushes and says, "God, you're going to start flirting unabashedly with me again, aren't you?"

"Probably," James says, doing that chin thing to Michael and kissing him on the nose.

Gosh, they're cute. I love them. I wish Ryan were here.

Tears well in my eyes. "I don't even know if Ryan loves me back."

Why can't he love me? What is wrong with me that he can't love me? I'm just unlovable.

Michael notes my posture and pulls me close to him. "Hey, Celeste. I can see on your face that you're spiraling. If Ryan doesn't love you, that's not because of you; it's because of him, you understand? You are lovable."

How does he always know what I'm thinking!?

James now catches on and hugs me close, too. "Yeah, you are more than lovable."

Michael continues, "Exactly, we love you. If that doesn't prove you're lovable, I don't know what would."

James looks at Michael like he's gone crazy, then Michael realizes what he's said. Michael stutters then rambles, "I'm sorr—I mean, I love you. Shit, I messed that all up. And, obviously, I can't speak for James's feelings. God, I suck at this. Why do I always forget how to speak around you, Celeste?" he laughs at himself. I smile at him; it's so incredibly endearing.

James sighs at Michael once again, "It's okay, Mikey, I do love her." My face flushes a deep, burning red, and I'm overcome.

"I think…I think I love you two, too," I say, smiling. "So, I really, really do want this to work."

We embrace for a long moment, kissing, and I watch as their dicks rise, ready to go another round.

"But—" I say, realizing we got a bit off topic.

"You also love Ryan," James adds.

"Yes," I say, tears welling in my eyes.

"What if…" James begins thoughtfully, "You have an honest conversation with Ryan? Not about us, specifically, but about your feelings for him. Clear the air."

"Tell him you love him," Michael translates. "See what that leads to."

The thought makes my stomach clench with anxiety, but I know they're right. "That would be the fair thing to do," I agree reluctantly. "But what if it ruins our friendship?"

"True friendships can survive honesty," James says gently.

I'm not saying no," I tell them both. "To us, I mean. I just need some time. And I need to talk to Ryan first."

Their faces light up with matching expressions of hope that make my heart flutter.

"I'm just worried. What if he says he loves me, too, and demands I be with him? I…I don't think I can make the choice: the choice between him and the two of you," I add.

"That is definitely a possibility," James adds. "I don't know the inner workings of his brain, but…he doesn't seem to be completely on board with the way things are now. There is a hostility coming from him that doesn't line up with his words. But then again, he and I have always kind of butted heads."

"Ryan needs to be honest with you and himself. He's been running from this for twenty years. It's time he grew the fuck up and worked through his shit," Michael says.

"And Celeste, if you have to choose him over me…over me and Michael. I will understand," James says.

"Yeah, I won't be happy about it, but I'll understand," Michael replies.

I nod slowly, knowing they're right but still dreading the conversation.

"If that were the case, Mikey, perhaps you and I could…" James says.

"Not a chance. I like cuddling on Friday nights, not waiting up by the phone," Michael says curtly. "Or at least not waiting by the phone alone," he adds, giving James a more flirtatious smile.

"I'm pretty sure he's not interested in men…" I say, finally admitting to my last reservation of bringing Ryan into this poly relationship.

"Sex doesn't have to be between all of us," James states. "We could work something out. Like I said, it doesn't have to be much different from things as they are now. For him, anyway."

"I'll talk to him. Soon. Before we…before we decide anything concrete about us," I say.

They both seem to relax slightly at this. James reaches out to squeeze my hand. "There's no rush, Celeste. Despite what my actions earlier might suggest, we're all capable of patience. I've been waiting 20 years for you. I can wait a little longer."

"Speak for yourself," Michael jokes, but his eyes are kind. "But yes, take the time you need. We're not going anywhere."

I become acutely aware of our situation—three adults having a serious relationship discussion while crammed naked on an office couch.

"Maybe let's get dressed and off this couch now," I suggest, a laugh bubbling up despite the weightiness of our discussion.

"Yeah, my back is cramping," Michael approves, stretching his arms above his head in a way that draws my eyes to the lean muscles of his torso.

"Okay," James agrees, pressing a light kiss to my shoulder before standing to collect his scattered clothes.

We dress in companionable silence, occasionally catching each other's eyes, smiling. It should be awkward, but somehow it isn't. There's a comfort between us that defies the newness of whatever this is. As I pull on my socks, I find myself wondering what a relationship with both of them would actually look like. Dates with one or the other or both? Holidays? Living arrangements? Kids? It's overwhelming if I think too far ahead, so I pull myself back to the present—one step at a time.

"Coffee?" James suggests once we're all decent again, though his hair still refuses to return to its usual perfect style.

"God, yes," Michael says with feeling.

"Should we go to Sarah's?" I ask.

James chuckles, “Yeah, the coffee here is terrible.”

Michael adds, “Sarah and Andy are going to have a field day when the three of us walk back in looking like this.”

James nods, “I think they’ve been silently trying to orchestrate this, honestly.”

60

I'm sprawled on the floor, knees against a stack of boxes, wearing what could charitably be called a "slutty Ash Ketchum" costume. I considered putting a tiny dick in a Pokéball to really emphasize exactly what I'm trying to catch 'em all of, but if you gotta' go that far to explain your jokes, are they still funny?

My jean shorts are as uncomfortable as they are short, and the baseball cap is already giving me hat hair, but I can't have anyone saying I'm not fully committed to this bit.

I do look pretty hot, if I do say so myself.

I strategically position the phone camera to include tits and legs. I try on three different selfie faces (peace sign, the "who me?", and the classic "just found a shiny dick, I mean shiny Pikachu" gasp), and settle on the gasp.

This is the first year since I was a teen that I've dressed up for Halloween, and I have never had the opportunity to do the "be someone else, but slutty" tradition. These pictures will serve to both immortalize the occasion as well as…hopefully, catch some Pokédick.

I throw my first Pokéball, a.k.a. sexy selfie text, at Ryan, because he's my gaming buddy and probably the most likely to fall for this bait.

He replies almost instantly, as if my phone vibrated before I even hit send, "You did NOT."

"I absolutely did. wuu2?"

"Wishing I was in Goosetown, ripping those tiny shorts off you, that's for damn sure."

Shit, he's out of town?

"wya?" I text with that emoji that looks like it's on the verge of tears.

"Bar in Minneapolis. Met with a few artist friends who are helping me promote the gallery opening."

Why didn't he tell me he was heading out of town?

He continues, "Just had an impromptu interview with an art critic! Was all dressed up in my costume, though." Then sends a single rolling-on-the-floor laughing emoji.

"Costume?"

There's a full minute before his photo comes through, and it is extremely worth the wait. Ryan is at some impossibly hip bar in Minneapolis, ringed with little devil horns (realistic, rubber, and sculpted to look like they're bursting through his scalp), a black suit, and a red dress shirt. A red cocktail glows in his hand. There are a few impossibly beautiful women in the background.

Jealousy rips through me, but I try to quell it, "Damn, now I'm wishing you were here, too. FUCKING HOT."

"You didn't wish I were there already? I'm crushed."

"Of course I did. You think I was just trying to show you my costume?"

Ryan replies, "Wuu2? Other than…touching yourself, hopefully," followed by a winky kissy face.

"Waiting for the sun to set so I can pass out candy. What's in the glass? It looks radioactive."

"It's called an Inferno. Tastes like ass."

Unable to stop myself, I ask, "Who's the brunette in the devil tail?"

"My agent, Rebecca. She's the one who set up this whole thing."

"I notice you two are thematic? Couples costume?"

"Coincidence."

I look at the picture longer, trying to decide if I believe him. Trying to decide if I have a right to be jealous. Should I be casual and text, "Well, wear a condom?" Because if he does fuck her, it does affect me and James and Michael…

As I am typing a message I'm sure to regret, "I could be home by midnight if you want?" appears, causing me to erase what I've typed.

"No, you stay. I don't want to get in the way of your shameless self-promotion and networking," winky face.

"I'm not interested in her, Celeste."

"I didn't ask."

"Didn't have to."

Fuck. Am I so transparent?

He texts again, "I'm gonna be jacking off thinking about the best brunette in booty shorts there ever was later. No time for that kind of networking."

He knows just how to get me. Alliterations and video game references.

"Pics or it didn't happen."

"You asking for a dick pic, Celeste?"

"Maybe."

"Maybe I'll send one, then."

"Good. Have fun, Ry Guy."

"You, too, Star Girl."

I ignore the warmth in my chest and the teensy voice that still worries he'll be sleeping with the cute devil.

I wander to the couch and send the selfie to Michael. He responds with no words, just a photo of himself in an all-black tracksuit, holding a plastic hockey mask and a (what I hope is fake) hunting knife in front of his face. He must be wearing contacts, which I don't see often. Usually, I only see him without glasses when we're having sex, so to see him without them instantly turns my mind to sex. *Fuuuuck, it's hot.*

I text, "You look like a stalker with a heart of gold from a cozy dark romance."

He replies, "Good. It's what I was going for."

"Michael, are you trying to thirst trap me?"

"Yep."

"Mission severely accomplished."

He replies with a GIF of a Pokéball shaking three times and then clicking into place. "Yours, too. Want me to come over?"

"Yep."

"Should I pretend to break in?"

"Oh fuck yes."

"20 minutes."

I glance out the window, and the sun has yet to set. The trick-or-treaters should start in about an hour. I probably won't have time to fuck Michael before they start lining up. *Damnit.*

There's one person left to text, and I hesitate before sending it. I know he won't come over, but I think he'd still like to see this.

"Trick or treat," I text with the image.

"Well, that's a treat if I ever saw one," he replies almost instantly.

"Thanks. You got a costume?"

"Honestly, I forgot it was Halloween tonight."

"Bummer. I was hoping for a picture of you in a sexy costume," I reply with a sad face.

"Well, here's a consolation prize," he replies with a picture of himself in his home office, papers sprawled across the desk. The blue light of his computer screen brings out the gold in his hair and the ridiculous, devastating warmth in his smile.

"There's no dick in that picture!"

"Is that what my baby wants?"

"Yes, please," I respond with a red-faced drooling emoji.

A picture with the hidden ink feature comes in, and the text "Thinking about that pretty tongue rolling over it." I clear away the invisible ink to find James's perfect dick, hard, standing tall, his thumb running over it.

I respond, "ty" and the three hearts around the face emoji.

"What are you up to tonight?" he asks.

"Other than drooling over that dick? Michael's going to come over and pass out candy with me."

"Wish I could be there."

"I know. Me, too."

I think I'm getting what Michael meant about waiting by the phone for James on a Friday night. I pout at the phone, realizing it is Friday night.

"Have fun, baby. Pics of the two of you would definitely make my night."

"I'll think about it," I send with a winky face.

I lean my head back against the couch, close my eyes, and reach my hand into my shorts for just a moment, thinking about all three of the sexy men on my roster.

I'm startled by a knock on my window—slow and deliberate. The sight of a masked man standing at my window scares me so badly that I scream and fall off the couch. My phone clatters to the hardwood. Watson, next door, barks.

"Celeste, it's me! Fuck, I'm sorry!" Michael says, removing the mask.

I clench my chest. My heart is pounding so hard that I contemplate the probability of a heart attack, given my age and health.

I break into uncontrollable laughter at the look of pure terror on Michael's face. The fact that I'm easily jump-scared did not occur to me.

"Come in," I shout to him, unable to control my laughter.

He rushes in and joins me on the floor.

"We didn't think that through, huh?" he says, joining me in the laughter.

"No, not really."

61

Michael surveys the towers of cardboard boxes that have become permanent fixtures of my home. They, along with every other horizontal surface, are blanketed in bags of chips, full-size candy bars, and soda cans.

"Wow," Michael says. "Did you buy every item of junk food they had at Glendos's?"

I laugh. "I ordered it online. Is it too much?"

"Well, you'll definitely be the popular house tonight."

The doorbell rings, and we both jump at the scare.

"Celeste, dear, are you okay? I heard you scream," Mrs. Heart's voice sounds from behind the door, followed by a bark from a concerned Watson.

I call out, "Yeah, I'm okay. Just got startled," as I lift myself to answer the door. I open it to reveal probably the best couple's costume I've ever seen. She's wrapped in a fur-collared coat: she's gone full Cavalier King Charles Spaniel, black and tan ears sewn onto a cap, and a velvet collar with a fake diamond tag that reads "Good Girl." Even Mrs. Heart goes sexy on Halloween, it seems.

Watson, wiggling with excitement beside her, is not to be outdone. He's in a tiny blue cardigan and a powder-white wig. He's got a pair of arms that make him look like a human holding a felt apple pie; lashed to it is a ribbon that reads "First Place."

"Oh, my God, you two look amazing," I say, beaming at them.

"Why, thank you, dear. I've been working on it for a while. I'm happy that I could actually put that ribbon on the pie," she says, beaming. "You're looking absolutely gorgeous." She leans in, spotting Michael, "You, too, young man. Did I interrupt anything?" she asks in that look that indicates she knows I'm a slut.

"No, we were going to pass out candy."

"Oh, can I join you? I forgot to get candy this year."

"Sure, that'd be great," I say.

Michael approaches, "Love the costume, Mrs. H." She smiles even bigger.

Mrs. Heart's eyes open wide when she wanders in and notices the piles of candy and other junk foods, "Good heavens, that's a lot of Snickers."

"Overachiever, I guess," I say, slightly embarrassed.

"Oh, that's fine, dear. We'll just have to give each kid a few things. I think you got more stuff than there are kids in the whole town."

"Let me get a picture," I say.

Mrs. Heart poses like she's on one of her calendars and asks, "Should I do December 1975?" Another chaste yet slutty pose, "Or October 1978?"

"October 1978," I say, giggling, and snapping a picture of the two. Mrs. Heart looks really hot, not just for her age, but for a woman of any age. Watson, on the other hand, seems deeply unimpressed by the whole affair but stands beside her dutifully.

Michael leans in and looks at my phone. "My dad had the '78 calendar," Michael says, looking slightly uncomfortable and slightly aroused.

I grab my plush Pikachu from the couch and hang on Michael so Mrs. Heart can take pictures of the two of us.

"Okay, dear, let's get one for James," Mrs. Heart says.

I bend over in front of Michael, ass at crotch, and point my tits at the camera. Michael must look abashed because Mrs. Heart says,

"Michael, look like you know what to do with her. Celeste, make an oh face. Awww, you two are so cute. James will love this."

She shows us the phone, and it is incredibly sexy.

Michael smirks at the photo, and I send it to James in our group text.

"Thanks, Mrs. H.," Michael says, and attempts to adjust his glasses, but he's not wearing any.

Mrs. Heart peruses the horde of treats, and I whisper to Michael, "Well, now you know where I got it from. That's the nerdy perv that practically raised me." He laughs and looks at his phone when James texts us, "Holy fuck that is hot. Thank Mrs. H for me."

Together, we prepare the bowls I bought and move to the porch, three guards ready to meet the onslaught of goblins and ghouls demanding treats.

I'm ready.

Trick-or-treaters descend in waves, and Mrs. Heart is in her element. She compliments every costume. I'm surprised she forgot to get candy. This has always been her favorite holiday. I'm happy I get to spend it with her and Michael, though. Watson, meanwhile, is a magnet for attention. Little kids and drunk teenagers alike fawn over his "Granny" look, and he soaks it up with a kingly patience, basking in the petting and compliments.

Half an hour in, Mr. O'Connor shouts from his porch. "Duck! You're making me look bad. Full-size candy bars AND pop cans!?" His porch is decked with orange lights and a portable fire pit. "All I've got is a bowl of root beer barrels and off-brand suckers."

He's dressed as if he fell right off the cover of Top Gun. Pair that with the daddy energy he always exudes, and he could give Ryan a run for his money in the handsomeness department.

"Sorry, Mr. O'Connor," I call back.

He grins. "Next year, we're joining forces!"

"Sounds like a plan!" I shout back.

"Oh, yeah, the three of you could make a whole big scene," Michael chimes in. "Maybe make your own miniature haunted yard."

"That'd be fun!" I say, looking to Mrs. Heart.

She frowns slightly at the idea. She's always been a big fan of the season, but she's not into spooky stuff. "Yeah, maybe," she replies with a polite smile.

"Mrs. Heart doesn't really like scary stuff," I reply.

"Oh, I guess you don't either. Scratch that idea," Michael says, handing candy and soda to a crew of tiny fairies.

As the flow of kids ebbs, Mrs. Heart perches on the step beside me, smoothing her wig with a practiced hand. She glances up at the house, then at the street, her energy suddenly drained.

"You okay?"

She shakes her head. "Oh, yeah, I think I might call it a night early. It looks like they're slowing down, and I'm feeling a bit under the weather today." She pats my hand, and her palm is warm and dry and gentle. "Thank you so much for letting me join you tonight. I had so much fun."

We exchange goodbyes, and she and Watson disappear into her home. I watch her windows as the curtains draw and the lights turn off. Warmth spreads through me as I feel grateful to have her in my life.

A wolfpack of middle schoolers barrels up, and I distribute the last of the peanut butter cups. I stand and stretch my legs. I ask Michael to man the porch while I go inside to get provisions. As I turn, I see it: a police cruiser, parked across the street with its headlights off.

I nudge Michael. "See that?"

He follows my gaze. "Probably making sure no one eggs Mr. O'Connor's house again. He always has the worst candy."

But as I watch, a shadow flickers in the front seat and realization dawns on me. *They're watching my house.* I shiver, and not from the cold.

I try to ignore it, but after thirty minutes, the cop car is still there, and it's all I can think of. I lean into Michael and say, "Michael, I'm nervous."

Michael looks up from the child he's giving chips to. "You think they're here for you?"

"I don't know."

My phone buzzes. I half-expect it to be a message from Goose

Grove PD, but it's not. It's James. "So, I was thinking about calling it a night early and joining you two. Michael still there?"

I glance at the cop car, then at Michael, then back to the screen. I tell Michael, "James wants to come over."

Michael looks beyond surprised, "Wow, really? That's great."

I reply, "He is. We'd love for you to join us."

"Great, be there soon."

"There's a police car parked across the street. Should I be concerned?"

"Your outfit is sexy, but not arrest-worthy."

I begin to reply that I'm legitimately scared, but he texts again before I get a chance, "Don't worry, baby, I'll be there soon. They can't do anything without cause. They might just be trying to intimidate you into doing something."

Twenty minutes later, I'm pulling the last bit of supplies to the porch. "I can't believe we gave it all out."

Michael replies, placing a soda in the pillowcase of a Power Ranger, "Most of these kids have been here multiple times. Either that, or Power Rangers are cool again. Which, I doubt." As the kid skips down the street, he reflects, "I was the Red Power Ranger in the third grade."

"Aww, I wish I could have seen tiny Red Power Ranger Michael. I bet you were cute."

"I was not." I look at him, and I highly doubt that. There's no way that man was ever not pretty.

A car pulls up, slowly driving due to the children, and stops in my driveway. The door opens slowly, and James exits with the flair of someone in a movie. A six-foot-two picture of chiseled virtue, dressed in a knight costume that looks like it fell off a movie truck.

There's even a sword strapped to his hip—probably plastic, but intimidating. The sight is so incongruous with the usual lawyer look that I almost choke on my own laughter.

He bows theatrically. "Fair maiden, I heard you were in distress."

"Are you going to slay the cop car?" I ask.

He looks over at the vehicle, then back at me. "I was considering running someone through, but not with this." He removes the helmet and runs a hand through his hair, which is somehow even more perfect after being trapped inside medieval headgear.

Michael snorts from the porch. "Of course you're a knight."

James bows with practiced ease. "I thought you'd appreciate it."

I snort. "Where'd the costume come from?"

"Costume from a few years ago. I liked it so much I couldn't get rid of it."

Michael asks, "Wanna' pass out candy with us?"

James grins, "That'll be fun."

I say sadly, "We're almost out, but it's getting late, so I think it'll be okay."

James leans in and says quietly enough that no children can hear, "That's fine. The candy isn't really why I came anyway."

62

The temperature drops, and while my shorts are sexy, they are not fit for a Minnesotan, near-winter-like, Halloween. We crowd together at the top of the steps, and our breath puffs in the air. At least three parents in the last half hour have brought up the Halloween Blizzard of 1991, and I'm feeling like it's about time to call it a night.

Michael emerges from within the house with a space heater and sets it near where he and I have been stationed. James apparently runs hot and doesn't seem phased by the cold, and has participated fervently in the "ha, you think this is cold, you would have…" ribbings that Minnesotans of a certain age are obligated to find hilarious. But, he's also a bit more protected from the cold in his knight costume than I am in my booty shorts and Michael is in his "I stalked you, but lovingly" tracksuit.

A little witch with silver star tattoos on her cheeks takes one look at our crew and declares, "You're the best house on the block!"

James bows deeply. "Thank you, my lady. We strive for excellence."

The girl giggles and skips away.

This night ended up better than I expected. It's been so much fun.

I laugh at the way James and Michael work together to get the current group of kids the perfect distribution of candy, soda, and chips.

A man and a woman holding a baby and a toddler wait by the curb, congratulating the children as they run to them, proudly declaring their spoils.

A fuzziness warms in me at the sight of the family, and my eyes tear up.

I ask both of them at once, more choked up than I expect, "You ever think about having kids?"

James blinks, surprised. "All the time," he says, a little too fast.

Michael, caught off guard, sputters. "You mean, like, in a theoretical sense? Or actually, like, actual kids?"

"Both, I guess?" I say. "Sometimes I see a baby and just—my ovaries go feral."

James laughs, then turns serious. "I want them. More than anything. But I worry I'd be a terrible father."

"Same…" Michael replies.

"That's ridiculous," I say, and I mean it. "You'd be incredible fathers."

James looks at his hands, the confidence gone. "I work too much. We all know that about me."

Michael watches him, eyes thoughtful. "You'd do better than you think. Even if you weren't there all the time, you'd be a better dad than your own. Better than mine."

James grins at him. "Low bar, Mikey."

Michael laughs sadly. "True."

James adds, "You'd make a great dad, too, you know. The nurturing, bookish kind. Probably bake cookies for the PTA."

He shrugs. "Maybe. I don't hate the idea."

There's a long pause, during which I realize I am very much in love with both of them, and also that I've never said this out loud to anyone.

Maybe Halloween is about taking off your mask, not putting one on.

"I want kids, too," I say softly. "I want a whole house full."

James nods, then looks at Michael. "You know," he says, "if there were someone there…for my kids…"

Michael raises an eyebrow and almost snaps, "Ah, so you want me to babysit your girlfriend and your kids, huh?"

"I was more thinking they'd be OUR kids," James says, waving his hand between the three of us.

"Huh. That's an idea," Michael says, looking toward the moon wistfully.

We sit like that, for a while, absorbing the idea. I let myself picture it: the three of us, a family, a whole pack of kids. I absolutely love it. But a thought blocks me from fully latching onto it. *Where would Ryan fit in this whole thing, though? Uncle Ryan? Or Dad number three?*

The last round of trick-or-treaters are mostly teenagers pretending to be too cool for costumes, but willing to humble themselves for a full-size Snickers. We reward their effort with extra Skittles and some light heckling. We hand out the last of the candy and start the elaborate process of cleaning up and moving things back into the house.

As I'm tidying up the last bit of things, I notice that James is staring at me with the kind of hunger that tells me his thoughts have drifted to the filthy. His jaw works, like he's chewing on a problem, and every so often his gaze flicks to Michael, then back to me, then down to my bare legs.

I catch his eye and smirk. "Got something on your mind, James?" I ask, folding my arms and leaning against the banister.

He shrugs. "Sorry. That Ash Ketchum outfit is just too sexy."

Michael slides next to him. "Nothing to do with the idea of knocking her up."

James just laughs. "That certainly didn't hurt," he says

"Maybe you should do something about it," I say, voice low and deliberate.

James reaches for my hand, slow and theatrical. He pulls me gently from my perch against the banister and kisses me, messy and real. His mouth is warm, and the stubble on his jaw scratches against my cheek in a way that makes me ache in places that have nothing to do with nerves.

Michael watches, head tilted, and then, without breaking eye contact, stands up and moves in behind me. He wraps his arms around my waist, one palm spread over my stomach. I feel the tension melt from my body, replaced by a current of pure, electric want.

"Bedroom?" Michael asks, his voice rumbling against my ear.

I shake my head and reply, "No."

They both look into the living room, and James asks, "Should we talk about that?"

"Not now," I say, running my fingers over his costume.

James pulls me into his lap the moment we hit the sofa. The breastplate is already unbuckled, and his shirt rides up as I straddle him, thighs bracketing his. He bites at my lower lip, his hands on my ass, and I grind against him until the friction makes me gasp.

Michael sinks beside us, his hand sliding up my back and into my hair. He tugs gently, making me arch, and kisses the curve of my neck with a tenderness that borders on reverence.

"You want us?" Michael murmurs, breath hot against my skin.

"Yes," I breathe. "God, yes."

James groans, and the sound vibrates through my entire body. "I want you, Celeste," he says. "All of you."

He means it, and I believe him. For once, I'm not afraid to be wanted.

I let them undress me, piece by piece. I'm left in my bra and panties, both barely-there, panties soaked through from anticipation. James slides his hands up my thighs, kneading the flesh, while Michael kisses a trail down my shoulder to the small of my back.

James finishes taking off his breastplate and shirt, revealing that perfectly sculpted body. He hooks a finger under my chin and brings my mouth back to his, while Michael peels away his own shirt over his head.

The next thing I know, I'm sandwiched between them on the sofa. James kisses me until my lips go numb, then moves down, mouth on my breasts, tongue flicking against my nipple through the fabric of my bra. Michael runs his hands up and down my sides, fingertips playing along my ribs, then circles back to my stomach, like he's memorizing every inch.

They're talking, too—low, filthy encouragements, words that make my skin burn.

"You're so soft," Michael murmurs, dragging his hand up my thigh.

"You're perfect," James agrees, and bites lightly at my collarbone.

My head spins. I can't keep up with the sensations: hands in my hair, mouths on my skin, the heat building with every breath. I moan, loud and unashamed, and that only makes them work harder.

We stand, a tangle of hands and mouths, so we can more easily undress.

They strip me of my bra and panties, tossing them to the floor. James fumbles with the pants of his costume, clearly impatient, and I help him out, giggling as I struggle to figure out the buckles in my eagerness. His cock is thick and flushed, the tip already slick. He sits back on the couch to watch me undress Michael.

Michael's pants are significantly easier to remove, and with a gentle tug, I have them on the floor. I kneel and take Michael's cock into my mouth.

"Fuck, you're both so hot," James says, voice ragged, as he absent-mindedly strokes his own cock.

I suck hard, the way I know Michael likes it, and his knees buckle. Michael moans, "Holy fuck, Celeste. You're so beautiful on my cock." He reaches up to push his glasses up, but they're not there, something he's done multiple times today. He laughs at himself. "No wonder you're so fucking beautiful right now, you're in focus." I giggle around his cock and suck harder, bobbing my head.

James reaches forward, placing his hand on my head, feeling the movement of my head on Michael's cock.

Michael cups my cheeks with his hands and says, "You're too good at that, sweetheart." He pulls me upward so he can kiss my mouth, then sits on the couch next to James.

They admire me for a moment, sitting together, before their hands find each other's cocks and stroke each other, slow, deliberate, in unison.

They're so fucking hot. I want to taste them both. I want to be split open and filled, taken by two men who know exactly what I need. "Could we…could we try something?" I rasp out.

They look at me, waiting for me to elaborate.

"Could you both be inside me…at once?" I ask.

They smirk in unison, then share a look.

"Oh, baby, I've been waiting for you to ask for that," James replies. He reaches for me with his free hand and asks, "You think you can take us both?"

I nod—the excitement, overwhelming me.

"Let me see," He says, pulling me toward him. He grips my hips, positioning me so that I'm standing directly in front of his face. He slides his fingers between my folds, hooking into me and making me fold forward so I have to brace myself on the back of the couch.

"God, you're so wet for us, baby," James says, almost in awe.

Michael watches as James strokes me, his eyes dark and hungry.

James pulls me forward, his tongue darting out to taste me. He starts slow, gentle flicks, then builds to a relentless rhythm that makes me writhe and whimper.

James holds me steady, one hand on my hip, the other stroking Michael's cock.

Michael kisses my hip and joins James's fingers inside me with his own. He whispers dirty stimulations in my ear. "Come for us, baby," he says. "You love it, don't you?"

I can't answer. Their fingers are inside me, and James's tongue is against me. The heat is building, building, until I can't hold back. I come with a gasp, thighs trembling, and they don't stop until I'm begging them to.

I collapse, and they guide me to the couch between them. They look at me, proud and a little in awe.

James stands and kneels in front of Michael before nodding. "I think she's ready." He leans down and gives Michael's cock a single kiss, then pulls back, allowing Michael the space to pull me into his lap.

Michael buries his face in my breasts. "Ready for us both, sweetheart?"

I nod. "Yes."

Michael slides in easily, the slickness making it effortless. The stretch is delicious. He fucks me slow at first, savoring it, then picks up speed, one hand clutching my ass, the other tangled in my hair.

James rises behind me, pulling Michael's hair out of his face so he can kiss his ear and neck, then James positions himself behind me so he can rub his cock against my entrance.

James whispers in my ear, "If it's too much, I need you to tell me to stop, okay, baby?"

"Okay."

He pushes forward, and the pressure at my entrance is followed by a sharp pop as his tip enters me. "Oh, fuck," I gasp out. The feeling is almost too much.

"More?" James asks.

"Yes, but slow…" I say.

He pushes deeper, slower, stretching me until I'm filled completely. The two of them inside me feel so full, so amazing, reaching every single crevice of my anatomy.

"You're perfect," James says, almost reverent. "You two were made for this."

"Holy shit, the two of you feel so good," Michael says.

"Can I keep going, baby?"

"Please," I gasp, and he doesn't hesitate. He moves with a rhythm, slow and gentle.

I begin to buck, trying to get even more of them inside me.

"Oh, baby," James says, voice barely more than a growl. "I need to fuck you, Celeste. Can I?"

"Yes," I rasp out, "Harder."

His movements speed up, getting rougher, his hands gripping my hips hard enough to leave bruises.

Michael kisses my neck and begins to press circles on my clit with his thumb. I reach up and pull him down to kiss me, and he lets out a muffled groan as our tongues meet.

James pounds into me. He bends down, kisses my shoulder, and whispers, "We're gonna fill you up, Celeste."

The words hit me like lightning. I gasp, shivering under him, and Michael grins, clearly delighted by my reaction.

"You like that?" Michael says, voice teasing. "You want us to put a baby in you?"

I nod, too overwhelmed to form words.

"Say it," James orders, voice sharp. "Tell us you want it."

"I want it," I moan. "God, I want it. I want you to come inside me. Please."

Michael comes first, hips jerking, squeezing his eyes shut, and spurting into me, burying his face into my chest.

James loses it then, he says, "That's it, Mikey, fill her up," thrusting harder, deeper.

The sensation sends me over the edge. I come again, squeezing around them so tight they both gasp for breath, and James pulses and shudders inside me. He comes with a guttural groan, then collapses on top of me, chest heaving.

We lie there, tangled and exhausted, bodies slick with sweat and cum. No one speaks for a while.

James pulls out and collapses beside us on the couch, stroking both of us as I lie spent on Michael's heaving chest. James places his head on Michael's shoulder and pulls me so that I'm sitting on both of them, tucking my head under his chin.

"I love the two of you so much. I'm so happy I came over tonight," James says, kissing Michael on the cheek.

"I love you two, too," Michael says, squeezing me tight against his chest and slowly placing kisses on both of us.

They don't ask me if I love them, but I do.

"I…I love you two, too," I say, tears welling in my eyes.

We embrace for a long time, waiting for our breath and heart rate to return to normal. All overwhelmed from orgasm and emotion.

Eventually, James whispers, "I meant what I said, you know," he whispers. "I want a family. With you. With both of you."

Michael threads his fingers through mine. "It's not the worst idea I've ever heard."

I laugh, a little teary. "I think I want that, too."

My phone chimes. I rise from our tangle of limbs and lean forward to retrieve it from the coffee table. It's the dick pic Ryan promised. I blush and turn the screen to my chest, worried James and Michael saw it.

Come on, Ryan, you gotta invisible ink a dick pic.

James must have seen it or at least deduced it was from Ryan. *Who else would be texting me at this time of night?* Because he asks, "Have you talked to Ryan yet?"

No. I'm scared.

"I will, I promise," I reply, unsure if I'm lying or not.

63

The weight of a hundred stares presses against my skin as I step into the town hall. I never came to these meetings when I was a kid, but my parents were regular staples. I know these gatherings are hotbeds for scuttlebutt. I'm hoping to learn more about the investigation into Richard's murder and learn a little town gossip on my own.

Marcus sits stiffly at the head of the hall, chatting quietly with Sheriff Kim and Angela. Daniel Stevens sits to his right, and Marcus appears to be fully ignoring him. While this meeting aligns with the regularly scheduled one, the fact that the two cops are at the head of the hall assures me the murder will be discussed tonight. In front of them, an ancient podium stands, its microphone tilted at an awkward angle, waiting for someone to begin the meeting.

Marcus's expensive suit looks out of place among the flannel and denim that dominate the room. His eyes are sharp, calculating, scanning the crowd like he's tallying votes rather than concerned citizens. When his gaze catches mine, a chill that feels like I stepped back outside runs down my back. His face softens, and he smiles at me. His hand twitches against his thigh, fingers drumming a nervous pattern before he forces them still. A nervous tic I remember well. I recall it tapping away at his thighs right before the first time we slept together.

The crowd seems restless tonight and is packed at capacity, likely due to the murder investigation still being ongoing after so many weeks. Folding chairs are arranged tightly and filled with bodies. I scan the room for open seats and familiar faces. I'm early, so I'm surprised how full this place is. I don't see Mrs. Heart, Sarah, Andy, or any of the guys.

Honestly, I'm relieved I don't see the guys. I'm pretty sure all three of them will be here tonight. It's been a few weeks since Michael, James, and I discussed going "official" with our triad. We've discussed a lot of the logistics concerning it. Thanks to James and his breeding kink, I think I know more about the legal ways we could protect any future offspring between the three of us than any other layperson in the world. However, I still haven't spoken to Ryan, and, as understanding as they are, they do seem to be getting a bit impatient with me. The drama of deciding between sitting with Michael and James or Ryan is not really something I want to deal with at the moment.

The front rows are fully packed, so I don't dare explore them for an open seat. I squeeze past a cluster of middle-aged women whose whispers fall silent as I pass, to sit in a large group of open seats in the middle of one of the back rows. I note a newspaper lying on one woman's lap, the bold headline visible: "MURDER IN GOOSE GROVE STILL UNSOLVED." Her eyes follow me as I squeeze past her to the empty seat. I feel a familiar discomfort creep up my spine—the sensation of being simultaneously the outsider and the spectacle. Some things about small towns never change, no matter how long you've been away.

"They're saying he was stabbed with garden shears," a man in a row ahead of me mutters to his companion. "Right through the heart."

"He had a heart?" someone laughs.

"I heard it was that Moon girl. You know, the rich one," comes the reply. My heart sinks. I sit in the middle of the cluster of open seats and feel eyes on me. My hands are cold despite the overheated room, and I tuck them between my knees.

"I hope they're going to tell us they've caught the murderer," I hear another disembodied voice say.

The open seats around me begin to fill, with the two on both sides of me remaining open. “Watson!” I hear a child cry out and look to the door. Mrs. Heart and Watson stand at the door, patiently allowing a child to pet him.

I wave to Mrs. Heart, and she sees me. She politely excuses herself from the child and squeezes through the crowd to sit next to me. Everyone on the row visibly brightens as Watson strolls by and receives his head pats. Mrs. Heart says hello by name to each person. She sits next to me and says, “Didn’t expect to see you here, dear.” I give Watson his usual hellos.

“I was hoping to learn more about the murder,” I say.

Mrs. Heart bristles and then nods, bending down to pet Watson, who now sits perfectly between her feet. “I hope they don’t dwell on such morbid talk too long. Just so you know, I saw your three beaus outside. They should all be entering right at the same time.” And, as if they all came in together, they’re standing at the door, scanning the room. I suspect James and Michael may actually have come together. Ryan is actively avoiding the others in quiet competition.

All three scan the crowd, eyes darting with purpose. They’re looking for me. Each is trying to find me first, I suspect. My heart lifts and twists. I look at the single seat next to me and envision the three running toward it, jumping over people, and fighting for it. I watch them from the corner of my eye, silently hoping someone random will find the open seat beside me first. I’m anxious that if I lock eyes with one of them, the three of them will cause a scene, fighting over who gets to sit there. There’s a group of open seats right behind me, and I hope they all just silently and non-dramatically sit there. I really don’t want to be any more the talk of the town than I already suspect I am.

“Celeste?” Ryan calls out, never one to worry about drawing attention to himself, and I turn instinctively.

Ryan sees me first. His eyes catch mine, and I know I’ve been found. He doesn’t hesitate and launches toward me. James and Michael spot me only due to Ryan’s progress toward me, and both look visibly defeated. *Well, that solves that problem.* Ryan moves through the narrow aisle in the same way Mrs. Heart wove her way to the seat next to me, saying hi to everyone. Michael and James shuffle through the row behind me with markedly less enthusiasm than Ryan.

Ryan claims the seat at my side. He squeezes my leg and gives me a peck on the cheek, with a "Hey."

"Good evening, everyone. Let's come to order," Marcus says, silencing all the current murmurs, just as Michael and Jame reach their seats.

When Michael and James sit in two seats behind me, Ryan smirks at them—as if he's bragging that he won the coveted seat. Their disappointment is silent, but it hums through the air—a quiet defeat.

I turn, mouthing a hi to Michael and James, causing them both to brighten and lean back in their seats. They almost lean into each other, but not in an overt way. I know they aren't really too keen on making their relationship public knowledge.

Ryan's hand does not leave my leg, and the warmth of him burns like a thousand suns. Or perhaps that's the burn of the other two's eyes on it.

God, I really need to speak to him.

Marcus continues, "Thank you all for coming out tonight. We've got a full agenda tonight. First, we'll be talking about the status of the Goose Grove Revitalization Project—"

A heckler in a middle row interrupts, "You mean the Goose Grove Gentrification Project!"

Marcus, undeterred, continues, "And second…we'll be hearing from Sheriff Kim concerning the ongoing investigation of the tragic death of Richard Holbrook."

"Murder!" someone shouts from my right. "Call it what it is!"

"Tragic, my ass," I hear someone to my side whisper.

Marcus keeps his cool and addresses the heckler this time, "I'll remind everyone to be respectful. We're here to listen, ask questions when appropriate, and support one another. Let's keep this meeting constructive." He pauses and lets everyone get their last bit of grumbling out of the way. "And please, let's follow the protocol I know I have reiterated multiple times concerning comments." He pauses, while everyone murmurs.

Ryan leans in and whispers, "He's been trying to get them to stop shouting and use the mic since he got elected." He points at a mic positioned in the middle of the aisle. "I'm surprised he hasn't given up on it."

Marcus continues, "I want to start by thanking you for your patience and continued support as we work to improve our community through the Goose Grove Revitalization initiative. As many of you know, this project has been delayed longer than any of us expected or wanted. Tonight, I need to share something difficult, but necessary. We've discovered that a significant portion of the funds originally allocated for this project has been misappropriated. In plain terms, the money was stolen. This is not only a betrayal of public trust, but also a direct blow to our progress and our shared vision for this community."

Gasps in the crowd cause Marcus to pause and wait for silence. I turn back to glance at Michael, whose eyes widen. James's lips remain pursed while he watches Marcus.

Marcus continues, "I want to be clear: we are working closely with law enforcement and auditors to investigate exactly what happened, and we will pursue every available avenue to hold those responsible accountable. But I also want to hear from you. If you have any information—anything at all—that could help us understand how this happened or who might be involved, please come forward."

The murmurs grow, and Marcus waits patiently. Well, those who don't know his nervous tic would call it patience. The tiny taps he's doing on the podium tell me he's anxious. He continues, obviously hoping his voice can just carry over the crowd, "You can speak to me directly, or contact the city's anonymous tip line. We're not giving up on this project. And we're not letting this setback define us. With your help, we'll get back on track and ensure this community gets the improvements it deserves. Before I open the floor to questions, I will give Daniel Stevens, who has been helping to manage the Goose Grove Revitalization initiative a moment to address you all. Mr. Stevens, you have the floor."

Daniel stands and replaces Marcus at the podium. He's looking markedly more haggard than the last two times I've seen him. It's almost like he's aged decades in these few weeks. "Good evening, everyone. I wanted to provide an update on the various development projects spearheaded by Golden Wingspan Development, given the current funding situation. I realize that the original timeline we proposed has expanded significantly," he pauses and clears his throat. "We understand that these half-finished projects cause great concern to the community. We are making our best efforts to determine how we can get things to an appropriate state, given the current funding available to us. I promise you, I want to get construction back on track as much as everyone in the community does. My team will be creating a new timeline to maintain full transparency. I greatly appreciate your patience and want to assure you that the trust you placed in Golden Wingspan Development to complete this project was merited. Thank you, I will return the floor to Mayor Adams." He sits down, stiffly, not waiting for comments.

Marcus seems a bit taken aback by the quick retreat and approaches the podium to address the rumbling crowd. "As Mr. Stevens stated, a new timeline will be proposed. As with the original timeline, this will be brought to the community for a vote before approval is finalized. However, I want to personally assure you, this project is my highest priority. I am doing everything in my power to seek funding from new sources, funding that will not come directly from the community, from tax money, to get this completed on a timeline that doesn't deviate too far from the original." His eyes flick at me.

"What happened to all our tax money that already went to this project?!" a heckler asks.

Marcus looks agitated and right on the edge of losing his mayoral cool. "Please, everyone, I would like us to maintain our protocol of approaching the mic to ask a question."

Principle Gandy…I mean, Gus…approaches the mic at the center of the room, "I think Bob asks a valid question. When we discussed this before work began, we were given the budget. What happened to all that money? What happened to all that taxpayer money?"

Marcus clears his throat and looks at Daniel and then Sheriff Kim. "Unfortunately, the money provided by the town was included in the stolen funds." He clears his throat as gasps and murmurs streak through the crowd. "That investigation is still ongoing. I understand this is upsetting. I am just as upset as the rest of you. Unfortunately, we do not have any more answers at this time. We promise to update you when we do."

64

Marcus waits for any further questions before proceeding, "Since there appear to be no more questions at this time, I will call Deputy Angela Martinez and Sheriff Kim to the floor."

Angela shuffles to the podium, her uniform crisp and her expression carefully neutral. She looks like she's multiple weeks overdue, but she doesn't let her extreme pregnancy reduce her authoritative look. Behind her, Sheriff Kim takes a position like a shadow, his weathered face revealing nothing.

"Thank you all for coming," Angela begins, her voice steady despite the feedback screech from the microphone. "We understand the community's concern regarding the death of Richard Holbrook."

"Murder!" someone shouts from the back.

Angela's face doesn't change, but I notice her fingers tighten around the edges of the podium. "We are conducting a thorough investigation into Mr. Holbrook's alleged murder," she corrects, giving the word its due weight. "Sheriff Kim is leading the case, and we assure you that all resources are being devoted to finding who is responsible."

Sheriff Kim steps forward, adjusting the microphone with practiced ease, each word measured and precise. "At this time, we are pursuing several leads. We ask for your patience and cooperation. If anyone has information that might be relevant to the case, we encourage you to speak with us privately after this meeting."

A murmur ripples through the crowd, dissatisfaction evident in the shifting bodies and exchanged glances. The room smells increasingly of sweat and impatience.

"Several leads? That's police-speak for 'we've got nothing,'" a woman to my left whispers loudly to her companion.

"There's a murderer on the loose in this town, and that's all you have to say to us?" someone chimes in.

Angela attempts to regain control. "Patrick, we understand—"

"What are you doing to ensure the town is safe?!" a woman shouts.

"We believe this is an isolated incident and the general public has no need for concern," Angela responds.

Someone stands at the mic. Angela sighs, obviously not wanting to answer whatever question this person has, "Yes, Janice," she says.

"Janice Finklers, The Goose Grove Gazette. Is it true that Richard Holbrook was responsible for the quote-unquote misappropriation of funds earmarked for the revitalization efforts?"

A man near the front stands, "Richard Holbrook was stealing from citizens of this town for years. YOU knew it, and nobody did a thing," he says, pointing at the police. "Now he's dead, and suddenly everyone's concerned about justice?"

The man's voice cracks with emotion. "That man convinced my brother to sell his house while he was undergoing cancer treatment. He owned the company it was sold to, undercut him, then sold the property to Golden Wingspan Development the next week for double the value."

This triggers a cascade of voices, each louder than the last.

Of all the rumblings, I'm only able to make out, "He cheated my mother out of her savings!"

After the crowd dies down, Sheriff Kim states, "We do not have a comment concerning that rumor at this time. However, I assure everyone that we are investigating that as a possibility."

The reporter continues, "Would that be a plausible motive for murder?"

Sheriff Kim states, "I cannot speculate on such things, Janice."

"Nearly everyone here had a reason to want that rat bastard dead," an elderly man whose trembling finger points accusingly at no one in particular. "Whoever killed him did this community a service."

The room descends into chaos, voices overlapping in a tangle of grievances both personal and communal. I sit frozen in my seat, the weight of their words pressing against my chest.

Mrs. Heart grabs my hands, hers trembling, the energy of the room getting to her.

Sheriff Kim's voice cuts through the noise, somehow commanding without shouting. "We are aware of the allegations against Mr. Holbrook. They are part of our investigation. But vigilante justice is not the answer."

My attention drifts back to Marcus, who now leans forward in his chair, eyes narrowed at the podium. The fluorescent light catches the sheen of sweat on his forehead, highlighting the tension in his jaw. When someone mentions property developers, his hand twitches again, this time forming a fist before deliberately relaxing. It's subtle, but in this moment, I'm sure he's hiding something.

"You let him get away with this for years!" The cry comes from multiple voices now, a chorus of demand that seems to swell and fill every corner of the room.

Mr. O'Connor stands, his silver blond hair catching the harsh light. His usually gentle face is transformed by anger."Richard Holbrook was a thief in a three-piece suit," he says, his voice carrying strength. "He stole more than money—he stole people's dignity, their security, their peace of mind."

His words hit me with unexpected force. There's something raw and personal in his tone. Ryan tenses at my side, his face is twisted in anger. I place my hand on his atop his leg, and he relaxes, smiling at me, putting his arm around me, and kissing me on the head.

Before I can consider it further, another voice joins the fray, and then another, until the meeting becomes a storm of accusations and demands.

I sit in the middle of this tempest, watching faces contort with emotion, catching glimpses of private pain made public. The air in the room feels thick, almost solid with tension. My chest tightens with a creeping anxiety, not just from the chaos around me but from the dawning realization that in a town this small, with grievances this deep, everyone is a suspect.

Sheriff Kim attempts to restore order, his stoic exterior finally showing cracks of frustration. "We will update the community as the investigation progresses. For now, we ask that you remain calm and allow us to do our jobs."

"How long?" someone demands. "How long before this gets swept under the rug like everything else in this town?"

I catch Angela's eye briefly across the room. There's something there in her pained expression—concern, maybe warning—before she turns away to confer with Sheriff Kim. The whispered exchange between them looks tense, and I wonder what they're not telling us.

The meeting continues its spiral into disorder, with Marcus finally rising to join the officers at the front, his mayoral authority an attempt to impose order that only seems to fuel the crowd's frustration. His perfectly practiced smile doesn't reach his eyes as he asks for patience, for trust in the system.

Watson becomes extremely agitated, expressing a fear I've never seen in him before. He whines at Mrs. Heart's feet. She stands, "I should get Watson out of here."

I feel suddenly exhausted, drained by the emotional current running through the room. I stand, "I'll come with you."

65

Mrs. Heart wraps a fuchsia scarf around her neck and shuffles ahead. Watson's leash pulls tight as he wants to remain hidden under the chair. "Come on, Watty, let's go, boy," Mrs. Heart urges, but he's too afraid to leave.

Ryan stands, says "I got him, Mrs. H," and scoops up the dog, holding his head to his chest. "It's okay, boy, let's get out of here."

I look back at Michael and James. James whispers something to Michael, and Michael stands, leaving James in his seat and shuffling out as well.

Why is James staying?

Ryan, always impossible to ignore, loops his finger in my back belt loop and leans close, his voice low. "Ever notice how Marcus's right eyebrow does that jump whenever someone calls him out on his bullshit?" He arches his own, which is more golden than anyone's eyebrows have a right to be.

I snort, which is mortifying. Ryan grins, mission accomplished. *He always knows how to make me feel better.*

Michael moves faster than Mrs. Heart and gets to the double doors before she does. He opens them for her, and she thanks him, ducking out as quickly as she can. Ryan and I follow suit. Ryan looks at Michael in confusion, as we funnel through the double doors into the stingy November air.

Once the closing doors block the din of the crowd, Ryan sets Watson down, and Watson seems immediately relieved. The last of the leaves is in defeat at our feet, a thin brown carpet leading to the parking lot. There's a tree near the curb that's now just a skeleton in the moonlight, all its leaves having fallen. Mrs. Heart pauses beneath it to re-tie her scarf. Watson immediately sets about sniffing every square inch of exposed root.

Ryan loops his arm through mine. "Nice night for that raincheck hayride, huh?" His voice is soft, but I can hear the smile behind it.

For a second, the only sound is Watson sneezing into a pile of dead leaves. Michael stands silently beside me, waiting for my response. "Oh, um, sorry, Ryan," I say, glancing toward Michael. "I, uh, have plans already."

Watson snuffles at my shoe, and Mrs. Heart gives me a discreet thumbs-up before retreating, silently. I wave to her and Watson as they walk home.

The double doors swing open, and James storms out, toward us. Walking with a brisk purposefulness.

James stops at us and clears his throat. "Celeste, I'm sorry I won't be able to join you two tonight. Something urgent came up." His eyes flick briefly to Michael—who's already scowling—and then to me, where they linger. "Work, of course."

Michael's arms snap tight across his chest, the fabric of his jacket straining with the effort. "Of course something has," he says, but it's not a question. His lips pull thin. "Something always does."

Ryan looks between all of us, the realization of what our plans were appearing to dawn on him.

James doesn't blink. He just shifts his weight, that lawyer's stance like he's about to cross-examine the wind. "I'm sorry, but it's really important," he says. There's an undercurrent to it—a sort of practiced regret, like he's had this argument a hundred times with a hundred people, and no one's ever believed him.

Michael doesn't let it go. "It always is." He glances at me, then back at James.

James steps toward Michael, and touches Michael's arm—gentle, apologetic—then leans in and kisses his cheek. "It doesn't mean you're not important, Mikey. We talked about this. This is why you and Celeste have each other."

Then, without skipping a beat, James turns to me and does the same. It's soft and electric and over before I can process it. A flush creeps up my neck.

The world seems to tilt, just a fraction. James's eyes widen momentarily when he realizes the gravity of what he just did. "Oh, um…" he says and looks around to see who saw him kiss Michael, then looks at Ryan to take in the expression that crept onto his face in response. I haven't talked with Ryan yet about the relationship elevation of Michael, James, and me.

I smooth my hair behind my ear—classic nervous tic—and turn to Ryan, who looks like he's watching a car accident in slow motion. His jaw flexes. For once, the usual Ryan smirk is absent.

"Bye, babe," James says. Then kisses me on the cheek again, this time whispering, "I'm sorry." He nods to Michael and walks back into the municipal building. *Why's he going back in there?*

Ryan's nostrils flare. He gives a tight-lipped smile and lets out a breath through his nose. He stares at the horizon, then at Michael.

We all stand awkwardly, none knowing what to say.

"How's the book going, Michael?" Ryan asks, his posture changing, and he's back to his usual charming, goofy self.

Michael responds, "Pretty well." He scrunches his eyebrows, confused as to why Ryan is talking to him.

"Nice. It's a murder mystery, right?"

"Yes, it is," Michael deadpans.

"Using me for inspiration for one of your characters?" Ryan asks, with a huge grin. "The devastatingly handsome sexual rival punched the victim, so he must be a murderer."

Michael sputters, "I'm sorry about that, Ryan, you have to underst—"

"No worries, man. If I had seen you punch Richard, I would have told her, too," he says, putting his arm around me and squeezing.

Their banter is slightly barbed, like a fencing match where neither wants to score a hit, and it's making me uncomfortable.

Ryan's eyes dart between me and Michael, and I can practically see the lightbulb go off. "Listen, I kinda jumped the gun and paid for the hayride already. Why don't you both come? I think tonight might even be the last night."

I blink. "You want Michael to come with us?"

"Sure," he says with a smile too big for his face, "The more, the merrier." I feel like he's trying to hint at something with that last statement.

Michael lifts his glasses. "I'm not much of a hayride guy."

Ryan leans in, lowering his voice to a theatrical whisper. "Come on. It'll be a hayride-slash-whodunit discussion. Who knows, maybe I can be of help. I know you two are trying to solve the murder. Being the son of the town gossip has its perks, after all. I know everything about everyone. Even you…Mikey." I'm not sure if this is a threat. And Michael stands taller, not sure how to take it either.

Michael looks to me for support, a deer in the headlights. I say, "Ryan, don't you think it would be kind of weird for Michael to join us on a date?"

"Nah, like I said, I don't mind sharing you," he says with a smirk and a tone that sounds like a challenge. "Based on what James said to Michael, it seems like Michael doesn't mind sharing either."

I open my mouth to protest, but Michael beats me to it. "Fine by me," he says with a deep forcefulness that I am taken aback by, but there's a sly curve to his mouth. He's accepted Ryan's challenge, and I really have no idea what's going on.

Ryan's smile is devious and strained, like he didn't expect Michael to actually take him up on whatever this is. "Perfect! Let's go now. We'll take my truck."

"Um…okay," I say, suddenly aware that both men are watching me like I'm a prize up for auction. I follow Ryan toward his truck. Michael trails close behind.

Michael gently grabs my arm as I open the truck door, ready to scootch into the center seat, and whispers, “What is Ryan up to?”

I shake my head, looking at Ryan, who’s turning the truck on with a scowl, “I have no fucking idea.”

66

The hayride wagon waits by the red barn, a weathered chariot of wood and straw. It's smaller than the crowded tourist wagons that circle the property during peak hours—just a private cart with metal wheels and hay bales arranged in a U-shape, pulled by a single tractor.

The driver, an older man in overalls who introduces himself only as "Pete," gives Ryan a look of confusion when he notices Michael standing behind us.

"You can pull three on this, right, Pete?" Ryan asks with a smile, hooking arms around my and Michael's shoulders.

Pete simply nods and grunts.

"Thanks, Pete," Ryan says, helping me climb aboard.

Ryan's hand lingers at my waist as I settle onto a hay bale, the dried grass crinkling beneath me. Ryan climbs in beside me, snuggling up to me and warming me against the chilled air.

Michael hangs back, obviously contemplating whether he still wants to call Ryan's bluff or not.

"Scared of the dark, Mikey?" he asks, and I note that he uses the nickname James often calls Michael.

Michael squints at him and simply says, "No," while leaping up to the cart and sitting at my other side—warming me further. *Ooo, this is cozy.*

"Michael, I'm sorry, I don't know what he's up to," I whisper, rubbing my hands up my arms, still cold despite their body heat. *I wish that human furnace James were here right now.*

Michael pulls out his phone and quickly types something before returning it to his pocket. I'm pretty sure he's messaging James. I saw him doing so in the truck, but I wasn't able to get a sense of what they were texting about.

Ryan reaches behind us, producing a worn plaid blanket from a wooden box. "Cold?" he asks me.

"Yes," I respond, my breath condensing in the air.

He unfurls the blanket with a dramatic flourish, letting it settle over both our laps.

"You can get under there, too, Mikey," Ryan says, leaning forward and tapping his knee with a smirk.

Michael pulls the blanket over his lap and simply says, "Thanks."

"All set, Pete," Ryan says. Pete turns to glance at us, then puts what I suspect are noise-canceling headphones on before turning on the tractor. The engine sputters to life, belching before settling into a rhythmic rumble.

"He can't hear a thing," Ryan says, thumbing at Pete behind him. "Can you, Pete?" he shouts. Pete doesn't respond.

"Ride this thing often, Ryan?" Michael asks, deadpan.

Ryan doesn't respond; he just lifts his lip in a half-smile and shrugs wordlessly.

With a jerk, the cart's wheels creak to life, and we all lurch forward. Michael, less so, his stiff posture stopping him from moving forward too far.

"Still cold?" Michael asks as I pull the blanket higher, tucking it around my waist.

"A little," I admit, though the chill in the air isn't the only reason I want the coverage. Ryan and Michael's proximity has my skin tingling with awareness. I'm really not sure what Ryan is up to, but the privacy of the blanket draped over all our laps feels like an invitation.

Ryan slides his arm around my shoulders, pulling me against his side. "Better?"

Michael glares at him, trying to figure out what his game is.

"Okay, Ryan, spill it. What are you up to?" I ask.

"What do you mean?" he says, pushing hair out of my face.

"Why did you invite Michael on this date?" I ask.

"Why don't you ask him why he accepted?" Ryan responds.

Michael opens his mouth to reply, but I cut him off. "Ryan!" I say with a less-than-jovial tone.

"I told you. So we can talk about the murder together. I want to help, too," Ryan responds.

"Bullshit, Ryan. I know you, and this is some passive-aggressive attack. I just can't figure out your angle," I say, turning so that I'm practically sitting in Michael's lap and poking Ryan in the chest with my finger.

"Celeste, you wound me. Literally, that kinda' hurt," he says, rubbing where I poked him.

"God, Ryan, I am…I am so over your shit. I don't know why I came. Michael, I'm sorry," I say. "I'm going to get off this thing." I stand and turn, yelling, "Pete!"

Pete doesn't hear me, and Ryan grabs me, pulling me back down to sit. "No, wait, wait. Celeste. I'm sorry. I'm serious. I just wanted to spend time with you tonight and…I wanted to show you I'm okay with this whole thing," he says, pointing between me, him, and Michael. "And I really did want to talk about the murder with you two."

"So, what did you expect was going to happen on this hayride, Ryan? I can tell by the headphones and the blanket that you had a whole thing up your sleeve. What were you gonna do? Finger me while Michael just what? Sat there and didn't say anything?"

Michael just sits there and doesn't say anything, eyebrow cocked in amusement and a half-smirk plastered on his face. He's enjoying me yelling at Ryan and probably also enjoying the idea of the scenario I just described.

A shadow crosses Ryan's face. "Okay, I'll admit. I didn't…I didn't think this whole thing through," he says, turning his head from me and looking out to the horizon.

The smirk on Michael's face turns to a full-toothed, devious grin when he says, "Or, we could both finger her." His voice is a warm rumble against my ear. My head whips to Michael. Ryan turns to look at him as well.

I blink, genuinely confused. That was such an un-Michael thing to say. Did my perverted brain imagine it? "What did you just say, Michael?" I ask.

"I said, we could both finger you," Michael replies, his finger tracing idle patterns on my upper arm.

Ryan laughs, the sound reverberating through his chest and into mine. "I suppose we could do that."

Heat warms my belly at the idea of this. "You can't be serious," I protest, addressing Michael and shifting closer to Ryan. Ryan replaces his arm around my shoulder and squeezes me close.

"I'm incredibly serious," Michael counters, plucking a stray hay strand from the seat and twisting it between his fingers. "In fact, I'd love to see how fast the two of us could unravel you if we worked together."

Under the blanket, Ryan's free hand finds mine, our fingers intertwining with familiar ease. The hayride rounds a bend, taking us past a small pond where the sunset reflects in perfect symmetry, doubling the beauty of the fading day.

"Hmm, that is an interesting proposition," Ryan says, brushing a stray hair out of my face. "I gotta warn you, Mikey, this is the pussy I learned on. I'm kinda a pro at it. Whadda' ya' say, Star Girl? You down?"

"Um...okay," I say softly, unsure if they really are serious.

"Relax, Star Girl. We got you," Ryan whispers into my ear, tilting my head toward his shoulder. I nod and rest my head against his shoulder.

The hayride continues its leisurely pace, carrying us through a section of young apple trees not yet open for public picking. My hand falls to the side and rests on Ryan's thigh, and his fingers trace my collarbone.

Michael's finger circles my knee before he gently pulls my leg toward him, our ankles hook together beneath the blanket. Each touch, while not yet crossing the threshold of risque, feels charged by new awareness.

"I've always had a bit of a thing for doing it outside," Ryan admits, his thumb stroking the sensitive skin of my inner wrist.

"You do, too, don't you, Celeste?" Michael says, wrapping his other arm around my waist, and referencing our Harvest Festival shenanigans.

Michael reaches between me and Ryan to latch around my midriff, his fingers graze Ryan's abdomen. Ryan sighs, his breath stirring my hair and fogging Michael's glasses, at the touch. Ryan's arm tightens around me. I turn my face up to his, finding his features softened by the golden light.

"Well, I guess we're doing this," Ryan says, leaning down to brush his lips against mine. His kiss tastes of cinnamon and comfort and desire, a combination that makes me melt against him. My fingers curl into the fabric of the blanket.

When the tractor engine suddenly quiets, I pull back, blinking in confusion. We've stopped at the highest point of the farm, a scenic overlook that offers a panoramic view of Goose Grove in the distance.

The horizon burns orange and pink. The town's lights twinkle, a constellation of human existence, decorating the silhouette of darkened buildings.

Beautiful.

"Ten-minute photo stop," Pete calls over his shoulder before climbing down from the tractor and wandering a discreet distance away, pipe in hand. Never looking toward us.

"Very considerate of him," Michael murmurs as Ryan pulls me tighter and I snap a picture of the sunset.

"Very," Ryan agrees, his voice husky. "Especially since I specifically requested a break at this spot."

Under the blanket, Ryan's hand finds my knee, then slides slowly upward along my thigh. Michael does the same on the other side. The warmth of their palms seeps through my jeans, branding my skin beneath.

"Oh my," I whisper, my voice catching as their fingers trace the inner seam of my pants.

I shift slightly, allowing my legs to part just enough to grant them better access.

Michael's sharp intake of breath is immensely satisfying when I lean forward to kiss him.

The blanket creates a private world for us, concealing the increasingly bold exploration of their hands. Their fingers travel higher, tracing patterns that make my breath catch and my pulse quicken. When Ryan finally cups me through my jeans, applying gentle pressure exactly where I need it, I have to bite my lip to keep from making a sound.

"Michael, we've only got ten minutes. Think we can get it done by then?" Ryan breathes against my neck, his teeth grazing my skin.

Michael kisses my neck and smiles against my skin. "Definitely." This is a side of Michael I didn't know even existed.

"Let's see whose name she calls out first," Ryan says, always making everything a game.

"You're on," Michael replies.

Sigh. Boys and their games.

Michael's fingers join Ryan's under the blanket, both of them stroking me through my jeans with maddening slowness. I arch into their touch, my hips lifting slightly off the hay bale. Together they explore me with teasing, feather-light touches that make me writhe.

"She's so responsive, isn't she?" Ryan asks Michael.

"Yeah," Michael responds, as Ryan's fingers work the button of my jeans. When he pulls the zipper, the sound is obscenely loud in the quiet evening. I glance toward Pete, but he remains a distant figure, his back to us as he contemplates the view and puffs on his pipe.

"He can't see anything," Ryan assures me, his hand slipping beneath the denim but still outside my underwear. "Lean back," Ryan murmurs, his lips brushing the shell of my ear.

Michael's hand slides under my sweater, his palm warm against my stomach, just above Ryan's, deep in my pants.

Ryan's hand moves more confidently now, fingers tracing the edge of my underwear before finally, blissfully, sliding beneath the fabric.

"That's it, let us take care of you," Michael whispers, looking me deep in the eye.

I hold my breath, every nerve ending alight with anticipation. When Ryan's fingers finally slip inside my folds, I have to stifle a moan.

"She's so wet already," Ryan marvels, his voice rough with desire. "So ready for us."

Michael's hand joins Ryan's inside my underwear. Ryan gently teases my clit while Michael's long fingers slide over Ryan's hand, teasing at my entrance. I gasp at the combined touch.

Michael smirks, "I love making you gasp, making you tremble."

In answer, I lean forward and kiss him deeply, my tongue meeting his in a heated exchange that leaves no doubt about my desires. I gasp against his mouth as his fingers find slick heat, plunging into me in a way that makes my hips rise involuntarily against their hands. Ryan kisses the side of my neck.

"That's it, Celeste," Ryan murmurs appreciatively, his thumb circling exactly where I need it. "Let go."

The dual sensations of the cool evening air on my face and their warm fingers between my legs create a delicious contrast that heightens every feeling. I'm aware of every detail—the rough texture of the hay beneath us, the weight of the blanket, the distant silhouette of Pete, the rhythmic movement of Ryan and Michael's hands that's quickly dismantling my composure.

"Do you like this, Celeste? Having both of us?" Michael whispers, his voice both teasing and tender as he hooks within me, hitting that perfect spot within. Ryan increases his pressure and speed, as the two stroke me from both sides of my pleasure point.

I can only nod, words beyond me as tension builds, coiling tighter with each stroke of their knowing fingers. My head falls back against Ryan's shoulder, my eyes closing as I surrender to the sensations.

"Oh yeah," Ryan encourages, his lips at my ear. "Come for us, Star Girl."

The childhood nickname, spoken in this intimate context, is somehow the final push I need. Release crashes over me in waves, my body trembling as Ryan holds me steady and Michael nuzzles at my breasts. Their fingers work me through each pulse of pleasure until I have to grab their wrists to still their movements. I push them deep and hard against me as I lift from the bail.

"Shh," Ryan soothes as a slight sound escapes me, covering it with a kiss that swallows my gasps. His free hand strokes my hair, gentling me as aftershocks ripple through my body. Michael strokes my hair from the other side and kisses my shoulders.

When I can breathe normally again, I open my eyes to find Ryan and Michael watching me with matched expressions of wonder and satisfaction.

"You're so beautiful," Michael says softly, withdrawing his hand and helping me readjust my clothing beneath the blanket.

"Especially when you come apart like that," Ryan adds, removing his hand, as well, and zipping up my pants for me.

Heat floods my cheeks, but it's not embarrassment—it's a mixture of lingering pleasure and absolute befuddlement. *What just happened?*

They press twin kisses to my temple as Pete returns to the tractor.

Ryan chuckles. "Perfect timing, Mikey." He brushes the hair from my face, and, always one to remind you of whatever goofy game he's devised, quips, "Dang. She didn't say either of our names."

I groan. How this dork ever convinced anyone to sleep with him is beyond me. I look at him to tell him his joke is stupid, then remember: *Oh, yeah, he's hot as fuck.*

Michael, seems to find him funny though, and chuckles, "Next time."

Next time? I look between them and ask, "Um…what about you two? Should I?" as my hands rest on their laps.

"I'm satisfied," Michael shrugs as the engine roars back to life.

"Maybe later. We should probably actually discuss the murder," Ryan laughs, "I wasn't kidding when I said I could help."

"My place?" Michael adds.

"Sounds good," Ryan replies.

They look to me for confirmation.

As the hayride begins its return journey, I curl against Ryan's side, and Michael leans slightly against mine. The cold returns as I come down from my climax, but my body is still humming with satisfaction and anticipation. Above us, the first stars puncture the darkening sky. I pull the blanket closer to myself and wonder if they really are satisfied or plan to do much more.

67

Michael opens the door to his place, and the smart lights illuminate the room.

Ryan whistles and says, "Swanky," as we all remove our shoes and jackets.

"Would you two like some wine?" Michael asks. We both answer in the affirmative, and I follow Ryan as he strolls into Michael's living room, eyes locked on his painting.

"Huh," he says, putting his hands on his hips, and looking at it.

"What?" I ask.

"That's one of mine," he says.

"Yeah, I know, he told me," I reply, watching Ryan's face.

"Did he also tell you what he paid for it?"

"No, why?"

"No reason…"

"There must be a reason."

"He overpaid," Ryan replies, and I'm confused by the comment.

"He's got another in his bedroom," I say, unsure how Ryan will even respond.

He simply says, "Cool," and acts like he doesn't care, but I sense he does. He slowly sits on the couch, and I join him.

"You okay?" I ask.

"Perfect," he replies, and I know that is a lie, but I don't feel like trying to drag it out of him right now. He's been so hard to read since we left the orchard.

We rode to Michael's place in complete silence. Michael silently texted while Ryan white-knuckled the wheel. Ryan's emotions, like always, were an enigma to me. If he caught me looking at him, he'd smile, but otherwise he looked…mad? Nervous? I don't know.

I just sat between them, in the truck's center seat, fondly remembering sitting between them on the hayride while they fondled me. Every time Ryan reached for the gear shift between my legs, I felt an intense heat that indicated I wanted more of them.

I got a glimpse of Michael's phone, and I could tell he was texting James—likely letting him know what transpired—possibly checking with James to see how he'd feel if things escalated. We talked about bringing Ryan into the fold, but as a plus-one for me. We hadn't even considered Michael and Ryan hooking up as a possibility.

Michael returns with three glasses of wine. He hands us our glasses, then places coasters in front of us before sitting in the adjacent chair.

"So…" Michael says.

"You two don't have some board with all the suspects listed out? Or like, a wall with a bunch of yarn connecting people?" Ryan asks, looking around.

"No, I don't really know how that would be helpful," Michael chuckles, putting his wine down.

"I dunno, a good visual aid sparks inspiration or something. You're the murder mystery writer. You tell me," Ryan says.

"Yeah, and I know that it's really a visual aid for film and television and doesn't usually serve much purpose in most cases."

"Bummer, I thought I could have been good at that part," Ryan laughs. "So, who are your suspects? Who do you need dirt on?"

"Well, you were a suspect, but not anymore, obviously…" Michael says, trailing off.

"What about James?" Ryan asks.

"Not James," Michael says.

"Why not?"

"Just because it can't be."

"Come on. Dude is always so 'busy'—that's suspicious," Ryan says, putting busy in air quotes.

Michael bristles at the word busy. "It's not James," Michael says curtly.

"Okay, sorry I struck a nerve. Then who else do you suspect?"

"Well," I say, interjecting, "There's something going on between Nicole and Daniel Stevens. I overheard them discussing the Riverside Development Project. She said something about Richard and how Marcus would never let her see her kids again if he found out what they did."

Ryan smirks. "Ha, yeah, that's true, there certainly is something going on between the two of them."

I lean forward. "What? You know what she was talking about."

"Yeah," he laughs.

"What? Spit it out."

"They're fucking. Have been for a while now."

"Wait. What?"

"They meet at the Lakeside Motel every Tuesday and Thursday while Marcus is in council meetings. Daniel's his best friend…well, at least Marcus thinks he is."

"How do you know this?"

Ryan shrugs, a too-casual gesture. "Small town. People talk."

"I'm guessing you use that charming smile of yours the same way your dad does to get people to spill their beans," I assume, remembering his childhood habit of eavesdropping.

He grins, unrepentant. "Well, in this case, my studio has a perfect view of the motel parking lot. Purely coincidental."

I ask, "So Nicole is having an affair with Daniel…what does this have to do with Richard?"

Michael chimes in, "If I had to guess, he was her lawyer. Maybe her divorce lawyer?"

"Bingo!" Ryan adds.

"What, you know that, too?" I ask, incredulous.

Ryan grins, so incredibly pleased with himself. "Well, that little bit I picked up from Angela."

"Angela told you?" I ask.

"No. But, Michael, I don't think you're entirely right about that whole board of suspects thing. When I went to tell Angela about punching Richard, I saw a diagram on her computer. I couldn't see much before she flipped it off, but it indicated Richard was Nicole's lawyer. He's a lot of people's lawyer, actually. Or was."

I think, "Well, shit…that makes…total sense. When I met with Richard, she was leaving his office crying! And then she was whispering with Daniel…"

Michael adds, "That would remove any motive Nicole would have for killing him. Why would she kill the guy who is helping her get a divorce?"

I muse, "That's all assuming she's filing for divorce. James might know. We could ask him."

Michael shakes his head, "If he knew, he wouldn't tell us."

Ryan laughs, "Really? She couldn't, like, squeeze it out of him?" Ryan makes a crude gesture with his hands.

Michael and I roll our eyes at him. Michael says, "No. And, he and Marcus are friends. So, if Nicole were planning to divorce Marcus, they'd probably keep that information from James."

"Okay, so let's assume it's not Nicole for a minute…who's left?" Ryan asks.

"Daniel and Marcus," I say.

"I dunno. Marcus is just…not the type," Ryan says, cocking his head.

I sigh, "Well, that's not exactly evidence, Ryan."

"I guess not," he admits.

I respond, "He's so suspicious, though!"

Ryan asks, "How so?"

I say, "Whenever I meet with him, he gets all sweaty and stuttery. He seems like he's hiding something. Plus, he told me to my face that he asked the cops to check in on me."

Michael and Ryan both chuckle.

"What?" I ask.

"I think you make our fearless leader nervous," Michael grins.

I squint at them. "Probably because he killed Richard and he's trying to pin this murder on me…"

"Celeste…really?" Ryan asks.

"WHAT!?"

"He is still in love with you," Ryan says.

"You keep saying that, but it can't be true. He broke up with me a million years ago. How could he be in love with me?"

"Celeste, you broke up with him."

"No, I didn't."

Ryan leans forward. "Yes, you did. He confronted you. Asked if we were still fucking. You said something like, 'If that's how you feel, we're done.' He ran off crying. It was…pretty sad actually."

"That sounds like he broke up with me…"

Ryan shakes his head. "Not to anyone else, Celeste."

"Oh…" I say.

Ryan playfully taps Michael and points at me, "Just keep that in mind if you ever think she breaks up with you."

"Thanks for the advice. I'll let James know," Michael says with a chuckle. Then gives me a tight, grimaced smile, realizing he accidentally broached the subject I've been putting off broaching.

Ryan sighs, "Soooo….elephant in the room. What's going on with you three? Are you, like, a throuple?"

"We prefer triad," Michael answers. I glare at him, causing another apologetic, grimaced smile.

"We…we're exploring something a little more…official," I say, watching Ryan's reaction.

"More official, like how? Are you three in love or something?" he laughs as if it's ridiculous, but the smirk wipes from his face when he sees our reaction.

I steel myself. "Ryan, I've been wanting to talk to yo—"

Ryan goes sheet white and asks, "Does that mean you and I need to call off our arrangement?"

I shake my head. "No, things don't have to change."

"Cool. That works for me." He looks at his watch and stands abruptly. "Well, I'm going to head out. I'll see you two later." He kisses me on the top of the head and rushes to the door.

I rise and ask, "Ryan, wait, you're leav—"

He cuts me off while hurriedly putting on his coat and shoes. "Well, I'm all out of useful information, and I should let you two do whatever it was you originally planned."

In a distinctly non-Minnesotan way, he grabs the doorknob the moment his shoes are tied—skipping four of the five Minnesota Goodbye stages.

"Thanksgiving?" he asks, already in the hallway, closing the door.

Dumbfounded, I simply nod, "Yeah, see you then."

The door clicks closed and feels like a slap in the face.

"Fuck. Is he always like that?" Michael asks me.

Tears well in my eyes. "Yeah…"

"Dude has some attachment issues."

"No shit," I say through sobs.

Michael hugs me.

I continue, "He didn't even let me ask him about any of it…about our relationship, if he wants to be with me, none of it."

Michael grabs some tissue and pats my eyes. "It's okay, love. He probably just needs a little time."

68

The Farmer's Market has moved indoors for the rest of the season. Mrs. Heart, Sarah, Andy, and I stroll through the stalls. Watson trots alongside us as we chat and catch up.

"We're going to try a combined family dinner this year. Pray for us," Sarah grimaces.

"Yeah, Nicole is putting this whole thing together. I'm not sure what's gotten into her, but she's been so insistent..." Andy rolls their eyes. "She keeps going off about the importance of keeping family together."

Huh, does that mean our theory about her wanting to divorce Marcus was off base?

Mrs. Heart runs her hands over a windchime. It sounds low and melodic. She chimes in, "Gus told me he was going, too."

"Yeah. Nicole's even insisting both our dads be there," Sarah grimaces.

I ask, "What? I thought you didn't talk to your dad, Andy."

Andy groans, "I don't...but, she claims he's ready to look past my life choices and accept me, even if he doesn't agree with them...she didn't even get defensive when I told her how passive-aggressive that was."

Sarah shrugs, "So…we still might pull out at the last minute, but the plan is to go and see how everything pans out."

Andy picks up a sparkly stone bracelet and holds it to the light. "Yeah, I mean, if I had a chance to fix things between us and then something happened to him…I'd regret that forever."

I swallow hard, and Mrs. Heart puts her hand on my shoulder.

Andy looks at me, realization dawning on them, "Oh, shit, Celeste, I'm…fuck. I'm so sorry. That was a shitty thing to say."

I shake my head. "No…it's okay. You're right. I do regret it. That's why…" tears threaten to escape me.

Watson rubs at my legs, and for the first time, when talking about my parents, I don't actually cry.

Mrs. Heart places both of her hands on my shoulders, "Celeste, it was not you who broke your relationship with your parents, so it was never your responsibility to fix it. I need you to understand that."

I sniffle and nod. "I know." And…maybe, for the first time, I'm not lying.

Mrs. Heart looks to Andy, "The same goes for you, dear. If this dinner doesn't pan out the way your sister hopes, it's not your fault. And you don't owe any of them your forgiveness if you don't want to give it."

Sarah and Andy beam at her. Andy chokes out, "Thanks, Mrs. Heart, I think I really needed to hear that."

Mrs. Heart says, "Of course, dear. And if you decide not to go, you're always welcome to eat dinner at my house."

"Thanks," they both say.

"Just make sure to bring Gus with you, I'm hoping to try his stuffing," she says with a wink and continues to walk.

We follow.

"Did she mean that…sexually?" Andy asks.

"Probably," I laugh, before taking some hurried steps to catch up with Mrs. Heart.

"Mrs. Heart, I was thinking of having Thanksgiving at my house. Would that be okay?" I ask.

She smiles and replies, "Oh, yeah, that'd be great, dear."

I smile at Andy, trying to prove there are no hard feelings, "The invitation extends to my place, you two."

I stop to marvel at some hand-knit sweaters when two matching young voices call "WATSON!" from my left. Watson and I snap our attention toward it, and Watson's whole body wiggles as he pulls me toward a pair of twins behind a booth holding a bunch of 3D printed dragons.

"Of course they have a 3D printer," Andy scoffs.

I follow Watson toward the twins, letting them hug him and tell him what a good boy he is.

"How's my little hero today?" one asks Watson.

"Better now that he's seen you two," Mrs. Heart laughs.

The other twin looks up from the dog, "Hey, Auncle Andy! Hey, Aunt Sarah." *Oh, these are Nicole and Marcus's twins. Now the hero comment makes sense.*

"Hey, runts," Andy says toward the kids as Sarah says, "Hey, kiddos."

One of the twins beams at Mrs. Heart, "Mrs. H., can I give him a T-R-E-A-T? I have some peanut butter and celery in my bag."

"Sure. He's getting spoiled today," Mrs. Hearts says, smiling at the kid who is hugging Watson with more love than I've ever seen him receive.

"Yay!" the child exclaims, jumping up from the cuddle.

"Just one, okay, Penny!" Andy shouts to the escaping kid as she runs toward a lunch box behind their table. The other hangs back, now petting Watson with equal fervor.

"How's business, Jenny?" Sarah asks the twin who hung back, while peering at the various trinkets expressionlessly.

"It's going okay, Aunt Sarah. We're about to close up, though, Dad'll be here to get us any minute. So if you want a dragon, you'll have to get one now!" Jenny says hopeful Sarah will bite at this sales tactic.

"Hmm, not this week, Jenny. Maybe next time." *Dang, even nepotism can't help them with their sale.* When Sarah sees the disappointment on the child's face, she caves and says, "I do all my Christmas shopping after Thanksgiving." This does the trick, and the child's mood visibly improves.

Andy smirks at Sarah, as if saying, "Do not give me one of these things for Christmas."

I see him before he sees me: Marcus, looking every inch the small-town mayor in his tailored blazer and campaign-ready smile, shaking hands with a farmer selling artisanal cheeses. Even from across the market, I can feel the gravitational pull he's always had—that effortless charisma.

"Sit," Penny says, returning to give Watson the celery with peanut butter. Watson sits immediately and is so still you'd think he were 3D printed.

"Good doggy," Penny says, giving the dog his prizes for being still as a statue.

"There's your Dad now," Sarah murmurs, following my gaze.

Andy makes a slight noise that might be a scoff. "Always on the campaign, even when it's not an election year."

"Thanks for the treat, Penny! Wanna go check out those quilts?" I ask, touching Sarah's arm to get her attention, hoping to leave before Marcus spots me.

But it's too late. Marcus has spotted us, his hand freezing mid-handshake as our eyes lock across the crowded aisle. For a split second, his politician's mask slips, revealing something unreadable beneath. Then the smile returns, brighter than before, as he excuses himself from the cheese vendor and starts making his way toward us.

"Too late for a strategic retreat," I mutter, straightening my shoulders. Watson, sensing my tension, presses closer to my leg.

"Celeste," Marcus calls as he approaches, arms opening as if for a hug. "Andy, Sarah, Mrs. Heart! What a pleasant surprise."

I step back slightly, avoiding the embrace. Marcus smoothly transitions the gesture into straightening his blazer, not missing a beat.

"Marcus," I reply, my voice cool. "Out pressing the flesh?"

His laugh is practiced, designed to disarm. "Just supporting local businesses. The backbone of our community." *God, what a fake, fucking dork.*

Marcus glances down at Watson, who's eyeing him with uncharacteristic wariness. Usually, he seems to like Marcus. "Hello, Watson," Marcus nods, his expression appropriately respectful. "How are you doing, Mrs. Heart?" he asks.

"Managing," she says with a bit of weariness that surprises me.

Is she feeling under the weather?

An awkward silence falls between us. Watson sits, leaning against my leg. The market continues to bustle around us, shoppers flowing past us, not bothering to stop at the twins' stall.

"About ready to go, kiddos?" Marcus says, breaking my gaze. The twins nod dejectedly and begin packing up their stall.

Marcus turns to me. "Celeste, I'm happy to see you! I've been wanting to talk to you."

Sarah clears her throat. "Well, we should probably check out the flower stand before they sell out of those sunflowers I wanted."

Andy picks up her cue immediately. "Right. For the cafe counter. Mrs. Heart, can you help us with this?"

"Oh, yes, sure. Watson, I'm just going to look at the flowers," Mrs. Heart replies.

"We'll just be over there," Sarah tells me, nodding toward a stall about twenty feet away. "Take your time."

Before I can protest, they're moving away and leaving me alone with Marcus. Well, not completely alone—Watson remains steadfastly by my side, his warm presence reassuring.

Traitors. All of them. Leaving me alone with him like this.

Marcus watches them go, then turns back to me with a more intimate smile. "It's good to see you, Celeste. Really good. You're looking well," he says a little quietly, glancing at his children, who are out of earshot now.

"What do you want, Marcus?"

"Oh, well…I wanted to check in on you. See how you were doing."

"Cut the crap, Marcus," I say quietly, meeting his gaze directly. "I know what you're doing."

His eyebrows rise in what appears to be genuine confusion. "I'm sorry?"

"I know that you're the reason the police are always hanging around me. Watching me." I say, keeping my voice low and intense.

Marcus's expression shifts from confusion to shock. "What? Celeste, that's—"

"Too convenient?" I interrupt. "That the woman who just moved back to town, who had a meeting with Richard days before his death, suddenly becomes a suspect in his murder? Despite having no motive and barely knowing the man?"

"I had nothing to do with—"

"You're the mayor. The sheriff reports to you."

"Actually, he doesn't. If we had a police chief, sure, they'd answer to me. But Goose Grove doesn't even fund a police department—we've got a sheriff. And the sheriff doesn't report to me, he reports to the voters."

"Marcus, you told me you sent the Sheriff to 'check in on' me!"

Marcus looks around, clearly uncomfortable with this conversation happening in the middle of the farmers' market. Several shoppers have already slowed their pace, curious about the mayor's intense discussion.

"Celeste," he says, lowering his voice and stepping closer, "this isn't the place. I've got to take my children home, but why don't we get dinner tonight and talk about this properly?"

The suggestion is so absurd that I almost laugh. "Dinner? You think I want to have dinner with you?" I look at his children, who are packing slowly and obviously trying to eavesdrop on our conversation.

He shuffles me away from the children and next to a wall at the edge of the market.

"We used to be close," he says, his voice softening, edged with nostalgia. "Very close."

"That was a lifetime ago," I reply, though something twists in my chest at the memory. Marcus and I had been extremely close.

"Some things don't change," he insists, his eyes holding mine. They're the same blue that used to make my teenage heart stutter, now crinkled at the corners from years of campaign-trail smiles. "I thought we were friends. Let's have dinner. I've got so much to discuss with you."

"I'm not interested in dating you, Marcus," I snap.

A flash of genuine alarm crosses his face. "What are you talking about?"

"Marcus," I lean closer, lowering my voice. "I'm not going to sleep with you. Stop asking me out. I might hate Nicole, but that's against my moral code."

His expression shifts to understanding. "Oh, Celeste. There's a misunderstanding. I just wanted to catch up and talk to you about investing in the town."

"Why, so you can steal my money, too?"

Watson growls softly, picking up on the tension between us. Marcus glances down at the dog, then back to me.

He says loudly, with a laugh, ensuring passersby hear, "You always did have an active imagination, Celeste." His voice lowers and is almost tender. "It's no wonder your company was so successful."

The abrupt change in tactics—trying to make me feel foolish by praising me—only strengthens my resolve.

"Don't patronize me, Marcus. This isn't about my imagination. It's about a dead lawyer who stole a bunch of money, possibly with your help. And now the cops seem to think I am guilty of something."

He sighs, running a hand through his carefully styled hair. "Look, I know coming back to Goose Grove after your parents' death has been difficult. Grief can make us see conspiracies where there are only coincidences."

His condescension makes my blood boil, but I keep my voice steady. "My grief has nothing to do with this."

"Doesn't it?" His eyes soften with practiced sympathy. "You lost your parents, lost your company, moved back to a town full of memories, and now you're feeling isolated and targeted. It's natural to look for someone to blame. I'm not sure why you've chosen me as the target. I thought we were on good terms."

"I'm not blaming you for my parents' death," I say sharply. "I'm accusing you of abusing your position as mayor to frame me for a murder you might be connected to."

Watson barks once, sharp and authoritative, as if punctuating my statement.

Marcus's face hardens, all pretense of warmth vanishing. "You're making serious accusations based on nothing but speculation."

"Am I?"

Marcus takes a step back, his expression cooling. "I think this conversation has gone far enough. I understand you're under stress, so I'll overlook these accusations," he says, exasperation edging into his voice. "God, you've always…always thought the worst of me. I'm not sure why."

"If you stole that money and killed Richard, I'll prove it," I assure him.

For a moment, something like genuine fear flickers in his eyes. Then it's gone, replaced by the practiced confidence of a man used to getting his way. The mayoral charm returning like a mask sliding back into place.

"Celeste, you're being a bit irrational." His voice drops, becoming intimate again. "We have history. Despite everything, I care what happens to you."

"Is that what you tell Nicole when you're reminiscing about our 'history'?" I ask coldly.

His jaw tightens. "My marriage is none of your concern."

"And my life is none of yours. So stop interfering with it."

Marcus glances over my shoulder, his expression shifting. "Maybe he can talk some sense into you."

I don't turn around immediately, unwilling to break eye contact first.

"But my dinner invitation stands. If you want to discuss this like adults, you know how to reach me," he says quietly.

Watson suddenly perks up, his tail wagging as he looks behind me and barks. I follow his gaze and feel a complicated mixture of relief and tension as I spot a James approaching. Marcus notices my expression change and smiles, waving at James, his shoulders stiffening almost imperceptibly.

69

James approaches with the easy confidence of a man who knows his worth in the world. He's wearing a casual button-down rolled up at the sleeves, revealing strong, tanned forearms. Even as my heart does its usual skip at the sight of him, my anger from talking to Marcus doesn't quell.

"James," Marcus says, his tone shifting from the intensity of our confrontation to something smoother, more collegial. "Good timing."

"Hey, Marcus," James replies with a slight nod before turning to me. His smile softens, becoming the one I've come to look forward to. "Celeste, baby, are you about ready for lunch?"

We planned for him to meet me here so we could all walk back to the cafe for lunch. My argument with Marcus made me completely forget about it.

Watson's tail, already wagging, picks up speed.

"Yeah," I acknowledge, not wanting to drop my guard just because he's here.

"I didn't mean to interrupt," James says, glancing between Marcus and me with a perceptiveness that makes me wonder how much of our tense exchange he witnessed.

"Perfect timing, actually," I say coolly. "Marcus and I were just finishing our chat."

Marcus clears his throat, straightening his blazer in a gesture I recognize from our high school days—his tell when he's uncomfortable but trying not to show it. "James, do you have a minute? There's that matter we discussed…"

James nods, his expression giving nothing away. "Of course." He turns to me with an apologetic smile. "Would you excuse us for just a moment, Celeste? I promise I'll be quick."

Before I can respond, the two men have already stepped away, moving just far enough that their conversation won't be overheard but remaining within sight. I watch them, a strange uneasiness settling in my stomach.

I feel…a bit abandoned. I'm upset, and he just…left.

"Well, that was interesting," Sarah says, appearing at my side with Andy and Mrs. Heart in tow.

Mrs. Heart asks, "You okay, dear? You looked really upset with Marcus."

"I'm fine," I say, my eyes still on the two men. "Just confronting Marcus. I feel like Marcus is the reason the cops have been hanging around outside my house."

Andy raises an eyebrow. "Marcus? Really?"

"Why would he do that?" Sarah asks, curious.

I hesitate, not ready to share all my suspicions, "It has to be related to the stolen money from the revitalization fund. Richard stole it, and maybe Marcus and Daniel helped him."

Mrs. Heart places her hand on my arm, "Dear, I really don't think he has anything to do with that."

Andy watches the two men with narrowed eyes. "Yeah, he's been losing his mind over that missing money. He's really not that good of an actor."

James and Marcus stand with their backs partially to us, but I can see their profiles—James listening intently as Marcus speaks, hands moving in small, controlled gestures. Neither looks particularly hostile toward the other.

Are James and Marcus friends? Is James in on this? Was that whole "I've loved you since I was seventeen" thing just a ruse to…to what? Frame me?

That's ridiculous, Celeste. He wouldn't. Would he?

I think I'm spiraling. Maybe Marcus is right; the stress from my parents' death is getting to me.

Or is he gaslighting me?

"I don't know what to believe anymore," I sigh.

Mrs. Heart says, "Celeste, dear, are you perhaps still holding onto some of those old feelings from when he hurt you a long time ago…"

My head snaps to her, and I say with pursed lips, "He didn't hurt me."

She just smiles gently at me.

She's right. He did hurt me. He was the first person who ever loved me, and he left…

But…

Ryan says that's not what happened…

Watson nuzzles my leg, and I squat down to hug him.

Maybe they're right. Maybe I'm just crazy.

Too emotional.

A pathetic little mouse…

An embarrassment.

Watson looks at me with his big brown eyes and rubs his head on my chest, looking right up at me the whole time.

At least he likes me.

Across the way, the conversation continues. James says something that makes Marcus nod vigorously, then clap him on the shoulder—a gesture of agreement, possibly even gratitude. The casual intimacy of it seems wrong somehow.

"What do you think they're talking about?" I ask, not really expecting an answer.

Watson whines softly, sensing my growing unease. I scratch behind his ears absently, my eyes never leaving the two men.

James suddenly gestures in our direction, and both men turn

slightly, looking our way. I resist the urge to pretend I haven't been staring.

Are they talking about me?

They're probably talking about how crazy I am.

I internally mock Marcus's voice. *How could a crazy slut like that have run a company? Thank God I dumped her all those years ago. I thought Nicole was bad.*

To which James replies: *Her mother was right about her. I need to run now while I still can. I'll just use work as an excuse to get rid of her. Thanks for letting me know, bro.*

Marcus says something else to James, his expression serious. James nods, then reaches into his pocket and pulls out what looks like a business card. He writes something on the back before handing it to Marcus, who pockets it with a nod of thanks.

Andy and Sarah stand nervously beside me, not really sure what to say.

They probably think I'm crazy, too. Everyone hates me.

No. That's not true.

I just need to breathe. Calm down.

They're my friends.

Mrs. Heart says, "Celeste, dear, why don't we go home?"

James glances at his watch, then says something that appears to conclude their conversation. They shake hands—not a formal, business-like handshake, but a friendly one that borders on a hug.

I stand from petting Watson and say, "No…I'm supposed to go to lunch with James. I'm okay, I think I just…I had a moment…"

James loves me.

He wouldn't be saying those things…

Your brain is just being mean to you, Celeste.

Marcus waves the twins to him. They've completed their packing and flank him, holding small boxes of their wares. He wraps his arms around each of their shoulders, and they walk away, disappearing into the crowd.

James watches Marcus go, his expression thoughtful. Then he turns and heads back toward us, his smile returning as he approaches.

I find myself studying that smile with new eyes, looking for signs of insincerity or manipulation, still struggling to regulate my emotions.

"Sorry about that," James says as he rejoins our group. "No rest for the wicked, as they say."

"Funny you'd state it that way," I say, looking at him wearily.

Watson, apparently having no such trust issues, nudges James's knee with his nose, demanding attention. James obliges, crouching down to scratch the dog's ears.

"At least someone's still happy to see me," he says, glancing up at me with a hint of question in his eyes.

I don't know how to respond.

He leans in, "Baby, let's go talk, okay? I think I need to explain some stuff to you."

My heart races.

Why does that sound so menacing?

Sarah clears her throat, breaking the awkward silence. "Is everyone ready to head out?"

James straightens, his attention politely shifting to Sarah. "Yep, my afternoon is clear."

Watson's tail thumps against my leg, his canine vote clearly cast.

I hesitate, torn between caution and curiosity.

Are James and Marcus conspiring against me?

No…that's…

I'm being ridiculous.

My suspicions are just paranoia born of stress and grief…

I should let him explain whatever he wants to explain.

Mrs. Heart leans into me, "Are you going to be okay if Watty and I go home? I can cancel with Gus."

She has plans with Gus for lunch. I can't ask her to cancel that just because I'm being stupid.

"Yeah," I say, faking a smile, my voice more neutral than I feel. "I'm okay. I just…I was just having one of my moments."

Mrs. Heart takes Watson's leash from me, looking at me as if she doesn't believe me.

James's smile widens, reaching his eyes in a way that makes me doubt my doubts. "I got her, Mrs. Heart." He wraps an arm around my shoulder.

Mrs. Heart pats his arm and smiles gently at him before walking away slowly, turning to check on me after only a few steps.

James and I settle at a round table near the window, while Andy and Sarah return to work. The cafe is busy but not crowded, with a pleasant hum of conversation and the occasional hiss of the espresso machine creating a soothing backdrop.

James sits across from me, appearing completely at ease. Like, he has no idea that I've been spinning up increasingly irrational conspiracy theories since he arrived.

"So," James asks conversationally, "Marcus told me what you said…"

"Oh, really…what did he say?"

"That you think he stole the money from the revitalization fund. And that he's framing you for Richard's murder."

"Well, yeah…I did say that…"

"Baby, why…why do you think that?"

I keep my lips sealed. Feeling a bit foolish, but also worried that I'm right in my accusations and James is helping him.

James sighs, "I'm sorry, I knew you and Michael were looking into Richard's murder, but I didn't know to what extent. I didn't realize that was the conclusion you and Michael had come to. I should have asked…"

To be fair, this was a conclusion I came to all on my own…just a little while ago…

"So…Marcus didn't steal the money? He hasn't sicced the police on me? You're not in cahoots with him?"

"No, no, baby. Let's roll back. I need to explain." His eyes hold mine, serious now. "First of all. Marcus did not steal that money. I've been investigating Richard for a long, long time. I was actually gathering evidence to present to the bar association when he died."

This revelation catches me off guard. "You were building a case against him?"

James nods, his voice dropping lower. "Richard's practices had become increasingly…questionable over the past year. Several colleagues and I were concerned, especially regarding his elderly clients."

James takes a sip of his latte, leaving a small foam mustache that he quickly wipes away. The slight imperfection in his otherwise perfect presentation makes something twist inside me—a reminder that he's human, not just a collection of charming gestures and possible ulterior motives.

He sets down his cup. "Marcus did not steal the revitalization money. When he found out the money was missing, he came to me about it. We figured out pretty quickly Richard was responsible. He was helping me build my case against Richard."

"Wait…so is that what you two have been meeting about?"

"Yes."

"But Richard is dead, why are you still meeting?"

"We didn't know if Daniel was an accomplice. We thought maybe he was…" he smirks, "in cahoots with Richard."

"Is Daniel an accomplice?"

"We still aren't sure, but it's looking like he's been…up to other things."

"You mean like fucking Nicole?"

"Oh, you know about that?"

"Ryan told me."

James just laughs. "How do those O'Connors seem to know everything?"

I say, counting off on my fingers, "Hotness. Friendliness. And in this case, proximity to motels."

He chuckles and takes another sip of his latte.

I sigh deeply. "So, Marcus hasn't been convincing the police to investigate me?"

"No." He shakes his head. "He can't make Sheriff Kim do

anything. He asked the Sheriff to check on you, as a friend, because he's worried about you."

I place my face in my hands.

God, I'm so stupid.

"Then why are the police focused on me?"

"I don't think they are, Celeste." He squeezes my hands between his. "I think it just feels that way for everyone who the police question. You've been through a lot, and it's an extremely emotional experience. I really don't think you have anything to worry about. Any evidence pointing to you is extremely circumstantial."

I sigh. "He's just always so…I don't know…jittery around me."

James tilts his head and says in the most soothing voice he can, "You make him nervous. I think he's still got feelings for you. Plus, he's really hoping you'll donate to the town, but every time he tries to talk to you…you get combative…or erratic." *He means sexually aggressive.* He strokes my hand and continues, "He's just really anxious to fix the town and is worried about you."

I groan. "I feel…like such a fucking fool."

"Celeste, it's okay. You're under a lot of stress. A lot more than I realized. I'm sorry I didn't tell you about my case against Richard. I didn't know you were coming to these conclusions. I should probably talk to Michael, too; that mystery dork has probably exacerbated all of this."

"Fuck…I need to apologize to Marcus. He must think I'm such a… Fuck."

"Marcus is a lot like Watson; he sees the best in everyone. I'm sure he doesn't think whatever it is you were about to say."

"Ha, is that how he tolerates Nicole?"

James releases a reserved laugh. "Maybe."

70

I hurriedly throw all the pillows and blankets I've accumulated around the couch I insist on sleeping on into a laundry basket, when Ryan groans loudly. He's heaving a box labeled "Books: YA, Crime, WC, SOS," from the dining room floor.

He asks, "Okay, Star Girl, I'm guessing YA means young adult, but what does WC and SOS mean?"

I blush, "Oh, um…why choose and sentient object smut."

He pauses just long enough to flash me that movie-star grin, "Ah, so, that's why it's so heavy. It's got all your erotica in it."

"They're not erotica. They have a story and relationship building."

"Oh, excuse me."

"That's my erotica over there," I say, pointing at the larger box with a drawing of an eggplant and a spicy pepper.

"That one heavy?"

"Yeah, that box is why I needed you," I grin.

Ryan raises an eyebrow. "You realize your bedroom has, like, negative square footage now."

"If you can't find the floor, you're not stacking high enough." I shoot him a look that's supposed to be authoritative, but judging by his snort, it's not achieved.

"Definitely not planning to ever sleep up there, huh?"

"Yeah, I think I'm just going to get a mattress for in here."

"You know, my dad has a couch kinda like that. It pulls out into a mattress. I'm surprised this one doesn't."

I fling the cushions off the couch, revealing a fucking pull-out bed.

God. Fucking. Damnit. This whole time!?

I lean back and groan with my entire body. "NOOOO. It's a pull-out. You couldn't have said something two months ago!?"

Ryan tromps upstairs, the floorboards creaking like an old ship under his weight. "I just assumed you checked." His laughter rings out from above.

I drop the cushions back into place and sit, allowing myself to wallow in my failure.

A thunk from upstairs suggests Ryan has located a spot on the floor to place the box.

"Remind me," he hollers down the stairs, "why do you have so many books?"

"Because I read them!" I yell back.

"Never heard of a Kindle?" He appears at the top of the stairs, chest heaving just enough to prove that the box wasn't empty, but not enough to look like he's trying.

I stick my tongue out at him as he bounds down the stairs, ready to grab another box. "You're making great time, you know. All those pushups are coming in handy."

He flops onto the armchair, dramatically wiping imaginary sweat from his brow. "I need a little rest before I get that box of erotica." He grins, squinting at me through a loose tangle of blond hair and yawns.

"No worries. We have a few hours until anyone gets here. Why are you so tired?"

"Other than the fact that you have me carrying a million pounds of smut upstairs at the crack of dawn? I was up late working on something."

He leans back, closing his eyes, and I openly stare at him. The way his chest is heaving as he's stretched out across that armchair makes me want to straddle him.

He opens one blue eye and peeks at me, leaning forward."Getting ideas about other ways to wear me out."

I duck my head, fighting a smile, and focus on stuffing the remaining blanket into the storage ottoman. "Nope."

He groans, stretching his arms over his head. "Oh, man, I can't wait to try Mrs. Heart's prize-winning pie. She's bringing it, right?"

I sigh. "Yeah. I hope she brings the crumble top, too, though."

He laughs, and the sound bounces off the high ceiling in a way that makes the whole place feel a little less like a mausoleum covered in piles of junk.

I gather up the stray shoes, sweaters, stuffed Pokémon, and hand-held video game consoles that have accumulated across the room since I moved in.

"Hey," Ryan says, more quietly, "you know you don't have to be a hostess with the mostest, right? It's okay if it's a little messy."

"I know. I just want to make sure everyone has room to sit," I mutter, but he gives me a look that makes me instantly sheepish.

He stands up, brushing his hands on his jeans. "Alright. Back to work. Maybe I'll start on the kitchen when I'm done with the boxes. Unless there's something else you'd like me to do?"

"Could you take that—" I pause, gesturing helplessly at the piano, "—out back and burn it?"

Ryan walks over to the piano, and he lays his palm on the blanket draped over the keys. "Sorry, Star Girl. I'm not strong enough to carry a grand piano."

"Mini grand."

"Can't carry that either."

My throat tightens in a way I hate. I muster a casual shrug. "Got an axe?"

"Not on me."

I nod. He doesn't push. Instead, he sidesteps and hauls a few more boxes up the stairs. After the dining room is finally clear, for the first time since I've moved in, I can see the dining room table.

Ryan wipes his brow again. "Alright, that's the last of 'em."

"Thanks, Ryan. I appreciate it."

"No prob, Celeste."

He flops back in the armchair, kicking one leg over the side. "So, what's next? Keep cleaning or…" he waggles his eyes at me.

I try to look stern, but he's impossible to scold when he's being this adorable. "Let's clean the table off first."

He sits, watching me fuss with the dining room table for a minute, spraying and wiping away the dust, then stands up and crosses over to me.

I say, "I suppose I should set the table. I guess it's good we never got around to putting those plates in storage."

He places both hands on the table, like he's bracing himself for a big reveal. "Actually, I brought you some presents."

"Oh, yeah?"

He smiles at me bigger than I've seen in a while. "Be right back."

He dashes to the door, swings it open, and jogs down the front walk. I watch from the window as he rummages in his pickup, then returns with a big cardboard box, haphazardly taped.

I laugh nervously. "Just what I needed, another box."

"It's not the box, dork."

He sets it on the table, peeling the tape with a flourish. "Ta-da."

Inside is a set of ceramic plates and bowls, each hand-painted with tiny blue stars and gold flecks. They're breathtaking.

"Ryan." I lift one out, holding it up to the light. "These are—wow."

"I made them for you."

"Really?"

He beams. "Glazed 'em myself. Dishwasher safe and microwavable. Put as many hot pockets as you want on them."

I run my finger over the rim. "They're beautiful. I can't believe you did this for me."

He shrugs, grinning a little sheepishly. "Well, I figured, what do you get a billionaire who can get whatever she wants, right? Handmade gifts! And, I thought…since you said the other plates had so many bad memories, you'd like some you can make new memories with."

I stare at the plates, throat aching. "Thank you, Ryan. Really."

He unboxes the rest, arranging them carefully on the table. When all the plates and bowls are out, he reaches into the bottom of the box and pulls out a roll of fabric, splattered with paint.

"What's this?" I ask.

"Drape painting," he says. "It's a thing artists do. You put it over something and it's supposed to change how you see it." He glances at the piano. "You could use it instead of the blanket, if you want."

I look at the piano, then at the painting—an explosion of warm oranges and reds, like the beautiful foliage of a Minnesota fall. I nod.

Ryan lifts the blanket, folds it, and sets it aside. The piano underneath is oppressive in its size—grinning at me with its malicious, toothy keys. Before I can spend too much time looking at it, he drapes the painting over the lid, tucking it so the colors spill down the side. He steps back to evaluate his handiwork.

"It's perfect," I say, and mean it. Tears well in my eyes.

He stands next to me, "I'm glad you think so."

"You're a really good friend, Ryan," I say, turning to bury my face in his chest, allowing myself to cry, while he hugs me.

He takes a deep breath and raises his hand to my hair. He's shaking. I look up at him, and he's crying, too. "I love you, Celeste. Not like a friend. Not like a friend with benefits, but hopelessly and pathetically in love with you since we were children."

The confession crashes into me like a meteor. My heart stumbles, caught in the shock. My brain turns over his words, not quite believing he actually said them. I open my mouth to respond, but the words tangle and knot. Ryan squeezes my shoulder. His expression is a mix of hope and fear as he searches my face for any hint of reaction.

"I know it must be a lot to hear," he says, a slight crack in his voice revealing just how much he's risked in telling me. "Especially since I've been…such an ass."

I swallow hard, still processing the shift in our reality. "Ryan, I…"

He interrupts gently, as if afraid to hear the rest. "Please, let me explain."

I nod, my head spinning, but the warmth of his chest against me, anchors me.

Ryan's gaze doesn't break from my face. "I didn't plan on telling you like this," he admits, his voice threaded with vulnerability. "But, it feels like it's time to stop hiding."

He hesitates, and I can see the struggle in his eyes, the decision to lay himself bare. "I've always loved you, but I didn't know it until you started dating Marcus. That's when it hit me. I was a dumb kid who thought he wanted to sow his wild oats, but I didn't. I just wanted you. It felt like Marcus took you from me."

My breath catches as I remember all the conversations we had. "But, after Marcus and I broke up, you…"

"After Marcus, you were so adamant about never dating again. I just couldn't ever find the right time. You were so focused on school, and I didn't want to screw that up. Plus, we were living together and sleeping together, what did it matter if you were my friend and not my girlfriend? It felt like the same thing."

"It felt like the same thing to me, too," I admit.

"I had this big plan. We were going to graduate from college, move back to Goose Grove, make lots of babies, and live happily ever after. But then, you said you were going to California to be a big-time video game developer. You said you never wanted kids. It felt like another time you were choosing someone, something, other than me."

"I wanted you to come with me, Ryan. I wanted you to make games with me."

"Fuck, I was so stupid. I was so angry and so hurt. I tried calling. I tried texting. But every time I did, I just couldn't think of what to say. All I wanted to do was beg you to come home to me."

"Ryan, I'm sorry…"

"There's nothing for you to apologize for. I was the stupid one. But when I got cancer. I realized how short life was. I was lying there, alone, scared, with all these tubes in my arms, and the only person I could think of was you."

"That's when you started texting me again?"

"Yeah," he admits.

My breath catches, "But, why…why have you still been insisting on friends with benefits? I don't understand, Ryan."

"Because you said you wanted kids. I…it felt nobler not to complicate that for you. It was stupid. I know, I'm always so stupid."

I gape at him again, trying to articulate everything I want to say. But, I can start with, "Ryan, I love you. I love you, too."

We embrace and kiss, crying into each other.

He whispers, "And…I know you're in love with Michael and James."

My heart stops. *Fuck. He's going to make me choose between them.*

"I don't know what to say," I whisper, afraid anything I say will make him run away. "Michael…and James…they're…"

He sighs, hugging me tighter. "Life's too short, Celeste. I'm going to stop hiding from you. I'm going to stop running. I love you, and if they're part of our lives, so be it." His eyes search mine, vulnerable and waiting. "I'm happy as long as I'm with you."

I just look into his eyes, searching for the right words. Fear crosses his face, and he says with a self-deprecating laugh, "Fuck, maybe one of them can give you babies."

"Ryan, don't minimize yourself like that. You're more than—"

"I know, Celeste."

"Shut up and listen to me for just a second. I love you. I love you for who you are. Because you are my best friend and always have been. Even when we were apart, I loved you. I don't love you for your ability to impregnate me. I love you because I love you."

71

I wipe my hands on my jeans, which are already dusted with flour, to open the door to Mrs. Heart. Her beaming smile is only slightly outdone by the aroma wafting from the pies she cradles in her arms. Watson sits with his tail gently swishing behind him, wearing a pumpkin-orange bandana and the unshakable confidence of a dog who knows he's about to receive a ridiculous amount of table scraps.

"Happy Thanksgiving, dear!" Mrs. Heart sings out as she crosses the threshold.

"Happy Thanksgiving," I reply, already eyeing the pies.

She holds up the two pies—one with a perfect lattice, the other with a golden brown crumble top. "I brought my award-winning pie and the crumble. I know you always pretend to like the lattice, but you're a crumble girl at heart."

I can't even protest, because she's right. She always is.

She hands me the pies and sets to work removing her gloves and shoes. Watson gives a little twirl of excitement and noses his way into my house, clearly on a reconnaissance mission spurred by the smells coming from the kitchen. She removes her pea coat, and her hand stops at the hooks by the door. "That's a lot of coats."

"Ha, yeah, the guys are all here," I say, gesturing with my elbow, since my hands are now occupied with pie. "They're in the kitchen."

As if on cue, there's a raised voice from the kitchen, followed by the unmistakable sound of something being set forcefully—though, thankfully, not shattered—onto the countertop.

"Are you seriously arguing that a pop-up timer is better than a thermometer?" James asks with a level of annoyance that luckily is never directed at me.

Ryan shoots back. "The pop timer's good enough."

Michael, in the background, provides a running commentary. "It's fine, James. Some people really prefer a surprise when it comes to their turkey. Personally, I love the idea of not knowing if I'll get food poisoning or dry meat."

Mrs. Heart smiles as if she's stumbled onto her favorite soap opera already in progress. "My goodness, it's lively in there."

"It's been like this for an hour," I say. "Dinner's gonna' be late."

We step into the kitchen, where the three men are gathered around a turkey, a spread of roasting pans, and thermometers (one digital, one old-school glass) arranged like surgeon's tools.

James is in the process of aggressively crushing ice so that he can calibrate the thermometer that I doubt Ryan will let him stick in the bird. Ryan is basting with reckless abandon, painting the turkey as if it's an art project. Michael is sipping coffee, leaning against the counter, and looking vaguely amused.

"Good morning, boys!" Mrs. Heart says.

"Mrs. Heart, please tell him a pop-up thermometer is sufficient. He'll listen to you," Ryan says. He wipes his hands on a towel, streaking it with a mix of melted butter and paprika.

"Ryan, dear, I really hate to be the one to tell you this, but you need a thermometer," Mrs. Heart says, patting him on the shoulder.

"Thank you!" James groans.

Ryan looks positively defeated, his shoulders slump, "Fine, I'll concede. But if we use the thermometer, we're gonna stuff it with stuffing."

"Noooo!" James all but wails, gripping the counter, and I have never seen this side of him. It's actually quite fun.

"Okay, boys, that's an argument I'm not going to get in the middle of," Mrs. Heart says.

Michael chimes in, "I don't even like stuffing."

Ryan and James both look at him as if he's lost his mind.

"I don't like it either," I laugh, and they look absolutely horrified.

Watson has already circled the kitchen twice, devoured a few dropped carrot peels, and is currently staring up at Michael, hoping for a piece of the green beans he's now snapping.

James turns to me, irritation written all over his face. "You want to talk some sense into him?"

"Fiiiine! We can do it your way this year, but for Christmas, we're doing it my way," Ryan says, hands up and backing away from the turkey.

Christmas? He's planning on having Christmas dinner with us.

"Thank you!" James says, taking Ryan's place at the counter. Ryan simply stands behind him, watching him work, hands on his hips, obviously waiting for something to criticize.

There's a heavy booming knock at the door.

I open the door to a handsome blond wall of fleece and plaid, topped by the only face in town that smiles wider than Ryan. "Duck!" he booms, enveloping me in a bear hug that lifts me off the ground for a second. "Happy Thanksgiving! Thank you for inviting me!"

I laugh, genuinely, and gesture for him to come inside. "Happy Thanksgiving, Mr. O'Connor."

Mr. O'Connor stops, stunned, at the kitchen door. "I came early, thinking you'd need an extra pair of hands, but it seems there's already too many cooks in this kitchen."

"We've got it, Dad. You can relax," Ryan replies, opening all the cabinets looking for God knows what.

"Okay, well…I'll just be watching the parade then. I'm here if you need me," Mr. O'Connor says, looking absolutely crushed that he can't help.

"Celeste, why don't you join him. We got this," James says, finally placing the turkey in the oven.

"You sure? Umm, okay," I say, super excited because I fucking hate cooking.

"Why don't you take Watson with you? He keeps getting underfoot, looking for treats," Mrs. Heart says, opening a bag of cranberries.

"And Ryan!" James says, nodding to the blond hovering at his back.

Mr. O'Connor wanders into the dining room and runs his finger along the edge of one of the plates I've laid out on the table. "These are the plates you made, Son?"

Ryan looks up from whatever trouble he's causing for James and beams, "Yeah."

Mr. O'Connor nods, visibly impressed. "Beautiful work, Son. I'm proud of you."

"Thanks, Dad."

Mr. O'Connor puts his hand on my shoulder, "I'm happy you're back, Duck," and I feel like he knows what these plates symbolize—a commitment from Ryan.

We fall into an easy rhythm after that. James and Mrs. Heart eventually kick everyone out of the kitchen, finding all of our help to be less than helpful. James has told me he enjoys cooking, but I didn't realize how much he enjoys it. The two spend the rest of the morning and early afternoon discussing cooking techniques.

For a light lunch, Ryan and Michael team up to assemble a "charcuterie situation" that is, almost too beautifully arranged to eat. While we wait for the food to finish cooking, Mr. O'Connor and Mrs. Heart regale James and Michael with stories of my and Ryan's youth. It's only semi-embarrassing.

At some point, Mrs. Heart slides up next to me and says, "You seem happier, dear."

"I am," I say, grinning so large my face hurts. "It's just having everyone under one roof. I like it. This is how I always wished Thanksgiving could be."

She squeezes my hand, warm and steady. "I'm glad, dear."

Once the turkey is done, I do a few final finishing touches to arrange the tableware. I turn toward the piano, covered in Ryan's drop cloth painting, and for the first time, I don't feel an empty pit in my stomach when looking at it.

We serve ourselves and sit around the table, allowing Mrs. Heart and Mr. O'Connor the head seats. Watson sits under the table, tail wagging furiously as he waits for one of us to "accidentally" drop food. Ryan sits at my side, and Michael sits at James's opposite us.

There's a lull as everyone tucks in, broken only by the clink of silverware and the occasional sound of Watson gnawing on contraband.

Never one to let me off the hook, Mr. O'Connor asks, "So, Celeste, you decide what you're going to do next yet?"

"Actually, I think I have," I say, swirling my wine. Everyone holds their breath waiting for my response. "I apologized to Marcus for… umm…accusing him of murder, and we had a really good talk about his plans for Goose Grove. I'm going to help fund the revitalization efforts."

Mrs. Heart smiles, "That's wonderful, dear!"

I continue, "I told him I want to make sure the money I provide is used to improve the town in ways that benefit everyone, not in ways that make money. You know, things like fix Main Street, renovate the park, start another community garden, stuff like that. But also, some small business grants. There's a clerk at town hall who could use some capital. I'm sure there are tons of Goose Grovians in the same boat. Oh, and we need a skatepark."

Everyone laughs.

"Gonna pick up skating again, Celeste?" James asks with a wink.

"Maybe," I smile into my glass.

"You mean, grinding, dear," Mrs. Heart corrects with a laugh.

I add, "I was also thinking the Glendos Mansion, while great as a haunted house and museum, maybe it could be used to help people who need a place to go. I don't know. Marcus and I have some ideas. But I want to use my money to help people. I'll start here in Goose Grove and see where that takes me. I'm ready to get back to work. But I want to work for others. Not work to hide."

Mrs. Heart pats my hand, "That sounds wonderful, dear!"

There's a pause while everyone thinks about what I said for a moment. "Speaking of work," Michael says, side-eying James, "You didn't have any to do today?"

James smirks at him, "I do. It never ends. But, I'm trying these things Celeste taught me called 'work-life balance' and 'self-care.'"

Ryan playfully scoffs, "Celeste taught you that?"

I smirk, "It was a 'do as I say, not as I do' type conversation."

"Obviously," Ryan chuckles.

We continue like this, eating and chatting for quite a while, each of us getting seconds, some getting thirds.

"Soooo, I have to know, what's up with you two? Why don't you like each other?" I ask, slightly tipsy and pointing my glass between Ryan and James.

James chuckles, "Well, Ryan's hated me since…what? Since I came back home from law school? Not sure why, though."

Ryan replies, "What!? I never hated you. You hated me."

James replies, "I mean, I've always thought you were a bit of a fuck boy and was jealous you had Celeste, but I didn't hate you."

"Ha, that's rich, you thinking someone was a fuckboy," Michael laughs.

"How am I a fuck boy!?" James asks, turning to Michael and looking seriously affronted.

Michael rolls his eyes, "Come on, James. Being 'married to work' doesn't absolve you of your other fuck boyeries."

Mr. O'Connor chimes in, "Okay, so what is a fuck boy?"

Mrs. Heart answers, "A man with a lot of sexual partners who is emotionally unavailable, doesn't take accountability, disregards his various partners' feelings, and uses grandiosity to mask deep-seated attachment issues."

James enters full-on lawyer mode and begins to lay out his defense, chopping one hand into the other with each point, "Okay, I may be emotionally unavailable and have deep-seated attachment issues, but I have not had a lot of sexual partners, I am accountable for my actions, and I do not disregard my partners' feelings."

Michael sighs and sips his wine. "Fine. I retract my previous statement. You may scratch it from the record."

"Thank you," James says, sitting back in his seat with a look of smug victory.

I try to get the conversation back on track. "So, wait!" I laugh, "You just didn't like each other because you thought the other didn't like you?" I hiccup. "Did that make sense?"

Ryan and James look between each other. "I guess that is what happened," James chuckles.

Mr. O'Connor chimes in, "To be fair, Ryan has always been a bit of fuck boy."

"Dad!" Ryan rolls his eyes. "I'm almost forty. I'm a fuck man now." He winks and sips his wine.

Mrs. Heart shakes her head. "You kids are hopeless."

Watson barks in agreement, and we all collapse into laughter again.

Once the plates are clear, Mrs. Heart claps her hands for attention. "All right, everyone. We have to say what we're thankful for."

"You first, Mrs. Heart," I say, tearing into a dinner roll.

"I'm thankful for winning the pie contest," she says, lifting her fork in triumph.

Everyone laughs, and then she softens. "But more than that, I'm thankful you came home, Celeste."

Ryan chuckles, "Maybe we should just skip that one, since we're all gonna say it anyway."

I blush and shoulder him, "I don't mind hearing a few times."

Ryan adds, "Alright then, I'm thankful to have you back in my life, Celeste. And, this is more of an announcement," he pauses, and turns to his dad. He places his hand on his shoulder. "Dad, I bought the orchard back."

"What?! Son, are you serious?"

"Yeah, when I was in the city promoting the gallery opening, I presold a few pieces. That was the last bit I needed."

Mr. O'Connor launches himself toward Ryan, engulfing him in an unrestrained hug characteristic of the pair. "I'm proud of you, son." Mr. O'Connor goes next, wiping tears from his eyes, "Well, I'm thankful for my son working so hard to get back our orchard. I'm thankful for Duck, too. I've missed you, Duck, and my boy needed you to set him straight. I'm grateful we're all back together again."

"Dad," Ryan rolls his eyes, as he always does to his dad.

James chimes in, "I'm grateful to Celsete for reminding me that taking care of myself and the people I love is just as important as my duty." He and Michael smile at each other.

Michael goes next, "I'm thankful for second chances and those who facilitate them." He grins at me. "Which is code for Celeste, of course." We all laugh.

It's my turn, and I can feel all their eyes on me. For a second, I panic, but then it comes to me. "I'm grateful to have all the love I could ever have hoped for. For all of you. And Watson, of course." I say, looking at the happy little spaniel. "I'm just thankful to have a family—a family I chose."

There's a pause, and I think I might actually cry.

I add, "And, I hope I can show you that I deserve you all."

Mrs. Heart looks at me, and I can tell a small, soft-spoken lecture is on my way, so I beat her to it, "Sorry, Mrs. Heart. I know I deserve love and don't have to earn it. Mr. O'Connor. I forgot to add earlier. I'm also going to go to therapy and work on my negative self-talk."

Ryan gives me another one-armed hug, and Mr. O'Connor raises his beer, saying, "To Celeste. The reason we're all here."

We all bask in the warm and fuzzies of it all.

72

After saying my final goodbyes to Mrs. Heart, Watson, and Mr. O'Connor, I click the door closed and turn to face them. All three of them. In one room. Each with a half-full glass of wine, and none of them in any rush to leave.

"Well," Ryan says, stretching and folding his arms behind his head, "I suppose we're gonna hash this out now, huh?"

Michael smiles. "I was told there would be a postprandial dissection of feelings. Did I misread the invitation?"

"Mine mentioned something about discussing the parameters of our relationship," James quips, eyebrow raised.

I roll my eyes and flop onto the couch, motioning for them to join me in the living room. Ryan claims the space next to me, sprawling like he owns this couch. James perches on the armrest of the armchair, perfecting his confidently uptight vibe. Michael settles into the center of the opposite couch, leans forward, elbows on knees, and stares into his wine as if it will protect him from this conversation.

"So," I say, "we're really doing this, huh? The four of us."

Ryan shrugs. "Seems like we are."

James takes a slow sip, then says, "I think we need to talk logistics."

"Polyamory project management," Michael deadpans.

James nods, entirely serious. "Exactly."

Michael snorts. "You want to schedule our sex life in a Google calendar, don't you?"

James opens his mouth, then closes it. "No comment."

Ryan leans forward. "Not that I'm against it, but what are we even calling this? I mean, is it a quad? Are there rules? Is there a group text? And do I have to, you know…be nice to James?"

Michael asks, "I thought we established that you don't actually have a reason to hate each other?"

"Well, I still think he's a fuckboy," James replies.

Ryan shrugs, unapologetic. "Some people process trauma with art. Some people process it by getting laid. I just happened to be good at both."

James grins despite himself. "You're an ass."

Ryan quips, "And you're a tightass."

Michael, "Are you two flirting now? I can't tell anymore."

I reply, "Me either."

I feel the tension dissolve, replaced by something warmer, looser, and utterly unlike the rivalry up to this point.

James changes the subject, "Back to Ryan's questions. Quad seems right to me, any objections?"

We all shake our heads.

I speak up. "So…um, that Google Calendar and group chat actually sound really nice. You have no idea how hard it was to juggle you all over the last few weeks."

Ryan asks, "But what are we scheduling on this calendar? Time with Celeste? Are we actually scheduling sex with her?"

James thinks, "We could have different calendars for each person. They can be color-coded. Then—"

Ryan cuts him off, "Holy shit, that sounds annoying. Who's setting this up? Mr. Busy over here? Maybe we should all just move in together."

Michael and James both look at him, then at each other, then at me, and for a second it's as if a spell is broken.

I ask, "Wait, are you serious, Ryan?"

He replies, "Well, I was joking…but it does seem like it would be easiest."

Michael asks, "Where would we live?"

James replies, "Well, your place would be too small for all of us, Mikey. So, here or my place. What's your place like, Ryan?"

Ryan shakes his head, "Not my place. It barely fits me."

James adds, "So here or my place."

"Not here," I say flatly, looking at my hands. "I think…I think I should sell this house."

Ryan turns to me and places his hand on my elbow, "Yeah? You think you're ready to let it go?"

I look up from my hands. "I am." They wait for me to continue as I collect my thoughts. "I think we should build a place. The perfect place for all of us."

Ryan chuckles, "I keep forgetting money is no object for you."

I reply, "Maybe we can move it with James in the meantime?"

Michael says, "I'd like that."

Ryan asks, "Is there a place I can paint?"

James thinks for a moment, "I have a really nice sunroom I never use. Overlooks the lake."

"I'm sold," Ryan says, slapping his legs. "There's only one other thing I want to know the answer to before we commit to this." Three heads swivel to him. "Sex. How's that gonna work?"

James clears his throat, "So, the three of us have been having sex. Sometimes together. Sometimes separate. And then sometimes she has sex with you. We could continue like that if that's what you want."

Ryan smirks, "You say that like there's an 'or' coming."

Michael says, "Or you can have sex with us, too."

Ryan replies, "Oh, huh…" then, in his characteristic deflection-using way, asks Michael and James, "Are you two saying you want to have sex with me?"

James replies matter-of-factly, "Of course we want to have sex with you, have you seen you?"

Ryan's eyebrows shoot upward as if this new information gives him a significant amount of power he has yet to realize he holds. He leans back, sprawling his arms across the back of the couch again.

Michael looks annoyed at James, and James replies, "Oh, sorry, I shouldn't speak for Mikey."

Michael sighs, "You saw the painting. You already know my answer."

Ryan purses his lip and nods, thinking.

"What? What does that mean?" I ask.

Ryan answers, "That painting he's got in his living room. It was the first one I ever sold once I started my shirtless painter videos."

"How does that answer the question, though?" I ask, confused.

He clears his throat. "Well, first, there was a bidding war. Then an anonymous bidder spent waaay too much on it."

Michael blushes, but then laughs, the kind of laugh that is half embarrassment, half relief. "And when I bought it, I sent an incredibly embarrassing note, please do not tell them what it said. I never thought you'd find out it was me." He puts his face in his hands and groans.

James taps Michael's shoulder, "What? You never told me that. Come on, tell us."

Michael just shakes his head in his hands.

Ryan let's out a single laugh, "Don't worry, Mikey. It's our little secret."

"No fair!" I laugh, tickling Ryan.

Ryan cackles. "Hey, stop! I don't know how quad bro code works, but it's gotta be stronger than regular bro code. I'm not gonna tell."

"Definitely stronger," James adds.

"Okay, that's really not fair. I'm going to be severely outnumbered in this," I say, fake pouting.

For a while, we just sit there, the four of us, watching the fire and feeling the edges of something new and hopeful knitting itself together.

Michael, his bravery returning to him, says, "So, Ryan, really, it's up to you. What do you think?"

Ryan bites the inside of his cheek, "I mean, I'm mostly straight. But I think…if Celeste is part of it…I'm interested."

Michael looks at me, then at Ryan, then at James. "Can we agree on one thing? Can we agree that if anyone wants to bring someone else in—emotionally, physically, whatever—we talk about it first?"

I say, "I want this to work. I want all of us to be happy. And I'm okay with us…being exclusive. At least until we figure out what this is."

Ryan says, "So, full quad exclusivity, at least for now."

James nods. "That's reasonable. It will give us peace of mind concerning unprotected sex. And I like the idea of stability, especially if kids are going to be in the picture."

Ryan tilts his head, "Kids?"

"Oh, yeah, sorry, we've talked about kids," James says, pointing between himself, me, and Michael. "But Celeste wanted to wait until we talked to you about…all this, before we proceeded."

Ryan looks to me. "What did you all decide?"

I scoot closer to him, ready to grab him by the collar if he bolts. "We want to be a family. All of us."

Michael chimes in, "Essentially, the kids would have two dads. Three if you want."

Ryan's hand tenses, "I…I do want. But…I…can't…"

"It's okay, Ryan, we know," Michael says. "James watches your lives, too."

"Now who's speaking for whom?" James asks, wiping his legs to flatten an invisible wrinkle.

"And you two are okay with that? With me…just being around… your children?" Ryan asks, his voice cracking a bit.

They both nod.

I grab his hand. "James already has all the paperwork sorted out that we'd need to protect parental rights of any non-biological fathers. It's not one hundred percent, and a court could possibly choose to reject it, but—"

"But I'm a really good lawyer," James interjects.

"Okay then," Ryan says.

"Okay then," the rest of us say in unison.

After a devastatingly long moment of silence, Ryan leans back and stretches his arms overhead. "I don't know about you guys, but it feels like we're all gearing up to fuck."

Michael, not missing a beat, says, "I thought that was also on the invitation."

73

"So, are we all just standing here like this, or should I at least pull out the couch?" Ryan's tone is so casual, I can't tell if he's stalling or actually making a practical suggestion. With Ryan, it's always both.

"There's a pull-out mattress?" James asks.

"Yeah, I just found it this morning," I say, with a sigh. "Don't say anything. I know."

Ryan makes a dramatic show of cracking his knuckles, then scoots the coffee table out of the way with his foot, muscles flexing through the threadbare knees of his jeans. He crouches, wrestles with the hide-a-bed lever, and the couch lets out a mechanical groan as it flattens into a makeshift mattress.

James grins at me, that little dimple in his left cheek deepening, and Michael's eyebrow goes up like he's privately placing bets on how long this will stay awkward. I glance between them, suddenly hyper-aware of how close we all are in my living room.

The faded, floral-printed sheet is the same one my mom used to put down for sleepovers. God knows how long it's been there.

"Oh, I guess I should go get some new sheets," I say, "Hold on."

Three pairs of eyes track me as I disappear down the hallway to the linen closet and grab a fitted sheet.

I jump to the bathroom, rummage in one of my toiletries bags, and come up with a nearly full bottle of lube.

When I come back, the three of them are still standing where I left them, and I'm struck by how beautifully awkward this is.

I hold up the bottle. "I'm just going to assume we'll need this," I announce, and put it on the end table like a trophy.

Michael nods, but I notice he's looking at James when he says, "Probably smart."

James is already moving, pulling the sheet off the bed and folding it to place it on the other couch.

"How do you want to do this?" he asks, and I know he doesn't mean the logistics of the bedding.

Ryan grabs the new sheet I brought and snaps it open, letting it fall to the mattress. The four of us work to snap the fitted sheet around the edges. *Well, that's a benefit of this relationship structure: fitted sheets don't stand a chance.*

There's a moment—a big, hungry, uncertain moment—where no one quite knows who should make the first move. I look at Ryan, who's always been the instigator, and for once, he hesitates.

James reads the room (as he always does) and turns to Ryan. "So, can we assume your response earlier means you don't want Michael or me to touch you during this?"

Ryan shakes his head, and for the first time tonight, the joking stops. "I mean, you can touch me, but preferably don't kiss me. Let's just say I'm okay with hand stuff. Maybe more." He shrugs, but his voice is steady. "Honestly, I'm not sure where I'll land in the moment. So, if it feels like you're crossing a line, I'll let you know."

James puts a hand on Ryan's shoulder, squeezes it once. "Good enough. We're all just figuring this out."

And then it starts, not with fireworks, but with a gentle, familiar gravity. James pulls me in, and his lips are warm and certain on mine. *God, this man knows how to kiss*. He waits for me to open, and then his tongue is there, asking before taking. He pulls me against his body, and his cock is already hard against my hip. There's nothing tentative about the way his hands slide down my back.

Behind me, I hear Michael move. He's quiet. So quiet that it takes me a second to realize he's come up behind James. Michael's hand slides up the back of James's neck, and he leans in and kisses him.

James breaks away from Michael and grins at Ryan, who is hovering at the edge of the couch like he's still not sure if he's allowed on set. "Get over here, O'Connor," James says, holding out a hand.

Ryan snorts but obeys, sitting beside me. For a second, he just watches. Then, slowly, he leans in and kisses my cheek. It's almost chaste, but then he pulls back, and his eyes are mischievous. I laugh at how innocent it is, considering how filthy things are about to get.

He kisses me for real. Ryan's kissing is different than James's—it's hungry, unfiltered, like he's making up for lost time. His fingers thread through my hair, tugging gently, and then his tongue slides into my mouth, and I moan into him, not because I mean to, but because it feels so good to be wanted this way.

The three of them circle around me, and it's dizzying, the way their hands and mouths trade off, each taking a turn with me, with each other. Michael kisses James again, his hand slipping up under James's shirt.

Ryan's shirt is the first to come off—I suspect he's excited to appease his three eager fans. He yanks it over his head and tosses it onto the armchair, then grins at me. "Your turn."

I reach down and pull my sweater off, and immediately Ryan's hands are on me, warm and soft and reverent, like he can't believe I'm real. "You're gorgeous," he murmurs, and I believe him, because I want to.

James is already half-naked—his chest is broad and dusted with hair, and I want to run my hands over it, so I do. He lets out a pleased little sound when I touch him, then returns the favor by unhooking my bra with a one-handed flick.

"Show-off," I mutter, but he just laughs and bends down to take my nipple into his mouth, and then I'm not saying much of anything.

Michael hovers for a moment, shirtless and uncertain, staring at Ryan's chest. "You're…fuck, you're hot," Michael says. For a second, Michael's hand hovers above Ryan's chest, then Ryan gives a tiny nod and Michael rests his palm there, fingers splayed, and Ryan's whole body shudders. Michael grins and looks to James like he's saying, "Hey, look what I get to do!" *Seems like I'm not the only one who has Michael as a fan boy.*

They work together, all three of them, to undress me. I lose track of whose hands are whose, whose mouths are where, and it doesn't matter because all I feel is the warmth of bodies, the rush of skin and breath and want. By the time they've got me out of my jeans, I'm soaked and tingling, and I practically collapse onto the bed, arms over my head.

The three of them stand above me for a second, and it is, without a doubt, the hottest thing I've ever seen in my life. Michael's cock is long and curved and already leaking; James is thick and impressive and standing at attention; Ryan's perfectly matches his own bravado. I want all of them. I want them now.

"Holy fuck," I say, out loud, because there's nothing else to say. "I want all three of you inside me."

James rubs his thumb over his head and says, "Touch yourself, baby. Spread those lips and show us how wet you are."

My face flushes, but I do as I'm told, fingers gliding between my thighs, finding myself already dripping. They all three just stand and watch me, languidly stroking themselves.

James sits on the bed beside me. Ryan sits on my other side, his hand joining mine, index finger pressing gentle circles into my clit. "Jesus, Celeste," he says, voice gone husky. "You're fucking ready."

James's hand pushes Ryan's aside, and for a second, they almost squabble over who gets to touch me, but instead, they work together. Michael kneels between my legs and lowers his head, his mouth joining their hands.

Michael's tongue is precise, flicking and swirling and—God—so fucking good. Someone slides their fingers inside me. I can't even tell how many, but I'm stretched and full, while James and Ryan kiss my nipples and neck. I'm crying out, clutching at the sheet, at their arms, anything I can reach. I come so hard and so fast I think I might black out, and when I open my eyes, all three of them are watching me, and I've never felt more beautiful or powerful or wanted in my life.

I grab Michael by the shoulders and flip him onto his back, which is harder than it looks, but he laughs and rolls with me until I'm straddling him, his cock pressing hot against my thigh.

"Impatient?" he says, voice rough.

For you, Michael? Always. "You have no idea," I say, and I reach down and guide him inside me.

It's perfect, the way he fills me. He grabs my hips and sets a rhythm, slow at first, then faster, and I ride him, eyes locked on his, until I can barely see straight. Ryan and James kneel on either side of us, their cocks slick and hard, and I reach out and take one in each hand.

It's a lot to manage, but I'm nothing if not efficient. I pump them both, alternating strokes, and when I lean forward to take James into my mouth, Ryan's right there, his own cock pressed against my cheek. I switch between them, sucking one, then the other, feeling the power in how they groan and grab at my hair and shoulders.

Eventually, James and Ryan line up, both pushing the heads of their cocks against my lips at the same time. I open wide, and they both slide in, not all the way, just enough that I can taste them both. It's overwhelming and perfect and so, so filthy.

"Jesus Christ, that is the sexiest thing I've ever seen," Michael says, closing his eyes, as if he's unable to bear the sight of it any longer.

James and Ryan slide deeper into my mouth, and I suck as hard as I can.

"Oh, baby, you're too good at that," James says, and I feel him start to throb.

"Holy shit, this is…fuck," Ryan gasps, and then they both come, mouths open, hands gripping each other and me, and I swallow as much as I can, the rest dripping down my chin and onto Michael's chest below.

Michael, not to be outdone, grabs my ass and starts thrusting up into me, his pace frantic now. I ride him hard, chasing my own orgasm, and when it hits, it's like a lightning strike—I scream, I claw at his shoulders, and then he's coming too, pulsing inside me, burying his face in my neck.

For a minute, the room is silent except for the sound of heavy breathing and the distant whir of the fridge. Then Ryan falls backward, arms spread like he's making a snow angel, next to Michael.

"Fuck," Ryan pants. "That was amazing."

James collapses beside me, planting a slow, lazy kiss on my temple. "Thank you, baby."

Michael sits up, encircling me and pulling me down so that I lay on top of him. "Come here, love," he says, so quietly I almost miss it.

I can't stop smiling, even as exhaustion starts to set in. "Ryan, Michael is an aggressive cuddler, so, fair warning," I say.

"It's like a post-coital cute aggression," James laughs, lying next to Michael and letting him wrap an arm around him before Michael kisses him hard on top of the head.

"I can't help that you two are so cute, you make me want to cry," Michael says, pulling us closer.

Ryan rolls to his side and places his hand on my back before closing his eyes. "We never used the lube," Ryan says.

James, "There's still time."

Ryan smirks, "Wanna bet who can get it up again first?"

God, he makes everything a game.

74

I can't even muster a fake laugh. I'm too blissed-out. My head's pillowed on Michael's chest, his skin cool and damp beneath my cheek, and every few breaths I feel his heart lurch like it's remembering a panic it forgot to have. He's still inside me, not hard anymore, just resting, and I'm grateful for the excuse to stay draped over him like a blanket someone forgot to fold. James is curled up beside us, his leg tangled between mine and Michael's, his arm resting on my ass, and his other hand tucked between, stroking Michael's arm. Michael's hand is in James's hair, absently threading through it. His other arm is squeezing me tight. From the angle of James's jaw and the flush on his neck, I know he's fighting sleep and losing.

Ryan's not quite touching anybody, which is very Ryan. Ryan asks the ceiling. "So, umm…are any of you allergic to cats?"

"Nope," we all say dreamily.

"We should get a cat," Ryan says, still looking at the ceiling. "I'd like a cat."

James's hand glides up my spine. "I think I'd like a dog," he mutters, not bothering to open his eyes.

"One like Watty," Ryan says. "That is the chillest fucking dog I've ever met."

Michael's chest vibrates under my ear with a low, embarrassed laugh. "He's kind of like a cat-shaped dog," he says.

"Let's get both," I say, nuzzling into Michael's chest.

It's all too much. This idea of our future: them, cats, dogs, kids. It all feels too perfect. I close my eyes, already half-convinced everything that's happened since I came back to Goose Grove has been a fever dream I'll wake from.

"Hey." James's voice is softer now, barely above a whisper. "Mikey. Celeste. Look at me."

Michael shifts under me, the movement making something inside me twitch and ache in a way that says I'm going to be grinding on him again soon. He turns his head, and I do too, so that we're both facing James. James's eyes are open now, and whatever joke he was about to make is stuck somewhere in his throat.

"Fuck, Mikey," James says, and the words come out shredded, like he's never said them before. "You are so beautiful. I love you."

Michael blinks once. His lips part, but for a second, he can't find anything to say.

He presses his lips to James's, slow and gentle, their foreheads touching at the end. James looks at me next, and suddenly I'm the one pinned by the weight of his attention. "You, too, Celeste," he says. "I love you so much."

Michael recovers enough to squeeze James's wrist. "You get sentimental when you're tired," he says, "But I love you too."

Ryan is silent for a beat, which is unusual enough that I twist around to look at him. He's half-turned away, like he wants to respect the moment and isn't sure what to do.

Michael notices, too. His arm releases me and reaches for Ryan. "Speaking of beautiful, Celeste and I get cold. Come here," he says, and pulls Ryan toward us in one surprisingly forceful tug.

"Whoa!" Ryan yelps, and then he's face-to-face with the rest of us. "Okay, okay, I'll cuddle."

"I told you," James says, "post-coital cute aggression."

"Jeeze, Mikey," Ryan says to him, not quite meeting his eyes.

"You're much stronger than I suspected. I didn't think you were hiding all this under all those old-man sweaters."

"Part of my mystique," Michael says, deadpan.

Michael wraps his arm around Ryan's shoulders, pulling him so that he's face-to-face with me on Michael's chest. Ryan looks surprised, chortles, and doesn't pull away. His thigh presses against mine, and his arm slings around my waist with a possessiveness that feels playful and romantic.

Michael still has his hand on Ryan's shoulder, thumb making lazy circles against his skin. James is lightly snoring at our side. He spent the whole day cooking, so I'm not surprised he's zonked out.

Ryan glances at me, then back to Michael. His fingers trail down my back, and for the first time, he doesn't make a show of being cool or ironic. His touch is careful, deliberate, the kind that says what his mouth won't. When he finally speaks, it's to me, not the group.

"Hey, Star Girl," he says. "I love you."

"I love you, too," I say, my eyes drifting closed as he tucks the hair falling in my face behind my ear.

I don't want to move—if I could sink right into Michael's ribcage and live there, I would. I can feel every heartbeat, every shift of breath, and every squish and trickle of bodily evidence between my legs. I squirm and shift, trying to remove myself from Michael's grip.

I whisper, "Hey, Michael, are you awake? I should go clean up.

Michael doesn't answer, his arm a dead weight on my back, locking me in place.

Ryan pushes himself up, hair in a wild haystack, "I'll go get you a warm washcloth."

"Thanks, Ry Guy," I say.

James's arm clamps tight around my waist. "Absolutely not," he says, with mock seriousness. "Nobody's cleaning up until I've had my turn."

Michael wakes, making a small huff of a laugh.

Ryan blinks, genuinely thrown. "Huh?"

James's fingers drag slowly down my spine and down my ass until they stop right at my pussy. "She can't clean up," he repeats, "until I've had a chance to cum in her."

There's a sharp beat of silence, and then Ryan cackles. "Oh, you've got a creampie kink, too?" He lifts an eyebrow at Michael. "What about you, Mikey?"

I guess he's Mikey to Ryan now, too. Should I start calling him Mikey? Maybe I'll call him Mike. Nah, he's Michael.

Michael lifts his head and gives a minute shrug. "I'm just happy to be included," Michael says.

"It's not a creampie kink, exactly," James says, and there's something proud and goofy about the way he juts his chin. "It's more of a breeding kink."

Ryan nods and considers this like they're discussing the most mundane thing. "I think I might have one, too. I know I can't knock her up, but…I fantasize about it every time."

"Well," James says, "maybe we should put a baby in her together, O'Connor."

"I like the sound of that," Ryan says, his voice hitching. He glances downward, and I can feel the heat radiating from the two of them, even without looking. "Did I win the bet?"

James is already hard again, pressed against my thigh like a promise. He chuckles, sliding his dick between me and Michael, "I think it's a tie."

I try to say it in the most deadpan voice I can, "Actually, Michael has been hard inside me since he woke up."

James asks, "Why didn't you say anything?"

Michael speaks up, his voice quiet but smug. "I didn't want to brag. But, what do I win?"

The boys snort in unison.

I bury my face in his chest and am not sure I'm prepared to live with a bunch of dudes if this is what life is going to be like.

Ryan leans over, lips to my ear, and murmurs, "You like the sound of that, Celeste? You want me and James to put a baby in you?" It's almost a joke, the way he says it, but also not a joke at all.

"Yes," I say.

Ryan's fingers are warm and careful as they slide along my spine, then down, tracing the curve of my hip. I shiver, muscles clenching. Michael's hand moves to my breast, lazy and proprietary. James slips a hand between my legs, fingers dipping into the mess there with a groan of appreciation.

"We're going to make you so fucking full," James says, almost reverent. James scoops me up and rolls onto his own back, pulling me on top of him. It's practically a wrestling move, except for the part where he's impossibly gentle, guiding me with hands that know exactly how much I can take and exactly how much I want to be taken.

"God, you're perfect," he whispers, his cock already pressed against me, and I can feel him twitching in anticipation. My body's already open, wet, and he slides in with an effortless, needy thrust that makes me arch and gasp.

Beside us, Michael props himself up, chin on my shoulder.

James turns his head and captures Michael's mouth in a kiss that is nothing like the gentle ones from earlier. This one's hungry, almost bruising, and Michael answers it with a heat that makes me feel like I'm a live wire caught between them.

"Fuck," James breathes, breaking the kiss to rest his forehead against Michael's. "Oh, God, Mikey, I love to feel your seed inside her."

Michael gives a little half-laugh, half-groan, and his hands slide down my body to my hips, gripping me firmly. "You want a refill?" he asks, voice dark and teasing.

James's eyes are wild, a little unfocused. "Yes," he says, not caring how desperate it sounds.

There's a moment of shuffling, James rolling to his side, still inside me. Michael reaches for the lube on the coffee table and slicks his cock, all business, no ceremony. He moves behind James, spooning us and kissing his shoulder as he positions himself. With a slow, deliberate push, he enters James. James's whole body tightens, a shudder running through him, and his cock pulses inside me so hard I nearly lose it right there.

"Oh, fuck," James says, eyes slamming shut.

Michael thrusts into him, slow and steady at first, then faster as James's groans rise in pitch. I can feel the whole thing, every tremor and push, and it's dizzying. The feeling of James inside me, Michael inside him—it's like being plugged into some circuit I never knew existed.

The next thing I know, Ryan is behind me, gripping my hips, breath warm on my ear. "Can I, too?"

"Yeah," I breathe out. He slicks himself with a generous pump of lube, then presses a careful, insistent hand to my ass, spreading me open. He lines up and, after a moment's gentle pressure, slides into my pussy with James. It's a lot, but the sting fades quickly, replaced by an overwhelmingly right fullness.

"Holy shit," I breathe, shuddering.

Behind James, Michael picks up the rhythm, thrusting into James, who thrusts into me, and Ryan matches their tempo so that every movement is amplified, layered, a chain of sensation. I'm pinned between them, filled from every angle, and it's almost too much—except I never want it to stop.

James's hands are on my waist, his grip so tight I suspect I'll have bruises in the morning, and he's chanting my name under his breath like a prayer. "Celeste, Celeste, Celeste, fuck—"

Michael's voice is a low growl. "You're close, aren't you?"

"Yeah," James gasps, "so fucking close."

Ryan's hand slides up my belly, finding my clit, and he strokes it in tight, practiced circles that almost make me scream. "Can you come for us?" he murmurs in my ear.

"Yes," I gasp, barely able to get the word out.

And then I'm coming, a shuddering, blinding explosion that knocks all the air out of my lungs. James loses it right after, pulsing inside me with a ferocity that is so delicious. Ryan groans as he follows, then Michael, who bites down on James's shoulder and pours himself into him.

We collapse, a heap of sweat and limbs and laughter, every nerve ending raw and alive. No one speaks for a long minute—there's just the sound of our collective breathing, ragged and animal.

James is still clutching me, his whole body shivering with aftershocks. "God, seventeen-year-old me never would have imagined I'd be doing that one day."

Ryan rolls off, chuckling. "Seventeen-year-old me didn't even know DVP was a thing."

James kisses my forehead. "You did so good, baby." He turns and kisses, "You, too, Mikey. Thanks."

Michael turns so he's sprawled on his back, eyes closed, a satisfied smirk on his lips. "You're welcome," he says to the ceiling.

Ryan asks, "Can I get her that washcloth now?" already halfway to the bathroom.

James calls, "Get two."

Michael adds, "Three. And a blanket. And don't think for a second you are getting out of cuddling."

75

I awake just after sunrise and slink out of bed to return my clothes to my body. James, Michael, and Ryan are all naked under the world's least adequate blanket. Their snores are a discordant trio. The sheet we put over the pull-out mattress has popped off a corner by Ryan's head. Michael is spooning James, nuzzling into his back, and, now that I've removed myself from the pile, Ryan now rests his hand on Michael's ass—not quite part of the cuddle pile, but not detached from it either.

I tiptoe through the gauntlet of clothes and make my way to the front door. Mrs. Heart will be awake by now. I tug on a hoodie (James's, from Yale, way too big, which means it covers the not-insignificant amount of hickies on my neck), slide on a pair of leggings, and slip outside.

I spot her already on the porch, wrapped in a pink bathrobe and sipping from a mug with a sassy cat on it. Watson is asleep by her side and doesn't even stir when I approach. His tongue peeks out just enough to make him look blissfully drunk, and I want to squish his face. She gives me a big, squinty-eyed smile. "Well, good morning, dear," she calls. " I just made tea."

I love her. I really, truly do.

I settle onto the wicker chair next to her. "Morning, Mrs. Heart."

She pats my hand, peering over the top of her mug. "You look like you had yourself a night. I notice all three of the boys' cars are still in the driveway."

"Ha, yeah," I say, "They're all still asleep on the couch. We had fun."

She laughs. "I'm glad you had fun, dear." Her hand tightens on mine, just for a second, and her smile fades to something a bit more intense. "I love seeing you so happy."

"I'm thrilled," I say. "I was going to wait for a good time to tell you, but I don't think there is a good time for some of this. So here it is: I'm selling the house."

Mrs. Heart blinks, then lets out a low whistle. "That's big news. Where are you going to live?"

I bounce my knees, nervous. "Um, nowhere far. We're—well, I—um. Okay, so, you know how I was getting kind of serious with James? And also Michael? And also Ryan, kind of, but it got more complicated, and now—"

She holds up her hand, smiling back in full force. "Stop. I'm old, not dead, Celeste. I know what a poly relationship is. Good for you!"

I snort. "It's less complicated than it sounds. James has a house out on the lake, and the plan is for all of us to move in, get our ducks in a row, and then build something together. Like, actually build a house. In Goose Grove, not somewhere far away. I want to stay here. I want—" I swallow. "I want to make a home."

Her eyes get glassy. "You sure know how to make an old woman cry before breakfast," she says, dabbing at her lashes. "I'm so happy for you, Celeste. And you want to sell your parents' place? That's good. That's really good. You don't need to carry all that on your back."

I look at my feet. "I was holding onto it because I thought…I don't know. I was trying to prove I wasn't the terrible daughter I always thought I was."

"You were never a terrible daughter, dear."

"Well, anyway, I'm not going to let my guilt and grief make me rot in that place anymore. I'm going to sell it, along with everything in it. I have no emotional attachment to any of it. No good emotions anyway."

She puts a hand on my cheek. "You go make a family. You deserve it, dear."

Family: the word lands heavy and sweet.

I clear my throat. "Oh! Also, we're going to try to have babies. Like, plural. Not all at once, probably, but…yeah. That's the plan."

Mrs. Heart does cry, now. Not a lot, but enough that she has to set her mug down and compose herself. "Well, that…I hope I'm around to see that."

"You will be, Mrs. Heart!" I say. I stand to hug her in her rocking chair. "I'm not going far! I'll still visit all the time."

When we quiet down, I let the silence sit for a moment. "You know, I was worried you'd be upset," I admit. "About me moving, and about…everything."

She shakes her head. "Never. Not about you being happy, Celeste. And besides, I'll still have Watson. The two of us will be just fine."

We sit like that for a bit, letting the chill burn off and the sun get stronger. I'm about to stand and go back inside when I remember the other reason I came here. It's the part I dread, but I have to do it.

"Mrs. Heart, can I ask you something kind of awkward?"

She squints at me, like she can sense the change in mood. "Sure."

"I know things have been…tough, financially. You don't have to say it, but I know. I don't want you to worry about money, okay? I've got more than I'll ever need. I want to help you out."

She starts to object, but I cut her off. "Please, Mrs. Heart. You've taken care of me my whole life. Let me take care of you for once. And don't give me that look, because I've already decided, and there's nothing you can say to change my mind. I'll buy the whole fucking town if that's what it takes."

She just looks at me, really looks, and her eyes are so blue and so full of things she'll never say. "You always were stubborn as a mule," she finally says, but her voice is shaky. "Alright. I'll let you help. But only because it's you."

We sit quietly for a few more minutes, sharing the sunrise.

I lean back in the chair, feeling lighter than I have in years. "I'm excited to get to work. I'm meeting with Marcus on Monday to discuss further how I can assist with the revitalization efforts. I'm going to do some good here. I want to do things like James. I want to help people."

Mrs. Heart laughs, but there's a brittle note to it. She grips her mug a little too tightly. "That's wonderful, Celeste," she says. "This town is lucky to have you."

That's when I notice her hands are shaking. I reach over, cover them with my own. "Hey. What's wrong?"

Her eyes dart to mine, then away. She lets out a long, shaky breath. "You ever have one of those days where you just wish you could go back and make a different choice? Just one little thing?"

"Pretty much every day since I was twelve," I say, trying to make her smile. She doesn't.

"I did a bad thing, Celeste." Her voice is barely audible. "A really bad thing."

I wait, because I can feel the heaviness coming off her in waves, and I know if I interrupt, she'll clam up.

She closes her eyes, takes another breath. "The night Richard Holbrook died, I was in the community garden. I was shaping one of the hedges. I don't usually trim the hedges, but it was looking scraggly. He found me there."

I swallow hard. Holding my breath.

"He'd always gotten a little fresh with me. Whenever he'd find me alone…he'd bother me. I tried to ask him about the money from the dealership. It's been so long. Why haven't I gotten it yet? He said something flippant, I…I can't for the life of me even remember what anymore," she continues. "We yelled at each other."

I can't speak. I just squeeze her hand harder.

He grips her cup tighter. "I don't know what happened. I really don't. Watson was with me. I tried to leave, but Richard got in my face. He grabbed my arm and tried to take the shears from me." She's trembling, now. "Then Watson…I think he tripped over Watson…he fell forward. Right onto the shears."

She covers her mouth. "There was so much blood. If I had just tended to my tomatoes like I intended…and left that scraggly hedge alone. The sheers…” She shakes her head, blinking back tears. “I thought…I thought maybe I could help him, but I couldn’t. He was gone, just like that.” Her voice breaks. “I panicked. I thought they’d put Watson down, or send me away. I didn’t know what to do. So I dragged him into the bushes, covered him, and then I just…went home.”

She’s crying, but it’s quiet, contained. I’m crying too, but only on the inside. Outwardly, I’m all focus and resolve.

“You didn’t mean to, Mrs. Heart,” I say softly. “It was an accident.”

She laughs, a harsh, broken sound. “Try telling that to the cops, dear. ‘Sorry, my dog tripped over a lawyer, and he fell only on my hedge shears.’ And after the town hall, when I heard everyone saying what he’d done…I realized I would never see that money from the sale. The cops would never believe I didn’t do it on purpose. They’ll lock me up till I’m dust.”

“No, they won’t,” I say. “Because no one’s going to find out. Not unless you want them to. I won’t tell a soul, Mrs. Heart. I promise.” *And I mean it with every fiber of my being.*

She looks at me, hope and terror warring in her eyes. “I can’t keep hiding. I have to tell the cops.”

I wipe her tears. “Okay. We can do that. I’m going to get James. He’ll know what to do. He’ll protect you and Watson, no matter what. And if he can’t. I’ll hire every fucking lawyer in the country if that’s what it takes.”

She lets out a weak laugh, then hugs me, clinging hard. “It’s okay, dear. I’m ready. I just wanted to win that pie contest and see you get out of that house. I can go now.”

“No…no, you can’t. I need you.”

“No, you don’t, dear.”

We hold each other and sob.

Between sobs, she says, “Promise, you’ll look after Watson for me.”

Watson perks up at his name.

“Of course. Of course,” I whisper into her hair.

76

I step into Sarah's Cafe and am immediately hit by the familiar scent of cinnamon rolls and espresso. I've barely made it past the threshold when Andy pops their head up from behind the counter at the sound of the bell.

"Well, well, look who finally graced us with her presence," Andy calls, snapping a tea towel in the air and grinning with that half-ironic, half-genuine delight that only they can muster. "Sarah! Celeste is here."

Sarah pokes her head out of the kitchen, the ends of her braids bouncing as she does a double-take. "Celeste! I haven't seen you in forever! Now that you have a bunch of boys to feed you, you don't need us anymore!"

"Sorry, I haven't been around much," I say, frowning. "Things have been so busy with Mrs. Heart and the move and the new charity I'm starting up."

Andy leans on the counter, chin in hand, eyes sparkling. "How are the house plans going?"

I reply, "Pretty good. We're still finalizing the design, but we should be ready to start building once the snow melts."

Sarah slides up next to Andy, planting her hands firmly on the glass case of baked goods. "How's Mrs. Heart doing? I saw her and Watson in the grocery store last week."

I smile, but it's the brittle kind. "She's…okay. She's honestly better than I thought she'd be."

Sarah exchanges a loaded glance with Andy, who lifts both eyebrows. "We heard she got out on bail?"

"Yup," I say. "They only held her for a couple of days. James says, worst case, she'll get house arrest. He's working his magic already."

Andy whistles this time, low and admiring. "Your guy's a real white knight."

"You have no idea, Andy," I laugh, then look at Sarah, who is already grinning. "But yeah. He's good."

"And Mrs. Heart—she really did it? I mean, not to gossip…" Sarah says, using her most innocent voice, which fools absolutely no one.

"She did." I take a breath. "It was an accident. Richard tripped over Watson, and he fell onto her sheers. She freaked out, worried she'd go to jail and they'd put Watson down, so she hid the body."

Sarah looks stricken, but only for a moment. "Maybe she thought no one would believe her. But she's seventy-three and weighs, what, ninety pounds soaking wet? There's no way she overpowered that man."

I swirl my coffee, letting the steam hit my face. "James says the only real problem is that she hid the body. And then didn't report it. Since it was an accident, he says not to worry. The preliminary hearing won't be until early next year, so she'll be around for the holidays, which Mrs. Heart is happy about."

Andy stares at me over the rim of their mug. "You think she'll walk?"

I nod. "If James has anything to say about it. Between her age, the fact that she'd never even gotten a speeding ticket, and the whole 'the victim was universally despised' factor? He's already prepping for a plea deal, but he doesn't think it'll even go to trial. And if it did, I doubt a jury would convict her."

Andy looks around conspiratorily, "I hate to be the one to say it, but…that dog did this town a favor. You know, my nieces always call him the hero of Goose Grove. I think they might be right."

We all chuckle softly, afraid to laugh at the morbid joke, but all wholeheartedly agreeing with it.

The bell above the door jingles a little too violently, making Sarah wince and Andy drop the lid to the sugar canister. There's a flurry of noise, followed by a pile of baby blankets, diaper bags, and a determined, sleep-deprived woman with a halo of curly hair.

Andy practically vaults off the counter. "Holy shit! It lives!"

Angela fixes Andy with a death glare, but it's undermined by her triumphant smile. "Oh my God, I need some coffee. Please."

"Sit, sit we got you, girl," Sarah deadpans, but she's already pulling up a chair at a corner table for Angela to sit.

Andy circles Angela, arms wide. "Give. Now," Andy commands, reaching for the baby carrier.

Angela surrenders the bundle with a look that says she's too tired to fight, but she stands back, arms hovering just in case Andy does something reckless, like toss the baby in the air. "Careful, Andy."

Andy beams down at the baby—small, soft, with the chubbiest cheeks I've ever seen—and coos in a voice I've never heard before. "You. Are. Perfection. I love that new baby smell."

Angela sits in the chair Sarah pulled out for her as if even succumbing to gravity takes more energy than she has left. "I know I wanted this. But, wow, I'm so tired."

Sarah rushes to the counter, "Triple shot coming up."

Angela says, "I probably shouldn't…I'm breastfeeding and I don't want her to be up all night." She sighs and melts further into her chair. "Fuck it. Pumping and dumping. Hit me, Sarah."

I watch the scene play out, half-amused and half-stunned.

Andy removes the baby from the carrier and hugs her close to their chest, bouncing and twirling like holding a baby is the only thing they've ever wanted to do.

"May I…?" I ask, pointing at the baby, suddenly self-conscious.

Angela nods, and for the first time, her eyes meet mine. There's a pause—awkward, but not unkind—like we're both calculating how much emotional weight to throw at each other after everything that's happened.

"Of course," she says, voice softer than I remember. "She likes new faces."

I perch next to Andy, careful not to crowd, and peek at the baby. I give her a single finger wave near her face. The baby is wide awake, big brown eyes blinking at me with the existential confusion of a creature who's only been outside for five minutes. She grabs my finger with terrifying strength.

"She's beautiful," I say, and I mean it.

Angela laughs, the kind that starts as a snort and blossoms into something musical. "She's a spitfire."

I ask, "What's her name?"

Angela straightens up. "Olivia."

Andy is already chanting "Livy. Livy." while doing a little dance with the baby.

Angela rolls her eyes, but she's beaming. "First time out in public," she says, her voice suddenly thick with pride and anxiety. "She was born, like, two days after the Town Hall meeting. And she's finally allowed around people—you know, germs and stuff."

She trails off and sips the coffee now in her hands.

I take the opening. "I wanted to apologize for generally being…a lot. During the investigation into Richard's murder."

Angela's shoulders lift, then drop, as if she's letting go of some grudge she'd been clutching for years. "I don't know if I can say this, but if I get in trouble, I'll just blame baby brain. Benefit of working in a male-dominated field: you can blame anything on 'woman stuff' and they just cover their ears and say, 'okay, okay' and run away. For the record, you were never a suspect. Not even for a minute."

I stare at her. "Really!?"

She nods. "Really. We had eyes on Mrs. Heart from day one. We just didn't know how much you knew."

Sarah leans in. "So, wait, you knew it was Mrs. Heart? The whole time?"

Angela shrugs. "We had theories. But the minute we found out about Richard's history with Mrs. Heart, it made sense. We just didn't have any concrete proof."

Andy loses focus on the conversation. "Saaaaraaah, don't you think we need one of these!?" they say, turning the baby to Sarah. "Look how cute!"

Sarah, sigh, "Oh, God, I knew this was going to happen."

"Baby fever is contagious," Andy laughs. "How have you not caught it yet?"

Sarah approaches the baby and scrutinizes her face, "Okay, my ovaries do think she's pretty cute."

Andy lights up.

Sarah sighs, "That's not a yes, Andy. That's a…" she tickles the baby, "a strong maybe."

Andy smiles. "Now that I won't have the runt to shower my auncley affections on, I'm gonna be extra insufferable, just so you know."

Sarah rolls her eyes, but her gaze softens as she looks at Olivia, and I suspect that maybe she might turn to a yes pretty soon.

I sip my coffee, still staring at the baby. "Wait. What do you mean you won't have the runts?"

"Nicole's moving to Minneapolis," Andy says, delighted to be the bearer of gossip. With the twins and Daniel."

"Wait," I say, piecing it together. "Not with Marcus?"

"Nope," Andy says. "She's leaving him. She's my sister, and I love her, because I have to, but it would be nice to put some space between us. I'm really gonna' miss the runts, though. Luckily, I'll have Little Livy here to shower with all my surrogate auncle energy. Unless there will be other babies for me to cuddle?" They look at Sarah with a sly grin and a raised eyebrow.

Sarah just groans and walks away, waving them away with her hand and saying, "Maybe we'll talk about it tonight."

Andy's eyes light up, and they turn their gaze toward me, "What about you, Celeste? Any babies for me to cuddle?"

I laugh, "Ha, not yet. Soon, maybe? Hopefully."

There is a long pause as the awkwardness of the talk of babies and my multitude of men comes up.

Angela is watching me. "You know, Celesete…Ryan…it was like he had a Celeste-shaped hole in his heart. I'm happy for him. Happy he found what he was looking for."

"Thanks, Angela. I'll tell him."

77

I push the lockbox the realtor placed on the door aside so I can get to the lock. I pause, realizing this is likely the last time I'll ever open this door. I turn to take in the yard.

Ryan's at the back of his truck, slipping on the icy driveway and reaching for a stack of cardboard boxes. The snow comes down in sheets, muffling everything, even the curses that escape him as he grabs the side of his truck to stop himself from falling.

The crunch of tires on ice pulls my gaze to the curb, where James and Michael pull up in James's car.

Ryan rushes toward me, boxes under his arm, and drops the boxes on the porch—his breath ghosts in the air. "Moment of truth," he says.

"Yep," I say, with a tight grin.

Michael lingers in the car a little longer than James, reluctant to enter the cold. There's something uniquely Minnesotan about the way the wind knifes through every gap in your coat, like it's been personally insulted and wants you to know it. Eventually, he exits the car and they both trudge up the snowy lawn to stand with me and Ryan on the porch.

We stomp our feet, trying to remove as much mud and snow as possible. I push the door open and shed my coat. The boys do the same, revealing three perfectly packed pairs of grey sweatpants. "You can leave the boots on. We'll be going in and out, and the cleaners will take care of whatever we can't wipe up today," I say.

James immediately takes command. "Okay, here's how this is going to go," he says, grabbing a pad of sticky notes from his jacket. "The service we hired will be here tomorrow to pack up all the stuff we don't bring home today. They'll also sort through whatever we say stays to decide what gets tossed or donated. We've got two dots: pink and blue. Pink goes on what we'll take home with us tonight. Blue goes on what we want the movers to bring tomorrow. Anything without a dot stays and will get sorted."

He looks at Ryan, who just shrugs.

"Did you hear any of that?" James asks.

"I'll figure it out," Ryan says, wandering deeper into the house.

James just groans.

Michael slumps onto the couch, "I kinda feel like we should keep this couch—you know, for all memories."

"I wouldn't mind putting it in my studio," Ryan says.

"Blue dot," James instructs.

I walk through the house slowly, touching things as I go. It's chilly in here; the radiator obviously needs to be replaced.

Not my problem anymore.

I don't get the kick in the gut I expected—no panic, no urge to crawl into a pile of blankets or wrap myself around a dick—just a quiet sense of closure. I'm here, and it doesn't hurt. I look at the guys walking through the living room, and the desire to wrap myself around a dick does actually stir in me.

James claps his hands. "Celeste, where are the boxes you brought with you? The ones that used to be in the dining room?"

Ryan points a thumb up the staircase. "I took them to her bedroom upstairs."

James's eyes light up with sudden, completely un-ironic enthusiasm. "I finally get to see your teenage bedroom?"

Michael stands, stretches, and says, "I want to see it, too."

Before I can protest, they've both started up the stairs, boyish glee overtaking them.

Ryan leans in and lowers his voice. "You're doing great, Star Girl." He pulls me into a quick side hug and plants a chaste kiss on the crown of my head.

I let the hug settle in. The world feels less sharp, less cold. "Thanks," I say. "This…this seems a lot less scary than I thought it would."

Ryan's eyes go soft. "That's good to hear," he says.

From upstairs, there's a crash, followed by James's voice: "Oh my God. We have to keep this Backstreet Boys poster."

Michael laughs so hard it echoes through the floor. "This is a side of you I've never seen, James."

I roll my eyes and smile so wide my face hurts. The last day of fall in Minnesota, and I'm surrounded by idiots in sweatpants and bad jokes. But for the first time in a long time, I don't want to run away.

If there's an Olympic event for shoving as many boxes as possible into a pickup bed, Ryan and James would at least medal. They're tag-teaming loads: James at the foot of the stairs, Ryan at the truck, and Michael as a sort of mobile relay who keeps popping up in odd places—sometimes carrying a box, sometimes carrying just the lid, sometimes pausing to read through an old yearbook or, God help me, the diary he found in my desk drawer.

I've stationed myself at the command center: the dining table. Every time the door opens, a gust of wind brings in the scent of snow and distant wood smoke. It's familiar in a way that makes my heart ache, but it's a good ache.

There's a high, excited bark from the front step. Watson, unleashed, comes bursting in like he owns the place. Behind him is Mrs. Heart, carrying a pie.

"I figured these boys needed some provisions, given all the hard work they're doing," she announces, her voice bright.

She places the pie on the table. "Crumble top," she says with a wink. She smells like cinnamon and cold air, and underneath, a perfume I've always associated with hugs.

Watson does a victory lap around the dining room, letting out his covered-in-snow zoomies, then settles at my feet, big brown eyes fixed on the pie with silent hope.

"Mrs. Heart, you are a lifesaver," I say.

She waves a hand. "Oh, I'm only here to make sure none of these gentlemen starve to death before the job is done." She glances at the staircase, where Michael is currently hollering down to James that he's found "the motherlode of Beanie Babies, please advise."

Ryan follows the scent of dessert like a floating cartoon character, grinning. "We're taking a break?" he asks, as if the answer isn't obvious.

"Please," I say, "you've earned it." I find plates that we haven't yet sorted through and a pie-serving utensil.

The home fills with the sounds of pie being sliced and men gently ribbing each other. Mrs. Heart listens to us with that half-smile she always has. At one point, she reaches over and squeezes my hand. "You're doing all right, Celeste?" she asks.

"I am," I smile.

"And you?" I ask.

"Pretty good," she laughs.

"Sarah said she saw you at the grocery store. You've been comfortable leaving the house?"

"Yeah, I was worried everyone would be scared of me, but no one is. Those who acknowledge it thank me."

James stands and starts gathering plates. "All right, people, let's get the final stuff sorted. The truck won't pack itself."

Ryan groans, "Not every minute needs to be used to maximum efficiency. We can relax."

James doesn't even respond; he just hand-washes the plates. Ryan grabs a hand towel to dry the dishes as he finishes them.

I linger at the door between the dining room and the kitchen for a moment and watch the snow fall in fat, lazy flakes through the window over the piano—still covered by the drape painting Ryan made. I stare at it for a long moment before I walk toward it. I touch the cloth. "I…I want to take this painting," I say.

Everyone joins me in the dining room. Ryan says, “We can hang it somewhere. It’d make a nice piece for the den in the new place.”

James agrees, “Yeah, that’d be nice.”

“We can put it over the sex couch,” Michael says, then looks at Mrs. Heart, “Oh, um, sorry, Mrs. H.”

“Dear, you think I don’t know what the four of you did on that couch!?”

I grab the painting with both hands and whip it off, revealing the baby grand piano underneath. I bundle the painting in my arms and run my finger along the lid of the piano.

Without thinking, I open the piano lid, revealing the keys.

Silence, for a second.

I run my fingers along the keys, pressing just enough to make them all ring out.

Glissando.

Still perfectly in tune.

I always loved the sound.

The guys approach me and stand silently behind, waiting for me to react, with that understated, supportive energy that makes even the most awful feel okay. They’re waiting for me to break down. But I don’t.

“I’ll find it a good home, Mom,” I say, softly, to the piano. The feeling of despair no longer overtakes me.

I smile and turn.

The relief on everyone’s faces washes over the room in a wave.

I exclaim, “Let’s go home!”

Want to follow Celeste and the boys home?
Join my newsletter and get a Bonus Epilogue!

https://imogenknowed.com/newsletter

A Note from the Author

Hello, readers! Thank you so much for taking the time to read Dates and Dead Bodies. I recently went through a phase where my special interest was cozy murder mysteries. I devoured them, reading close to 300 in 2023. When I wasn't reading cozy murder mysteries (and, you know, doing my day job), I was reading why choose smut. This book was a way for me to combine my two great loves in reading.

I hope that you found it enjoyable and a mashup well worth your time.

Please leave a review of Dates and Dead Bodies on Amazon and Goodreads.

If you'd like to keep up with my work, follow me on social media and subscribe to my newsletter:

https://www.instagram.com/imogenknowed/

https://imogenknowed.com/newsletter

Special Thanks

I want to thank my husband for his unwavering support while I wrote this book. Without his support, I could not have hyper-focused on it, writing literally every moment of the day that I wasn't working or sleeping.

To my husband:

Thank you for enthusiastically discussing characters and plot with me. Thank you for being okay with the fact that my mind was lost to another world for a while. Thank you for always putting food in front of me when I get so lost in something and forget my own body has needs. Thank you for always being there to help me recover whenever my mind and body explode from the world being too loud, too distracting, and too scratchy. I love you.

About the Author

Imogen Knowed is an AuDHD girly who hyperfocuses on creating fake people in her head. Instead of letting them stay in there, she writes them down for others to meet. She spends her days programming video games and her nights reading and writing smut. When she's not writing smut or making video games, she's hanging out with her daughter, husband, dog, and/or three cats.

If you'd like to keep up with my work, follow me on social media and subscribe to my newsletter:
https://imogenknowed.com/newsletter

instagram.com/imogenknowed
threads.com/@imogenknowed

www.ingramcontent.com/pod-product-compliance
Lightning Source LLC
LaVergne TN
LVHW010553100826
845148LV00014B/2700